David McLaurin

was born in Sussex in 1963, a
had moved there from Trinidad where his father had been in the Colonial Police. He was educated in England, but passed most of his school holidays in Malta, where his family later settled. After reading English at Oxford he taught at various schools, most recently in suburban Essex. At present he is studying for the priesthood in Rome, where he now lives.

The Bishop of San Fernando, David McLaurin's first novel, was runner-up for the 1994 *Sunday Express* Book of the Year Award. *Mortal Sins* is his second novel.

By the same author

THE BISHOP OF SAN FERNANDO

DAVID McLAURIN

Mortal Sins

Flamingo
An Imprint of HarperCollins*Publishers*

Flamingo
An Imprint of HarperCollins*Publishers*
77–85 Fulham Palace Road,
Hammersmith, London W6 8JB

Published by Flamingo 1996
9 8 7 6 5 4 3 2 1

First published in Great Britain by
Gerald Duckworth & Co. Ltd 1995

Author photograph by *Express* Newspapers

ISBN 0 00 654864 4

Set in Linotron Janson
at The Spartan Press Ltd,
Lymington, Hants

Printed and bound in Great Britain by
Caledonian International Book Manufacturing Ltd Glasgow

For Catherine and Clive Richardson

ACKNOWLEDGEMENTS

For his help with technical details concerning the military life and routine, and about weapons, I owe a debt of gratitude to Francesco Speranza, who patiently answered my questions. I am also grateful to Alessandro Caspoli, who provided me with insights into the life of a friar. Any inaccuracies in this book are mine, not theirs.

CAST

The General, President of the Republic
General Hernandez, Minister for Foreign Affairs
General Messina, Minister of the Interior
Colonel Olivarez, Head of Security
The United States Ambassador

Roberto Enriquez, a captain of cavalry
Fritz Rodriguez, the same, friend of the above
Captain Zondadari
Captain Ximenez
Tanucci, a lieutenant in the Engineers
Strauss, an NCO
Major Williams, uncle to Ximenez
Ernesto Caballero, a journalist
Miguel, a police conscript
Hoffman, a medic and penguin expert

Don Alvaro, the Archbishop
Father Morisco, his secretary
Two Franciscan friars
A military chaplain

Maria Enriquez, Roberto's mother
Isabel de Calatrava, a social success
Nicola Nickleby, an English student
Elena Garcia, in love with Roberto
Carmen Garcia, her mother
Mrs Williams, the Major's wife
Sir Nigel, the British Ambassador

One

A young man sat on his bed polishing his boots. They did not need polishing, but he had been trained to polish them regularly, and he was dutiful. They were hard, heavy boots, made by blind people. It was a little past half past six in the morning, and very soon he would put them on as he always did. His father, he knew, had had a man to do such things for him; he himself did not, but tried not to resent the fact.

The room he slept in was small and bare; apart from the usual furniture there was a bookshelf containing some now neglected English novels, almost all from the last century, nothing modern, for most modern books were passed around from hand to hand wrapped in brown paper, something he did not approve of. There were other titles as well: a life of Pope John XXIII, a few manuals of a technical nature, and a book about natural family planning which he had been given some years previously, but never read. On top of the bookcase were some photographs: one, now thirty years old, was of his parents on their wedding day; another showed the sort of girl that a stranger would have mistaken for his sister; a third showed him and his best friend at some official function. Apart from that, there was a standard picture, the type everyone had, of the President of the Republic and next to it, a reproduction icon of St Michael the Archangel. A crucifix on the wall was the only other decoration.

He finished his boots, put them on, and stood up. He was ready to face the day. Not a single article of the clothing he wore was his own. It was all Government property. The last thing he did before leaving was to assemble his gun, a Beretta, and put it in his holster – for though he had never fired a shot in anger in his life, he was a soldier, and dutifully carried his gun as an officer should, putting it together every morning, and taking it apart, for safety, every night. He was never without it, though he had never needed it yet. But his was a dutiful nature. That was the way he had been brought up.

Downstairs he went; he was always up early, and the barracks were deserted. In the large echoing hallway, the man on guard duty, who had been there all night, stood to attention as he passed into the dining-room. The ageing Italian waiter approached him respectfully.

'No eggs this morning, sir,' he said apologetically. 'And Captain Rodriguez has just sent down, sir, to say that he has eaten a poisoned *empanada*, and won't be down to breakfast.'

'A poisoned *empanada*?' asked the young man. 'Is it serious?'

'No, sir. But he particularly asked me to ask you not to disturb him. The Captain, sir, has had a bad night. The quality of the meat in the *empanadas* some people serve, sir, isn't quite what it could be.'

'Then I'll breakfast alone,' said the young man.

He did so, not very well either, now that food shortages were beginning to affect even the Army; and his mind turned to his fellow captain's bad night. His brow, which was a remarkably fine one, contracted into a slight frown. It was really too bad of Fritz to go round eating suspect *empanadas*. They always had breakfast together, very early, and he did not like having his routine interrupted.

Not very far away, the President had had a bad night too.

The old Indian woman, who crouched next to his bed and hardly ever left his side, now that he could not eat without her help, shook her head. She knew what the doctors knew but would not admit. Medicine could not save him, and even magic was losing its powers. The doctors were doing their best, feeding the President of the Republic by drip; and every now and then they would inject him with clear fluids in the hope of keeping him alive. On the table next to his bed stood a statuette of Saint Michael the Archangel, the best of soldiers; but the old man was past caring and even his patron saint seemed to be emptied of his wonted powers.

The President's oblivion was not shared by the others in the vast bedroom. General Messina, who had been Minister of the Interior for the last twenty years, was worried, for if the old man died, what would happen to the rest of them? And General Hernandez, his colleague at the Ministry of Foreign Affairs, even General Hernandez felt a shiver of fear underneath his exterior calm. Uncertainty loomed ahead. The old man might die, and if he did, they might as well all die with him. Only Colonel Olivarez, the Head of Security, reckoned to be the cleverest man in the Republic, seemed to be immune from the general air of unease. He was thinking of the future, not of ifs but of whens, and he was making plans.

These three military men withdrew to the other end of the room, to a window which commanded a fine view of the Palace Square outside and the Cathedral beyond. They stood there and contemplated the prospect.

'I assume that we can trust all these people?' asked Messina, meaning the doctors.

'They can talk as much as they want to,' said Hernandez. 'But I have made sure they have no one to talk to. Not one of them leaves this building.'

'If there were a leak, and if rumours were to start,' began Messina.

'Panic would sweep the country,' said Hernandez. 'And we can't have that. Things are bad enough as it is.'

The two old men, who had been colleagues for almost twenty years, were known to dislike each other. But this was one thing upon which they could both agree. The country had to be kept calm. The slightest intimation that the President was dying could have consequences.

'Things are pretty bad as it is,' agreed Olivarez quietly. 'And I mean that whatever may happen here.'

Olivarez was considerably younger than the two Generals, and he stood at a little distance. The two old men gave him looks of loathing, the sort that are usually given by old men to rising younger ones. Neither of them liked Olivarez, which was another point of agreement between them, and this dislike was fuelled by the fact that they both knew that Olivarez was a man they could not do without. He was Head of Security, about fifty years old, and nearly always right.

'The fact is,' said Olivarez, 'that the system is running down. I don't just mean the General himself. Look at the way inflation has gone up and up – certainly we don't allow figures to be published and we have the newspapers in our pockets, but when people have to pay over a thousand escudos for a cup of coffee, while last year they paid only fifty, they do notice it. And the unemployed on the streets are only waiting to make trouble.'

'It's worse everywhere else,' said Messina, who was supposed to be responsible for the economy.

'And we have squandered our foreign reserves,' continued Olivarez remorselessly. 'God only knows what would happen to us if the North Americans and the British were to drop us.'

'Things were much worse in the old days,' said Hernandez. 'They had inflation of over a thousand per cent then. The North Americans will never abandon us. They know that the alternative is much much worse. They won't drop us, as you put it, simply because they don't want a Communist government here. It is as simple as that.'

'The Army has been in power for twenty years,' said Olivarez. 'I myself can hardly remember the Liberals; people will forget soon that the old days were worse. And as for Communists, they hardly exist nowadays.'

'Thanks to us,' said Messina.

Olivarez wondered if Messina had heard of the Berlin Wall.

'If you were to catch a few dangerous Communists,' said Hernandez slowly, 'it might do wonders. It might take everyone's mind off inflation.'

'Yes,' said Messina. 'You are the Head of Security. Find something for our younger men to do. It can't be right to have young officers sitting round all day doing nothing. They get discontented. Give them something to do. We need a war. You can't blame us for everything that goes wrong, Olivarez; Army morale is your department. We can't have disaffection in the ranks.'

'Of course,' said Hernandez, 'we are not as popular as we once were. People are so ungrateful, and nowadays military dictatorships tend to look old fashioned. People forget that we saved them from anarchy and dictatorship and mob rule. But if they really want democracy they can go and savour its delights abroad. How many people have done that in the last ten years? About a hundred, which goes to show that the vast majority are perfectly content with the life they have here.'

'And as I say,' put in Messina, 'if we did have a Communist government, things would be even worse. Look at what Allende did to Chile; and look at' – He searched his mind for a suitably chilling comparison, and the others wondered what he would hit upon – 'Look at Albania and Bulgaria. As Hernandez says, people simply aren't grateful. And if we do have trouble on the streets, we know what to do. Round them up, cut their hair and put them in uniform. It works every time.'

Olivarez was driven to reflect, and finally he spoke:

'There's no use expecting people to be grateful, as they have short memories. As for civilian trouble-makers, putting them in uniform only makes them into military trouble-makers. So many governments have failed simply because they lacked the corporate will to go on: look at Stroessner, and Pinochet and Galtieri. On this continent the examples are disturbing. And it is always for the same reason. The Army cracks under strain; its men grow bored and tired; their minds drift off thinking about democracy, peace and other empty notions. And the civilian classes are even more prone to do the same thing, especially if the Army isn't there to provide a lead. We all go soft simply because we've no longer got anything to fight for, and because we've got nothing to fight against. Perhaps we do need a war after all. If people had thought that Communism was a real danger they would never have got rid of Pinochet. But without the enemy, we lose our *raison d'être*.'

'Then perhaps you had better find it for us again,' said Messina.

Hernandez sighed. He did not enjoy this sort of conversation, which was becoming more and more common these days. He liked to think of himself as a gentleman, and he rather resented the fact that for the last twenty years his fate had been linked to that of Messina, who was undoubtedly a thug. The Junta had done many things that Hernandez personally disapproved of, but he quieted his conscience by telling himself that he would never have given his approval unless Messina and the President had not persuaded him to do so against his natural judgement. Although the Army had overthrown the entire Liberal Cabinet, it didn't follow that he had wanted them all shot. He had known several of them quite well, and was never easy when he thought of how he had countersigned their death-warrants. He hoped they had never known; it would have made him even more uncomfortable to think that several old friends had gone to summary execution knowing that he, Arturo Hernandez, had betrayed them. But he hoped not; he hoped that their last moments had been filled with blissful ignorance, and he was almost sure that they had been. After all, the Liberal ministers had been given little time for reflection, but been arrested, tried and executed with remarkable swiftness in the small hours of the morning some twenty years ago.

Hernandez lit a cigarette; they were English cigarettes, a type that you couldn't get in the shops, thanks to the balance of payments crisis, but which came via diplomatic bag. In these hard times he was driven to relying on the kindness of his friends for these necessary luxuries. Sir Nigel, the British Ambassador, was so thoughtful and generous. How on earth anyone managed to smoke the national brands without throwing up, General Hernandez could not imagine. He gratefully pulled on his Silk Cut. They said that the national brands were made out of sweepings from factory floors. Just like the tea that you got nowadays. Thank God for his Marks and Spencers Earl Grey, another present from Sir Nigel, who, though rather tedious, had his uses.

'Give me a free hand for a month or two,' Olivarez was saying. 'You'll see then what I can do.'

Hernandez looked at Olivarez. He supposed he ought to like the man for exactly those reasons that made him dislike Messina. According to his dear old friend Isabel de Calatrava, Olivarez was related to half of Spain. He looked at Messina, who doubtless was related to half of Italy, only the wrong half.

'Yes,' Hernandez said easily. 'Let's give Olivarez a free hand and see what he can come up with.'

Hernandez had not actually been following the conversation, but it seemed to him that Olivarez was a man to be trusted whereas Messina was not. And that Messina, he could tell, did not like Olivarez merely made him all the more sure that Olivarez was just the man to be given a free hand.

'Oh very well,' said Messina, a trifle ungraciously, or so Hernandez thought.

And with that the conversation ended. The three men went their separate ways, leaving the General, the Father of the Republic, in his state bedroom attended by the doctors and the Indian woman and his little statue of Saint Michael the Archangel; they left him, a huge rotting hulk of a man for whom nothing could now be done, for in a month at most, the long decline into death would surely be over. And already the old man was not important. He would die and be forgotten; he had been as good as useless ever since Hernandez had learned to forge his signature and thus deprived him of his last function on earth.

It had not ever been thus.

* * *

When Olivarez got back to his office he sat at his desk and stroked his precise military moustache. His office was housed in a drab building, once used as an Army Navigational School; it was the sort of building that presented an anonymous face to the world and did not arouse curiosity. Here Olivarez sat at his desk and thought of the General as he had been twenty years ago, when the military had first come to power. The General had been a man of vision then, a leader, a man who had been able to galvanise the entire army into concerted action. How easy it had been. The General (no one ever referred to him by his real name: he was always just the General) had driven to the Presidential Palace in the middle of the night and gained admittance to the then President's bedroom, where he had informed the poor man that a Communist coup was about to take place, and that the Army would protect him. Thus the President had consented to go to a military fortress and had been driven off like a lamb to the slaughter. The rest of the Government, never adept at organisation, had been picked up one by one, some to be taken away, some to be shot at once when they unwisely tried to resist arrest. It had been Messina who had supervised that side of things; and none of the graves had ever, to Colonel Olivarez's knowledge, been found.

The next day the Republic had been informed that it had been saved in its sleep from Communism and anarchy. The foreign Ambassadors had met the new President For Life and come away satisfied. The Republic had been saved; and if anyone complained openly of the fact, they did not do so for long.

Of course, there were complaints now, Olivarez knew perfectly well. People complained when there were periodic shortages. This month it was sugar. Last month it had been lavatory paper. But these were minor complaints from unimportant people. The real danger lay with the younger generation of officers in the Army, the young men in their late twenties and early thirties. They were bored, there was nothing for them to do, and some of them perhaps were already infected with silly ideas imported from North America. And when the General died, the link with the past would be broken, and what would their thoughts turn to then?

With this in mind, Colonel Olivarez began to work out his plan.

Two

Isabel de Calatrava, had she told the truth, which she did but rarely, found General Hernandez something of a bore; but despite this, he was still her dearest friend. Her reasons for this were almost entirely mercenary. Arturo Hernandez had never married, and as he had been over fifty when he had become Minister of the Exterior, he had felt it rather late in the day to start the search then for a wife who could have played the part of hostess at social functions. Instead he had prevailed on Isabel to take on the responsibilities for the social side of the Ministry, which, after a show of reluctance, she had done. Of course, she received no remuneration for her services but she did oversee the accounts; thus in her own dignified way she had ample opportunity of joining in what everyone else was doing, namely enjoying public funds.

Under her directing hand social events at the Ministry had taken a definite form, evoking what she hoped was a spirit of pre-war elegance. Her clothes were all of a piece with this idea; and if she imagined herself in any ambience at all, it was that strange never-never land where no one seemed to do anything except sip tea and eat crumpets, elegantly dressed in silk.

That was what she was doing at present. She was entertaining Arturo Hernandez to tea, something she did about once a week, and the dear General was confiding in her, something she enjoyed immensely. (Her English paying guest, whom she had taken for purely financial motives, was safely relegated to the kitchen, keeping the dog company.)

'Of course,' he was saying, 'you know everyone in the country. I know you do. You have such a good memory for names, and you know all their relations too and all that there is to be known about them. You're like a walking filing cabinet.'

'Yes,' said Isabel.

'Now, for example,' said Hernandez with what he thought was devilish cunning, 'if I were to mention the name of a certain Captain Roberto Enriquez, you would know exactly who I meant, wouldn't you?'

'Certainly,' said Isabel. 'I was at school with his mother; she was Maria Maitland and she married an officer in the Cavalry; he died, I think, and they had this one son. A very nice-looking boy, now about twenty-eight years old; but I think I heard that he hadn't really settled down as yet.'

'Indeed?' said Hernandez. 'That is doubtless because he is still only a captain and feels he ought to have been promoted. Apparently he is supposed to be one of the best young men in the Army; how they come to that conclusion I don't quite know.'

'You seem to know all about him,' said Isabel delicately, wondering if he would tell her more.

'If you know his mother, perhaps you could get him and her to come to the races this Saturday – invite them.'

'Certainly.'

'Colonel Olivarez will be there too.'

'Indeed?'

'Yes, this is all something of a thing of Olivarez's. He seems to have got the idea that it would be useful to spot some up and coming talent. That's why he's got this Enriquez boy on his mind and we have to arrange a meeting. I must say I have my doubts.' He paused. 'Do you know of a young man called Captain José Maria Rodriguez?'

'Yes I do. That young man is very well known. They call him Fritz. I seem to remember something about him, but I can't quite think what it was. Shall I invite him too? He's a great friend of Enriquez. They were at school together. Captain

Rodriguez's mother was a Schultz, I think. I can't think who the Schultzes were, and I doubt they were anyone. They had a ranch somewhere.'

'Of course there are all sorts of things that never get into military files, my dear,' said Hernandez. 'You ought to try and find out a bit more about Enriquez's character. The other one is less important, I think. Enriquez is the one that Olivarez is worrying about. Go and see his mother; of course, you're not a secret service agent, but you could see what you could find out . . .'

Isabel smiled. There was nothing she liked better than digging up scandal.

'And who knows?' said Hernandez rhetorically. 'You might find out something important and Olivarez might be grateful. We can't afford to underestimate Colonel Olivarez.'

This was the conclusion that he had come to that morning, which he had spent studying a series of files that the Colonel had sent him. There was no doubt that the Colonel was clever; what was surprising was that the Colonel had got so far by being so clever, for over the last twenty years the Junta had been careful not to promote clever people. Clever men were dangerous.

The files he had had in front of him were a case in point: each one of them represented a potential danger to the state. He had just been reading the file devoted to one Captain Zondadari. Captain Zondadari was rather a worrying figure, if what was written in the file was true. The Captain was a man of noted bravery, and much admired by some of his colleagues, the sort of man who ought to have been promoted years ago. But much worse than this was the fact that Zondadari's parents had come to South America from Spain at the end of the Civil War. That was a dubious heritage. Then there were the suppositions derived from it, and various reports of snippets of conversation attributed to Zondadari. It seems the Captain was something of a young Turk in the making. One particular remark struck Hernandez with horror: the Captain was reputed to have said that one day democracy would be restored to the Republic. The word 'democracy' was one that General Hernandez loathed. He had put Zondadari's file aside, after writing on it: 'This man cannot be trusted with any secret work at all.' That at least would frustrate Olivarez's plans for Zondadari.

The second file that he had dealt with had been that belonging to José Maria Rodriguez, known as Fritz, who was the only child of a Spanish father and a German mother, both deceased. It had told him that Rodriguez was something of an intellectual; Hernandez's suspicions were immediately aroused. Rodriguez had built up a reputation as a military historian and a tactician. He was twenty-eight years old, unmarried and possibly a womaniser. He was, the file noted, not an observant Catholic. Hernandez wondered what that could mean. He would have to ask Isabel.

A third file dealt with a Captain Ximenez, currently stationed at San Cristobal, far to the south. This made reassuring reading. This man was half Welsh and half Spanish, but wholly loyal, as far as Hernandez could tell; and he was a man whom others would follow. With admiration Hernandez read the long list of achievements that the file attributed to Captain Ximenez: he had been given medals and decorations and prizes for everything from shot putting to shooting. He was respected and feared. Though Hernandez was a sedentary and rather lazy man himself, he felt that Ximenez was much to be preferred to the bookish Rodriguez, and wrote a note to that effect on the file.

His final task had been to read Enriquez's file. He was the same age as Rodriguez and they had been to the same school. His father had been dead for over twenty years, and had been a colonel in his son's regiment, the Cavalry. Hernandez racked his brains and was eventually able to call to mind a Colonel Enriquez. He seemed to remember that the poor man had died of a chill when still young, a chill he had caught when spending a weekend shooting duck. How very unfortunate. For

Enriquez *père* had been a very promising man, all those years ago. And now Olivarez clearly thought the same thing of the son. Again Hernandez dipped into the file: it seemed that Roberto Enriquez had been the most diligent cadet in the Army at one time – and diligence was something Hernandez admired much more than intelligence. But despite the fact that he had got into the Cavalry, he had not been promoted beyond the rank of captain. This was not in itself unusual. Very few were promoted these days, simply because there were so few old officers who wanted to retire.

Hernandez himself was over seventy years old. All these young men were doubtless waiting for the President to die; that was when their hoped for opportunity would come. Hernandez had lit an English cigarette and considered what might happen. The President would die; there would be a power struggle; one side would lose it and be disgraced, and then there would be promotions galore for those who had supported the winning side. This was not a comforting thought. He did not relish the prospect of a power struggle with Messina; he was getting too old for that sort of thing, and sometimes wished that the President would outlive him.

The old General returned to the file; someone had clearly taken a great deal of trouble with this particular file. He wondered for a moment if it were the work of Olivarez himself. Olivarez was methodical, as only people who busied themselves with secrets could be; but perhaps Olivarez was an artist too, and had produced this file, which was a complete portrait of a hero. How lucky Roberto Enriquez was, thought Hernandez, to be born into a military dictatorship, and one that had such need of heroes. Apart from his promising background, half Iberian, half Scottish, Enriquez seemed to have all the right qualities. He was a strict Catholic, not given at all to dissolute habits, unlike so many of his colleagues. There was a young lady in the picture, which was probably just as well, but the file provided ample details about her, which left General Hernandez in no doubt that Captain Enriquez was a very virtuous young man. He wondered idly how such details had been gleaned. It was rather worrying to think how widespread telephone tapping might be in the Republic.

The file also furnished some photographs of Enriquez. While Hernandez had skimmed over the photographs of Zondadari, Ximenez and Rodriguez, these particular photographs gave him pause for thought. A face, he thought, could perhaps give far more information than any file. The face he now looked at was unusual not only for its looks (Spanish and Scottish, thought Hernandez, were a remarkable combination) but for its expression. Captain Enriquez had clear hazel eyes, and somewhat wiry golden-blond hair brushed back from a high forehead; his skin was as delicate as a child's and reminded Hernandez of the smooth light brown marble of southern Italy that he had once seen as a young man. But it was the expression that arrested him more than anything else. There was something so direct about the way that this young man stared into the camera; it was more than confidence, it was almost contempt. There was a slight curl to those lips which seemed to speak of a profound disenchantment with the world. He checked the file to see who his associates were, but he found only a reference to the officer everyone called Fritz. He felt instinctively that this was the man they were looking for, a man without friends.

His mind had turned to Olivarez's plan. He would have to speak to Olivarez in detail later on. But first he would go and see Isabel; and that was what he had done. The meeting at the races would be instructive.

Once tea with General Hernandez was brought to a successful conclusion, Isabel de Calatrava decided to go to work at once. Clearly Arturo Hernandez, and Olivarez too, wanted her to find out as much as she could about Captain Enriquez. Accordingly she would go and call on Maria. Such undercover work could hardly be done over the phone.

Isabel was not a natural undercover agent, being rather large and stout and far too expensively dressed. In fact she was just the sort of woman who attracted attention wherever she went. The ministerial car that she used for social calls had the same effect. Her clothes too, which were copied by long-suffering seamstresses from photographs in European magazines, reflected her personality, being striking in the extreme, and often making her recognisable from a considerable distance. Today she descended on Maria Enriquez swathed in various shades of pink, her only concession to discretion being her last minute decision to leave her dog at home. The dog, a rather troublesome animal, had formed an attachment to her English paying guest, Nicola Nickleby, who had come to the Republic to learn Spanish. This was useful, as it meant that both girl and dog could safely be left at home, thus disposing of two problems at once. (Having a girl to stay was such a bore, but her parents were paying for her keep in sterling, directly into Isabel's London bank account, which was a reassuring thought in these uncertain times.)

'My dear, it's been such an age,' she said when she did eventually gain access to the Enriquez flat. 'I was just passing – but I'm afraid that I am rather out of breath –'

'The lift hasn't been working all year,' said Maria, watching her visitor sink into a chair. 'I find that it gives me good exercise.'

Isabel smiled. She looked at what exercise had done for Maria. For there she was, thin, neatly dressed, with silvery blonde hair, and wearing nothing more exciting than a pair of pearl earrings. There was not a trace of make-up on her face, and Isabel thought that the overall effect was woefully underdone.

'I would so like it if you could come to the races, this Saturday afternoon,' began Isabel, as soon as her breath had returned.

'How –'

'And you simply must bring Roberto. I am dying to see him; and I can't remember when I saw him last. But he was so delightful then, and wherever I go I hear such glowing reports about him.'

'Roberto has never struck me as delightful,' said his mother thoughtfully. 'If you are born blond on this continent people seem to think well of you however unworthy you may be of their good opinion. I've noticed that in my own case. But' – she hesitated, realising that Isabel, who was blonde now, certainly hadn't been born that way – 'I think Roberto was spoilt as a child, *pobrecito*.'

'Really?' asked Isabel, fascinated by this maternal frankness.

'You see, boys are very strong willed. And in Roberto's case, his father had died when he was seven years old, and all his uncles and cousins felt so sorry for him that they would indulge him in every way. Boys are allowed so many things that girls aren't, I've noticed. If a boy is seen to be strong willed, that is thought to be quite proper. I always hoped that the Army would make him a little less cross.'

'And did it?'

'Not really. If anything, he has got progressively more cross, if that is the word, as he has got older. He is discontented. He has this terribly dull job at the Ministry of Munitions; I can never seem to get him to tell me exactly what it is that he does, but whatever it is, it is clearly not satisfying him. And he might be there forever. It would ruin his character for good. The only person who seems to be able to do anything with him is Fritz.'

'Fritz Rodriguez? Whose mother was a Schultz?'

'Yes. His parents have been dead for years, though. He was an only child too. They were at school together, so they have been friends ever since they were about thirteen. I think that Fritz can say things to Roberto that no one else can. But what I really hope is that he will get married sooner or later. Perhaps that will make him more human.'

'But to whom?' asked Isabel.

'There is someone,' said Maria confidentially, yet wondering why she was telling Isabel all this. 'The trouble is that Roberto shows absolutely no sign of wanting to get married, even though I think that she would like to marry him. They have been friends for almost five years now; I haven't met her, but I am sure that she must want to marry him, and I think the reason he's never let me meet her is because he is frightened that the two of us would together force him to get married. Roberto hates doing anything unless he's convinced that it is his own idea.'

'How odd,' said Isabel. 'And who is she?'

'She sounds perfect, and I would love it to happen,' said Maria. 'Her name is Elena Garcia. Her mother is the editor of a fashion magazine, and she herself is a journalist with *The Post*. The father has been dead for some time, I think. It was Fritz who met her first, actually, from what I can gather. She must be about twenty-five.'

'But does he love her?' asked Isabel.

'He's a mystery to me,' replied Maria.

'I love mysteries,' said Isabel. 'You must make sure that he comes to the races with you on Saturday.'

'I doubt he will . . .'

'But he must. General Hernandez will be there, and so will Colonel Olivarez. It will be a great opportunity for him.'

'And who is Colonel Olivarez?' asked Maria.

'Oh, he's someone in the Government. You will find that he's quite a charming man. Do persuade Roberto. And I tell you what: I'll send an invitation to Captain Rodriguez; I'm sure he'll come; he's such a sociable young man, and if anyone will persuade your Roberto to come it will be Captain Rodriguez and you, my dear. And now I really must go. I've left the dog behind at home and the poor animal does hate it so. Someone will bring you the tickets you'll need to get into the enclosure. *A bientôt*, my dear.'

Three

Roberto did not live with his mother, as might have been the case, but he did visit her very frequently, usually once every two or three days. He was fond of her, and a little in awe of her, because he sometimes thought that he admired her more than any other woman he knew. This was because he knew that she had never flattered him, but treated him with absolute truthfulness. He often wished he could have grown up to be more like her; he admired her calmness and remoteness. Roberto himself, having been given his own way in almost everything since his earliest youth by his other relations, his sycophantic schoolmasters and most of his few friends, now found himself unable to be remote about anything. Life was a constant series of infuriations, a long agony of annoyance. For here he was, a brilliant young man, excellent at everything he had ever done, from algebra to athletics, yet he was still stuck behind a desk at the Ministry of Munitions. There were no fields of glory waiting for him. His captain's uniform was purely for show; he spent days pretending to deal with pieces of paper which were supposed to be connected with an Army that in the last two hundred years, ever since independence, had never once fought a war. Sometimes he wondered why he carried on at all. But the cruel fact was that in the Republic there was nothing outside the Army. The Army had expanded to fill all the available space in the country. One simply had to be patient and wait for opportunities that might never come.

And he was patient; for though he was frequently

infuriated, he never allowed anyone to see it. That was the way he had been brought up.

On top of this there was the fact that Elena loved him. This was not his fault; she had, as they said, fallen in love with him. Roberto imagined that falling in love was rather like falling off a cliff, something people did involuntarily. Once it happened that was it; and Elena was resolutely in love with him, and though theirs was a far from ideal relationship, she seemed to have no thought of ever giving him up. This was a pity, for he often felt that he would not make her happy, even though she was, more than anyone he had met, most naturally designed to make him happy. But he wasn't sure if he wanted to be happy. He was supposed to be lucky, at least that was what Fritz had told him several times, but he was unable to appreciate his good fortune.

Fritz had been instrumental in their meeting. Fritz was Roberto's closest and perhaps only friend. Fritz himself was the sort of person who was universally popular, and almost completely different from Roberto in every respect. Like Roberto's mother, he never seemed to be ground down by the tedium of daily life, but always found plenty to keep him happy. He was forever reading Sir Winston Churchill's history of the Second World War, or Clausewitz, or the correspondence of Prince Metternich, all for pleasure; and between times receiving passionate telephone calls from women who would never leave messages when he was out. In almost everything Fritz let himself be guided by Roberto, and he was so used to being guided by him that he never thought to resent anything Roberto might do.

Roberto had met Elena at a regimental ball; they had met as strangers, for Elena had been invited to the ball by Fritz, who at the last moment had fallen ill and asked Roberto to go in his place, which he had done as a favour, for generally Roberto hated social occasions. Thus it had turned out that the girl's nascent affections had fixed on Roberto, not Fritz. But Fritz, despite a considerable sense of disappointment, did not resent this; he was used to having little success with younger women, just as he was used to dealing with the advances of older ones; it was not what he would have chosen, but nevertheless something he had got used to. Besides, Fritz was rather short, well built and with a shock of reddish-brown hair that was already thinning somewhat on top; he had a pleasant face and a charming smile, destined to melt the hearts of any military wife past her fortieth birthday. By contrast, Roberto was tall and blond, with a perfect physique, and therefore it seemed quite natural to Fritz that Elena should fall in love with his friend rather than with himself. Furthermore, being a military historian, Fritz had an almost exalted idea of friendship between comrades in arms, and was resolved never to let any rivalry develop between him and Roberto. Thus he had retired from the field, from time to time hearing about Elena with interest, but taking the trouble never to see her.

And so it had gone on for five years. Roberto sometimes wished now that he had never gone to that ball in Fritz's place. The last time he had seen Elena, she had suggested that they go away together to America; she had the habit of referring to the United States as 'America'. He had reminded her that they were already in America as it was. That had been over two weeks ago, and he had not seen her since.

'We've been invited to the races,' his mother was telling him. 'Isabel de Calatrava came round to do so specially.'

'How peculiar,' said Roberto, looking at the tickets his mother had passed to him. 'And why should General Hernandez want to see us? I see it is for his box.'

'I wonder if he will be there. Isabel seemed to think he would be. Isabel said someone called Colonel Olivarez would be there too. Do you know who he is?'

'He's the Head of Security. God only knows what he does all day. I can't imagine that a country like this is swarming with foreign spies. There isn't anything to spy on. I should quite like to see what Colonel Olivarez is like at close quarters.'

'Then you will come with me? I gather Fritz is invited too. Did he tell you?'

'I haven't seen Fritz just recently. He's recovering from being poisoned by an *empanada*.'

'*Pobrecito*,' said Maria sympathetically. 'But you will come, won't you?'

'Yes,' said Roberto. 'There may be something in all this. I don't expect I will like Colonel Olivarez, though.'

'Isabel says he's charming,' observed his mother.

Roberto laughed. Colonel Olivarez presumably was responsible for many uncharming things.

'And how is Elena?' asked Maria, as she always did.

Roberto's good-looking face assumed a frown of abstraction.

'I don't really know,' he said. 'She hardly ever talks about herself these days. Mainly she talks about her mother.'

'And do you tell her about me?'

'No. She is far too busy telling me about her own mother. It seems that Mrs Garcia has contracted political fever – not dangerously so – but enough to make her dull. She has adopted the view that soldiers never did any good. I think she's got it into her head that I am ruining her daughter's life, and she may be quite right about that. She thinks that Elena ought to find some nice young man to marry.'

'She has, *chiquitito*.'

'I don't think I am particularly nice,' said Roberto, a hard look coming across his face. 'But Elena can't see that. It is odd, isn't it? Her mother has even tried suggesting some alternatives she might consider.'

'Who?'

'Again they are all officers,' said Roberto. 'The first was Fritz, of course, but that is quite hopeless from all points of view; Fritz is far too loyal to me to do anything like that. She suggested a few other nice young officers she had met. But none of them will do. They spend most of their time hanging around with very disreputable people and sniffing strange substances, not that Mrs Garcia would realise that.'

'So Elena is better off with you, after all,' said Maria.

'Mrs Garcia doesn't agree; she says the Army is ruining the country, and she blames me. Of course, she may be right, but it is hardly my fault. If it is someone's fault then it is the fault of all these senile old men like Hernandez. But I think that it is no one's fault at all. A country like this is destined to be misruled. It may be something in the weather.'

'I hope it doesn't rain on Saturday,' said Maria. 'I haven't been to the races for a long time. They say that the General is very unwell.'

'Who says so?' asked Roberto. 'All the newspapers say that he's absolutely fine.'

'I know they do, and no one believes them the more they say it. Poor old man, he must be over eighty now.'

It had never crossed Roberto's mind that the Father of the Country, the President for Life, was nothing but a poor old man.

'If he is dying,' said Roberto, 'what will happen to the rest of us?'

He was a young man, and in the prime of life, yet again and again this feeling of helplessness crept up upon him. He envied the way his mother could be so calm and sit there and feel sorry for the old man, unworried about the future. The General might die, they might be catapulted into some unknown fate, and here she sat in her comfortable flat, unruffled by thoughts of the future.

'*Chiquitito*, I can't help wishing that you would get married soon,' she said suddenly.

'To Elena?'

'Yes. I am sure that I'd like her.'

'I am sure that you would,' he said.

'And you like her too, don't you, dear?' asked Maria.

Of course he liked her. But that wasn't the point. The point was, that he didn't love her, but that was not something he could tell his mother. Besides, he wasn't sure whether it was true. Perhaps he did love her, after all. But if he did love her, why did the realisation that she loved him – he knew she did because she had told him so often enough – why did that make him so uncomfortable?

He could not answer her question. All their conversations ended like this. Roberto got up to go. He carefully put on his cap and kissed his mother on the cheek. He wished that he could satisfy her dearest wish, to which she referred every time he saw her. Perhaps he would telephone Elena. He could feel a brand new five hundred escudo coin in his pocket; it was one of the new coins they had minted recently, and seemed to buy nothing more than a telephone call. Perhaps he would find a public telephone box that was working and call her, on his way back to his dull existence at the Ministry of Munitions.

Four

Elena was at work; that is, she was in the offices occupied by *The Post*, the Republic's only English-language newspaper. She was drinking tea with a man who was known as Young Caballero. He enjoyed the epithet 'Young' because he was the grandson of the Editor, Old Caballero. Very little ever happened at *The Post*, and this was one of those idle hours.

'He never phones,' she was saying. 'I keep on leaving messages for him at the Ministry, but he never replies.'

Young Caballero nodded sympathetically. Elena was tall, dark and beautiful. It was quite easy to be sympathetic to her.

'I can't think why I never hear from him,' she was saying. 'You see I made a point of telling him that my mother was going away for two weeks. He could phone me at home and that would mean there would be no risk of her picking up the phone. I know he doesn't want to speak to her, and that's not entirely his fault either, but now he seems not to want to speak to me either. Why?'

'Military men are a strange lot,' said Young Caballero, who had had various experiences in that field.

'There's no reason for it. Everyone here is slightly mad,' said Elena. 'I can't think why you didn't stay in America.'

Young Caballero had spent some years in California, but he had decided to come back. The delicate reasons for his return had never really been explained to Elena. But she had never been sufficiently interested in his emotional life to press him about it. The mystery of Caballero's private life would attract her attention briefly every now and then, but then she would always be brought back to the one topic that dominated her waking hours, namely, Captain Roberto Enriquez.

'It's no use saying I should leave him, because I can't,' she said decisively.

Caballero, who had said nothing, sighed.

And then the telephone rang; Young Caballero discreetly crept out of the room, sure that it would be him. The poor girl was a little bit mad today, he thought; but in this country, everyone was. So Caballero crept out of the room, wondering when this collective madness would end, and if the country would ever regain its senses. He stood in the corridor outside his office and looked out of the window. A few hundred yards away he could see the Presidential Palace, the Marine Gardens to the north of it, and the fine sweep of the Bay along which the city was built. In the Palace, if it was true, and it was hard to tell what was true these days and what not, an old man lay suspended between life and death. Perhaps he was already dead, and they were keeping it a secret. Perhaps, even if he died, the whole absurd system would go on without him. Perhaps, as some people were whispering, there would be a civil war. Why there should be a civil war was not clear, but that was what a few people were saying. It would be the final absurdity. It was as if they lived in a land under a cloud; something had come between them and the sun, a shadow had fallen between them and reality, and in that shade they were all condemned to live.

Five

Saturday came, and with it the promised afternoon at the races. In the past Roberto had always set Saturday afternoons aside for Elena, as he was a creature of habit, but he had told her over the telephone that he was engaged that Saturday, and to assuage her disappointment he had agreed to come to dinner at the Garcia flat afterwards. Her mother was away, and it seemed best to take advantage of her absence. Mrs Garcia, editor of *Moda*, was on a business trip to Europe; he would never have agreed to come to see Elena at home had her mother been present. It was odd that he saw so little of her; it was almost as if he wanted to avoid her, even though he was fond of her. But the fact that she loved him frightened him. The normality of her affection was completely out of place in the life he led when he was away from her. He feared that he would never be able to love her and marry her, and he felt accordingly that he ought to have been able to cultivate her with a spirit of detachment, lest she lead him into frustration and unhappiness.

This strange frame of mind was a result of his odd upbringing. He lived in a world where impersonal duty was considered paramount. The nation existed to do its duty, and his mother had been unable to compete with the idea she had tried to instil in him that personal things were more important. The Junta had won; the Junta was everywhere. It was the entire life of the nation, and much as he despised the old men who ran the country, nevertheless he had imbibed all that the Junta stood for. The life of a soldier had always seemed to him to be the best sort of life, an ordered life; and everything else opposed to it seemed to him naturally to tend towards anarchy. He had become used to the discipline of keeping the passions at bay. The idea of being guided by anything as irrational as love filled him with horror. It would be so very feckless to allow oneself to drift in a way one could not control.

His passion for order made him rather dislike General Hernandez at first sight. On entering the box he had had a formal little talk with the old man, but had not been impressed by his evident fondness for champagne. As soon as he was able to do so, he had taken his glass and gone to the front of the box to pretend to look at the horses. Roberto decided that Hernandez was soft, and that it was no wonder that the country was becoming more and more inefficient with such men to rule it. He had noticed that his mother was already there, deep in talk with an ageing colonel of her acquaintance, and had decided not to join her. He wondered where Fritz was; he had rather hoped Fritz would have got there before him; but Fritz had been a little mysterious about his movements that afternoon, when thcy had discussed it at breakfast.

'Well, you have seen him?' asked Isabel de Calatrava.

'Yes,' replied Hernandez; 'A very fine young man. I wonder what Olivarez will make of him. Is there any sign of Rodriguez? I wanted to ask you some more about him. What is he like?'

'Very charming,' said Isabel, with a little smile. 'Recently he has been spending a lot of time with the wife of one of your colonels from the Ministry. At least that is what I hear.'

Hernandez was thoughtful.

'Which colonel?' he asked.

'Colonel Mendoza,' said Isabel candidly.

General Hernandez looked towards the aged Colonel Mendoza, who was still deep in conversation with Mrs Enriquez. There was no sign of his wife, and the General grew thoughtful again.

Colonel Olivarez was not long in disengaging himself from

the British Ambassador, leaving him among the champagne bottles with his American counterpart, and coming up and joining Roberto at the front of the box. It was a large box and they were quite removed from the noise of the party in progress behind them. Olivarez put his untouched champagne glass down on the ledge next to Roberto's. This was a place for confidences.

'Do you like champagne, Captain?' he asked.

'Actually, sir, no. I've never really drunk it before now, so the fault is probably mine,' replied Roberto politely, not knowing who this friendly colonel was.

'Never? I thought that all our young officers spent most of their time revelling in foreign luxuries. Or am I wrong?'

'I hope you are, sir.'

'And why do you hope that, Captain?'

'There's something worrying about a country where the ruling class becomes soft, sir.'

'And is that happening to us, do you think?' asked Olivarez. 'But don't answer. I know you would not want your words to be misinterpreted. But there are many who would say that you were absolutely right; there's a sense now that things can only get worse. Look at the men who are conscripted into the ranks these days. There's no doing anything with half of them: they're mentally unfit or physically unfit, or both. There's not much officer material there, I can tell you. And then there are the officers we have, especially the younger ones. Morale is low. So many of them start off so well but then get infected by strange ideas; and even if you stop them from travelling abroad, and the value of the escudo does that more completely than any law could, somehow or another they lose their dedication to duty. It is no wonder that the Americans and the British think we are doomed.'

'Do they think that, sir?'

'They do. Do you see that man over there? The lugubrious looking chap with the moustache? He is called Sir Nigel something or another. He is the British Ambassador and a great friend of General Hernandez. He seems to have observed our decay at first hand. We listen to his telephone conversations; not that we really need to, as he is very indiscreet: but he gives us a few more years and then –'

Olivarez snapped his fingers.

'Unless we do something soon,' said Olivarez after a pause for reflection, 'it will be too late. There's already a *fin de siècle* feel about all this.'

'And what can we do, sir?' asked Roberto, looking round the box, noticing the elderly officers quaffing champagne, and Isabel de Calatrava's voice, high and insistent, detailing some latest snippet of gossip. His eyes were looking for Fritz, but Fritz was not there.

'We will revamp our intelligence services,' said Olivarez shortly.

'That will be a job for Colonel Olivarez, sir,' said Roberto.

'My dear young man, I am Colonel Olivarez.'

Roberto was surprised. He had not expected the Colonel to be so ordinary a man. He wished now that he had paid more attention to the conversation, for he could not be sure what answers he had made, what he had said, and whether he had said the right things. For one thing was certain: there were no casual conversations with Colonel Olivarez, there were only examinations.

'Have some champagne,' Sir Nigel said to the rather dull looking North American standing next to him. 'I'm sure our hostess won't mind our helping ourselves. Besides she's stuck with a frightfully boring colonel that I have just left her with.'

'Thank you,' said the North American, who happened to be the Ambassador of the United States.

'Quite a good party this,' said Sir Nigel conversationally.

'Yes,' replied his companion.

'As long as you don't get stuck with some frightful bore that is,' said Sir Nigel. 'Does Isabel invite you often?'

'Yes.'

'Yes, yes, I suppose she must do,' said Sir Nigel, now

remembering where he had met the dull little man before. 'Look, have some more to drink, no one will notice. We might as well drink as much as we can. There could be a revolution tomorrow, and then where would we be? Do you have a helicopter?'

'I do,' said the North American.

'Really?' said Sir Nigel with sudden interest. 'What a useful thing to have. You never know when you might need one. One has seen it in films of course – the helicopter on the embassy roof, panic-stricken women, old retainers heartlessly being left behind. But sometimes one feels that films come perilously close to reality.'

'I've never been one for the cinema,' said the United States Ambassador.

'I've heard,' said Sir Nigel, lowering his voice, 'that the Old Man can't last much longer. You know what that means. Our passports section is very busy these days. All sorts of people have been round using the shakiest of connections to try and get Her Britannic Majesty's little blue book. Even, between you and me, our hostess there.'

The United States Ambassador looked at Isabel with renewed interest. Isabel was wearing a frock copied from Norman Hartnell, and had a glass of champagne in one hand and a Pekingese in the other.

'Did you say she was a friend of your Queen?' said the American.

'No. Not at all. It was a manner of speaking.'

The United States Ambassador now began to look around himself, wondering how he could escape this Englishman. He sometimes wished he had never accepted a diplomatic post. He did not feel at home in this strange land of double meanings.

(By happy contrast, Nicola Nickleby was beginning to feel much more at home in this strange republic. She was starting to enjoy the party. No one was paying the slightest attention to her: her youth and the fact that she wasn't in military uniform, but merely in a dress her mother had bought her in

Godalming, made her quite insignificant. But this had its advantages; it meant that she was able to drink as much champagne as she liked without her hostess noticing, and she was also free to admire the guests. Perhaps the champagne was going to her head, but there was one young officer there who was divinely handsome. She hoped that she would get to see him again; perhaps he would be present at other parties given by Mrs de Calatrava. She did hope so. She was fast beginning to lose all affection she had ever felt for her hostess's dog.)

Conversation ceased for a while. Attention momentarily shifted to the race-course where a few decrepit horses began to run round the dusty track. This, after all, was what they had gathered to see. Maria Enriquez borrowed a pair of binoculars and followed the race intently, as had been the manner of her youth. The more polite guests did the same. Roberto, who imagined that there would be nothing that would interest him, now began to wonder in earnest where Fritz had got to. This new habit of his, disappearing for hours on end, was rather annoying. He was keen to see Fritz so that he could discuss Olivarez with him, and began to feel more annoyed than ever that Fritz had not turned up. He would go and see whether he could find anything out; he left the box in the company of the aged Colonel who had so bored Sir Nigel, and who had been waiting for his wife (a woman many years his junior) all afternoon in vain.

At the back of the box, undisturbed, General Hernandez and Colonel Olivarez were enjoying a few quiet words.

'Enriquez is what we are looking for,' the Colonel was saying. 'An impeccable background, and from what I've been careful to ask about him, generally liked, though he does have a reputation for reserve as well. That is no bad thing. A man should be liked but he shouldn't owe anyone any favours. And the same goes for Ximenez. But I suppose you saw the files?'

'I did,' said the General. 'You can use Enriquez by all means. And Ximenez. But Zondadari is out of the question. The man has liberal ideas.'

'Which was why I wanted him,' said Olivarez. 'He won't be very liberal by the time I have finished with him. We have to turn opinion round among the younger officers.'

'No,' said Hernandez stubbornly. 'Zondadari is dangerous, he's too well liked, and he must be kept away from the centre of the action. What does he do at present?'

'In charge of the City barracks.'

'Then leave him there, where we can see him. I wouldn't trust such a man in the provinces; but in the City, under our noses, he can't do any harm. It is Rodriguez I want to talk about. The man is impossible. Isabel invited him here this afternoon, and he hasn't shown up. Poor Colonel Mendoza was here too, expecting his wife, and she didn't turn up either. She's about forty-five, I believe. I've just spoken to Isabel and she told me she wouldn't be surprised. We can't have this sort of thing going on, you know. I've known Colonel Mendoza for years, and while I think he made a terrible mistake marrying a woman years his junior, all the same . . .'

'Rodriguez is a very clever man,' said Olivarez.

'There are others,' said Hernandez. 'I want you to get rid of Rodriguez. Send him out of this city to some place where he won't be comfortable, with superior officers who will give him hell. Send him to teach the military cadets something useful in San Cristobal. That's where Ximenez is, isn't it? I can read between the lines: Ximenez is a brute. Send him there.'

Thus the fates of Fritz and Roberto were both sealed on the same afternoon, in different ways.

Six

Roberto had tried to telephone Fritz, but without success, and had wasted several thousand escudos in the process. He looked at his watch and saw that it was past six o'clock. He decided he would not go back to the box, and that if he were to slip away, no one would wonder where he had gone, for they would all be too busy watching the races. Besides, Elena would be expecting him soon, and he had wasted enough time trying to get hold of Fritz. So he left the race-course and began to walk towards Elena's flat, which would take him about half an hour. He would arrive early and surprise her. He was glad Mrs Garcia would not be there. Under normal circumstances her absence alone should have made him light-hearted. But these were not normal circumstances.

He had met Colonel Olivarez and that filled him with dread, for he knew that he would surely meet him again. He had not imagined that the Colonel would have been so urbane, so unremarkable. He had heard the name of Olivarez often in the past, but never imagined the Head of Security to be of such benign aspect. It was as if the dreaded Olivarez had adopted the most cunning disguise of all, that of conventional normality. Olivarez had not been there to see the horses. Roberto wondered if he had said anything that could have been misconstrued, if he had allowed himself to fall under suspicion already. But as far as he could remember he had said hardly anything at all, and certainly nothing incriminating. But why had Olivarez spoken to him? Ought he to be worried? Or ought he even to be pleased?

He rang the bell of Elena's flat, resolving to set the question of Olivarez to one side. He would try and enjoy himself instead. The door buzzed open, and he went up, not noticing the car parked opposite and the two men who were inside it.

The flat was filled with the welcoming aroma of garlic, one of the few things of which there was no shortage at present.

'Someone sold me a rabbit,' she said to him. 'They did – really. I know it was a rabbit, because I saw him kill it before my very eyes. One has to do so nowadays, otherwise they'll sell you anything, even cats. How were the races?'

'Dull, as far as races go. And Fritz ought to have been there, but didn't show up.'

'Then it must have been really dull,' said Elena. 'Fritz livens things up wherever he goes, I imagine.'

'He does. But I'm glad to see you.'

Later, after they had eaten the rabbit and drunk some Cuban vodka that had brought tears to their eyes, she said:

'I wish it could always be like this.'

'What do you mean?' he asked gently.

'I mean, I wish life would be a little more kind to us. I know we are relatively well off – but I was on the telephone in the office the other day, and I was sure there was someone listening.'

'You're mad,' he said. 'But that is the way I like you.'

'I thought I was mad too. The telephones are often strange. And I think I've noticed a man following me in the streets sometimes.'

'There could be a perfectly good reason for a man following a beautiful girl.'

'I know. Perhaps I am a little bit paranoid. Mother is, and I am catching it off her.'

'Don't worry, you're safe here with me now. You can even fall asleep.'

'But you're hardly ever here, Roberto.'

'I know,' he said. 'If I had any sense I'd come and see you more often; but I think I'd bring you bad luck. If I had any real sense, I'd suggest we pack and go somewhere else tomorrow.'

'Where would we go?'

'I don't know. Brazil, Australia . . . It hardly matters where. There isn't anywhere I could go, really . . .'

Elena had fallen asleep. What was stopping him emigrating to Australia? Of course, he wouldn't have any money, but he could get some sort of job. But all this was idle thought. He had to stay where he was; he could not desert his post.

He was jolted out of his calm reflections by an insistent knocking on the door. Elena woke with a start. There would be no escape after all.

'Who is it?' asked Elena, going to the door. 'It is almost midnight.'

'Let me go,' he said, doing up his shirt buttons, going towards the door.

There were two men, one a lieutenant, another an NCO, both armed, both waiting patiently for him to open the door. Both were unknown to him.

'You are to come with us at once, sir,' said the elder of the two, the NCO.

'Where to?' he asked.

'You will know when you get there, sir,' was the reply. 'Come.'

'I need to put on my shoes,' said Roberto. 'I've been asleep.'

'We know that, sir,' said the man. 'But our orders are to take you at once. Get the rest of your clothes, and quickly.'

Roberto went into the sitting-room, where he had left his shoes and socks, and his tunic. He began to put them on, while the younger of the two men, a youth of about twenty in the uniform of the Engineers, watched him, his hand resting on his pistol.

'What is happening?' asked Elena.

'I don't know. I can only guess.'

He was about to reach for his holster and put it on, when the young officer held out his hand for it.

'I'll take it, sir, if you don't mind,' he said, a little apologetically.

'I suppose I am being arrested,' said Roberto to Elena. He looked at the younger of the two men, the one who seemed to have the kinder face. 'Lieutenant,' he asked, 'can I make a telephone call?' For he had suddenly realised that he had left the races without saying goodbye to his mother.

'Certainly not,' said the older man, the NCO, more to the Lieutenant than to Roberto. 'It is time to go.'

Dazed, Roberto got up to go.

'I'd better do as they say,' he said to Elena, half-way to the door, but by the time she had thought of what to say in reply, he was gone.

As soon as he was outside, he was put into the back seat of a car, and the young Lieutenant got in next to him, holding his arm, and with his other hand, sticking his Beretta pistol against Roberto's ribs. He wondered where he was being taken, and hoped to God that the lad's grip was steady and that the safety catch was securely on. The Lieutenant looked very young to him, and inexperienced in handling firearms. This then was what happened to people who were arrested. He knew that such things did happen, and he had pictured them, but he had never imagined them happening to himself. He felt an odd sort of curiosity about it all. These then were Olivarez's men. He was in the hands of the Security Department.

The older man, the NCO, was in the driving seat, and presently turned round to speak to the prisoner.

'If you are wondering who I am, sir,' he said, 'my name is Strauss. We may meet again after this, who knows.'

So perhaps he was not going to be shot after all. He did not like the look of Strauss, but he would hardly have introduced himself if their acquaintance was going to be speedily brought to an end by a summary execution.

'And that, sir,' said Strauss, turning round again, gesturing to his colleague, 'that is Lieutenant Tanucci. Now he's a great friend of the Colonel, aren't you, Tanucci?'

Tanucci laughed, showing off some indifferent dentistry. Roberto noticed that Strauss had not called Tanucci 'sir';

clearly Strauss, despite his inferior rank, was the real one in charge.

'The reason we took your gun, sir,' Tanucci said to Roberto, 'was to stop you trying to kill yourself. We've got to deliver you intact. The Colonel expects it.'

'And do people shoot themselves rather than meet the Colonel?' asked Roberto.

'Sometimes,' said Strauss. 'It depends what the Colonel wants. We try to take no risks, sir. It upsets the Colonel when someone does.'

The car sped on through the darkened streets – there was no street lighting anymore, thanks to fuel shortages – and presently they arrived. Large gates opened to admit them, and immediately shut behind them; they were in a courtyard. Without being given any time to recognise his surroundings, Roberto was hustled into the building. There was a long corridor, which they took at a run as soldiers did when carrying out orders in the Army, then a door, then a bare room; bare except for filing cabinets and a desk, a few wooden chairs, and Colonel Olivarez seated behind the desk. A single light bulb dangled above him, illuminating the whole.

'Good,' said Olivarez gravely, without looking up for more than a few seconds. 'Did you know that Mrs Carmen Garcia is the widow of one Hector Garcia, a man who committed suicide while in Army custody, held on political charges? I don't suppose you did. Is Miss Garcia politically minded?'

'No, sir.'

Roberto was doing his best to stand respectfully to attention. He was being held by his two captors, who were gripping his arms tightly. Olivarez was studying certain files open in front of him.

'You are right,' said Olivarez mildly. 'Miss Garcia says very little of interest on the phone, at least when it comes to politics. She spends most of her time talking about you. I hope it amused some of our men to hear what she said. There are some real gems in her conversations, but I'll spare you the embarrassment of reading them out. Well, that seems all in order,' he said, and shut the file he had been reading.

Olivarez looked up at Roberto and considered him for a moment.

'I want to ask you a question,' he said. 'I am a little puzzled. You speak Spanish and English, don't you?'

'Yes, sir.'

'That is in your file,' said Olivarez. 'Your mother was a Maitland. I suppose you spoke English at home, didn't you? Yes, that is in your file too. What puzzles me is this: why can't Captain José Maria Rodriguez speak German, when that was his mother's language?'

'His mother used to speak English, sir,' said Roberto, confused by this unexpected question. 'They never spoke German at home, as far as I can remember.'

'Curious,' said Olivarez, and then shut Fritz's file. He then looked up at Roberto. 'Do you know why you are here?' he asked.

'No, sir.'

'Well, it isn't to ask you questions about Rodriguez. What if I were to tell you that you were to be shot at once for being a danger to the State?' he asked calmly.

'I would ask to phone my mother, sir,' said Roberto. 'And also to speak to a priest.'

'Would you?'

'Yes, sir.'

'I am afraid to tell you, Captain, that those are two things that we never allow. No one is allowed any communication with the outside world once they are brought here. When people disappear without trace, they do just that. They disappear.'

The Colonel paused as if for thought; then he looked suitably grave for a moment; then he gave a slow deliberate nod. Roberto found that his arms were being released from their tight grip. But no sooner had this new sense of release come to him, before he could quite understand it, the evil-faced Strauss had roughly pulled off his cap. As he was wondering what he ought to do in these circumstances, he felt Tanucci's hands slip around his waist and very quickly pull out his belt. Before he was able to protest, his belt was being tightly buckled around his chest, pinioning both his arms very effectively, and he, with the uncomfortable sensation that his trousers might be coming down, was being forced to run down another long corridor. This took a matter of seconds, and suddenly they were outside. He saw a post, and a wall, and knew what was going to happen. Twenty-five minutes ago, he had been dreaming of freedom in Australia; now, for some careless words he could not call to mind, he was to be shot. Tanucci was tying him to the post. He noticed Strauss carefully checking his M-12 rifle. Tanucci's boyish face was very close to him: Tanucci was, with a look of concentration, fixing the target to his tunic, just on the spot where he had felt for his heartbeat. He knew then, as he saw the look of concentration in the boy's eyes, that he was to die. He tried to say the act of contrition, but could not remember the words. A terrible fear came over him, and Tanucci pulled the hood over his head.

There was a sound of retreating footsteps, distant voices, a moment of silence, and then the sharp report of rifles. Then there was only blackness.

Seven

Elena, after a frantic search through the telephone directory, had at last found the number she had been looking for. She would telephone Roberto's mother, and tell her what had happened. She was a military widow, and she would know what to do, who to see, what steps to take. This doubtless was what Roberto would have wanted her to do. But when she picked up the receiver, she discovered that the line was dead. They had cut her off, and the realisation that there was nothing she could do reduced her to tears of despair.

A long way away, as if approaching from an infinite distance, he could hear the sound of laughter, high pitched, immature laughter, belonging to Tanucci.

A bucket of cold water and a gentle prod with a boot roused him from his faint. Hands were undoing his bonds. He had slumped to his knees and found it impossible to stand.

'Come on, sir,' he heard Strauss's voice say. 'You have only fainted. And like all the rest you've ruined your trousers.'

Then he realised that Strauss was talking to him.

The next interview with Olivarez was far more pleasant than the first and took place some hours later. He had been allowed the luxury of a bath and a few hours' sleep. His uniform was being cleaned somewhere by expert hands. He was sitting in a dressing-gown, and had just finished a substantial breakfast. Round his neck hung his military identification tag and the medal of Our Lady of Lourdes that he had been given as a boy, and he had worn constantly since as a charm against bad luck. He felt as if it had protected him once again. He was glad to be alive.

'We do it to all our new men,' Olivarez was saying. 'It shows what a man is like. It is a test of character. Quite a few don't make it, you know; they break down, they start to plead. But you were excellent, Enriquez. Tell me truthfully, though, will you ever get to like Strauss and Tanucci?'

'I doubt it very much, sir,' said Roberto.

'Strauss has something of a history,' said the Colonel. 'He had a slight criminal record when I discovered him. Not a good family either: this Strauss comes from a long line of Viennese thugs who were pretty glad to come here in' 45. Nothing at all to do with the composers. Strauss is a rather distasteful character, but he will do distasteful work – under your command, of course. If he ever disobeys you or gets out of hand, I'll have him hanged. Strauss is there to be used. Tanucci is somewhat different. I won't tell you how I met him; you can use him too. You'll find that he's young and malleable. He's not stupid, even though he might seem so to you. He's supposed to have won a prize for mathematics – he was in the Engineers. From the lower classes, of course, and despite the name, common Italian stock. He won't be any trouble to you or anyone else. But Strauss will need careful control. Ah, here come your clothes.'

An orderly entered with a pile of freshly laundered clothes.

'Get dressed and we'll go to the Palace. I can explain things to you on the way there.'

'The work you are going to do,' said Olivarez, when they were in the back of the official Mercedes, 'is of the utmost importance. That is why the Minister of the Interior himself will explain it to you. You will see General Messina and possibly someone else as well. He will tell you details, but all the time you will be working for me. You will have to take an oath of secrecy and you will tell no one about your work: certainly not La Garcia, nor even your mother. Do you want to ask me any questions?'

'Yes, sir. What exactly am I going to do?'

'For a start you will not even go back to the Ministry of Munitions to clear your desk. You will be reporting to the building that we have just left, the old Army Navigational School, where you will live and have Strauss and Tanucci under your command. It will be your job to oversee the rooting out of those engaged in anti-Government activity. It will be a political job, the type that can only be done by men of the highest trustworthiness. I've told you about Strauss and Tanucci – they will do the actual work of questioning and arresting prisoners, but you will be the one to see that they do it properly and effectively. I don't intend to let them loose on the population without any safeguards, do you see?'

'I see, sir. What means are we to use to question prisoners?'

'Any and every means,' said Olivarez. 'Strauss is something of an expert at that.'

'And after they have been questioned?'

'For some of them, the majority perhaps, there will be no afterwards,' said Olivarez shortly. 'You are to ensure that they disappear.'

'All of them, sir?'

'Yes, unless you can think of some civil charge against them and hand them over to the Police; but you are not to be a policeman. You are a soldier and this is a war.'

They arrived at the Palace. It was early in the morning, and Roberto felt the tiredness pass over him. His head was swimming. It was not every day that he was shot and brought back to life. They were once again going down very long corridors, but walking this time, passing uniformed men who sat at desks, and who, seeing Olivarez, stood up hurriedly and saluted. At last they reached their destination, and before them was Messina, a short stout figure in a uniform a little too tight for him, which perhaps explained his acutely uncomfortable expression. Olivarez and Roberto saluted.

'The Republic is in peril,' said Messina, getting down to business at once. 'Even the Security Department can't be entirely trusted. You may find that some of your duties will be unpleasant, but we expect you to put your sense of duty first. Is that clear, Enriquez?'

'Sir,' replied Roberto.

He thought he understood. This was the long expected call, the call to do something for his country.

'We are facing economic sabotage,' continued Messina. 'We have to find the men who are behind it. Olivarez will deal with the propaganda side of things, but you will actually catch the men responsible, and you will do everything in your power to uncover the network they have in the country. They must be accounted for. You will work practically alone, but that is vitally necessary, as the Army itself is riddled with Liberal sympathisers. We have names already, and they will be encouraged to betray their friends.'

Olivarez then gave the General a questioning look.

'Very well,' said the tubby little man. 'You had better follow me.'

Another corridor, more men on guard, all of whom saluted as they passed; and finally there was a door that seemed more important than any other. Messina knocked, but received no reply. He hesitated a moment, and then went boldly in, the others following.

It was a very grandly furnished room, shrouded in brocade. His eyes took in a huge and hideous four poster bed, a dusty stuccoed ceiling, and a vista of tarnished mirrors. It was the sort of room that in his imagination Roberto had always seen inhabited by doomed sovereigns or the lonely Prime Ministers of dying regimes. In rooms such as this, insulated by Divine Right and deaf to the cries of the mob beyond the palace gates, a generation of Bourbons had passed away. But the sound he could hear now was not that of a mob, but was rather the brash North American accents emerging from the only modern and discordant thing in the room, a television set. Before it sat a man of great age, propped up in his chair by cushions; next to him, like a tutelary deity guarding the hearth, sat an old Indian woman, her black and uncomprehending eyes fixed on the screen.

The General was watching television.

Messina approached and turned down the sound. The Old Man, who had not seemed to be aware that anyone had come into the room, turned his head slightly and looked at Messina, as if wondering who he could be. The old Indian woman sat on, motionless. Messina bent over the Old Man and whispered a few words in his ear. Then he turned and beckoned Roberto to come forward. Over the thick carpet, into the silence, he came. Messina placed Roberto's hand into the Old Man's. The pale blue eyes looked at him; Roberto, who had not seen the Father of the Country for some years, noticed that he was wearing pyjamas that were hardly clean. The General's hand was weak and pale in his own.

'There,' said Messina, bringing the encounter to a close.

They withdrew a few paces and bowed. Then they turned to leave.

'He's very pleased,' said Messina. 'I told him who you were and he quite approves.'

From behind the closed door they could hear the television, now louder than ever.

After that there were a few official papers to sign. Roberto was told that this was routine; one of them concerned the oath of secrecy. Olivarez told him that someone would remove his personal effects from his present barracks and transfer them to the Army Navigational School. Then he was told that he was free to go. He stepped out into the Palace Square, his head still light. He went to a café and sat down and ordered a cup of coffee, and wondered what he had better do. It was Sunday morning and only ten o'clock. Only ten hours had passed since he had been arrested the night before, and yet it seemed like a lifetime. He had died and been revived. Around him the bells of the Cathedral rang out into the clear early summer air.

In the Cathedral the Archbishop was preparing to say Mass. His secretary, a small dark priest called Father Morisco, stood at his side to remind him that the Mass was to be one of thanksgiving to mark the General's restoration to good health, news of which had just been announced. The Archbishop, who had never been a worldly man, nodded his head gravely.

Roberto sat on in the café until the bells had stopped ringing. Then he decided that he would have to make a few telephone calls; but after paying for his coffee, he realised that he did not have enough money. He would walk to his mother's flat and phone from there; that was where he usually had Sunday lunch anyway.

The first person he tried to phone when he got there was Fritz; but Fritz was away, he was told when he got through to the barracks, and no one quite knew when he would be back. A slight tremor of worry took hold of him when he heard that, and he put down the telephone and was silent for a few moments. He hoped to God no one had arrested Fritz. His mother was out, doubtless still at church; perhaps he had better phone Elena to let her know that he was safe. But something gave him pause. He suddenly felt his cheeks go hot at the memory of what Olivarez had told him the night before. Elena's phone was tapped and she had spoken about him – but to whom? – on it. He could imagine the subject of her conversations. Women did discuss things amongst each other which men would never mention amongst themselves. He and Fritz, for example, had never spoken about sex; but doubtless Elena did to her various female friends. And these conversations were now recorded for the vast amusement of his new colleagues in the Security Department. The fact that he was blushing made him feel even more annoyed with himself. Despite the fact that he was tanned, his skin did have the northern habit of turning colour; he remembered how he had felt the colour drain from his face when Tanucci had pulled the hood over his head. It made him annoyed that his feelings should be so visible; and it made him annoyed that Elena should speak about him over the phone: for though he had faced a firing squad last night without disgrace, though he knew his bravery was beyond question, he had certain secrets that he had hoped would never have been told.

The phone rang, disturbing his thoughts, and he picked it up.

'Hello,' he said.

'Bobby, this is Fritz.'

'I've been trying to get hold of you. Where have you been? They said you weren't in barracks.'

'I've been trying to get hold of you,' said Fritz. 'But no one seemed to know where you'd gone. That's why I thought I'd try your mother's. I am afraid that I'm in a bit of a jam. That's why I didn't make it to the races.'

'What, again?'

'Look, it's a long story and it's rather complicated –'

'They always are, Fritz,' said Roberto good-humouredly. 'Was it another poisoned *empanada*? Anyway, I am glad that you're alive. Look, where are you now?'

'I'm in San Cristobal.'

'Yes, that is complicated,' conceded Roberto. 'When will you be back?'

'That's just it,' said Fritz's voice. 'I was sent here late last night and as far as I know I am not coming back. You see, I got into a bit of a scrape with someone I don't think you know called Colonel Mendoza and he's had me more or less exiled to this awful place. Old Mendoza must have used his influence: there can't be anywhere worse than San Cristobal, unless it's December Island, I suppose. I'm supposed to teach the cadets military history – but that is just an excuse. I had a talking to when I arrived from that ghastly man Ximenez. He's a big noise down here, and they say he's just been made something to do with the Security Department –'

'Fritz, we don't know who could be listening,' said Roberto, cutting him off. 'For God's sake be careful and whatever you do, don't offend Ximenez.'

'I've never offended anyone in my life,' said Fritz truthfully. 'At least not intentionally. Not even Colonel Mendoza, I suppose. But you know what Ximenez is like, or perhaps you don't. I don't think he likes me one little bit. I got the impression he'd love to put me up against a wall and have me shot. Do you remember he once tried to pick a quarrel with me in the bar of the Military Club, about five years ago?'

'No, I don't,' said Roberto, who could never keep track of the Fritz mythology. 'But listen: just keep out of his way. One must be careful these days. I'm in a bit of a jam myself, but I can't speak on the phone.'

'A bit of a jam?' asked Fritz. 'I'm the one who gets into trouble. You were the Head Boy at school, Bobby. You never got into trouble then.'

'Our schooldays are over now,' said Roberto sadly. 'I'm not sure what I ought to do, and I wish you were here to tell me. I'm not quite sure what I've got into, but I can't talk about it over the phone, understand?'

'Look, Bobby,' he could hear Fritz's voice say – Fritz was the only person who used his old childhood name these days – 'Whatever you do, just do your duty and no more or less.'

'And the same goes for you, Fritz. I'll speak to you soon. You won't be able to phone me. I won't be at the Ministry any longer, and I'm not in barracks, either, as far as I can see. I'll phone you at the cadets some time. I'd better go, before my mother comes back.'

'Goodbye then, Bobby,' he heard Fritz say.

'Goodbye, Fritz.'

The line went dead.

He could feel himself grow hot around the face yet again, and was glad that there was no one there to see it. Ximenez, whom he knew by reputation, was not the sort of person who would take to Fritz. But Fritz was on his own now, over a hundred miles to the south, and Fritz would have to look out for himself. They were all in danger to some extent or other. What Fritz had done to annoy Mendoza, he could not imagine; but Fritz was always saying what he thought, and that could be dangerous. He hoped to God that he would keep his mouth shut in San Cristobal. But if Ximenez was engaged on secret work too, then Ximenez would hardly have time to bother with Fritz, which would be a good thing.

He supposed he ought to ring Elena and tell her that her phone had been tapped – but then he could hardly do so over the telephone. And then he felt a renewed wave of embarrassment over the subject of her telephonic indiscretions, and, as he bathed his now scarlet face in cold water in the bathroom, he thought that he would not phone her at all – at least not for the moment: he felt a sudden angry desire to let her worry about him for a little bit longer.

Eight

The Army Navigational School, where Roberto had had his brush with death, was one of those buildings from an earlier age; but its days of glory were long past. The cellars had once been filled with wine, but that had all been drunk now, and the little man who had presided over the dusty bottles was gone too, leaving only abandoned galleries and myriads of cobwebs in his place. The officers who had drunk the wine were similarly departed. They had been a small band of men, who, some six years ago, had been formed into a committee and put in charge of urban planning. They had planned very little and the little they had planned had never been realised; the public money that had been allotted to them had disappeared, as public money had the habit of doing. Yet when word from above had eventually brought their fruitless but nevertheless convivial activities to an end, a certain nostalgia had gripped them. They would be separated and scattered in other Government departments, and would meet no more. No more would they play chess in the shady courtyard under the oleanders, nor would they sleep away idle afternoons in the bedrooms above. They would be dispersed and other men, less worthy than they, would take their places and use the building for other purposes.

And so it was. The urban planners had gone, Strauss and Tanucci had come. Olivarez had come too, from time to time. The Army Navigational School was ideal for his purposes: it was far from the centre of things, in a neglected part of the City which was half town and half degraded countryside, wholly disastrous from the point of view of urban planning. It was in some ways as remote as Siberia. The cellars were deep underground, and from them no sounds would ever escape; the walls were high, and the very few windows that looked onto the outside world had bars on them. It was a place that Olivarez had had in mind for future use for some time.

There were prisoners there; when Roberto arrived he found that there were only three of them in this Bastille of a place, under the watchful guard of Tanucci and Strauss. There was also an old and profoundly deaf cook, who was assisted by one kitchen boy. And that was all.

The first prisoner, along with his other colleagues in misery, had been taken from his residence at midnight and bundled into the boot of a car. He had resented this. He had been kept in solitary confinement since his arrival, and as a result had rather lost track of the time that had passed; there was no light in the cellar either, so he was unable to tell whether it was day or night. Despite this disorientation, the prisoner was in no mood to talk, and proving remarkably stubborn. At least he had said nothing of interest, nothing anyone wanted to hear. But on other subjects he had been eloquent: he had complained about the food, his cell, and even demanded a lawyer.

'You are holding me here illegally,' he had said, when Roberto came to visit him, and he repeated it every time.

'Are we?' asked Roberto, the third or fourth time he heard it. 'Would you like me to call the police?'

The prisoner was thoughtful. The officer sitting on the chair in front of him seemed to be a decent sort of chap, but with the police, one could never tell. People who had been arrested by the police were said to end up dead at the bottom of mineshafts, victims of overenthusiastic questioning.

'You see,' said Roberto, following up the advantage that he had sensed in this pause, 'I have had your flat searched since you have been here, and the police would be shocked to see what was discovered there, shocked but also very interested.'

He said this in rather a laconic tone. He was not enjoying this intelligence work. It was remarkably dull. In the week he had been doing it, a week in which summer had arrived in all its glory, he had been cooped up in a wine cellar interviewing people who clearly did not appreciate his efforts on their behalf. Upstairs Tanucci and Strauss were wasting their time sunbathing on the roof or playing cards in the courtyard, bored, waiting to be told that the prisoners were proving stubborn.

'And what did you find in my flat?' asked the prisoner, now a little less sure of himself, but hoping to bluff it out.

'I'll tell you,' said Roberto. 'They found a book that is banned in the Republic. It was a foreign publication, and presumably you imported it. Importation of banned books carries a prison term of about three years.'

'That's absurd,' said the prisoner. 'Don't you know anything about art?'

The prisoner was getting arrogant again. Roberto sighed.

'Art?' he said. 'I've tried to read it and it isn't even interesting. But whether it is art or not isn't the point. The Government has banned it and you have broken the law. And that's besides all the other things you are supposed to have done but refuse to tell me about.'

'What sort of government is it that bans *Lady Chatterley's Lover*?'

'A sensible one, as far as I am concerned,' he said, feeling himself getting annoyed, but unable to help it.

Roberto was losing patience with the prisoner. His dealings with him were rapidly convincing him that the man deserved his present incarceration. But the prisoner seemed quite unable to grasp this developing lack of sympathy.

'I am not here to discuss literature with you,' he said slowly. 'What I want are the names of the people you went to see in California the last time you were there, what you discussed, what they said about the Government, and who you passed that information on to when you got back here. That's what we want to know.'

'So you can arrest them too?'

'Yes. Who are your friends?'

'So, a social life is against the law now as well, is it?'

'Are you going to tell me?'

'I don't think I am,' said the prisoner rather grandly, thinking of his artistic integrity, for, before his arrest, he had been a man of letters.

'But these people are opponents of the Junta,' insisted Roberto.

'So they are,' said the prisoner unwisely.

'Then you do associate with enemies of the Government?' said Roberto, wondering if that could count as progress.

The prisoner was silent.

'Don't you realise that you could be shot for that?' he asked suddenly, wondering if threats would work. 'I could have you shot right now.'

The prisoner looked away superciliously, as if to signify that he was quite ready to be a martyr for art.

Roberto felt he could stand it no more. The colour in his face was beginning to rise. He got up, walked out and slammed the door behind him. Then with the dismal clang sounding in his ears, he went up the stairs and out into the courtyard. It was early evening, and there was a fountain in the courtyard. He splashed some cold water on his face to make the embarrassing inflammation go away. Then he lit a cigarette. On the other side of the courtyard, Strauss and Tanucci were playing cards. He looked at them with hearty dislike. He had not forgotten his experiences at their hands.

It was going to be a warm night. Neither Strauss nor Tanucci were properly dressed; both were in shirt-sleeves, which was strictly against the rules. He had not given them permission to sit around in shirt-sleeves and play cards. The irritation he felt against them merged with his annoyance with the prisoner. Let them all punish each other, he thought.

'You two men,' he said. 'Go down and see that first prisoner. He has been wasting my time for days.'

Strauss stood up; Tanucci seemed a little dubious, but he stood up too.

'Tell me if he says anything before supper,' said Roberto.

Then he went up the staircase to his bedroom and lay down on the bed. The room was quite bare; his 'personal effects', which had been brought there from his previous barracks, lay in a cardboard box, unpacked. He stared at the ceiling. He had no idea that this sort of work would be so dull and yet so infuriating at the same time. He wondered what Strauss and Tanucci would do to the prisoner. At least he was not there to see it; and besides the prisoner had brought it on himself. He could have spoken, or at the very least he could have tried to be a little less provoking. He ought to be taught a lesson.

He wondered about Elena. He has seen her once since his arrest and mock execution. He had told her she was not to try and contact him, that the phones were tapped. Humbly she agreed to this arrangement. Any conversation, he had stressed, was dangerous and liable to misinterpretation. He had seen guilt in her assent; perhaps it was her fault, this mysterious new job he had, about which he had said so little. Perhaps something (what?) that she had said had damned him by association.

Fritz too, he had told her, had been sent away, for some mysterious misdeed. That, he saw, frightened her. And it frightened him too. He was alone now.

In the cell below, deep underground, Strauss, assisted by Tanucci, was preparing the prisoner's lesson. The prisoner was now tied to the chair in which Roberto had sat, and was blindfolded. A few simple articles lay about the cell: a metal bucket, a hammer, a length of knotted nylon cord and a few harmless pieces of wood. With these Strauss set to work as evening fell, instructing Tanucci in the art of torture.

A little less than three miles away the Older Set were having a party. Only the very best people in the Republic belonged to the Older Set. There was as yet no younger set. Young people were far too busy working, or being in the Army, or leaving the country, to make much impression. Isabel de Calatrava knew very few young people, except by name, and she saw little reason to get to know any despite the fact that she had a young English girl staying with her. Thus it was that she was completely insincere when she asked Maria Enriquez about her son.

'I haven't seen you for ages,' she said, though they had in fact only met ten days ago. 'And how is dear Roberto?'

'I haven't seen him since the races,' said Maria. 'He seems to be very busy.'

'Such a good-looking young man,' said Isabel.

'Who?'

'Your son, my dear, I meant your son. It was so good of you to bring him to the races. I hope that from now on we will see him often.'

('We' signified Isabel and General Hernandez; but Maria, who was not as well informed about these matters as she should have been, did not know this. In fact she had little idea why Isabel had invited her to this present party. Such attentions, resumed after a lapse of many years, were most confusing.)

'Of course,' Isabel was now saying in what was supposed to be a conspiratorial whisper, but sounded rather like the effects of a sore throat, 'I quite understand what you mean when you say he is very busy.'

'You do?' asked Maria. 'I think it's all my fault that he hasn't been to see me all week. He used to come three or four times a week, but I think I have frightened him away, because the last few times I urged him to get married. He hates being reminded of things. And I think since then he has tried to avoid me, if that isn't too strong a word. I can't get hold of him at all: the Ministry of Munitions were very mysterious about him when I finally got through on the phone. Can you believe it, they actually tried to convince me that he didn't work there?'

'But you've seen the newspapers, haven't you?' asked Isabel a little sharply.

'Only *The Post*,' said Maria.

'You should read *El Mercurio*, my dear, as that is the paper that is fed its information directly by the Junta. Lately it has been full of the most interesting things. But it is best not to discuss it; and you are quite right not to; only I am sure you must be very pleased that Roberto is so busy in the service of the Republic. I gather that rather awful Captain Rodriguez has been sent away. I never liked him. Oh look, there is Colonel Olivarez!'

And there he was: for Colonel Olivarez was, much to his surprise, something of a centre of attraction at this particular party. He was surrounded by adoring ladies, all somewhat older than himself. He felt as though he was the hero of the hour. For the Republic was in danger – *El Mercurio* had said so – but Colonel Olivarez would save them all.

Somewhere in the background, his favoured position, observing but unobserved, stood the short dark figure of Father Morisco, carefully eating an olive. Next to him was the British Ambassador, likewise engaged. (Next to the Ambassador was Nicola Nickleby, allowed out for the party as a special treat, and munching her way steadily through the *empanadas*, unnoticed by anyone.)

'Good party,' said Sir Nigel. 'Olives not bad either.'

'Yes,' said Father Morisco. 'We might as well eat them while they last.'

'I gather that your boss has worked a miracle,' said Sir Nigel jovially.

'The Archbishop?'

'Yes. They say he has caused the dead to rise – almost.'

'The Archbishop has that reputation,' said Father Morisco carefully. 'You hear so many stories about miracles these days. I have to make reports on all of them. I suppose you are thinking of the old woman in San Cristobal?'

'No.'

'She was up and about and digging her vegetable patch the other day,' said Father Morisco. 'Quite an achievement for her.

But whether that was caused by the Archbishop praying for her, I wouldn't like to say.'

'I was thinking of a case in this very city,' said the Ambassador. 'Hasn't the Archbishop's intervention brought a very old man back from death's door recently?'

'Oh, the President. I think the connection is far too tenuous to justify this talk of miracles. People will believe the most unreasonable and extraordinary things, I find. I suppose it is because they find real life is so unbelievably awful.'

'I enjoy life,' said Sir Nigel, helping himself to another olive. 'What I want to know is how much longer all this is going to go on for.'

'I think,' said Father Morisco, 'that things will always go on much as before in this country.'

'That won't be too bad, then,' said Sir Nigel.

'I think it will be worse than anything. Eventually people will lose faith even in miracles and then where will we be?'

Out of the corner of his eye, Father Morisco noticed that one of the middle-aged waiters, thinking himself unobserved, was greedily helping himself to *empanadas*; some he put into his mouth, others he wrapped in a napkin and put into his pockets, busily chewing the while.

'Olivarez knows what he is doing,' said Sir Nigel, a little puzzled by the mystical flights of the priest's conversation.

'The Communists have met their match in Colonel Olivarez,' opined an old lady in a pearl choker.

Maria Enriquez heard it and wondered. For suddenly the talk was of Olivarez, and the small dapper Colonel had replaced food shortages as the chief topic of conversation. Olivarez realised it and smiled, knowing that his plans were already achieving a success of sorts.

The first prisoner seemed to have suffered somewhat at the hands of Strauss and Tanucci. Roberto looked at him through the spy-hole drilled through the door for the purpose: the prisoner was lying on the floor, undressed and motionless, in a pool of urine.

'What have you done to him?' asked Roberto, wondering if the man was dead.

'Nothing much, sir,' said Strauss. 'Nothing that could be called torture.'

'What exactly?' asked Roberto.

'You tell him,' said Strauss, looking at Tanucci.

For Strauss could see that Tanucci was looking ashamed and ill at ease, and thought it best for him to overcome these feelings as soon as possible.

'Strauss put a metal bucket over his head and banged it with a hammer,' said Tanucci. 'It's not painful, Strauss says, sir, but it is meant to put them into a more tractable frame of mind. And then after doing that for about twenty minutes, we put a sort of tourniquet around his temples and tightened it.'

'The knout,' explained Strauss.

'And did he say anything?' asked Roberto impatiently. 'I can't see any point in mistreating the man unless he's going to tell us something useful. I hope to God you haven't gone too far.'

'Gone too far?' asked Strauss sullenly.

'You know what I mean,' said Roberto. 'Anyway, let's go in and see.'

'He'll talk, sir,' said Tanucci with a touch of desperation.

And indeed he hoped he would. It had been Tanucci's first experience of interrogating a prisoner, and he had not yet begun to enjoy the process.

They went in.

The prisoner did not stir. His eyes were open but appeared to be sightless. Strauss and Tanucci picked him up and put him in the wooden chair. Strauss held the prisoner's head up. Apart from a few bruises, Roberto could detect no sign that the man had been mistreated. He was not dying, he was merely stunned.

'Are you surprised that this has happened?' he asked.

'Yes,' said the prisoner, in a new voice.

'These two officers,' said Roberto, now noticing that Strauss had a nut-cracker in his hand, one of the type that were shaped like small vices, 'these two officers will put you to torture unless you give me that information I want at once. Unless you speak now, there is nothing further I can do, and certainly nothing I can do to stop them.'

There was a pause. Roberto nodded, and Strauss put the nut-cracker over one of the prisoner's thumbs and began to screw it tight. At once the prisoner began to recover from his stupor. He was beginning to talk. Roberto took out his notebook and began to write down names. Progress was being made.

Over the next few days, further progress was made, and by the time Olivarez arrived to inspect the work, all three prisoners had spoken, and Roberto had obtained three lists of names. At least twenty names appeared on all three lists; these were shown to Olivarez, who nodded his approval. But before new arrests could be made, there were the old prisoners to be disposed of, and of that Olivarez said nothing.

The first prisoner could be handed over to the police and be dealt with by a civil court, which would give him at least three years in jail for possession of an illegal book. That would take care of him. The other two prisoners presented different cases. While in the first case, no law had been broken during the interrogation, with the other two, several illegal things had been done. Tanucci and Strauss – and Roberto was inclined to blame the NCO more than the Lieutenant – had gone too far. They had used electricity. There would be very little point in discharging those two prisoners. But Roberto hardly liked to object to what Strauss had done, now that it was over; it had after all obtained quick results, unlike his own gentle questioning of the first prisoner; and he did not want to appear squeamish in their sight. He could remember still the experiences that he had undergone at their hands the first night he had met them. He did not want to compromise his reputation for bravery. Thus he thought he would let Strauss and Tanucci deal with these two prisoners themselves.

'I will hand the first prisoner over to the police,' he told them. 'As for the other two, release them. Deal with it yourselves.'

'Very well, sir,' said Strauss, after a moment's hesitation.

'Oh Strauss,' said Roberto. 'What was it you were once put in jail for?'

'Rape, sir,' said Strauss, and left.

After they had gone, after the sound of the car had faded away into silence, Roberto sat alone in the dark courtyard with his thoughts. It was late, but he had no desire at all to go to bed. He was beginning to wish that he had never met Olivarez. For Olivarez had in a strange way captured him. Olivarez had known something about him that Roberto himself had hardly known; Olivarez had known that he would follow orders to the bitter end, no matter how much he disliked doing so. Olivarez had been right, and Roberto had been wrong, for up to then Roberto had always imagined that there were certain things he would never do. He had always thought that a cold-blooded killing was beyond his nature, but now even that did not seem so very remote. Perhaps he would do it, in the course of duty. Perhaps there was nothing he would not do in the course of duty.

He wondered about the Communist plot. The lists of names seemed to show that there was a network of disaffection in the country. In fact, there was so much to be discontented about, that one could hardly doubt that disaffection did exist on a wide scale. None of the names of the people who would shortly be arrested were particularly surprising to him. For there they all were: the intellectuals, the sneerers, the conscientious objectors, the scoffers, the people whose friends all lived in England or California. He had never had much time for intellectuals; a soldier, a good soldier, he supposed, never did. Of course, it was true that Fritz with his Tacitus and Livy, his Clausewitz and Churchill, was something of an intellectual –

but it was a hobby with Fritz, a way of passing the time, not an end in itself. And Fritz was an excellent tennis player too. Intellectuals were never good all-rounders; and he despised them for it. In his limited experience he had found that they generally returned the compliment. He knew that Carmen Garcia despised him. She fancied herself an intellectual – and her magazine, instead of sticking to knitting patterns, dabbled in all sorts of loathsome ideas. Several of those about to be arrested, he realised, were bound to be friends of hers; he was glad then that Elena knew nothing at all of what he was doing. But even so, the prospect of damaging the happiness of Carmen Garcia did not horrify him as it might have done; perhaps it would teach Mrs Garcia to be a little bit more cautious in her approach to him in the future. It would do her no harm to be slightly afraid of him.

As for Elena, who wanted to marry him – and he too wanted to marry her, if only he could bring himself to do so – perhaps his misgivings would vanish if he could somehow prove to himself through his work that there really was nothing that could frighten him. For, despite everything, despite his infinite good-breeding, his fine looks, his rank in the army, despite the fact that it was an open secret that women liked him, and that men regarded him as a natural leader – despite all these grounds for unbounded confidence – Roberto was always a little afraid in his dealings with Elena. Five years they had known each other, and for five years she had told him that she loved him; they should have been married years ago. But on his side there were constant misgivings. Intimacy always fell short, because intimacy embarrassed him. Because of this, he had always tried to see as little of her as he could – they rarely met above once a week, and since he had come to the Army Navigational School, they had not met at all. It was odd: he had not been frightened, openly frightened at least, when he had been prepared for what was to be an execution, his own execution; and yet he was afraid of – quite what he could not be sure – he was afraid of failure, if it could be given so grand a word. In fact what frightened and embarrassed him was simply too trivial for words, and because it was so, he could not find the words to explain why it should be so. But the fact was this: when he was with her, he dared not let his feelings become deeply engaged, but he attempted to keep her at a distance – for when his feelings were engaged, he would find himself turning bright red, something which he could not bear, simply because it was so difficult to control. And he did not want anyone to know his weakness, not even her.

Perhaps if he could shoot a man in cold blood, as Strauss could doubtless do, or administer the knout without seeming to feel it, as Tanucci had done (for Tanucci, feeling betrayed by Colonel Olivarez, under whose protection he had thought himself permanently secure, felt little pity for anyone but himself), perhaps if he too could act with perfect control, perhaps then he might break the barrier and really become a good soldier and a man of courage. He would have to prove to himself that there were no things he would not do in the course of duty, and that there was nothing that could make him blush.

Nine

Elena found her work at *The Post* most congenial and thought that she had been lucky to get the job. Very few worked for *The Post* nowadays. Back in the 1940s, those heady days of glory, *The Post* had been a flourishing concern. Old Caballero, the Editor, had been a young man then, and circulation had been high. At one point *The Post* had even overtaken its Spanish-language rival, *El Mercurio*. *The Post*, of course, had supported the Allies in the war, while *El Mercurio* had stood by the dictators. Something of the Anglo-American glory had settled on *The Post* then, as indeed had something of their funds; but those days were now long gone. The grandiose offices in the centre of the City remained, now half empty; Old Caballero was still at his desk, and the declining but faithful readership still thought that the paper was rather liberal in its views – by which they meant that it was not a mouthpiece of the Junta. But the days of glory were past, and the fact that *The Post* was the last independent newspaper in the Republic was more a tribute to its obscurity than anything else. The Junta had never thought it worth their while to buy it or to close it down.

This apart, *The Post* provided a pleasant refuge. Elena knew that she ought to have worked for *El Mercurio*, had she really wanted to get on in journalism. Or else she could have worked for her mother at *Moda* – but that would have meant being tied to a desk in a crowded office, where she would have had to fulfil the role of boss's daughter, as well as being restricted to writing about only one thing. At *The Post* her talents were allowed free range. She could more or less do as she pleased.

Naturally, everything that she wrote was checked by someone or another, but, that apart, she could write about what interested her. Hers was a creative form of reporting, and her speciality was foreign affairs. In the Republic, she had noticed, no one really cared about foreign affairs, being too bothered about the quality of the coffee or the latest shortage. They knew that the North Americans would always be there, and that was all they knew or cared about the world beyond them.

Elena generally dealt with news from North America and Europe. (South American news only got into the paper when it was particularly bad – good news from their neighbours might count as subversive.) Reporting on Europe and North America was simple enough and did not involve leaving her desk. She simply read the press releases and then made them up into articles. Alternatively, she read the foreign newspapers and if she came across anything of interest, she adapted it – that was a particularly useful way of writing features. Hardly anyone noticed that the news was always a little out of date, as they had little else to compare it with. If anything had to be really topical, there was always the World Service of the BBC. She had sat up an entire breathless night 'reporting' a Royal wedding that way.

Today she was sitting at her desk reading an American magazine, hoping to glean something useful and interesting, when Young Caballero came in. He quite often did this. It was one of the chief advantages of working for *The Post*: she had an office all to herself, and little work that could be classed as urgent. There were no deadlines for her, and as a result several hours a week could always be devoted to long conversations with Caballero.

Elena, without ever feeling the danger of falling in love with him, liked Caballero enormously. He was a person she could confide in, and there was nothing she had not told him. His manner, attentive and sympathetic, invited confidences, and she always knew that he was the soul of discretion where her affairs were concerned. On other topics, she was less sure, and she had already warned him about the danger of discussing politics over the telephone. Politics, of course, was a wide category, as they both knew. To say that there was a shortage of sugar in a less than cheerful tone might be construed as a sign of political disaffection.

'I've brought you *El Mercurio*,' said Caballero, putting both himself and it down on her desk.

'Anything in it?' she asked.

'The usual rubbish. But page three has an interesting murder,' he said thoughtfully. 'Some man in San Cristobal has confessed to chopping his wife and mother-in-law up and storing them in his deep freeze.'

'I could do something with that,' said Elena.

'And he has said that he will do it again if given the chance, and that he intends to die unrepentant. He will certainly hang – but the fact he intends to do so unrepentant is rather unusual, don't you think?'

'I could write an editorial,' said Elena. 'Five hundred words or so on human brutalisation, condemning it of course, and perhaps ending up with a little quote from the Pope.'

'That does sound a good idea,' said Caballero. 'The trouble is, someone is bound to read it, think that you are blaming the Government for our obvious degeneracy, and come and take away our licence.'

'Yes,' said Elena. 'I suppose they would.'

One had to be realistic.

'I was thinking of an editorial on the Channel Tunnel,' said Caballero. 'It could end with a eulogy of Mrs Thatcher. That always goes down well; they seem to prefer her even to the Pope nowadays.'

'There is something a little absurd about the idea of a Channel Tunnel,' said Elena, seeing that the theme had definite possibilities.

'The absurd is the one thing that everyone in this country really likes,' said Caballero. He picked up the photograph she kept on her desk. 'How is the Captain?' he asked lightly.

'I haven't seen him for ages,' she replied. 'You know how it is. He seems to have gone ex-directory, so I can't even phone him. And there is something else too. You know Roberto has the idea that our telephones here are being tapped.'

'Really?' he asked. She had told him about this strange idea of the Captain's before, and he hadn't taken it seriously then, either.

'Yes, really. I do think you – I mean we – ought to be careful about what we say.'

'Did the Captain say so?'

'He did.'

Caballero smiled: 'The Captain is an odd fellow,' he said lightly. 'I can't imagine that anyone could be remotely interested in what I say on the phone, or what you say for that matter. No one is going to come in the middle of the night to take us away, my dear. What surprises me is that the Captain should think so.'

'I wish you would take Roberto seriously,' she said, a little reproachfully. 'There could be real danger,' she added, wishing she could make him understand her fears.

'I have tried to take the Captain seriously,' answered Caballero. 'But there seems to be something about him that isn't quite on my level. I dare say if I were to meet him, I might warm to him. But he's not in the same league as other soldiers, is he?'

'The last time I saw Roberto he talked about emigrating,' said Elena sadly.

'Take a look at the front page of *El Mercurio*,' said Caballero suddenly. 'We are in the midst of a political crisis, in case you haven't noticed.'

He put the front page before her. Elena had never been interested in politics, which was just as well, since most political activity was illegal in the Republic. In a country where there were only two possible opinions about anything, the Junta's and the wrong one, there was not much room for discussion. But despite that, she did as she was told and read what was in front of her.

The front page of the paper spoke to her of another world. 'Grave threat to State Security' was the headline. She read as follows:

> 'This newspaper has been authorised to state that in recent days a serious threat to the internal stability of the Republic has been discovered. Steps are being taken to deal with this threat. Various elements, consisting of left-wing sympathisers and hardline Communist revolutionaries have already been taken into custody. For security reasons, and because the operation is still in progress, no names have yet been released. Further moves to ensure the stability of the Republic are expected shortly. Yesterday the President of the Republic called on the people to rally to the defence of the nation in its hour of need. "Nothing," he declared, "must distract us from the important task of dealing with the enemy within. All other concerns must come second. Any dissent would only give comfort to the enemy. With this in mind the Junta has published the following decrees . . ."'

Elena scanned a list of new laws with little interest.

'Well,' asked Caballero, 'what do you think?'

'Think?' she said. 'They are getting hysterical. Not that I try to think about them much.'

'Quite,' agreed Caballero. 'It seems to me that it is only a matter of time before the entire thing collapses.'

'Do you mean that there really will be a Communist revolution?'

'No. There aren't any real Communists left – at least not here. They all live in New York or London, I suppose. I wonder who they are going to arrest. But perhaps your Captain is right and we should be careful about what we say on the phone.'

And then they turned to discussing the Channel Tunnel once more.

* * *

Roberto too was reading *El Mercurio*.

The political news did not interest him; in fact, he was sitting in the Military Club, one of the few places that still sold drinks at a reasonable price, and he had come there to get away from the oppressive atmosphere of the Army Navigational School. He had been a member of the Club ever since getting his commission. It was a large and palatial building in the centre of the City, and at this time of the afternoon, it was deserted. He sat in the smoking room, undisturbed, reading an item of news in the paper. It seemed that a young man in the police force had shot himself accidentally in the leg while waiting for a bus. He had been absent-mindedly playing with his gun. That, thought Roberto, would amuse Fritz. Fritz made a point of never carrying his Beretta – or if he had to, and Army rules dictated that officers should, he made sure it was never loaded. For Fritz lived in terror of accidentally shooting himself and never could quite trust himself with a loaded weapon. By contrast, Roberto had no such fears. He always carried his gun, and always made sure it was loaded, just as the rules stated an officer should do. Guns did not frighten him, simply because he was always in control of himself, and would never pull a trigger without actually wanting to. Fritz, though, was always doing things that he never quite intended to do. He wondered if Fritz would read the article and feel a little tremor.

Someone came into the room, and glancing up, he saw it was Captain Zondadari. He looked down at the paper again. He did not quite know what to do. He knew Zondadari only slightly, and was not sure if he wanted to engage in conversation with him. But at the same time, he was bored to death, wishing something would happen. This, after all, was one of the afternoons that would have been filled by Fritz's company; Roberto was a creature of habit, and had not quite worked out what he might do now that Fritz was not there. He was missing Fritz's company. He had even thought of going to call on Elena, whom he had not seen for weeks, but decided against it. He did not like sudden meetings.

He could feel that Zondadari's eyes were on him, and wondered if his solitude was going to be interrupted. But there was something a little bit gauche about Zondadari, something uncertain in his manner, and Roberto thought that the man would not dare to speak to him. After all, even though Zondadari was thought to be a fine officer, one of their best, everyone knew that his parents had been poor people from Barcelona on the wrong side in the Spanish War, which was the sort of thing anyone would find hard to live down. In fact Roberto was fairly surprised that Zondadari was a member of the Military Club at all, even though he was in charge of the City barracks.

But he was wrong. Zondadari was going to speak to him. (In fact, Zondadari had been wanting to speak to him for some time, and was preparing to take this unlooked for opportunity.) He could tell that the man was hesitating, and he put down his newspaper, so that the thing might be got over with as soon as possible. He looked at him, and Zondadari seemed to quail before him for a moment, and then recover his courage.

'Enriquez,' he said, 'I wonder if you'd heard anything from Fritz Rodriguez.'

'Not a word,' said Roberto. 'I keep meaning to phone him – but I haven't done so yet. And the lines are always so bad.'

Zondadari placed himself in a neighbouring armchair.

'It seems odd that he was sent to San Cristobal so suddenly, doesn't it?' he said.

Roberto said nothing; and his impassive face gave nothing away.

'I was wondering whether it might have been something political,' said Zondadari.

'Political?' asked Roberto, genuinely mystified. 'What on earth has Fritz got to do with politics? What have any of us to do with politics?'

'Perhaps more than we ever expected,' said Zondadari quietly. 'It just occurred to me that Rodriguez's devotion to Sir Winston Churchill might have got the better of his judgement, that is all. Perhaps I had better explain: if someone felt that Rodriguez sympathised with liberal ideas such as democracy . . .'

'Fritz – democracy?' asked Roberto almost angrily. 'For God's sake, Fritz never gave things like that a thought in his life. He is too good a soldier to bother with things that don't concern him. Of course, he isn't the world's most discreet man, but even so . . .'

'Even so, he would never express a political opinion?' said Zondadari, finishing the sentence for him.

'Yes,' agreed Roberto, wondering whether he could go back to his paper without appearing rude.

'But the fact is,' said Zondadari with a great effort, 'that the General will die soon and then someone or something will have to replace him.'

'I suppose so,' said Roberto, grudgingly.

'And who is it to be?'

'That is hardly my concern, but if it is to be anyone, it will probably be Colonel Olivarez – eventually. He would be very efficient.'

'I suppose he would,' said Zondadari. 'So you would like another soldier? Not elections?'

Roberto was suddenly cautious.

'Go on,' he said.

'It seems to us,' said Zondadari, using a telling plural, 'that this system cannot go on much longer. Our economic problems are terrible, and before very long the United States will stop helping us – probably when there is a new president there. They can be quite touchy about human rights, you know, and they could wash their hands of us. But we can prevent all of that by giving up military rule once the General has died.'

'Who are *we*?' asked Roberto.

'There's a group of us who think like this,' said Zondadari. 'We have some contacts with people who could work something out, some sort of transition to proper government.'

'And is Fritz involved?'

'We thought you might like to be,' said Zondadari, ignoring the question.

'And why me?'

'People would take notice of you, Enriquez. They know who you are; they admire you; they know you are a good soldier, and they know that you aren't some crack-pot revolutionary. In short, if the regime were to lose your support, and the support of all the officers like you, it would be finished.'

'And it never will,' said Roberto quickly. 'You can have all the ideas you and your friends, whoever they are, want to have, but you can be certain that we will never be disloyal.'

'Disloyal to what?'

'The Army.'

'And the country?'

'The two are the same thing. This place would be ruined by a civilian government. I don't know how you could even think of it. And if you ever mention this to me again, I will have you denounced as mutinous, do you understand?'

Zondadari got up and walked quietly away. His mission had not been a success. He had expected better of Enriquez. Enriquez was a clean living young man, a good Catholic, just the sort of young man who ought to realise that the regime was going too far.

Zondadari closed the door of the smoking room behind him, and Roberto was left alone, a little surprised by the vehemence of his own reaction to what the man had said. Zondadari's words had been full of common sense. The country was going to the dogs; but there was nothing that Roberto despised as much as common sense. It made the world prosaic. Common sense would ruin them all. In addition to this he could not imagine a world where all were equal: it would be monstrous and unreasonable if both the heroes and the cowards were to be treated alike. Zondadari had plainly gone mad. Of course, he had spoken to him in confidence, so he would say nothing to anyone about it. But he resolved with a frown that he would never speak to Zondadari again. The man was an anarchist, and there was nothing more terrible than disorder. In fact, of all things that he feared, disorder, that complete loss of control, was surely the greatest.

Elena had tried to get hold of Roberto that very afternoon, hoping that he would be at his mother's, but the telephones had as usual been impossible. Dispiritedly, she had abandoned the attempt, which she had made so frequently of late, and settled down to do some work. Several hours must have passed in quiet concentration, for she was unaware of the passage of time. Once, Caballero put his head round the door rather hurriedly to tell her that he was just going out for a few minutes; by the time she looked up it was to see a young man standing in front of her, a stranger.

'Yes?' she asked, this seeming the best opening.

The stranger seemed ill at ease. He was a mere boy, not more than twenty, and dressed in the uniform of a lieutenant of the Engineers. When he spoke it was in an accent that marked him out as the child of Italian immigrants.

'Is Mr Caballero here?'

'Isn't he in his office?' she asked.

'They told me downstairs that he was out, but that you would know where he might be,' said the youngster, even more ill at ease.

She had seen him before, she now realised, but where exactly she could not remember. She wished she could place him. He was rather a pretty young man, she decided, despite having rather bad teeth; just the sort of badly-paid young man who might idle his hours away in some public place waiting for someone like Caballero to stand him a drink.

'Are you a friend of Caballero's?' she asked.

'Yes,' said Tanucci. 'I mean, no. I mean, I know him. I just wanted to see him.'

Blackmail, concluded Elena. A couple of thousand escudos

to be going on with – was that what he wanted? But the boy-officer, who now seemed almost terrified of her probing gaze, hardly seemed to have the self-confidence of a blackmailer.

'Is it important?' she asked.

'It is,' said Tanucci. Strauss was arresting Caballero that afternoon. He had seen his name on the list. It was urgent.

'If you leave your name,' the girl was telling him, 'he's bound to be back soon. He did say he was going out, but he never goes out for long.'

'I – no,' said Tanucci. Caballero had gone; it was already too late. He wished he could explain to her the urgency of the case, but how could he? 'I have to go,' he said lamely.

Tanucci turned and left.

Elena, as soon as he was gone, phoned the secretary on the door.

'Any sign of Young Caballero?' she asked.

'He went home because the police called. There has been a burglary at his flat.'

'Oh. Did you know who that young officer who was asking for him might have been?'

'Not at all,' said the secretary, who had been with the paper for many years and had no wish to gossip about her employers.

'Well, tell him to come and see me as soon as he gets in,' said Elena, thinking of the fun she would have in teasing Caballero about the young Lieutenant later on.

Outside the building, Tanucci walked blindly on, until his panic subsided and he found himself in Palace Square. He ought not to be there; he was supposed to be visiting his mother. He wondered if anyone had seen him. He ought not to have tried to warn Caballero – he had taken a terrible risk, and the fact that he had stumbled into a meeting with the girl he recognised as belonging to Captain Enriquez merely underlined the extent of the risk he had taken. But she had not recognised him – he felt sure of that. Caballero had been a friend to him, a friend of sorts, and one ought to take risks for one's friends. God alone knew what he might say once he was arrested; they said that arrested men always talked. Now that Caballero had been arrested, he too, Rodolfo Tanucci, was in danger.

He stared at the Palace facade, pretending to examine it with the interest of a tourist, and tried to reason. There were no letters, nothing written down, that could connect them; he had never had his photograph taken with Caballero. He could always deny knowing the man. Besides, he had done nothing wrong, technically speaking, in knowing Caballero. Caballero had committed crimes enough with other people: they would not be after him. And if any finger was ever pointed at him, he would survive. Olivarez would save him; the thing of which he was most ashamed would be his salvation. He would survive. Caballero would not. Men taken away by the police never did.

Caballero had indeed suffered the fate of the 'elements' mentioned in the newspaper; he had been taken into custody and it had happened like this.

As soon as he had heard the message left at *The Post* that his flat had been broken into and that the police were there, he had rushed home, only stopping briefly to tell Elena that he was going out. His flat was only a ten-minute walk away, and all he could think of was getting there fast enough before the oafish policemen destroyed the place in their clumsiness. He had terrible visions of his furniture being treated with scant respect. But when he had got there, he had found that the message was only partly true: the flat had been broken into, but there were no policemen there, only Strauss and two private soldiers, sifting through his personal effects. They had made a pile of embarrassing and incriminating objects on the floor of the principal room: several magazines that he had bought on trips abroad and smuggled into the country, several books, and some containers that held, he remembered with a sickening sense of recognition, various illegal substances. Then he was arrested, before he could protest at the intrusion.

The arrest had been brutal; he had scarcely feared that this might happen, and he had never imagined it happening in this way. As he was bundled, stunned by a blow from a rifle butt, into the boot of a car, he thought only of the fact that he had left his desk at *The Post* a mere twenty minutes before; that his pen was still there, and all the things that he had not bothered to tidy away. Of course, he knew that he had been foolish. He had been friendly with lots of slightly risqué people: literary types, intellectuals, drug-users, soldiers who would pass the time of day with him for a few thousand escudos, which was nothing to him, but what they were paid in a week. Of course, he had spent much of his early youth in California, which was bound to make him suspect. He had never been careful about his telephone conversations. But despite all this, he had not imagined that danger had been so imminent and disaster so near. None of his activities, or even all of them considered together, had amounted to the equivalent of enrolling in the Comintern. There was no logic to his fate; and as he felt himself being driven away to the Army Navigational School, he tried to cheer himself with the thought that, though he could feel one of his ribs was broken, yet everything would be alright. They would surely realise that he wasn't worth arresting, and in a few days he would be at liberty.

Ten

Time had passed, but just how much time, he was not sure. It was certainly more than a few days, he felt: the aching tiredness caused by constant sleeplessness was enough to assure him of that. But whether he had been there weeks, he could not tell. The despair he felt in recurring waves did indeed make it feel that he had been there for weeks, but the very fact that he was still alive told him that this was impossible. He tried to be logical, though logic was hard. There was no telling anything for certain. Because he had been constantly blindfolded, he did not know whether it was night or day. Time, which he had up to now experienced as a succession of passing moments, now seemed to be an enduring aeon, an endless duration. And even space itself had grown strange. He could not see, and his body was numb. He felt that he must be underground, because it was so cold and so silent. He had tried shouting to reassure himself that he still existed, but as hunger had come, and then gone to be replaced by a sense of pervading weakness, he had decided to conserve his ebbing energy by keeping silent.

In calmer moments he was able to think. The pain from his broken rib seemed to be easing, a sign that he had been there some time, if it was healing itself. He knew he had been stripped, and that he was bound. He was able to move with some difficulty and he tried to calculate the dimensions of the cell they had put him in. It seemed alternately very small or very large. Somewhere on the floor he found a puddle of not very clean water which he had lapped up like a dog, lest he die of thirst. This source of water he was forced to pollute with his own urine a few hours later.

As for his captors, he remembered the face of the NCO who had arrested him; it had been a coarse Germanic face, belonging to a man of about his own age – thirty-five or thereabouts. He tried to fix the face in his memory and wondered if he would see it again. Perhaps they had forgotten him, and were leaving him there to die of hunger and thirst. This became an obsessive thought in the dark silence, and with this in mind he fought the long and lonely battle against unconsciousness. He was tired, but he could not sleep as the place was too cold, but gradually he felt himself slip from consciousness, and fearfully he wondered if he would ever regain it.

He did. He came out of his stupor to feel a damp cloth being rubbed against his face, and some water in a glass being held to his lips. This was the first act of kindness he had received since his arrest and he felt a sense of gratitude for it that made him feel close to tears. He sensed that his blindfold had been taken off, but he was still unable to see, blinded by the harshness of what was in fact only a sixty watt bulb. He did not realise it, but he had been a prisoner for only forty hours. But he had no idea of time any more, and was far more aware of the pleasant odour of a foreign cigarette that now pervaded the cell. He was in fact acutely aware of that cigarette now, and he was sure he could identify the exact brand. It was a brand that he himself had smoked many times in California, but which was not widely available in the Republic; it was in short an officer's cigarette – not one smoked by a civilian or a private soldier.

'Do you know where you are?' asked a voice in detached but not unfriendly tones.

'No,' said Caballero, trying to find his own voice, and surprised by its tremulous quality.

'You are in the hands of the Security Department,' continued the voice. 'Do you know why?'

'No,' answered Caballero, knowing that much depended on his answers.

By opening his eyes, Caballero could now see a pair of military boots. He realised that he was still lying on the floor. Sensation was returning to his body. He could feel the ropes that held him. But the voice that belonged to those boots seemed strange and distant, as if coming from a long way away, conveyed by a far off megaphone.

'Try and think why you are here,' said the voice. 'Some of my colleagues may get impatient with you.'

'I have done nothing wrong,' said Caballero, with a great effort.

'That is what everyone says, and it is almost never true.'

'In my case it is,' said Caballero.

'They found all sorts of things in your flat. Do you remember that?'

'I have friends in the Army,' said Caballero. 'Ask them about me.'

'Who? Tell us about them.'

'They –'

Caballero realised what he was saying.

'Give me a name. Who?'

Caballero was silent.

'You'll tell me eventually,' said the voice.

Caballero found himself in darkness once again.

The next interrogation came some hours later. He was blindfolded again and tied to a chair.

'What are the names of your friends in the military?' Roberto asked him. 'If you tell me, I will give you something to eat.'

There was a smell of food in the room. Caballero could tell that his unseen tormentor was eating. His sense of smell had become acute, and he could tell it was the aroma of meat.

'Wouldn't you like something to eat?' asked Roberto. 'And afterwards you could have a cigarette, a proper cigarette, like the ones you must have smoked when you lived abroad. And you could even have a shower, if you told us something interesting. You could wash. Just tell me who your friends in the military are.'

Still Caballero said nothing.

'I probably know them already,' said Roberto. 'Perhaps one of them had you denounced and sent here.'

'They wouldn't,' said Caballero.

'They always do. They are very indiscreet. They tell things to people they trust, and they don't realise that those men are working for us.'

'Rodolfo's not stupid,' said Caballero, thinking of the least reliable of his military friends.

Roberto paused. Zondadari, he knew, was called Ramon. It would have been a long shot linking Zondadari with Caballero anyway. Zondadari was a married man with children. And if Zondadari was a traitor, he was hardly likely to be busy betraying the Army in the company of Caballero; they were too different. But somehow he thought that one day he would find someone who might tell him something of interest about Zondadari.

'Rodolfo isn't stupid,' Roberto agreed. 'Rodolfo would never let what has happened to you happen to himself. He has told us everything.'

'What has he told you?'

Roberto wondered what any associate of Caballero might have confessed to.

'He told me that you and he used to smoke cannabis together,' he said conversationally. 'Can you not smell this steak?'

'You have probably done the same yourself,' retorted Caballero.

'You don't know me,' said Roberto calmly; for it was true: Caballero did not know him, and as long as his identity was secret he was safe. No improbable insults would wound him.

'Tell me about Rodolfo and I'll give you some steak,' said Roberto again. 'There's no need for you to protect him. He has betrayed you, you know. He has done it to lots of people, I imagine. You meet some poor little conscript and are kind to him and all along he is only thinking of the money he'll get for being a witness at your trial.'

'I've done nothing wrong,' said Caballero, beginning to whimper at the unfairness of it all. And it was unfair. He had been nothing but kind to the Lieutenant; he had been kind to many such, but now his clouded mind fixed exclusively on Rodolfo Tanucci. 'Why don't you arrest him?' he asked.

'If he has denounced you,' said Roberto knowingly, 'he will be perfectly safe. It is you who are in trouble – nothing at all will happen to Rodolfo except perhaps a commendation for intelligence work. Informers are well rewarded.'

Caballero pictured it. Rodolfo must have been an informer from the start – but what lies had he told them?

'Damn Tanucci,' he said, overcome by the misery of it all. Roberto threw him a bit of steak and then left him alone once more.

By the time the third interrogation came round, Roberto was driven to reflect that so far he had made little useful progress with Caballero. This was not what the Government was looking for. It was true that he probably had enough information now with which to ruin Tanucci; Caballero had not actually admitted anything illegal in his friendship with the Lieutenant, but Roberto was sure that he himself could squeeze something of that nature out of Tanucci himself; but he was not sure that it was worth the effort. Tanucci was not important; there was something in him that shied away from the task of humiliating unimportant junior officers. Tanucci's affairs were not his business. Besides, the resultant scandal might have damaging repercussions. Tanucci had been, and perhaps even still was, a favourite of Olivarez. Such cases demanded tact.

Apart from this, the whole business of Caballero made him

uneasy. The man was a friend and colleague of Elena's – he knew that; and if it had not been for the fact that Caballero did not know who he was, Roberto would have felt even more uncomfortable. He did not want to have the man mistreated in any sort of way, but he felt he had to make some progress with him, if only to show that all this effort was not being wasted. Perhaps too there were other things that Caballero might know.

Two days had now passed, and Caballero kept his blindfold, but had been fed and allowed to wash. He was also dressed. Roberto hoped that this kindly treatment might bear fruit.

'You'll get about two years,' he said.

'What for?' asked Caballero.

'Importing pornography, possession of drugs and corrupting young soldiers,' said Roberto. 'Two years is very reasonable, I'd say. It could be much much more. And if you were to confess to that, there wouldn't need to be a trial, there wouldn't be all that unpleasant publicity. I expect you have relations, and you want to spare them.'

'And what else would I have to give you?' asked Caballero.

Roberto could see that the man's wits had revived. It was now possible that some sort of bargain could take place. Negotiations could begin.

'You've visited the tomb of Karl Marx in London,' he said.

'Yes,' said Caballero. 'A lot of tourists do.'

'You've hung around with well-known enemies of the Junta in California.'

'Yes,' said Caballero. 'I suppose I have.'

'And you have used the newspaper you worked for and which your family owns as a front for anti-Government activity,' concluded Roberto.

Caballero was silent. He could see the way things were going.

'All you have to do,' said Roberto, 'is to sign a statement to that effect, and then I'll have you handed over to the police, and you'll get two years.'

'And you'll close down *The Post*?'

'Yes.'

'And if I don't sign?'

'I think that you will,' said Roberto reasonably. 'If you do make trouble, there are other people here less gentle than I am, people you haven't seen yet. And in the end you will sign all the same. People always do. I have it all typed out for you to sign right now.'

Caballero considered. It might be his death warrant that he was signing. Perhaps as soon as his confession was signed, he would be shot. And then they would close down *The Post*, and perhaps arrest all its employees on the strength of it. But, if he did not sign, what would happen then?

'I'll sign it,' said Caballero. 'Take off my blindfold and give me a pen.'

Roberto removed the blindfold. Caballero blinked in the unfamiliar light, and took up the pen. His hands were numb and he had difficulty holding it. His eyes grew accustomed to seeing once more, and he looked at his captor, and at the same moment realised that he knew that arrogant handsome face. He had seen it in the photograph that Elena kept on her desk.

'Let me read what I have confessed to first,' he said.

'Certainly,' said Roberto, and pushed the man, still tied to his chair, towards a table, on which lay two flimsy typewritten sheets. Then Roberto leaned back in his own chair, and lit a cigarette. As he did so, he kept his eyes on Caballero. Soon the man would sign, and then it would be all over. The prisoner was still peering at the confession, hesitating over it.

'Go on,' urged Roberto. 'You'll be out of this place almost at once. It is a better fate than being shot, I can tell you.'

Roberto drew on his cigarette. He had been smoking rather a lot recently. He ought to try and cut down. He bore Caballero no malice. He owed as much to Elena. The very fact that Caballero had not been touched by Strauss was surely proof of the fact that he had been kind to the man. Of course, he could have the man shot, if he so wanted; but having

Caballero shot would serve little purpose. The main thing was to have *The Post* shut down. Elena was an impetuous girl, and he was sure one day *The Post* would get her into trouble; trouble should be nipped in the bud. Elena could go and work for her mother at *Moda*. She would be safe there among dress designs and knitting patterns, safe in a woman's world.

Caballero was still holding the pen, wondering what to do, his mind racing over the various possibilities before him.

'Before I sign,' he said suddenly, 'I'd like to make a telephone call.'

'That's impossible. Just sign and you can call afterwards. You can tell whoever it is that you've been arrested by the police.'

Caballero paused. To sign, he realised, would be death. They would shoot him at once. That was what they always did. No one ever came out of these interrogations alive. He had to be clever. He would probably be shot, but there was one slight chance of salvation. The question was, how best to use it.

'I want to speak to someone,' he said.

'Not Tanucci?' asked Roberto. 'His name doesn't even appear in your confession. He's got nothing to do with it.'

He was getting a little impatient with Caballero's evident desire not to be helped. He wished he could get the man out, without Tanucci seeing him. Things were complicated enough.

'No. I want to speak to a colleague of mine at work called Elena Garcia.'

'For God's sake, sign it. If you know what is good for you, you'll sign it.'

There was something rather urgent in Roberto's tone; Caballero sensed that his hesitation over signing had rattled his opponent. He was gaining the advantage over him; and now that he could see him, now that he knew who he was, they were pitted against each other on far more equal terms. He knew now that Enriquez wanted him to sign at almost any price; and as Enriquez wanted it so much, he ought not to do it, under any circumstances. He put down the pen.

Roberto felt a spasm of annoyance at the man's stubbornness. Perhaps Caballero was a Communist after all. Communists were well known for their blind adherence to mistaken beliefs. He felt that he was beginning to repent of his kindness; it was almost as if Caballero was determined on being tortured by Strauss. But he resolved to be patient. He would not call in Strauss if he could possibly help it. The gentler arts of persuasion must be used first.

'You must trust me,' he said. 'Look, I'll give you a cigarette. They're real cigarettes too. All you have to do is sign and then you will just go to prison for two years. You can't think that I'd get any pleasure out of having you shot, can you?'

Caballero took the cigarette into his mouth. He sensed that he was gaining time. He was, oddly, beginning to be fascinated by his predicament. It was rather like a game of chess.

'You might like to have me shot,' he said. 'There's such a thing as sadism.'

'Yes, I suppose there is,' agreed Roberto. 'I have seen it. But you have really no idea . . .'

'About what?'

'About what a kind person I really am. The man who arrested you and broke your rib, would he be doing this? I have never caused anyone a moment's pain in my life – except when it has been necessary, absolutely necessary.'

'Is this necessary? My arrest and imprisonment?'

'Oh yes. The Republic is in danger.'

'I don't believe you,' said Caballero. 'I suppose that is what you think; you have to believe you are doing this for reasons of State, because if you didn't, you'd just be left with your own motives.'

'What on earth do you mean?' asked Roberto coldly.

'If you invoke reasons of State, then when you arrest people without proper charges, lock them up, torture them, shoot them, or do whatever it is that you do to them, you can quite easily say to yourself as you do so that it is all done for reasons of State, and that you personally don't approve of it at all. You say: "This isn't my action, it's the State that is doing this." And that means that you avoid the responsibility.'

Caballero felt he had scored a point with this line of argument. Despite the fact that he was tied to a chair in a dark and unfamiliar room, he felt he was in his element. For this was what he was best at, dazzling the less gifted with his brilliant intelligence. Thus he had always been, and thus, even in the very jaws of death, was he still. He loved argument, he was addicted to it; he always won arguments and he would certainly win this one. He would run rings around the gallant and good-looking little Captain. He was beginning to feel quite sorry for him. The fact that the stakes were so high made the contest all the more exhilarating.

'There you have it,' said Caballero, spitting the cigarette stub out of his mouth. 'You project your responsibilities onto the State, this huge impersonal construct. You see yourself as some sort of servant of a higher destiny – just like Hitler.'

'Don't you realise I have the power to have you shot or to have you released?' asked Roberto, putting out Caballero's smouldering cigarette end with his shoe, and at the same time wondering why Elena had ever liked this bumptious little man.

'That's what you think, Captain,' said Caballero, too caught up by his own cleverness to stop himself now. 'You think you are powerful. But in fact you are the very opposite. You want me to be frightened of you, but in fact you are frightened of me.'

Roberto laughed.

Caballero, forgetting that Roberto was laughing at the sheer absurdity of his statement, and forgetting that he was tied to a chair and reeking of his own filth, became annoyed.

'I know what you are really like,' he said.

'Then you know more than I do,' said Roberto.

'Elena Garcia keeps your photograph on her desk.'

Roberto was silent; he had thought he was safe in anonymity. He began to feel that his cheeks were burning.

'I know why you are in the Army,' Caballero was saying, quite oblivious to the terrible mistake he had made. 'And I know why you are doing this. You feel you have to prove yourself, if not to her, then to yourself. You're an inadequate.'

Roberto felt the burning sensation in his cheeks spread to his forehead, his neck, his shoulders and even his chest. He screwed the typed confession up into a ball, and stubbed out his cigarette. He realised now what Elena had told this man about himself in those conversations over the telephone that Olivarez had mentioned; and that this odious creature in front of him knew things that he had never mentioned to anyone, not even Fritz. He was angry and the colour of his entire face must show it. All the feelings he had tried to keep under control were now erupting. His self-control, the work of years, was disappearing. And this odious man was seeing it happen. The process was quite involuntary. He was conscious that the ghastly and humiliating blush was now quite evident and that Caballero could see what he had never allowed even Elena to see. Caballero had stabbed him to the quick.

He got up and picked up the knout that was behind his chair, an instrument that he had never intended he should use. He stood behind Caballero and put the knotted cord around his temples, and began to tighten it. Caballero began to squirm with pain.

'What did she say to you?' asked Roberto thickly.

'She told me what you are like,' said Caballero.

'And what am I like?' asked Roberto, tightening the knout as fast as he could.

'Cold,' screamed Caballero.

The man had lost consciousness. Roberto reeled across the room and leaned against the wall; his breath came in thick heavy gasps. He desperately loosened his collar, in case he too fainted. But he could not blame himself. He would have let the man go, to please her, but the man himself had provoked him beyond measure. And now the man had seen him like this, as no one else had ever seen him. He had been reason itself, and this present catastrophe was not his fault. Caballero was starting to come round. Roberto let himself out of the cell, and thankful that there was no one around, went upstairs to his bedroom as quickly as he could, threw off his clothes and stood under a cold shower.

He was not a cruel man, he told himself when he had recovered, towards evening of the same day. But Caballero had provoked him. As a child, he had used to have a terrible temper; as an adolescent, he had learned to control himself perfectly. Things that had once moved him almost beyond endurance, now left him cold. Aged six, he had suffered from tantrums and writhed on the floor empurpled and screaming, a victim to his own hot blood. But maturity had brought self-control, and the blood had ceased to rush to his face; he had banished anger, he had divorced himself from passion, he had doused his face with cold water lest it ever give a betraying hint that underneath the calm exterior lay something beyond his powers. Everything he had done was done in a way that no one could reproach. He had faced a firing squad calmly; he dealt with people he didn't like calmly; he never let anyone move him beyond what he thought it was right to be moved. Even with Elena, over the five years he had known her, never had he given himself away. His skin had always kept its wonted honey-gold colour.

But now Caballero, in his stupidity, had defeated him. And with a little sigh of regret, he knew that Caballero would now never be released.

Eleven

Roberto stood alone in the middle of the Palace Square, surrounded by some rather uninterested pigeons fearlessly pecking away around his feet, ignoring his presence. He had a moment ago telephoned Elena from a call box, and she had told him that she would leave *The Post* and come to him at once. It was good of her, he reflected. Perhaps he did not deserve her; but she still loved him after all this time. If he had any real sense or if he really loved her, he told himself once again, he would break the whole thing off. Of course, she would be upset, but she would learn to forget him and find someone else. She would be happier that way. But it was not her happiness he was thinking of just then. Elena was about the last tenuous link he had with reality. His mother secretly disapproved of him, he felt; Fritz had gone; but Elena was still there. She believed in him still, and despite the fact that she had not heard from him for weeks, she was on her way to see him. That was some comfort.

She came to him across the Square. He watched her approach, and thought about Caballero; he had tried his best, he told himself yet again.

'I have been so worried,' was the first thing she said, kissing his cold cheek.

'About me?' he asked, a little surprised, but nevertheless pleased.

'Of course. They say the most awful things are happening.'

'Who says so?' he asked.

'Friends of Caballero. Apparently a lot of people have been

arrested, or have simply gone away, all over the country. I don't suppose you know anything about Caballero, do you?'

He felt his heart grow cold within him.

'What do you think can have happened to him?' he asked.

'They think he must have gone abroad. If Caballero had been arrested and had talked, why haven't the others been arrested themselves? So we are hoping that Caballero is safely in California, and perhaps can't get hold of us to say so. Besides, fleeing the country is a crime now, isn't it? So we wouldn't know if he had got away. It is the uncertainty of it all that is so worrying.'

'Try not to think about it,' said Roberto. 'Whatever has happened to him, you can't blame yourself for it, can you?'

'No,' she said.

'And perhaps you might give his strange friends the hint that they ought to be more careful in the future,' said Roberto. 'I mean . . .'

'Yes, I know what you mean,' she said. 'I know all about that, though Caballero did surprise me. It used to make me wonder, the fact that he wasn't married. But the homosexuals and drug addicts are perfectly safe in some ways, because they have an early warning system. They think someone will tip them off. They're quite sure about that, because someone tried to warn Caballero; and I think Caballero must have been warned by someone, if he has got away.'

'And who warned him?' asked Roberto.

'Some lieutenant called at *The Post* the day Caballero vanished,' said Elena. 'A rather guilty-looking young man. He was running a risk, I suppose.'

Roberto was silent; these revelations made him feel uneasy.

'Try and keep away from these people,' he said. 'And now let's go for a walk in the Marine Gardens.'

So they walked in the Marine Gardens, a public park that lay to the north of the Palace, fronting the sea. Because it was hot, they walked along the sea wall, until they came to the little jetty in which it ended, which commanded an excellent view of the seaward face of the Palace, and the other side of the magnificent bay on which the City stood. Opposite to them, on the south side of the Bay was the Riviera with its elegant line of hotels, separated from their side by a two-mile stretch of water. They discussed the distance, as people do, when their minds are full of important subjects: she thought that it was two miles; he imagined that it was nearer three. Neither had ever heard of anyone swimming it.

It was an odd sort of conversation, for neither of them was paying much attention to the subject. He was thinking of Caballero, and how she should never know. She too was thinking of Caballero, and wondering where he was. But Roberto's presence comforted her, and with him next to her, she thought that the nightmarish possibilities she had imagined could not be true. The faith she had in him made the world different for her. But Roberto had no such faith, and he looked at the Presidential Palace and felt a cold hatred towards it, for it had made him inhuman. And because he felt the loneliness of inhumanity, because he felt he had been driven to do things he had never wanted to do and that would never be understood should they come to light, he put his arm around her and held her tight in his embrace.

Twelve

Several weeks passed. Roberto brooded on the way things were going. Caballero was dead, but he tried to put that out of his mind by thinking about the information the torturers had extracted from their various victims. He put his mind to intelligence work, sitting in the courtyard of the Army Navigational School, trying to puzzle out the meaning of the various confessions. He sat in his shirt-sleeves in the sunlight, away from the sweet smell of decay that came up from the cellars below, trying to make sense of the transcriptions of human misery. His heart was now hardened to the things he had seen. He read with a professional eye accounts that had been forced out of prisoners by thumbscrew and electric shocks, and he did so wondering what he would pass on to Olivarez. For the Colonel had asked for a report.

Some of the information before him was simply embarrassing. Though all their prisoners had been civilians, there were several facts that had come to light about the members of the officer class in the course of their investigations. Nor was this all. Officers had been mentioned by name; and one of them even pointed to Olivarez himself. Of course, the prisoner had merely mentioned 'a very senior officer'; but Roberto had bullied the truth about that out of Tanucci. It was astonishing to think that the Head of Security himself was responsible for such a breach of security. But even so, Roberto put this particularly damaging piece of information to one side and burned it there and then with his lighter.

He was not interested in Olivarez's private life, nor in

Tanucci's sexual habits, nor in knowing who sniffed cocaine with whom. That was not his job; his job was to do with politics, not morals. But no matter how hard he tried to piece things together, there was always one piece of the jigsaw that was missing. Nowhere could he find any hint, let alone mention, of Zondadari; yet he knew from first hand knowledge that Zondadari was disaffected. Why then did none of the evidence they had gathered implicate Zondadari? The only serious threat to the State was a coup by disaffected officers, and yet he had uncovered nothing about that.

Instead he had to be content with endless details about who had had coffee with whom in California, and what they had said about the General and democracy; about how such a number of people had been to see Karl Marx's tomb in London; about how the following were guilty of importing illegal books, usually ones he had never heard of. Few, few were the references to an actual conspiracy against the State – there was only in fact one decent confession to go on, and that was one that had been made when he had not been present, and of which he had been able to make little sense. The date seeemd to indicate the afternoon he had spent walking in the Marine Gardens with Elena. It was in Tanucci's writing.

He called Tanucci.

The young man came and stood before him, eyes cast to the ground.

Roberto, sensing that Tanucci was not at his ease, resolved to use a conciliatory tone.

'You took this down,' he said, showing him the paper.

'Yes, sir,' said Tanucci.

'Now,' said Roberto. 'Can you explain to me why it is written in what I take to be Italian?'

'But I have never written in English, sir, at least not much; and the man was speaking so fast, that I thought it best to write in the language I was fastest at writing in.'

'So he spoke in English?'

'Yes, sir.'

'I wish I had been there. Is he still here?'

'No, sir,' said Tanucci.

Roberto ran his eye over the piece of paper again. The prisoner in question had given the details of an elaborate conspiracy against the state, and mentioned several members, organised into cells. But there was something about the whole thing that struck him as immensely improbable.

'I didn't know that you were Italian,' he remarked, taking his eyes off the paper. 'Tanucci doesn't sound a very Italian name to me.'

'It's from Naples,' said Tanucci.

'And you took down what he said exactly?' asked Roberto mildly.

'Yes, sir,' said Tanucci.

'Except,' said Roberto, 'you must have translated all the names too. You see the prisoner confesses to knowing several agents, I suppose you'd call them, and they all have Italian names: Carlo, Anna, Nicola, and even Firenze. He must have said Charles, Anne, Nicholas and Florence, I imagine. Oh dear, it is complicated. I am rather afraid that I can't make sense of it. Can you?'

He passed the paper back to Tanucci, and Tanucci took it, thinking that this was some type of test.

'It is clear, sir, to me,' he said. 'All these people are using code names from various English novels; and sir, if you look at the prisoner's name, you'll see that he was a professor of literature.'

'Ah,' said Roberto. 'And to think that I thought – at least I did not know what I thought. How clever of you to work that out. But that goes to show the whole thing is useless, for how on earth can you catch someone when you don't know what their real name is? It's like looking for a needle in a haystack.'

'There are descriptions, sir,' said Tanucci.

'Very vague ones too,' said Roberto. 'Let me see: it says here that the leader of the gang is of youthful appearance and goes under the name of Nicholas Nickleby; speaks English with a very strong British accent; has clear blue eyes, an innocent manner and blond hair, but is nevertheless very dangerous; of slight build, and of the Leninist-Maoist persuasion. Well – there can't be many people in this City like that, can there? You should have no difficulty finding him; only "Nicola", as you have taken down, is a girl's name in English. Nicholas is a boy's name. Which did the prisoner use?'

'I can't remember, sir,' said Tanucci a little diffidently.

'So, we don't know whether Nickleby is a man or a woman. Tell me, Tanucci,' said Roberto suddenly. 'Do you really think there are any Leninist-Maoists in the country?'

Tanucci was silent.

'If there aren't,' said Roberto reflectively, 'then we've been taken in very badly indeed.'

'Colonel Olivarez has given us this job, sir,' said Tanucci. 'When it's finished, we will see what happens then.'

Roberto sighed. He wished he could invite Tanucci to sit down and tell him what he really thought. Presumably Tanucci did think, and in a way that Strauss did not. But that would never do; so he sent Tanucci away and thought of all the various things that might happen. Perhaps foreign agents were at work in the Republic calling themselves by improbable Dickensian names. The whole matter of threats to State security now was beginning to seem to him to be almost entirely implausible. What were they doing? But what choice did they have, but to continue doing it? So he sat on and thought and did nothing, uncertain of what he could do.

He went to see his mother, and she looked at him and said: 'Are you worried about anything, *chiquitito*?'

'Yes, I am worried,' he replied.

But that was all. She dared not press him. Maria Enriquez, who had been a Maitland, had not been brought up to ask questions. Curiosity was rather vulgar; and apart from this deep-seated belief, she also knew from experience that curiosity was counter-productive. There was no telling what a strong willed young man might do if she were to try and probe too deeply. He would resent it; worse, he might go and do the exact opposite to whatever he might perceive that she wanted him to do. Interference would be disastrous. She already wished that she had never urged him to get married. There was something so stubborn about him, that she rather feared that he might never marry simply because he knew she wanted him to; he might remain a bachelor forever, simply to underline the point that no one at all, least of all his mother, could persuade him to do anything he did not want to do himself. Thus she decided she would keep her peace, and steered away from dangerous topics. Instead they discussed the usual problems, the food shortages and the abysmal quality of the olive oil. And at the back of it she hoped that one day he would tell her of his own accord about what was troubling him.

All around them the country was discussing the quality of the olive oil. The country was in ferment. It was widely assumed that the food shortages were caused by hoarding. An interesting – so it had struck Elena at least – story had appeared in *El Mercurio*. Two men had been killed by a mob in one of the poorer parts of the City. The mob, a word the Government newspaper seemed to enjoy using, had been under the impression that the two men, who had been shopkeepers, had had hidden stores of food in their cellar. The police had arrived too late on the scene to prevent the crime taking place; but not too late to make several arrests among the dispersing mob. The cellar, broken into, had turned out to be empty.

This sort of thing made disturbing reading.

Isabel de Calatrava read it and put a hand up to her pearls and repressed a shiver. She thought of mobs, in Paris and in St Petersburg; she thought of poor Marie Antoinette. And she immediately told Nicola Nickleby that she was not to go out of doors except accompanied by one of the servants.

Carmen Garcia read it, and thought that the whole thing had been stage-managed. She wondered what the Army would make of their opportunity.

Generals Hernandez and Messina read it, and were both immensely pleased. There was nothing like the utter arbitrariness of mob violence and sudden murder to make people trust the forces of law and order. A strong dose of fear was just what the people needed.

The British Ambassador read it and thought that this was the beginning of the end for the regime.

Colonel Olivarez read it and saw it as the first step towards the establishment of a new regime.

Father Morisco read it out aloud to the Archbishop, and both considered it in silence for a while and were worried.

And finally Roberto Enriquez read it and was eaten away with terrible anxiety, because he thought he saw in this new development something that no one else could see.

Thirteen

The British Ambassador was not the complete fool that most people took him for. He could see the way the wind was blowing as well as the next man, and liked to remind himself of this fact at regular intervals. On the day the executions took place – for they were hanging six of the rioters that they had managed to catch, on the grounds that they had had common purpose with the murderers who had killed the two shopkeepers, and they were hanging them with as much haste as possible, perhaps to show that retribution was swift – on the day of the hangings, Sir Nigel decided that something ought to be done.

He had quite given up hope; in the tradition of long gone Ambassadors like Lord William Bentinck, he had tried to advise the oppressive Generals that moderation might bear more fruit. But they had not listened. The hangings would take place, despite his advice.

Sir Nigel was in despair for another reason too. The Embassy was full of furniture. If he had had a wife, she might have been useful now – for someone would have to supervise the packing away of all these valuables. But he didn't have a wife. He had joined the Foreign Office long before the days when bachelorhood had become socially unacceptable. Perhaps, he thought, alternately stroking his huge moustache and rubbing his bald pate, he could draft in that useful woman, Isabel de Calatrava. But perhaps not. No doubt she would be only too glad to help, but, though Sir Nigel never underestimated anyone's kindness, he feared that if he were to apprise

Isabel of his forebodings, her mind would immediately turn to the preservation of her own valuables. People were like that; come war, revolution and civil disturbance, they immediately rushed to pack their own bags and not someone else's. Quite ordinary people became egotistical monsters, transformed by self-interest. That was why it was necessary to act now, before things got out of hand.

He walked around the Embassy a little sadly. He had collected so many charming things during the years he had spent in the Republic. In a country like this, where the currency collapsed with gratifying regularity, few things had been beyond the reach of the pound sterling. He had collected everything he could lay his hands on – Spanish silver, huge pieces of eighteenth-century furniture, crystal chandeliers – he had collected compulsively and promiscuously. Taste had never been his strong point; there had been no discrimination in his collecting, only acquisitiveness. The Embassy, a pretty Italianate villa on the far side of the Marine Gardens, on the north side of the Bay, would doubtless be burned down by some mob, and unless he could get its contents away, what a bonfire there would be. But it would take a battleship to carry all this back to England, he realised sadly, as he contemplated the future ruin of his possessions.

A battleship.

The idea suddenly took root in his mind. There were battleships in the Atlantic. Gunboat diplomacy and Britannia ruling the waves were things of the past, but there were still a few ships in the Atlantic, not too far away, and surely something could still be arranged, no matter how much times had changed? He would put the question to London.

London, however, was not as enthusiastic as Sir Nigel had hoped. They received his request with frigid politeness. The nature and extent of Government cuts were explained to him. Government cuts, it seemed, had more or less crippled the country. The days of Pam and Dizzy, he was told, were definitely over. In vain did Sir Nigel explain the nature of the danger: London was unmoved by his harrowing descriptions of rampaging mobs, revolutionary movements, coups and counter-coups. London remained inflexible in the face of the possibility of danger to British subjects and property. No battleship would be forthcoming.

It really was appalling. Here he was, an Englishman abroad, surrounded by unreliable foreigners, abandoned by the Government he was supposed to represent. London would not lift a finger, despite the way he had given full range to his descriptive powers. Perhaps he had better try Isabel de Calatrava after all. She had more influence with Hernandez than he did himself. Perhaps, as long as he did not tell her what it was for, he could get her to organise the loan of an aeroplane.

The substance of Sir Nigel's communication with London was made into a memorandum and put into a tray marked 'Urgent'. About a week later, one expert on South American affairs read it and said to another member of the same department:

'What's this about a revolution in the Republic of . . .?'

'Where?'

He explained where.

'Oh, I think they have quite a lot of revolutions there. I shouldn't let it worry you. Why do you ask?'

'Our man out there seems to be asking for a battleship to evacuate the British community.'

'Oh really? And is there a British community out there?'

'Do you think we should do something?'

'Oh, I don't think so, do you?' said his colleague. 'But if you really do want to do something, why not issue advice to British subjects not to go there? That would be just the thing. No one ever goes there, so it won't cause any inconvenience at all. It is the one place in South America no one has ever been to, as far as I can work out.'

'That's what I'll do . . .'

And so the problem was settled.

Fourteen

Nicola Nickleby was enjoying her stay in the Republic more and more. It had all been rather strange at first. The parties she had been to with Mrs de Calatrava were quite unlike the parties she had been used to at home in Godalming. There had been so many important people present, Government Ministers and Ambassadors, and she had done her very best to remain as inconspicuous as possible, which she felt was what her hostess expected of her. But really, Isabel had been quite kind, and she was glad that her mother had spotted that small advertisement in *The Lady*. There had been a few difficulties right at the start, though. Isabel, thanks to some confusion over her Christian name, had expected her to be a boy, not an eighteen-year-old girl. Apparently, in the Republic it was men who were called Nicola, with an accent on the last a. That was the Italian for Nicholas, and there were lots of Italians in this country. However, having come all this way, Isabel could not have sent her back home on the grounds that she was the wrong sex. Besides, though Nicola was not to know it, Isabel was very keen to build up her stock of pounds sterling at present.

Why Isabel should have preferred a boy student was explained to Nicola by the cook, once her Spanish had improved sufficiently to understand her. The Republic, said the cook, was not the place for young women, especially blonde girls from overseas. The danger consisted in Men. Boys could be allowed to wander around as they liked, but a girl was a different proposition, especially in a country so full of soldiers.

Nicola couldn't help but feel a little thrill about this information. Men were still objects of mystery to her. There weren't any in Godalming; at least there weren't any real men, like the ones you saw in South America. Godalming could boast persons who belonged to the masculine sex, men her father's age, or young men with beer bellies that you saw hanging around outside pubs on summer's days, or spotty youths who did various ill-defined jobs behind the counters of newsagents' shops – but there were no men like the handsome young officer she had seen that day at the races. She wished she had had the courage to go up and speak to him, but she hadn't dared. He had looked so remote, so distant, so beautiful. She had attempted to ask Mrs de Calatrava about him afterwards, which had immediately aroused her hostess's suspicions. In fact she had not had any success at all in finding out who he was – she had only planted the idea in Isabel's mind that she was a little man-mad.

Hence her present condition. Isabel had gone out to make a social call on behalf of General Hernandez, and Nicola was strictly confined to the kitchen with dog and cook for the day. For today they were hanging six men. The streets would be dangerous, swarming no doubt with police and soldiers. So she sat in the kitchen sipping wine and listening to the cook, who was explaining the political situation to her. It was very complicated, very foreign; she heard about Communist plots to destabilise the Republic, and how Mrs de Calatrava's friend General Hernandez was doing his best to deal with the situation. Nicola tried to imagine that mild old man – he always smiled at her when he came to the house, although he plainly had no idea who she was – dealing with anyone.

On a happier note, the cook told her that soon it would be the time for the President's birthday celebrations. That was always good fun, and she was sure that Mrs de Calatrava would not mind her going to see the celebrations. They could go together. Of course, Mrs de Calatrava always went to the reception in the Palace as befitted her rank; but the cook was of the opinion that the real fun was to be had in the streets outside. It was a public holiday, and everyone would be there. It would be such fun.

Nicola agreed, and felt that this would be a wonderful opportunity to see life in South America at first hand.

Elena was finding that life at *The Post* had become rather dull of late. There was no news, except the news of the hangings, and that, once its initial morbid fascination had worn off, didn't interest her for long. She was growing sick of plots and conspiracies and the ever more hysterical tones of *El Mercurio*. She could not believe what the paper said, and she could not believe that anyone sane could believe it either. What was worse, there was no Caballero there either to keep her sane. Caballero had known how to make her laugh; with him you were reassured: you knew you were sane and the rest of the world was mad. His mockery restored the balance. But Caballero, it now seemed certain, had gone abroad, and was probably even now lounging in some café in San Francisco, enjoying himself. It was rather selfish of him to have left her in this way, without even dropping a hint that he had been about to flee the country. She hadn't until now realised just how much she had depended on him. It was almost as if she had been in love with him – which of course was not the case. But some of the symptoms of love were there. She felt driven to talk and think about him. She had mentioned his name to other people who had shrugged their shoulders or just looked at her a little oddly. She had even tried to engage his grandfather in conversation about Caballero, but without success. She would have tried his friends, except that she had not seen any of them for some time now, and rather suspected that they were keeping low profiles.

It was this – a desire to talk about Caballero, and the inability to find anyone who would listen to her – that drove her eventually to speak to her mother.

'Do you remember Caballero, the Editor's grandson?' she asked over dinner one night.

'Vaguely,' said Carmen vaguely.

(She had so much on her mind these days. She felt sometimes that she was living in a miasma of vagueness.)

'Has something happened to Caballero?' she asked, suddenly forcing herself to think.

'Nothing has happened,' said Elena. 'He has just gone away rather suddenly. About a month ago he left the office and he hasn't come back since, and he hasn't told me where he has gone.'

It struck Carmen that her daughter was very unlucky in her choice of male friends. They seemed to have the habit of disappearing for longish periods and not leaving forwarding addresses. But this hardly seemed to be the time to mention it. She did not want to quarrel with Elena about Captain Roberto Enriquez yet again.

'Where do you think he has got to?' asked Carmen.

'Roberto had the idea that he was in danger. But I have hardly seen him since,' said Elena. 'I am sure that Caballero is safe, but if he wasn't so thoughtless, then he would have sent me a postcard at least just to make sure that I knew.'

'Men don't think,' said Carmen. 'But they do say –'

'What do they say?'

'The newspapers have been full of reports about people being rounded up. Of course, they never mention names and they never say why. That funny old man who taught English Literature at the University, apparently he was taken away, or so I heard at the office, and no one has seen him since. They just hope that eventually he will turn up . . .'

There was silence between them for a while. Elena felt that her confidence was wilting.

'I can't imagine anyone wanting to round up Caballero,' she said.

'Perhaps he told his grandfather where he was going, and the old man forgot all about it,' said Carmen.

'Of course,' said Elena, 'they tapped our phones. Roberto found out somehow and told me about it, but even so . . .'

She did not quite know how to say it, but what she meant to say was, despite the phone-tapping, there could not be anything so serious the matter. Of course, she assumed there were political prisoners somewhere, locked away, and that someone was responsible for it. But these were things outside her experience, and she could not believe that anything similar would ever involve people she knew.

Carmen was staring into her soup. Knowledge, that deadly commodity, had undone her many years ago. She hoped now that Elena hadn't liked Caballero too much; and more than that she could not hope. There was no undoing the past. She had, years ago, made the terrible mistake, in the belief that her daughter had to be protected, of concealing from Elena the true nature of her father's death. She had protected her only too well. Elena had grown up insulated from the real world, as if enclosed in some huge glass jar. She had never known, because no one had ever told her; and now Carmen feared that she might find out, not by being told, but by discovering for herself.

Elena did indeed go to bed more disturbed than she had been for some time. She now had the idea that Caballero might be in prison, forgotten by everyone, hoping that she would remember him. The conviction took root that she had to do something. And when she got up, she knew that she had to do something, if only because the suspicion was there in her mind, and unless she excised it, she would never get a moment's peace.

The idea of phoning hospitals or the police was patently absurd. They would never tell you anything at the best of times. The only thing for it, the only way to break the terrible sense of secrecy that gripped the country, was to gather together the few U.S. dollars she had been hoarding, and go and see Caballero's flat.

She had never been to his flat before; in the past they had met at the office, or in public places. The caretaker let her in on the payment of one dollar. The flat, she was told, had been sealed by the police; but the caretaker was evidently happy to let present gain outweigh future risk.

Elena stood in the midst of the unfamiliar flat, and she knew at once what had happened. Caballero had not gone on holiday. No one had ever gone on holiday in such a manner, no matter how hurried their departure. All the books had been thrown from their shelves, and clothes had been pulled from their drawers. The place had clearly been subjected to a thorough search, and it frightened her. Only the bathroom had been untouched. The toothbrush, the razor and the soap were eloquent testimony to their departed master and the suddenness of his going. Someone had taken him away, and given him no time to pack. But what had he done to deserve it? He hadn't been a criminal or a spy or a threat to State security. And where was he now? The desolate flat frightened her. The thought of where Caballero might be at present angered her; and blended with the anger was a sense of curiosity.

Fifteen

Roberto was sitting in the smoking room of the Military Club. It was a very fine room, and because it faced south, it received no direct sunlight. It was dim and cool. The ceiling was high, the armchairs were cavernous. Because it was a hot summer's day outside, the smoking room was deserted, which was just what he had hoped to find. He had no desire to be ambushed by a club bore, or worse, to meet Zondadari again. If he could not spend his afternoons in agreeable company he preferred to spend them alone.

Life was becoming intolerably dull. He wished that Fritz was not in San Cristobal. If Fritz had been there now, perhaps they would have played tennis, which was something Fritz did rather well, but not too well. Last summer they had played tennis a great deal together, almost twice every week, and Fritz had almost always lost. Roberto sometimes wondered if Fritz lost deliberately; but because he could see no real reason why he should choose to do so, he used to dismiss this from his mind.

He had escaped once again from the claustrophobic atmosphere of the Army Navigational School. He did not want to see his mother. She was a reproach to him; to look at her even would be to be reminded of the ideal which he had been brought up to follow, the ideal which had failed him. Once he had thought that to do his duty was the only thing to do, but now he felt adrift. His duty was no longer so clear. Olivarez had used them all. Tanucci had hinted as much. Olivarez took people up, and exploited them; then when he was done with them he threw them away. But even being thrown away by Olivarez didn't cure you of the malaise the man brought, for Tanucci plainly longed to be taken up again. Olivarez was like a magician: once met, he was never forgotten.

He thought of Elena, and blamed Olivarez for ruining that part of his life – not that there had been much to ruin. But the remote prospects he had once entertained about settling down with Elena to lead some sort of normal and domestic life now seemed more improbable than ever. How could he ever love her properly, how could he ever let her see his soul, when he had killed Caballero for doing just that? For he had killed Caballero; he had shot him in the back of the head, and he had died, and he had done so because Strauss had refused to do it for him, and because he had not dared to ask Tanucci. He had not wanted to seem a coward, and he had done it; and now he was as guilty as they were. Except, he felt no guilt; he felt nothing at all. Tanucci felt guilt, he was sure; he looked shamefaced much of the time. Strauss did not know what it was. But he, Roberto, felt no guilt. He knew he had done wrong, and he felt he would one day suffer for it as justice demanded, but he felt no grief for what he had done. His heart was cauterised by years of self-denial; and the fact that he felt nothing for what he had done, that he felt nothing for anyone at all, was perhaps punishment for his sins.

He sat on in his solitude, trying not to think of Elena. His mind turned instead to the plot or plots or whatever they were supposed to be. He was sure now that these could not exist in reality. If only Fritz were there; for Fritz would know. Fritz was sensible, and until now he hadn't realised that he had relied on Fritz's common sense so much. Of course, Fritz always did what Roberto advised and frequently got into trouble when Roberto wasn't there to stop him; but Fritz, though hardly practical in some ways, did have an instinctive knowledge of the truth. When they had been at school together, Fritz had been one of the only boys who had ever dared argue in school debates that it was a good thing that

Hitler and Mussolini had lost the war, despite the fact that his mother had been a Schultz. But Fritz was like that: he could recognise what was true, an ability which, even if he had once had it, Roberto now felt he had lost for ever.

Behind him he heard quiet steps. He sank as unobtrusively as possible into his armchair, and as he was facing away from the door he hoped he would not be seen or noticed. Two men had come into the room, thinking it was empty. Their voices were low but distinct.

'The British have landed us in a terrible mess,' one was saying. 'In fact I would go as far as to say that the British have done for us. They have put us into the same league with countries like Cuba and God knows where else. That sort of thing is hard to shake off and panic has a way of spreading.'

'It has certainly spread to you, General,' said the other voice.

Roberto, realising that he was overhearing something important, sat completely still. It was as if he was a little boy crouching at the top of the stairs, hearing his elders below discuss terrible things.

'I am not panicking,' said the first voice querulously, which was unmistakeably the tone of General Hernandez. 'The only reason that we are here and not in the Palace is because I feel sure that my telephone has been tampered with, and who knows what else. I don't want Messina to know everything I am doing. He has been at some of my men in the Ministry, I am sure.'

'Oh?' enquired the second voice, which belonged to Olivarez.

'This is important,' continued Hernandez. 'Unless we do something soon the game is up. Discovering non-existent Communist plots hasn't helped much; and hanging six innocent rioters won't do us any good at all – that was Messina's idea. The man's a brute. All we need is for a few questions to be asked in London and Washington, for the British and the North Americans to withdraw their investments, and then we are done for. Then there might really be a revolution. The escudo will vanish into thin air, even more so than at present, and then where will we be?'

'I don't see how I come in,' said Olivarez.

'Everyone knows that Security is the one Government department that still works. You can deal with Messina,' said Hernandez. 'If we have got to have a revolution, then let's do it our way, and do it quietly, like the last time. Get rid of Messina before he ruins us all.'

'A coup? When?'

'Before the General dies.'

'Is he dying?'

'He has been dying for years, you know that.'

'And what then?'

'Then I'll be President, as the last remaining member of the Junta, and you will be Minister of the Interior or even Prime Minister if you like. You can have a free hand, as far as I am concerned. Promote a few promising younger men. Get rid of all the rubbish Messina has clogged the Interior Ministry up with. But it has got to be done now, before the General dies, and before Messina himself decides to make a move.'

'When the Old Man dies,' said Olivarez after a lengthy pause, 'not before. As soon as the Old Man dies, that would be the moment for us to make our move. There will be such confusion just then that there should be no difficulty.'

'But what are we going to do *now*?' asked Hernandez.

'If as you say the British have advised their nationals not to come here and branded the Republic unsafe; and if people panic as a result – if let's say Isabel de Calatrava decides to lead a stampede to safety, and if there are more riots – that won't necessarily do any harm. People will only blame Messina, that is all. He is the Minister of the Interior and these things are his responsibility.'

'I suppose so,' said Hernandez. 'But in the meantime, stay in the Palace, and stay by the Old Man's bed. Messina is never far away, and that way you can watch him, and watch for the moment the breath leaves the General's body.'

'Certainly,' said Olivarez.

'Good,' said Hernandez. 'I suppose it was Messina who tapped my phone?'

'Of course,' lied Olivarez.

Roberto heard the two men get up. Their footsteps receded and the door shut behind them. When he was sure they had gone, he took out a cigarette and lit it. He sat and smoked, pondering what he had heard. In this way half an hour passed, the very deadest of the afternoon. In particular he pondered what Hernandez had said about non-existent Communist plots. What then had they been doing?

There was nothing worth fighting against, nothing worth defending either. He had thought so once but thought so no longer. He had lost his faith.

Sixteen

Nicola was distressed to hear that the Republic had become unsafe for British visitors. She felt that it was ridiculous. The local paper had said nothing about it, but she had had a telephone call from her parents, who, in the safety of Godalming, were filled with foreboding. Mum and Dad, she knew, had never been happy with the idea of abroad. The fact that Nicola was a pretty girl, blue-eyed, blonde, seemingly much younger than her eighteen years, always made them worried. Foreigners were not to be trusted; in the past they had always gone on holiday in Cornwall; and as if to prove how right they had been to be cautious, these particular foreigners in the Republic seemed to be on the point of revolution. Mr and Mrs Nickleby had rung the Foreign Office, and 'revolution' had been the word that had been used. (The Foreign Office was perhaps the only place in the world where the Junta's propaganda had found a receptive audience.)

To Mr and Mrs Nickleby, revolution meant blood in the streets, tumbrils, bread riots and death. They had begged Nicola to come home. Vainly, across the transatlantic wires, Nicola had tried to persuade them that there was no revolution. She had told them that it was a figment of their imagination, or someone's imagination. There simply was no revolution, she repeated; it was true that there had been a riot, but six people had been hanged for that, she had told them. Her father had always favoured the death penalty, she knew, but this reassurance produced a subdued shriek of dismay from her mother and what amounted to an order from her father. She was to come home at once, on the next flight too, no matter how much she was enjoying herself, and that was that.

Thus the call had ended.

With a heavy heart she had told Mrs de Calatrava the news. They went out to a travel agent. The next flight to London, fortunately, was some days hence. A ticket was bought, once suitable proof of identity was produced, in the name of N. Nickleby; you always had to show your identity when buying air tickets, said Isabel, so the Government could stop malcontents fleeing the country.

The fact that she was to go was very disappointing from a financial point of view, as far as Isabel was concerned. She had been counting on that money. Even Nicola, such a quiet girl, seemed subdued by the news, and as a result Isabel had not the heart to interfere in her plans to go to the President's birthday celebrations that coming Saturday afternoon. She'd be perfectly safe with the cook, and would come to no harm.

It was because he thought that General Hernandez had handled foreign policy so badly that General Messina had decided to organise huge celebrations for the General's birthday, to show just how efficient the Interior Ministry could be. He was not entirely successful, for no one had counted on the Old Man living this long, and all the preparations were made at the last minute; but Messina went on all the same, keen to show that he and not his rival was the coming man.

(The President himself was unaware of the trouble being taken on his behalf. He lay in his bedroom, hardly breathing. It was now a matter of indifference to him what the nation did over the chosen weekend. No matter how much noise the crowd might make in the square outside his windows, no matter how much noise the chosen few might make inside, he would not hear it now.)

All Government officials were suddenly informed that they were to have two full days' holiday. Even the Army Navigational School, thought Roberto, could suspend its activities for forty-eight hours. He was losing his appetite for the work. None of the information gleaned so far had come to anything. Olivarez's men had been combing hotel lists and flight lists for people with Dickensian names, but to no avail, and surely nothing would happen over the weekend of the General's birthday. The basements would stay empty as they had been for some days. A spirit of festivity was sweeping the City. The people, despite the fact that they were supposed to hate Messina, and that they were supposed to be terrified of plots and riots, seemed to be about to join in these birthday celebrations with surprising gusto. Perhaps they wished to forget the six men who had been hanged so recently. It gave Roberto an oppressive feeling; he wondered how they could be so easily seduced with the promise of parades and fireworks. The weather too had grown heavy, for it was now the middle of summer, the season when the City was usually empty. But no one was going away, at least not yet; there was an atmosphere of expectation.

The prospect of hot noisy nights, and the sound of fireworks made Roberto resolve to leave the City for the weekend. His first thought was that it might be possible to go to the cooler South, to San Cristobal in fact, and visit Fritz. He rang Fritz up and told him of his plan, but Fritz, rather infuriatingly, said he would be too busy that weekend to see him. It seemed that birthday madness was sweeping the country, and that Fritz had been given the job of organising a military parade in San Cristobal. Fritz would be busy.

His next thought was Elena; perhaps they could slip away to the country together. He had neglected her of late, and perhaps he ought to devote some time to her. He had never actually passed the night under the same roof with her; but now that he was beginning to think of himself as a lapsed Catholic, there was really no reason why he shouldn't. But these thoughts were interrupted by the orders that came from General Messina. The military parade was to take place in the

Palace Square on Saturday at two in the afternoon. Messina, having recently bought some second-hand tanks from an African dictator, was rather eager to show them off. There was to be a march past the Palace; Messina would view the spectacle from the balcony, with Olivarez next to him, sharing his splendour. And just so that everyone who mattered should know that the new tanks and their master were a force to be reckoned with, every officer in the City above the rank of Captain, and that included Roberto, was to be in the Palace, ready to hang out of the windows and join in the fun.

Roberto eventually was forced to realise that his weekend of freedom would have to begin once the parade was over.

And so it was; Messina stood on the balcony, Olivarez next to him, and below them the tanks lumbered past under the curious gaze of an immense and at times excited crowd.

'I hope you are enjoying this,' said Messina to his companion.

'Immensely,' said Olivarez.

'There are so many things you can do with tanks,' said Messina happily. 'For instance, I could blow up the Ministry of Foreign Affairs.'

'Hernandez is never there these days,' observed Olivarez. 'He never strays far from the President's bedside.'

'I have noticed that,' said Messina. 'That is because he is afraid. You know as well as I do that when the Old Man dies, there will be nothing for Hernandez to hang around for. I suppose you tap his telephones, don't you?'

Olivarez smiled.

At one of the windows, Roberto was watching the procession. The battle lines were already forming. There was a group of young officers around him, many of whom he knew.

'The Old Man is almost dead,' one was saying.

'If not dead already,' said another.

'The question is what will Olivarez do?'

'I'll follow him to the ends of the earth,' said one young man. 'And I don't care if Messina has got tanks or not. And all over the country,' he added without thinking, 'there are men like me, just waiting for the signal.'

'And you?' asked an officer, suddenly turning to Roberto, who was wondering what the signal would be, and when the coup would come. 'What will you do, Captain Enriquez?'

Roberto was silent for a moment, then said in tones which he hoped sounded utterly uninterested by the question: 'They say that Olivarez is the coming man.'

Roberto left the window, and walked over to a table where the wilting remains of the food still lay. His eyes searched for something edible among the uninviting comestibles. He saw a captain's tunic on the other side of the table, and raising his eyes he saw that it belonged to Zondadari.

'You here?' said Roberto.

'Under orders, like yourself,' said Zondadari. 'Much rather be with my wife and children.'

'Aren't you enjoying the tanks?' asked Roberto coolly.

'The tanks,' said Zondadari, 'don't work. I think they were sold to Messina at a knock-down price simply because they didn't work. Have you thought about our last conversation?'

'The tanks may not work,' said Roberto, carefully examining a sausage and wondering whether he was hungry enough to force himself to eat it. 'The tanks may be made out of cardboard, but the fact remains that the crowd outside is cheering. They don't mind who they have to cheer, as long as there is someone there on that balcony.'

'And why shouldn't it be you on the balcony, then?' asked Zondadari.

'I don't have the patience for that sort of thing,' said Roberto. 'Only the stupid or the misguided want to govern the crowd. I don't have any ambitions left. You're wasting your time with me, Zondadari. In fact, you are wasting your time altogether. As soon as that old man is dead, they all know what to do.'

The crowd in the square seemed to be bursting into new fits of applause and cheers. Roberto reflected that they could not have cared less about the man whose birthday they were supposed to be celebrating, and he was going to say something to that effect to Zondadari, when he noticed one of the Palace staff standing next to him, trying to catch his attention.

'You are wanted outside, sir,' said the man.

Roberto wondered what it could be, and thought that whatever it was, he could at least use it to make his escape. It was nearly three o'clock, and he thought that if he went away now, no one would notice.

'There goes Olivarez's trusted man,' he heard a voice say quietly, as he was leaving.

In the courtyard below, he found Tanucci.

'What is the matter?' asked Roberto.

'They wouldn't let Strauss in, sir,' said the Lieutenant. 'So he's outside. The thing is, some of the Colonel's men have sent us a report saying that they've found that a woman using a British passport in the name of N. Nickleby has booked herself onto the Monday morning flight to London.'

'Well?' asked Roberto.

'And she answers that description we were given, sir. It means that the information we've got isn't so fantastic after all. Strauss wants to make an arrest as soon as possible.'

'You'll never manage with the City in the mess it is at present,' observed Roberto. 'You'll have to wait until Monday; get her at the airport.'

'Strauss wants you to tell us to arrest her now, sir,' said Tanucci, a little insistently.

'Then Strauss has my permission to do as he likes,' said Roberto a little angrily. 'And one other thing. You won't see me until Monday lunchtime at the earliest. Do what you like.'

He turned away and began to go upstairs again. There was still some time to kill, before he could decently escape. He felt rather annoyed that something might be about to happen just as he was planning to drive into the country, having arranged to borrow his mother's car, to spend a few peaceful hours in the regimental shooting lodge, which today of all days would be absolutely deserted.

He went back to the window and lit a cigarette. The group of officers around him were engaged in a treasonable conversation.

'Hernandez would never do. He and Messina will have to retire gracefully when the Old Man dies. They only got where they are because of him, anyway. Olivarez is the coming man,' said the man who had inadvisedly mentioned signals before.

'Do Messina and Hernandez know that?' someone asked.

'Not at all. They're both too busy distrusting one another.'

'That will give Olivarez just the chance he needs,' said someone.

'And he won't be slow to take it,' observed someone else knowingly.

Their voices were gradually sinking into whispers; Roberto looked out of the window at the crowd below and stifled a yawn.

Seventeen

The crowd below the Palace windows that Roberto looked down upon was one of the largest that had gathered there in recent memory, and contained, did he but know it, Nicola Nickleby as well as Strauss and Tanucci.

Strauss had only been aware of the fact that Nicola had bought her ticket for a few hours. The security men employed by Olivarez checked all flight bookings regularly, but because the whole country was in chaos all weekend, thanks to the General's birthday celebrations, it had taken longer than usual for the report to be made. As soon as it had been, Strauss, with Tanucci in tow, had gone to the travel agent and found out where the suspect lived, which was not difficult, since Nicola, in case her flight had to be retimed or cancelled, had left her address with the travel agent. After that it had only been a matter of watching the block of flats and waiting.

It was thought best by Strauss not to arrest the woman at home. Nickleby was dangerous and she had associates. The operation that Strauss had in mind was designed to cause panic in the ranks of her associates; for Strauss resolved that Nickleby should be snatched in the street, and the large crowds everywhere that Saturday seemed to be a God-given opportunity.

It turned out to be easier than he imagined. A woman answering Nickleby's description had come out of the block of flats shortly before two, accompanied by another female. They were followed by Strauss and Tanucci as they made their way on foot towards the Palace Square. Strauss had stood next to

Nickleby in the crowd, and sent Tanucci into the Palace to inform their superior officer of what was about to take place – for if anything went wrong, Strauss did not want to be without support. He did not intend to act solely under the authority of a boy lieutenant. He was resolved to be as well covered as only a man who had once been sentenced to hang could be.

As soon as Tanucci had come back, bearing Enriquez's thoughtless consent, the plan was put into action.

Strauss approached Nickleby amidst the press of bodies, as soon as he could see that her companion was allowing her attention to wander. When he was near enough, he struck. Years of experience with hypodermics meant that Strauss struck cleanly and effectively. The small blonde girl gave a low scream; it was the only sound that she made before fainting under the effect of the tranquilliser.

Isabel's cook was several feet away and craning her neck to see the tanks the better when it happened.

'A young lady has fainted,' she heard someone say.

She turned. She saw a rather brutish-looking man in uniform.

'Clear the way, clear the way,' the man was shouting above the excited noises of the crowd. 'You, Lieutenant, sir, give me a hand.'

A younger man, an officer, was trying to do his best to push through the crowd and come to the rescue. The cook noticed that it was Nicola that they were helping. She caught sight of her pale blonde face for an instant, so noticeable in the crowd. She tried to attract their attention, but in the press – and there were some more tanks appearing now, and the crowd was applauding them deliriously – no one heard her. She tried to force her way towards Nicola, but unluckily the crowd was surging forward at that moment, and no matter how hard she tried, she found herself being carried away in the opposite direction. She screamed, but her scream was drowned by the cheering. Now ever further away, she saw Nicola's lifeless form being carried away to an ambulance, and the two officers getting in it with her. Then the ambulance drove off, sirens blaring, hardly noticed in the midst of the military festivities.

(The ambulance had been General Messina's idea. He knew women fainted in crowds on hot days. He had wanted people to think that the Junta thought of everything.)

After a few hundred yards, Strauss informed the ambulance driver and the medics that their vehicle was being requisitioned for military purposes. They did not argue. Then Strauss drove to the Army Navigational School, where he left the prisoner under the guard of Tanucci. He then returned the stolen ambulance to its station in Palace Square and decided to report his brave exploit to Captain Enriquez, who he knew would still be inside the Palace.

By lucky chance Strauss found Roberto just as he was coming down the stairs.

'Sir,' he said. 'We've caught her.'

Roberto looked at him coldly, for he was in that moment making his escape. Elena would be waiting for him at her mother's flat, and he had promised to be there in a few minutes. He did not want to be late.

'Oh very well,' he said. 'Don't do anything rash.'

'Will we see you soon, sir?' asked Strauss.

'I expect so,' said Roberto, knowing that it was not true, but hurrying away all the same.

'It is so hot!' exclaimed Isabel de Calatrava a few hours later. 'Do you like my hat?'

'Yes, and yes,' said Maria Enriquez.

Isabel was certainly dressed for the occasion. It was as if an overweight flamingo had settled on the lawn.

'We do seem to keep on meeting, don't we, my dear?' said Isabel. 'Of course, I know why.'

'You do?'

Both ladies were standing under the shade of a pine tree, where they were taking refuge from the broiling sun; it was now six in the evening, but still as hot as ever. They were at the garden party, being held in the Marine Gardens to celebrate the General's birthday. In the background a military band was playing excerpts from the operas of Verdi adapted for brass. Little flocks of overdressed people were visibly wilting in the sunshine, uncertain as to why they were there. The garden party had been another idea of General Messina's; he had heard of similar things being held in London.

'You see,' explained Isabel. 'Everyone is talking about Captain Enriquez. Your young man is so well thought of. He is quite the handsomest man in the Army; and he is so clever. They say that Colonel Olivarez has noticed him.'

'So you tell me.'

'I am sure of it. But I don't seem to have seen him here anywhere.'

'He hasn't come,' said Maria. 'He told me that he wouldn't come and that no one would notice his absence. He preferred to slip away once the parade was over.'

'So modest of him,' gushed Isabel. 'And also rather clever. Perhaps it is best to keep one's distance at present. Do you think the President will appear?'

'I really don't know,' said Maria. 'I am sure the poor man would rather be left alone to die in peace.'

'Talking of death,' said Isabel, 'there is the Archbishop.'

The Archbishop was standing a little apart, as Archbishops do. Father Morisco stood next to him, like a sentry on guard, very neat, smiling and black. He had just been speaking to Captain Zondadari.

The Archbishop was deeply troubled. He had hoped to see the President. That was why he had come. Instead he had seen General Messina who had given him bland assurances about the Father of the Country's health.

'I am wasting my time,' said the Archbishop quietly to himself.

'Your Grace?' asked Father Morisco solicitously.

'We are all wasting our time,' said His Grace.

'And time,' said Father Morisco, surveying the ladies in hats and the men in their medals and dress uniforms, 'time is running out.'

It was, thought the priest, the swan-song of the régime.

A feeling of doom hung over the Marine Gardens, for the party was having quite the opposite effect to the one General Messina had intended.

'You saw the tanks?' Sir Nigel was asking.

'No,' said the rather dull man next to him, who happened to be the American Ambassador.

'Quite right. Neither did I. They invited me to do so, but I refused. They were trying to prove a point I suspect. They want to show the people that they are still in business – a show of might. I was damned if I was going to be a party to that. They can go down the plug without me. Her Majesty's Government won't be very sorry to see them go, either.'

'My Government,' said the dull man, 'thinks the same as yours.'

'Have I asked you whether you have a helicopter?' asked Sir Nigel, with what he hoped was an air of indifference. (For Sir Nigel had given up hope for his furniture once Isabel de Calatrava had been unable to provide him with an aeroplane, and was now thinking primarily of himself.)

'You have and I do,' said the American; attempting a witticism he added: 'The balloon will soon go up.'

'He's had three strokes already, he can't eat solids any more, and he won't survive the week,' said Sir Nigel.

'I've heard the same,' said the American.

'He will die.'

'He will die,' echoed the American.

'Hernandez will take over,' said Sir Nigel.

'Messina will take over,' said the American. 'But it won't be a peaceful transition.'

'In a country like this,' said Sir Nigel with a rare flash of insight, 'things have been peaceful for far too long.'

Eighteen

Some twenty miles away, in the very hunting lodge that his father had caught his death of cold in, Roberto said: 'Caballero is dead.'

Elena had been talking about him, on and off, all afternoon. He had felt pushed past the limits of endurance. She had used the same phrase over and over again. She had been unable to bear the uncertainty any longer: she said that she had to know whether he was abroad, or in jail or dead. He had not come to the country to hear this, but to escape from it. He felt he had to stop her talking about Caballero. So he had told her.

She heard the words and was silent. She thought of Caballero alive and she tried to picture him dead, but failed.

'How?' she asked.

'The death certificate said that he was killed while attempting to escape from protective custody,' said Roberto shortly. (This was true.)

'Oh,' said Elena, numbed by the realisation that her very worst fears were now confirmed.

'I didn't know whether to tell you or not,' he said at last. 'But I supposed only the truth would put your mind at rest. There is something else that you ought to know as well; I think you ought to go abroad. They say there is going to be a war. The President is almost dead, and when he is finally dead, there will be a fight. I want my mother to go too.'

They were sitting on the terrace as he said these things to her; he kept his eyes on the view as he spoke and did not look at her.

'And you?' she asked, at last.

'I've got to stay here. And if I'm killed that will be that. It is no more than I deserve.'

'Why?'

'Everything has gone too far,' he said mechanically. 'I can't walk away from it now.'

He was thinking of Caballero.

'I won't leave the country unless you come too,' she said.

'Heroism doesn't mean anything any more. It's all false. If only you knew.'

'But knew what?' she asked.

'It is over between us,' he said. 'The only thing you can do for me now is to go away.'

'What?' she asked.

'I don't think we should meet any more,' he said lamely.

'But I want to know why not,' said Elena. 'Look at me and tell me why. What has happened? If you don't tell me why, I'll never leave you but hang onto you like a harpy.'

'I don't want you to hate me,' he said.

'Oh God, you are so vain,' said Elena in exasperation. 'You are so damned vain. You want to be so perfect, and you want me to go away because you can't bear the thought that I might realise that you are less than perfect. You expect me to be there whenever you want me, and now you expect the opposite. You think that you are so important.'

'Then why don't you leave me?' he said, looking at her now.

'I wish to God I could,' she replied.

He reached for his packet of cigarettes and lit one.

'You never used to smoke,' she said reproachfully.

'There are many things I've never done that I do now,' he said.

'There's one thing you've never done, certainly,' she said bitterly.

'Well go and find someone who will,' he said cruelly. 'I don't want you. I don't think I have ever wanted you really. It has been bad enough having my mother hanging over me all these years; but I don't want you making me into a hero as well. Don't you realise what I have just told you? Can't you see what has happened? I killed Caballero. I did it myself. I shot him in the back of the head, and I did it because I hated the man for what he had told me about myself. I am a murderer. Now leave me.'

Elena looked away and wept.

'How could you?' she asked.

'It was very simple.'

'But why?'

'You will never know, because I will never tell you.' Then he added: 'I lost my temper, but that isn't an excuse. I lost my temper because he told me that I was a sadist and that I couldn't ever love a woman properly, at least not you. At least that is what I think he said. I can't remember. It all seems so strange. Killing him was so easy, and I have never killed anyone before now; in fact I can hardly use a gun.'

He laughed uneasily and a little hysterically, amazed at the stupidity of it all.

'I never thought it possible that you could be violent or cruel,' she said, trying to understand him. 'You've always been so shy and reserved and frigid.'

'But I am not,' he said viciously. 'You've never known me.'

She got up and went into the house. Roberto was left to watch the sunset on his own. He knew he had done the right thing. He had told her the truth. He was a murderer and he was beyond her forever because of what he had done. He was cut off from the rest of humanity, just like the first murderer who had borne the mark of Cain. As he sat on the terrace realisation of the solitude of his existence swept over him. He was condemned to live among people he had no liking for, and he was separated forever from those who might have given him comfort. He thought of his long dead father, and of his disapproval; and he thought of his mother, who had brought him up as a hero's son, and was angry. She would condemn him, but she had made him what he was, because she had never told him that there were other things higher than the call of military duty.

But this last thing was not true; he was unjust to his mother, just as he was unjust to Elena. He was the way he was because he was still the boy who blushed, the boy who could never bear to be proved wrong about anything. And he could not admit that he was wrong now. He could not turn back: only a miracle could do that, and he did not believe in miracles any more.

He wondered where Elena was, and wondered how he could face her. He felt a glow in his cheeks. Behind him lapped the swimming-pool; and because he could not go into the house and confront her – for he had murdered her friend – he decided he would go for a swim instead to escape the heat and to eradicate the traces of guilt on his face.

From within the house Elena heard the splash of him diving into the pool. Her tears had dried now. Caballero was dead, and she felt that she too had played a part in his death. Caballero was dead, but even that could not break the bond that existed between her and Roberto. She could not and would not let him go. She was stubborn, and she loved him with all the stubbornness of love. So she took a towel from the bedroom, combed her hair and went down to the pool edge. There he was furiously doing his lengths, and eventually he noticed her shadow on the water and stopped. He took the towel from her, and getting out of the water used it to cover his shoulders. She noticed that he had gone for his swim still wearing those particularly hideous knee-length shorts that the military always wore under their trousers. He sat down by the edge of the pool, dripping and silent, and reached for his pack of cigarettes.

'I can get dressed and drive you home,' he said, lighting one.

'No.'

'Then I can get someone to come and pick you up, if the telephone is working.'

'No,' she repeated. 'I've decided that I've got to stay here with you.'

'You may wish you hadn't,' he said.

'If I do, I promise that I'll never tell you,' she said. 'Caballero isn't important to me anymore,' she added with an effort. 'But you are. And whatever Caballero said to you, isn't true. I – I believe in you.'

'Because you love me?' he asked.

'Yes.'

He contemplated his bare feet and wondered if love could redeem him after all. How odd it was to think that he had shot Caballero, and yet here he was, sitting in his shorts by the side of the swimming-pool, smoking a cigarette, with her next to him. He had broken all the rules. He was in a state of mortal sin, as he had killed another man; he was now a lapsed Catholic, something he had never been before. All his previous life seemed to have disappeared, but he felt no different. He had crossed some barrier, and found himself on the other side, and yet that other side was not the desolate terrain that he felt it ought to be. She still loved him; she would not leave him; and the thought of that almost made him angry once more.

He put his arm around her, as he had been in the habit of doing in the five years he had known her. He felt her warmth against him, and he wondered if he should continue to hold out against her any longer. Had there been any virtue in his long self-control? Could he not, at long last, be what she wanted? It could not make any difference to the state of his soul, after all. All that was finished. He had killed Caballero, and in the process he had killed his own soul.

Darkness fell.

Later, Elena watched the distant lights of the City, and knew that amidst the indifferent mass of humanity that composed it, lay Caballero's body. The clothes he had worn on that last day she had seen him, his watch, and the ring he always wore, perhaps these would be returned one day to his next of kin neatly wrapped in plastic, accompanied by some impersonal death certificate. Until then, Caballero had a tenuous existence in a sort of suspended animation. Until then he would be disappeared, not dead. Only he was dead, and Roberto had killed him. But she was forgetting that already, and felt a small residue of guilt for it, a guilt that concerned only herself. She had not realised how little Caballero had meant to her in comparison to Roberto. But this had always been the case. All those afternoons of conversation she had had with Caballero had been about Roberto. She had never really been interested in Caballero himself, only interested in him as an interlocutor for conversations about Roberto. And those conversations had cost him his life; her indiscretions had killed him. She was sure of that. And if Roberto had not killed Caballero he would not have made love to her either. One mortal sin led to another. That was equally sure.

Behind her Roberto lay asleep; she could hear the calm regular sound of his breathing in the darkness. He was very beautiful as he lay there. She wondered if she were pregnant; it was quite possible; in some ways she would rather like to be pregnant. It would be the definitive bond between them. The possibility of a child had never occurred before. On the very rare occasions when it might have arisen in the past there had always been enormous self-control on his part which had prevented it. She had never taken the various steps women were supposed to take for the prevention of conception; nor had he done what men were supposed to do; these things had never been necessary. Up to now there had been some invisible barrier between them; but this evening something had changed.

The barrier had dissolved between them. They now both knew each other. He had killed Caballero, and she was an accessory after the event. She had joined him in his crime, because she could not bear the thought of him being apart from her. It was as if she had given him that most precious thing of all, her soul. Perhaps she should have done as he had suggested and left him, but it was too late for that now, and she was bound to him forever.

Something that sounded like a bomb went off in the distance. He awoke with a start. She stayed at her window and heard him pad over to her on silent feet. He put his arm around her and she felt his warmth behind her. His chin nuzzled against her shoulder and she took his hand. His proximity comforted her and drove away the slight sense of melancholy that she was beginning to feel.

'They are letting off fireworks from a ship in the Bay,' he remarked. 'Twenty miles away.'

'Don't tell me that it is a clear night and that we have a wonderful view,' she said.

'Why not? It's true,' he said. He was not used to having his conversational opening challenged in this way. 'Are you feeling sad?' he asked her.

'Only a little. Are you?'

'Not particularly,' he said, knowing that this was not true. Melancholy had taken hold of him. Caballero was dead; there was a strange intimacy between himself and the murdered man, and now there was this new intimacy between himself and Elena. The way he had let Caballero see him had meant that he had been unable to hide from her any more as well. His isolation had been breached, and the days of his self-sufficiency were over. He was feeling sad. He had failed to be the complete man of duty.

'I'll resign my commission,' he said. 'Do you want me to?'

'Very much,' she said.

'There will be a war soon. I don't want to be part of it. I can't be,' he said, already feeling the hold she now had over him. He wondered if she was pregnant already, but did not know how he could frame the question without sounding as if he were already trying to squirm out of his responsibilities.

'You have gone all red,' she remarked, putting a hand on his cheek and holding it here, studying his face in the reflected light of the fireworks. 'Again,' she added, for he had been like that as he had made love to her.

He looked at her and began to long for his clothes and a

cigarette – it was uncomfortable this way she had of looking at him and seeing into his soul. She knew his secret.

'Marry me,' he said, reaching for his pack of cigarettes.

Nineteen

Not very far away, under the cover of darkness that was intermittently pierced by bursts of artificial fire, Nicola Nickleby was in the custody of Tanucci and Strauss.

Her return to consciousness had been painful, and had confused her. She did not know where she was. Nothing made sense. She could remember being in the dense crowd in the Square; then she had felt the world disappear around her. She had woken up to find herself in a different world, cold, blindfolded, and without clothes.

She had wondered if she was dead. The numbness of her body felt like what she had always imagined death to be, and so did her inability to see. But eventually sensation returned: she had felt the blindfold, the handcuffs, the freezing and hard floor beneath her. She had cried out repeatedly, but there was no one to hear her.

For what had felt like hours she tried to think. Her sobbing, which had sounded strange and unfamiliar to her own ears, distracted her mind. But exhaustion brought silence and a sort of peace. She was lost in eternal darkness, in a place without time, unsure whether it was night or day, with no idea of how long she had been there for. She tried to think of something familiar: of Isabel, of her parents, of home, of her University, of her dog in Godalming. She wondered whether she would ever see the dog again. She knew that something terrible was happening to her. But she had to keep calm. So she thought of the dog, fixing her mind on an animal of uncertain pedigree on the other side of the world, who could not possibly be aware of her fate.

At length a door opened. She sensed there was a man in the room. She felt hands laid on her, pulling her up. A voice said something in Spanish that she couldn't understand. The voice was indifferent, business-like and harsh to her ears.

The next thing was that she was being put in a chair; she heard another voice now, and felt that they were discussing her, but she did not dare speak.

Eventually something hot was directed at her face; her blindfold was removed and she was staring into a bright light. She was aware of her own nakedness now. Through the blinding light she saw the outlines of two men. She was terrified. Surely, in a country where Isabel de Calatrava gave such grand parties, where everyone was so nice, such things could not happen as were happening to her now?

'Why are you here?' asked one.

'I don't know,' she whispered.

'You had better tell us,' said the second.

Gradually in the ensuing silence her eyes became accustomed to the light. The first man was large, unshaven and had staring eyes. The second was much younger, her own age in fact, and sat next to him, indifferently smoking a cigarette. Both were in military uniforms.

'Who were you staying with?' asked the older one.

'Isabel,' she whispered, picturing her, so normal, so far away.

'Isabel who?'

'Isabel de Calatrava, calle Victoria, 12.'

She noticed that the younger man wrote this down.

'Where are the rest of them? Where is Dickens, for example?' asked the younger man, looking at a sheet of paper.

'I don't know anyone called Dickens,' she said.

'We're wasting our time,' said the older man. 'She won't talk yet.'

Nicola was only too willing to talk, but she was not sure what they wanted her to say. She noticed the two heads come together in whispered conversation. The first man seemed to be making some point rather insistently; the younger man looked a little doubtful. They were discussing her; and she had a sense of the unreality of it all, seeing these strangers deciding before her very eyes what they were going to do with her. Finally there was silence, and the last thing she heard the younger man say was 'Not without Enriquez'; then she noticed that he looked fearful for a moment, and then resigned to what was to happen.

The elder man had got up by now and was approaching her. His eyes transfixed her. While she looked at him, the younger one took her by the shoulders and pulled her up, and made as if to embrace her. Her face was pressed against his tunic, which was rough to the feel, and she smelled the perfume on him, which was not at all what a man smelled like, she knew, even though her experience of men was limited.

The other man was behind her now, and soon she began to scream, and her cries were stifled by the tunic pressed to her face.

The brutal experience was soon over, and Tanucci pushed her to the floor. He watched Strauss fastidiously doing up his trousers, and then knew that he was expected to join in, if only to prove that he was Strauss's partner in crime. Appalled by what he had just witnessed, Tanucci was unable to move. Then he felt his stomach rise.

'Bravo,' said Strauss sardonically, when the younger man had finished vomiting over the violated girl, and gave him a cuff on the side of the head.

Then the two men left, switching off the lights and locking the door behind them, leaving Nicola Nickleby alone in darkness and despair.

The next day, when Strauss, having decided to celebrate the General's birthday in true Teutonic style, was still sleeping off the gallons of beer he had drunk, Tanucci finally plucked up the courage to check on the prisoner. It was noon, and for most of that Sunday morning he had felt ashamed of his behaviour;

this was the day when the entire country was going to church, and he had just connived at rape of a most brutal kind. It was the nastiest thing about Army life, he knew, this being forced to join in things by other officers, so that you too had to share their guilt. Olivarez had done it to him; now Strauss had done it to him yet again. But this was worse. This was a woman. Men could stand pain, he knew, but women were different, and this one in particular had been a mere girl, at least to look at. He wished that Captain Enriquez had been there; for if something had gone wrong, Enriquez would have had to share the blame with him and Strauss; but Enriquez had gone God knew where, and if something had gone wrong, they would be blamed and would not have Enriquez to protect them. Of course, the Captain had known what they were doing, and had given them *carte blanche*. But *carte blanche* was easily given and just as easily retracted. Tanucci knew you couldn't trust the upper classes.

Tanucci stood uncertainly in the corridor outside the prisoner's cell, wondering what he would find inside it once he had the courage to unlock it. For he had the uncomfortable realisation that for once Strauss had gone too far. There had been something so horrible in the way the girl had screamed as the NCO had violated her, and he felt a shiver of guilt at the memory of the way he had stifled her cries against his tunic, embracing her almost, while Strauss raped her. He had never witnessed a rape before, but now he had seen the look of hatred in Strauss's eyes while he had committed that terrible parody of the act of love. It had frightened him, and revolted him, yet at the same time excited him. Now the memory of it shamed him.

He hated Strauss, just as he hated Olivarez. They had brought him to this. When he was seventeen, and merely been a quiet schoolboy with an aptitude for mathematics, he should have realised how well off he had been then, and rejected the lure of becoming an Army officer. It was true he was only a lieutenant in the Engineers, which was the lowliest of all the regiments, and that he would never be put up for the Military Club which was for Cavalry men like Enriquez, but the lure had been there. The Army had offered him advancement, and because he was only the child of a carpenter, advancement had meant much, for there had been no other paths open to him. But what had he advanced into apart from his own degradation? Despite his brains they had treated him badly; he spoke bad Spanish, with a heavy Italian accent; he spoke good English with an atrocious Spanish accent, and they never let him forget it; he had known nothing of sex and he had been exploited by Olivarez. Then he had been passed on to Strauss, when Olivarez had had enough of him; the only companionship he had ever known in the Army was either fleeting encounters in dark places, or the camaraderie of the torture chamber. Caballero had been kind to him – but Caballero was dead. He tried not to think of him. Now the final degradation was the part he had played in reducing the small blonde foreigner to the obscene heap that lay on the other side of the door.

He opened the door, steeled himself for the worst, switched on the light, and at once saw that the worst had in fact happened. It was twelve hours or so since they had left the prisoner, and she was dead. Her small body lay on the concrete floor, shrivelled, pale, naked and very dead, without even a hint of motion. He remembered what he had once learned at school about the soul being the motion that was in a body; this body had no soul any more, but was quite inanimate. He could not even feel frightened any more, but only curious. He tiptoed forward. Her face was turned to the floor, as if she had died in despair. He was glad he could not see her face, for he had held that same face close to his chest last night and seen the expression in it then.

The cause of death was clear. Around her head was a small pool of congealing blood, and scattered around the cell were the broken fragments of the rickety chair, which had been the only piece of furniture in the cell. It would not have taken much strength to have smashed the chair against the concrete floor, he realised; but it would have taken much courage fortified by despair to do what she had done. For the girl had stabbed herself in the jugular with a large carpenter's nail taken from the chair.

He backed out of the room, switched out the light and locked the door. He wondered why she had done it; for if she had been a criminal, and hardened, surely rape would not have driven her to such extremes. Or perhaps she had been a Communist spy who had been specially trained to commit suicide at the first opportunity after capture. But there was nothing professional about this death. It spoke only of desolation, and if he had had any tears he would have shed them for her there and then.

His first thought was that he had to tell Captain Enriquez as soon as possible. But Captain Enriquez had gone away somewhere, and he wasn't quite sure where. Strauss would know perhaps, but he did not want to alert Strauss to what had happened just yet. Enriquez was bound to come back sooner or later; it was the greatest of pities that he had ever gone away; for if Enriquez had been there, this would not have happened. He would have restrained Strauss. Enriquez at least had authority; he was cold and arrogant and did not make Tanucci feel at ease, but at least Enriquez was not brutal in the way Strauss was. But now what would happen? The Captain would come back, see what had happened in his absence, and both he and Strauss would be court-martialled and shot if the Captain decided against them. Tanucci was nineteen years old and he did not want to die just yet. He certainly did not want to die in the company of Strauss and for such a crime as this.

There was only one thing to do. It would be no use trying to hide the evidence of what had happened. He thought quickly and then ran upstairs. Outside the room Strauss slept in he could hear stentorian breathing. He opened the door, took the key and then locked it. The man was now a prisoner, but slept on unawares.

Twenty

While Tanucci was wondering where he was and what he might be doing there, Captain Enriquez was sitting down to Sunday lunch with his mother. The weather was less hot than it had been the day before, and Maria's flat was somewhat cooled by the breeze that came in from the sea. Somehow or another the food had managed to be excellent. How his mother had contrived this, he did not know, nor did he like to ask. He was, for the first time in years perhaps, feeling too concerned about other things to want to hear about food shortages, queues and empty shops. The freshness of the summer air, the calmness of the still city – for the population was in the process of recovering from the excesses of the first stage of the General's birthday party – brought to his mind memories of days of far off happiness, when he had been about seventeen years old, and when he had known nothing about politics, power and death. There had been a certain simplicity about his youth: it had been a time of simple desires that had found easy fulfilment, full of good books and food; riding horses in the country; going to church and sleeping soundly at night. It was odd how these details came back to him. It was some time since he could actually remember eating anything wholesome, or riding a horse, or picking up a good book: gone were the days when he had had a favourite author, or relished a set piece in Trollope or Scott, or a line of Coleridge; gone too were the days when he had slept soundly and passed untroubled nights, secure in the knowledge that God was in his heaven and that his bed was surrounded by benign angelic presences.

Between the ages of seventeen and eighteen, the age he had entered the Army, he had imperceptibly grown up. Maturity had arrived. Without realising quite why, he had succumbed to discontent. Happiness had ebbed away and its place had been taken by a sense of the injustice of his position. For the last decade of his life he had wanted other things. The restrictions placed upon him, first by his mother's presence, then by Army discipline and finally by his entanglement with Elena, had irked him to a degree that he had known was unreasonable. He had wanted to command, even to be feared. He had polished his ceremonial sword and known that he would never use it. He had sat behind a desk and dreamed of action. For Fritz, with whom he had more or less grown up, the transition into adult life had been much easier: Fritz had kept his adolescent pleasure in living: he had his military history to occupy him, and a keen sense of the adventurousness of the ordinary. Fritz was easily amused, and had never let his sense of duty interfere with his amusements. Fritz too had never been remotely religious, either as man or boy, but always carefree. It was true that Fritz had had his oddities as a youngster; he had hated any teasing reference to the slight physical difference that he alone had borne at school, and that had made him different from other boys; but that was merely something odd, not something that could ruin one's life. Roberto had been different even as he had grown up: bored, reserved, cold, longing for an outlet for all the passions that were trapped inside him.

That was why Olivarez's intervention, when it had come, had been welcome. He had seen it as a way out. But in fact it had merely been a way in, further into the world he had begun to loathe. He had blown Caballero's brains out, hoping that murder might lead him to freedom. Instead it had merely brought him face to face with impossibly intricate complications. He had wanted to be brave, to do his duty, to prove himself, to live to the full. Instead he had found himself in a darkened cellar, holding a smoking gun, sickened by his own sin, as far away as ever from the release he had sought.

Freedom, he realised, now lay elsewhere. There were simpler desires that could be more easily fulfilled. Happiness and freedom were within. His mother had this gift: a secret and comforting knowledge that she was loved, and, despite his father's early death, that she was beloved still. This was the discovery that he felt he was now and only now on the verge of making: happiness lay, not in trying to prove oneself perfect, or in deeds of heroic self-control, or in the keeping of some extraneous law, or stopping oneself from blushing and denying the emotions, but rather in surrendering oneself to love.

He could see his mother smiling at him across the table. It was a warm gentle smile; he did not know it, but her smile was a response to the look of warm satisfaction that suffused his own face.

'You look happy,' said Maria.

'I think that must be because I am happy,' he replied. 'Perhaps it is the food.'

Maria contemplated the huge joint of beef that lay on the table. There would be plenty left over; she had promised to give the remains to a convent of contemplative nuns, who had told her that they had not seen fresh meat for several months. It seemed they could never leave their cloister to shop; and shopping took such time these days. But she abandoned this train of thought and gave her attention back to her son. He seemed about to say something.

'I am going to get married,' said Roberto. 'To Elena.'

Maria smiled.

'Does Elena like pearls?' she asked. 'I always meant my daughter-in-law to have mine; but there is this farmer who is quite keen on them as well. This beef cost me three pearls, you know.'

'Pearls aren't important,' said Roberto.

'I agree. And I am very glad. Will I at last get to meet her? And soon?'

'Yes. I thought I would bring her to see you tomorrow

perhaps. We don't want to wait long. We've waited far too long already. I don't see why we shouldn't marry next month. No one can object. We can't have a party as there are such shortages, so we don't have to organise anything apart from the church side. And we might as well avoid the expense, as we are going to be poor. I have decided to resign my commission; I have decided to become a civilian.'

'Can you do that?' asked Maria.

'Yes. There may be something to pay, of course; but we are not at war. I shall go and see Colonel Olivarez on Monday.'

'What will you do instead?'

'I don't know,' he said lightly, for he still felt a little removed from reality by the experiences of the previous night. 'Going abroad is impossible. The escudos that I have in the bank wouldn't even cover the cost of the flights.'

'I have some money, you know,' said his mother. 'I mean real money, not escudos. It is in England, where your father invested it. And if you haven't forgotten about it completely, there is Torre del Mar.'

Torre del Mar was a country house some forty miles from the City. It had belonged to his grandfather. Thanks to the vagaries of the Napoleonic code, Roberto owned half of it. The other half belonged to his paternal uncle, who had used it as a summer house.

'Doesn't Uncle Francisco want it any more?' he asked.

'It seems not. Your uncle has got it into his head that he ought to emigrate to Argentina. He has been trying to sell everything he has here, you know, quietly of course, over the last few weeks. And he's offered to sell me his share of Torre del Mar; I know the place is terribly run down, but he's not asking much: about twenty thousand English pounds, which I can well afford. He would rather like to have some hard currency, it seems. And I think it would be a good idea to take him up on his offer before he changes his mind.'

'But if it is a ruin . . .'

'It is quite a charming and safe ruin,' said Maria practically.

'Whereas in this flat, one can never tell what might happen. I could give you half of Torre del Mar as a wedding present.'

'That would be kind. I could take up farming.'

He had not been to the old family house for some years. He did not think of the leaking roof, the grass growing in the courtyard or the general dilapidation of the place; but rather of long summer days and carefree evenings. If he were there to run the place himself, it might even be made to pay.

Then they began to discuss the question of the wedding. Delicately his mother began to suggest a suitable church; she spoke of Father Morisco, who was such a helpful man. Roberto had stopped going to church, recently, she knew, though she had not known why. It had surprised her, as he had always been very observant and dutiful before. But these things could just be a phase that young people often went through. Perhaps now he was to marry, he would be a good Catholic once again. And the same thought occurred to Roberto; he rather missed going to church; he ought to rejoin the rest of humanity. Perhaps one could be redeemed by love after all. Gradually the prospect of happiness began to take shape before him.

It was past four in the afternoon when he arrived at the Army Navigational School, resolved on tidying things up before his imminent departure. In this happy mood he encountered Tanucci, sitting at the table he habitually used in the courtyard.

'I've been trying to get hold of you, sir,' said Tanucci. 'Something has gone terribly wrong.'

'What?' asked Roberto.

Tanucci had been rehearsing what to say for hours, and now told the story in a modified form.

'I've locked Strauss up in his room, sir,' he said in conclusion. 'But he's awake now and roaring for lunch.'

As if on cue, Roberto heard hammering on a distant door.

'Is he armed?' asked Roberto.

'No, sir. He left his gun down here. NCOs are like that.'

'Thank God for that,' said Roberto wearily, feeling that happiness was slipping away from him. 'I had better go and see what is left of the prisoner.'

With bitter footsteps he made his way downstairs. Laid out on a table were the pathetic remains of a life. The girl's clothes, her wallet, and her British passport. He examined the name on the front cover, N. Nickleby, Miss. Tourists were meant to carry their passports at all times. He knew that: and this one had perhaps cost the girl her life; for he looked at the Christian name and discovered it was Nicola. Listlessly he examined the childish photograph. Then he glanced into the cell for a moment, and then turned hurriedly away. He sat down on a wooden chair, one of the same type that the prisoner had used to end her intolerable existence. With a slightly unsteady hand he lit a cigarette.

'This is horrible, Tanucci,' he said.

'Yes, sir.'

'And Strauss must hang for it. You say he raped her?'

'Yes, sir.'

'He deserves to hang. Did it occur to you that you might have arrested the wrong person?'

'No, sir.'

'The girl's passport says she is called Nicola; the suspect you were looking for was called, or rather using the name of Nicholas Nickleby, the name of a Dickensian character.'

'Were there two N. Nicklebys then, sir? Did we get the wrong one?'

'No,' said Roberto. 'There was only one, and that is her, in that cell. The other was a fiction.'

'If you had been here, sir,' said Tanucci suddenly, 'perhaps you could have stopped him. I wish you had been here. I had no idea you would be gone so long. Strauss was so impatient, and there was nothing I could do . . .'

Tanucci's voice trailed away hopelessly; Roberto said nothing at all. Of course, Tanucci was a lieutenant and Strauss only an NCO, but how could he have expected the boy to restrain the man?

'I suppose you were on duty elsewhere, sir?' said Tanucci.

Roberto said nothing.

'You knew Strauss was like that, sir. Everyone did. He has done it before and it stood to reason that he would do it again. And as for me, sir, you know that I'm only nineteen and I've never done anything like that in my life.'

'For God's sake,' said Roberto. 'Shut up. Sit down, take a cigarette, and get it into your head that I'm not going to have you hanged as well. And also get it into your head, you stupid boy, that no matter how much you try and blame me, it won't alter a thing, and that you were there and only you know what your guilt is.'

Roberto stopped shouting as suddenly as he had started. Shocked into silence, for he had never known the Captain raise his voice before, Tanucci sat down at the table and suddenly burst into tears.

Roberto had not seen a man cry for many years, if ever. Once, when they had bcen at school together, he remembered Fritz bursting into tears: but he had been twelve or thirteen at the time. Tanucci was nineteen, yet he was crying like a child. Roberto wondered what had happened in that cell, and he wondered at the events that could reduce a man to tears. When Fritz had burst into tears at school, he had given him something to eat. Now he lit a cigarette, and passed it over to Tanucci.

'Have one,' he said, wishing he could comfort the boy in his wretchedness. 'They're the ones only given to the Cavalry regiment. And don't worry; I won't let them hang you. Strauss will hang, but he deserves it.'

'We all deserve it,' said Tanucci miserably. 'Strauss raped her, but what we did to some of the other prisoners was worse. She killed herself. But the others . . .'

'She was a foreign national,' said Roberto. 'That will make a huge difference.'

'Let's bury her, and burn her clothes and forget all about it, sir,' said Tanucci desperately. 'If we don't everything that has gone on here will come out . . .'

'You arrested her in public, remember.'

'There was a crowd. No one ever observes things in a crowd. You can hardly send her body back to England like that. Let's get rid of it.'

'And Strauss?'

'That's up to you, sir. You are the one who gives the orders.'

Roberto thought: a few clothes and a passport would be cinders in a few minutes. And a body could easily be buried in the cellars; there were several there already, including Caballero's. And would Olivarez thank him if he knew that Strauss, the man he had been supposed to control, had murdered a British tourist while he had gone absent without official leave? He should have been there to have prevented such a silly pointless mistake. And what on earth was to be gained by making it all public? Strauss could surely be dealt with quietly, hanged for his previous rape conviction if nothing else. Perhaps Tanucci was right after all. And the fact remained that he was in charge, at least for now, of the operation. Whatever he did was technically legal; to admit a crime now would be to throw everything in doubt. And above all, while Strauss had been raping the girl, he himself had been making love to Elena, when he should have been at the Army Navigational School, preventing such things from happening. Tanucci was right: he had failed.

He sighed and put out his cigarette. From the cell came the gentle stench of decay.

'We'd better bury her,' he said. 'You can help me.'

Outside he heard the sound of petards. They were still celebrating the General's birthday.

The cook had been hysterical, and Isabel had had a hard job to calm her when she had got back from the Palace garden party, still wearing her huge hat and Balmain frock. Eventually she was able to calm the woman, send her away with orders not to tell anyone else, and then try on her own to make sense of what she had been told. She had very much feared that something like this would happen; girls were so very unstable, not at all like boys, always getting into trouble. And now this had happened just two days before the girl was due to return to England. What would happen if she was not on that plane? What would she say to the parents if the girl didn't turn up? If only Nicola had been Nicholas, this would not have happened. She remembered the races, and how the girl had taken such an interest in the Enriquez boy. And now she had caught the eye of some soldier. It really was too bad.

She wondered if she should phone Arturo Hernandez and ask him what she should do. He was the Minister for Foreign Affairs, after all – but he was so hopeless when it came to anything practical. And she would feel so foolish if she were to ask him to look for some flighty girl; after all, it was in a sense her own fault; she should have kept the child safely under lock and key, especially during her last few days. Because it was quite clear what had happened: the girl had eloped – but how was she to explain that?

As for the cook's tale, it was clear the woman was doing her best to make up a story that would let her off the hook. The cook should have kept her eye on the girl and not have lost her in the crowd. She would have stern words with her, and threaten her with the sack if she repeated this absurd story of a military kidnap. There simply could not be a grain of truth in that. The secret police would never have the courage to arrest a holder of a British passport; Isabel knew that for a fact – after all she herself had been to the trouble of getting dual nationality for just that reason. No: wherever the girl was now, she was not in the hands of the secret police. She was probably now in the arms of some young conscript with a winning smile. And if she didn't turn up by the time her flight was due – and Isabel could not quite imagine her daring to turn up chez Calatrava after what she was undoubtedly up to – if she didn't turn up, then that was what she would have to tell the parents. The girl was – she searched her vocabulary for a suitable word – a bit of a tart.

Isabel breathed a sigh of relief. Even she had been young once; she felt a little zephyr of sympathy for the girl, and her annoyance about her sudden disappearance began to wane. Military men were rather charming, and perhaps she was being over harsh in blaming her too much for what was essentially a sin of youth.

Twenty-one

Monday morning came; at seven the streets were deserted. The Palace Square was empty and chill, still in shadow. It was as if the entire Republic was still asleep, plunged into drunken slumber. All the officials, all the officers, all the people with Government jobs would not appear before noon. Their work could wait for them. Only at the Palace gates, two men stood resentfully on guard, much against their will. Neither of them wished to be there. Their sense of grievance was much increased by the knowledge that virtually every other soldier in the Republic had decamped or gone AWOL the previous night, taking advantage of the anarchy that had attended the final stages of the celebration. They would get no reprimands. But the two men on guard at the baroque gateway had not dared to slip away, chained to their posts by the knowledge that Colonel Olivarez was in the building, the one man who sat at his desk continually, working, never leaving the Palace, only waiting for the General to die. The two men at the gate did not even dare try to escape the boredom of guard duty by snatching a few moments of sleep; they knew that Olivarez was a man who interpreted rules strictly. Their bad temper and sense of oppression was further increased by the fact that neither of them had dared to have a drink either – drunkenness on duty being a punishable offence.

Roberto crossed the Square, knowing that the early morning was the best time to see the Colonel. He was challenged by the now sleepy guards, who asked him his business. At the mention of the name Olivarez they looked at him with respect. A third man presently appeared. Roberto was led away – first down echoing marble corridors, then down corridors lined with linoleum, the sort of corridors that were never seen by the public. Finally he was led into a huge room that contained a desk, a typewriter and a very young officer. The man who had brought him there turned and left. Roberto stated his business to the young man at the desk, who made a noise by way of reply which might have been yes or no, accompanied by a little shrug of the shoulders. Roberto said that he would wait. The young officer shrugged again, to signify that this decision meant nothing to him. Roberto sat down on a hard spindly-legged chair. From time to time the youngster at the desk looked up at him as if to see if he were there still, and regarded him with dark and suspicious eyes.

What seemed like a long time passed. He grew numb from sitting in the same position and he dared not smoke. The room was large, featureless and dull. Olivarez was not a man for grand places. He moved silently and unobtrusively. He was feared. In a country where nothing worked, like the Republic, Olivarez, the Chief of Security, presided over the one organisation that could reasonably claim to be efficient. God alone knew how many people passed through his hands, directly or indirectly; certainly no human being knew.

It was gradually getting hotter. Roberto felt the sweat forming into droplets under his armpits, soaking into his tunic. But this was the last time he would ever have to do this. Soon he would be free. Only Olivarez's consent stood between him and freedom. Deliberately he had stopped himself rehearsing what he would say. That would have been pointless. Olivarez was clever, and he would not be outwitted. Olivarez kept people waiting in dull rooms, in rising heat, subject to poisonous glares from their inferiors, all things, thought Roberto, exactly calculated to give him the advantage when they were finally admitted to his presence.

He tried not to think of the now buried Nicola Nickleby. That was too horrible. He had never until now seen anything that he had not been able to think about with a balanced mind. But now he thought that if he dwelled on her his mind might lose its immaculate self-control.

At last the young man behind the desk arose, and, clutching a sheaf of papers, left the room through the door behind the desk. A few moments later he reappeared and said laconically:

'The Colonel will see you now, sir.'

His tone bordered on the disdainful.

Roberto stepped into the inner sanctum. Olivarez sat at his desk, reading a newspaper. He looked up as Roberto saluted.

'Captain,' he said. 'I hope you haven't been kept waiting?'

'Not at all, sir.'

'Oh good. Some people are, I know,' said the Colonel confidentially. 'They sometimes keep them waiting a very long time. And some people never get to see me at all. But how glad I am to see you.'

Roberto continued to stand in front of the desk, as was the custom. Interviews were always conducted standing up in the Army, just as orders were always executed at a run. For the Army of the Republic never sat, but stood, never marched, but ran; Roberto had learned that when he was eighteen years old, during his early days as an officer cadet.

'How are things going?' asked the Colonel. 'Tell me.'

'Your orders have been carried out, sir.'

'Of course they have. I know that. I have had various reports, and I never expected anything less. But there have been difficulties . . .'

Olivarez's voice was half statement, half question.

'Strauss, sir,' said Roberto.

'Ah yes,' said Olivarez. 'A non-commissioned officer with something of a past. Has he been a nuisance to you?'

'Not entirely, sir. He has been a little . . .'

'Over enthusiastic? Is that it?'

'Yes, sir. He has raped a female prisoner, who later committed suicide in her cell.'

Olivarez nodded.

'Strauss,' he said, 'has been difficult in the past. I think he had better be disciplined. I suppose that has been troubling you?'

'Yes, sir.'

'Shall I have Strauss seen to? He already has a conviction for rape. A civil offence, which carries a civil punishment.'

'I think so, sir.'

'Good,' said Olivarez. 'I presume you have him in a safe place. I'll see to it that he is hanged even before he notices it himself. Not a bright man, Strauss. Not, as you say, wanted on voyage.'

Roberto was silent.

'And you, Captain?'

'Sir, I wish to return to civilian life,' said Roberto with some difficulty.

'You do?'

Olivarez seemed surprised.

'I would like to get married, sir,' continued Roberto. 'My family has a property in the country and I want to settle there and be a farmer.'

'Any soldier who has done eight years' service can get married, you know,' said Olivarez. 'That is in the rules and regulations. And who do you plan to marry?'

'Elena Garcia.'

'Yes,' said Olivarez. 'I know something about her. I presume then that it is all arranged between you?'

'Yes, sir.'

Olivarez stood up and went over to the window, and stared out at the Marine Gardens. Roberto did not move, but continued to stand to attention in front of the now vacated desk. Olivarez wondered whether it was worth his while to interfere in this little affair. If someone were to blacken La Garcia's character, would that dissuade Enriquez? Or should someone persuade her against him? But perhaps it had not come to that as yet. He wondered whether La Garcia knew if her future husband had executed Caballero. That might be a useful piece of information, the imparting of which might make her reconsider.

'Of course, I have no objection to you marrying, Captain,' he said, turning round. 'You have done your eight years of service. And I am sure you know the young lady's background; I am sure you haven't made an unwise choice. You would be surprised though if you knew about some of the things that do happen when soldiers think they are in love. Even quite senior men can make naïve mistakes. I'm sure you know about Colonel Mendoza, for example, who married a woman years his junior; and now he's the laughing stock of the Army. I have even had to intervene myself on one occasion, and get rid of his wife's lover for him. And even Generals too' – he thought of Hernandez and Isabel de Calatrava – 'can make bad mistakes. But I have no objection. You are not old and foolish in these things, I am sure. But I still don't see, Captain, why getting married should mean that you have to leave the Army and go and look after cattle.'

'I think the Army isn't for me any more, sir,' said Roberto lamely.

'And what would your father have said to that, I wonder?' asked Olivarez. 'I don't need to remind you of your duty. When I picked you out I thought you were just the type we needed. Intelligent, young, bright, well-bred, an excellent background, good-looking, rides a horse well. If we were to let you, one of our best men, give up Army life, what effect would it have on the others? We have already seen that men like Strauss are no good. But he's an NCO. But look at our young officers, look at men like Tanucci. A nice enough boy perhaps, but no background, no tradition to him; the sort of man who would betray what we stand for at the drop of a hat. And Tanucci is one of our best lieutenants, on paper at least. He came near the top in the examinations for entering officer training. Probably a mistake to make men of his class officers, if only officers in the Engineers, I know, but what choice have we? There seems to be no one else.'

'Sir,' said Roberto, 'I am none of the things you have said I am. I am not even particularly brave.'

'We won't discuss your personal accomplishments, Captain, if you please,' said Olivarez coolly. 'Perhaps you have just discovered that you have a certain disdain for the job you have been given? Strauss may be a criminal, but at least he has a strong stomach. Perhaps we need men like him after all. Perhaps you have just given Strauss a new lease of life.'

'Strauss, sir, is a murderer.'

'Miss Garcia's liberal principles have influenced you, I see,' said Olivarez contemptuously.

'Sir, Strauss's victim was a British national. I saw her passport. The British are supposed to be our friends.'

'Damn Strauss, then,' said Olivarez. 'You should have stopped him. Why didn't you?'

Roberto did not know what to say. He merely stared ahead and felt extremely uncomfortable.

'Answer,' said Olivarez coldly. 'If you knew she was a British national, why did you let Strauss rape her?'

'I wasn't there when it happened, sir,' said Roberto.

'Where were you?'

'I was in the country, sir.'

'Were you absent for more than eight hours?' asked Olivarez. 'And do you know what it says in Article Sixteen?'

'I was absent, sir,' said Roberto, 'for about twenty-four hours. Article Sixteen says that unauthorised absence of more than eight hours constitutes dereliction of duty, and absence of more than eight days constitutes desertion. The first is to be punished by a reprimand, the second by a term of imprisonment in a military jail.'

'Good,' said Olivarez. 'And your knowledge of the Military Code makes it even more inexcusable. In the case of officers who are absent without official leave for more than eight days, what happens to them?'

'They can be reduced to the ranks, sir.'

'Quite,' said Olivarez. 'I am afraid that you are not the man I took you for, Captain. You can go.'

Roberto saluted, and turned to the door.

'You shall hear from me,' said Olivarez as an afterthought. 'I have no use for men who allow themselves to pity our enemies.'

Roberto left.

Olivarez was angry, but he never let anger interfere with his judgement. He had made a mistake with Enriquez. He had thought that the man was ambitious and could be trusted with delicate matters. That had been true of Ximenez, who had done good secret work so far in San Cristobal; but in Enriquez's character was some flaw he had not been able to detect in time. But he could not simply get rid of Enriquez; to sack him, and leave him hanging around the City would be a recipe for disaster. Enriquez was too visible a person for that. He would become a focus for discontent. Another solution would have to be found. He would have to get the man out of the way somehow.

He sat at his desk and thought. Perhaps he could send Enriquez to San Cristobal. That would certainly be out of the way; but Rodriguez, the one everyone called Fritz, was there. The two men were close friends, and it would never do to have them share an exile, and grow discontented and disaffected together. Enriquez would have to go somewhere else.

After a few moments' consideration, he called in the venomous young secretary. They began to make out the warrant for the execution of Strauss and various other orders. Accordingly the young officer was the first to know of the downfall of the arrogant young Captain, to whom he had taken such an instant dislike.

Twenty-two

Roberto hesitated in the glare of the Palace Square, wondering what to do. He had made Olivarez angry: whether that meant he would be cashiered, dismissed from the Army, he did not know. That would be a desirable outcome; but equally possible was the prospect of arrest, for he had established himself as a man who was no longer trustworthy.

With this in mind he started to walk towards Elena's flat. It was only twenty minutes away, and it was still not yet mid-morning. He hoped he would find her at home and her mother absent.

'Well?' she asked expectantly, as soon as she let him in. 'Did you see Olivarez?'

'I saw him,' he said. 'But I am not at all sure what the result will be.'

It struck him then that Olivarez would easily guess where he had gone; it was possible that if he was to be arrested, they might arrive quite soon.

'But what did he say?' asked Elena. 'Tell me.'

'I think I told him something I shouldn't have,' said Roberto.

'What?'

'A mistake I made,' said Roberto, thinking of Nicola Nickleby's body. 'Olivarez may think that I know too much to be allowed to leave the Army. I think I may be trapped. And now that I have asked to resign, he may never trust me again.'

'Perhaps he'll sack you,' said Elena, feeling her confidence ebbing away, just when she had been convinced that everything was going to end well.

'Sometimes,' said Roberto, 'they never let you go.'

'We can still get married and wait for things to change,' she said.

But he thought of the girl in the cellar and knew that nothing could ever change that.

In the Palace, Olivarez had made up his mind. The Army Navigational School would have to close. Strauss, Tanucci and Enriquez would all have to be silenced. The death warrant for Strauss had already been sent, and he had just completed arrangements for the police to arrest him at the School. That would silence him, and forever too. There was no need for such severe measures with the other two – they were only accomplices to Strauss's crime, and were bound to want to keep the whole thing quiet, just as much as Olivarez wanted to. But they had been careless and they would suffer for it.

A girl was dead, a foreign girl. Foreign governments were notorious for objecting when their nationals were arrested without trial; he tried to imagine what their reaction would be to one of them disappearing. Once the matter became public, no matter how much you pleaded mistaken identity, or how much you denied the whole affair, foreign governments rarely gave up. They imposed sanctions, they broke off diplomatic relations, they reduced you to the status of a pariah nation. It would be a disaster if Strauss's incontinence were to have such effects. And for this reason, Olivarez was determined this whole affair would never become public. He was Head of Security, and his natural instinct was to keep everything secret. Added to this was the knowledge that the victim had only been a girl. There were numerous cases of girls disappearing abroad. Her vanishing into thin air could and would be attributed to numerous causes he was sure, before anyone stumbled on the truth.

The prospect of witnesses coming forward worried him; and so he was determined that witnesses there should be none. The circumstances of the arrest had been favourable, for he had just received a report of them from Tanucci. No one noticed anything in crowds. By tomorrow Strauss would be dead. No one else would speak. He would effectively silence both Enriquez and Tanucci too for the forseeable future. There might be some trouble, but it would surely not last for long. And if the worst came to the worst, if they were forced to admit that they were responsible for the girl's disappearance, then the blame could always be shifted onto Messina or Hernandez. The old men had been there long enough.

Olivarez signed the orders that he had had typed up. They were to be conveyed to Enriquez at once. He gave instructions to several men about where Enriquez would be. He was glad it was midsummer: his plans for Enriquez would not have been possible otherwise. He told his men exactly what they were to do, and sent them on their way.

When they were gone, he lit a cigar. He reflected on the closure of the Army Navigational School, and on the unexpected weakness of Captain Enriquez. But he comforted himself with the thought that he was being more cruel than kind.

Within twenty minutes two naval officers were ringing the bell of the Garcia flat, bearing sealed orders. Neither quite knew why they had been sent to pick up Captain Roberto Enriquez, but they had been convinced that they were to follow their orders to the letter. They were both polite young men, in smart summer uniforms, and Elena opened the door to them without feeling the misgivings that she had felt on first seeing Strauss and Tanucci. But even so, her heart sank somewhat, and she knew that these two polite young men now asking for Captain Enriquez were the bearers of disquieting news.

She let them in, and in they came, smilingly, with pleasant expressions and gleaming teeth. Roberto was standing on the balcony; he wondered if this was some sort of joke being played on him by Olivarez.

'We have an envelope for you, sir, with orders in it,' said one.

He held out his hand, and Roberto entered the flat to take the envelope. (The young naval officer had not gone out onto the balcony to give him the envelope, because he knew the temptations that an open balcony could offer to a desperate man.)

Roberto opened the envelope to read its contents; the officer who had given it to him stepped onto the balcony to admire the view, such as it was. The other withdrew to a discreet distance and took up a position near the front door. They had their orders, and they were making quite sure the Captain would not make a run for it.

When he had read what was in the envelope, Roberto impassively passed the letter on to Elena. This is what she read:

'Captain, You are relieved of your current position with immediate effect. Bearing in mind your duty as a soldier to obey orders, and your oath of loyalty to the Republic that you took when you received your commission, I order you to place yourself at the disposal of the two naval officers who bear this letter. They will arrange all the details concerning your next posting. You are to be Commander of our garrison on December Island, for the next six months, renewable for another six months after that; you will receive instructions about what you are to do in this regard, and you will follow them exactly. I am sure you will appreciate the honour done to you by being selected for this important command. Olivarez.'

'Where is December Island?' asked Elena.

'Somewhere near Antarctica,' said Roberto.

'Will it be for six months or a year?'

'I expect it will be for six months.'

He held her tightly against himself and felt her tears. He himself was too numb to feel anything.

'I won't see you for a long time,' he said.

'Go and speak to Olivarez,' she said, between sobs.

'They wouldn't let me; and I have the impression that this is final.'

The officer on the balcony coughed. Roberto went out to him.

'There are quite a few things for you to do, sir,' he said cheerily. 'I've been told to help you do them: things like collecting your winter clothes, and anything else you may need for a six months' stay in the South Atlantic. And there is also your new platoon to see to. I believe you know Lieutenant Tanucci already. He is going with you. The ship sails tomorrow at four in the morning, and you are expected on board tonight. We are to stay with you, sir, and help you in any way we can. If you wish, there's no immediate hurry, and we could wait in the hallway if you have any business here that you have to finish off . . .'

The prospect of spinning out the grief of parting turned his numbness to complete coldness.

'No,' he said.

He felt colder than even the frozen wastes that he imagined surrounding December Island.

'You can drive me to see my mother in a few minutes,' he added.

Then he went into Elena. He tried to kiss her, whispered the word 'goodbye' and presently was gone.

The two naval officers did their best to cheer him up.

'There is something about the sea,' said the first.

'An eternal fascination,' agreed the second. 'The first adventure man ever had was when he invented the boat and put out to sea in it. And now, sir, to your mother.'

Isabel de Calatrava was pouring herself a large drink. She thought she deserved it. She had just been on the telephone to Godalming. It had not been an easy conversation. Mr and Mrs Nickleby, in their rather blunt English way, had been appalled by what she had told them. They had spoken of coming out to

South America on the very next plane they could find. In vain had she tried to explain that there was no cause for alarm, and that their daughter's disappearance was simply par for the course. After all, this was South America, the land of adventures, a place where Surrey teenagers did do things which they would never dream of doing at home. But the Nicklebys had not been impressed by this line of argument; they had simply failed to understand; their daughter was a good girl, they had insisted.

Isabel sloshed the gin and tonic round her glass. She thought of England, such a refreshingly normal country, and she thought of her passport, and the money she had there in the bank. How inviting a prospect that seemed. She wished she could walk away from the nightmare she sensed was developing. It was too late now to phone Arturo Hernandez and ask for his help. He would not know what to do. There was only one man who could cope with an emergency like this, and that was Father Morisco. She picked up the phone again and hoped that she would not have too much trouble getting through to the Archbishop's Palace.

Twenty-three

By six that evening Roberto was on board ship. The cheery naval officers had put him there, and said goodbye, wishing him luck, almost envying him his voyage. His mother too had wished him luck, but in a more philosophical tone. Maria had thought that it might all be for the best after all. He was to be gone for at least six months; the wedding would have to be put off – but perhaps a delay would be beneficial. Happiness, said Maria, had to be earned, and it would be all the more sweet once it was earned. That his mother should be such a fervent believer in the old-fashioned doctrine of purgatory hardly surprised him.

'You have had things so easy until now, my dear,' she had said.

It did not seem that way to him. He felt now that his adult life had been nothing but a long series of frustrations. But this new turn in his fortunes was undoubtedly purgatory. He had seen the platoon he was to command, which was now below deck. He had not liked the look of them. He wondered where the Army recruited from these days. It was as if he had been given the command of a penal colony. But he felt that he deserved it: he should never have left the Army Navigational School under the nominal charge of Tanucci when he had known that Strauss was a convicted rapist, and that an arrest of a female prisoner had been made. He should never have gone with Elena to the country just then: but that was merely one in a long chain of things he should never have done. He wished he could know what his first mistake had been.

The setting sun played golden on the harbour waters. The view of the Bay and the City was as fine as ever; but in his pocket he could feel a sheet of crisp and expensive paper, of the type Government Ministers usually used. Without asking him or telling him, Elena had written to Olivarez, or seen him, he did not know which; she had attempted to intercede on his behalf. The reply had been delivered to him a few moments ago on the ship. He remembered the words without having to re-read them: 'The individual has no rights,' Olivarez had written. 'There is only absolute duty. The Army and the State are more important than the individuals who make them up. Your duty consists in obedience. Your feelings on the matter do not come into the question. I am sure that you will enjoy your time on December Island. You will find binoculars there, I hope. They tell me that the wildlife is spectacular. I am sure you will find the penguins fascinating.'

He took the letter out of his pocket and threw it overboard. Olivarez's smug cleverness sickened him. This was his last night in the country and he was spending it on board. They were to sail at four the next morning. Elena would sit down to dinner with her mother, without him; his own mother would sit calm and alone in her own flat as she always did. Elena would be miserable just as he was: but each was isolated in their own misery. He wished now that he had not left her so suddenly. The two Navy men would have waited by the door – but his sentence of exile had snapped his vitality. He was cut off, not for six months or a year, but forever. The pain of departure filled his body.

Tanucci joined him at the ship's rail. The fact that he was having to share his exile with Tanucci was another source of woe. Tanucci's presence would be a continual reminder of all the things he most wanted to forget. He wanted to be alone. But Tanucci could not know this.

'Have you heard about Strauss, sir?' asked Tanucci in a low voice.

Fear seemed to have made him more than usually respectful.

'No,' answered Roberto. 'What exactly has happened to Strauss?'

'They've hanged him, sir. They did it a few hours ago. I was there. The police came for him; they had been sent by the Colonel. And they took him out of his room, down to the courtyard, and they hanged him there and then. I didn't think that they could have done that, sir. I mean, I thought you had to be hanged in what they call an appointed place. It didn't seem legal to me.'

'He was under sentence of death already,' said Roberto. 'It couldn't have made much difference to him. Did you actually watch the hanging?'

'I tried to, sir, but I couldn't. But I heard it.'

'Did Strauss die bravely?'

'No, sir. He shouted and he kicked and he screamed right up to the very last moments. I don't think anyone dies bravely, sir, not when they know it is going to happen to them. I am sure I wouldn't. I am quite glad I am going to this island. We will be safe there. People say there will be a war soon. Besides, I quite like ships.'

Tanucci seemed to be cheering up already.

'I hate ships,' said Roberto. 'Have a cigarette.'

'The medical officer and the Chaplain have already come on board,' continued Tanucci, taking one of the proffered cigarettes. 'I saw them loading an enormous amount of cigarettes and cigars too, sir. And several cases of whiskey and brandy.'

'Really?' said Roberto, without interest, putting away his lighter.

'And the food too. I have never seen so much. Enough for six months, until the next ship calls.'

'We shall have plenty of time for eating and drinking and smoking,' said Roberto.

'That's what I hear, sir,' said Tanucci brightly, clearly not dismayed by the prospect.

Roberto felt a little contemptuous of these simple pleasures that gave such comfort to Tanucci. The Lieutenant, in fact, had been allowed to visit his family for a few hours before going away; the fact that his brothers and sisters who were still at home looked hungry had not been lost on him. And yet here he was now, smoking cigarettes, which, if they had been available in the shops, would have cost as much as his father earned in a week. He was one of the lucky ones; not as lucky as Enriquez perhaps, a man who had grown up in what was to Tanucci incredible luxury, but luckier than his own family.

'There is very little to do,' he continued. 'They say that it's an easy life. I was speaking to one of the NCOs about it. It seems the last Commandant of the garrison didn't enjoy it much.'

'Oh?'

'He killed himself,' said Tanucci, suddenly doleful again.

'Why did he do that?'

'No one seems to know, sir. They found him one morning and it was quite a surprise. He had gone into the bathroom and cut his veins. He bled to death in there.'

'The inactivity must have got him down,' said Roberto a little ironically.

The medical officer, Hoffmann, now came up and joined them.

'Plenty of activities,' he said conversationally, having overheard Roberto's last remark. 'For a start there are the penguins. Penguins,' he added, in tones of great conviction, 'are my passion.'

Roberto looked at Hoffmann. He was small, dark and of repellent aspect. Roberto was beginning to dislike him already. Tanucci too regarded the doctor with a look of uncertainty.

'Penguins, sir?' prompted Tanucci at last.

'Oh yes,' said Hoffmann. 'The chances you get on December Island are unique. As the place is uninhabited and indeed uninhabitable, the birds haven't learned to fear men. They are quite tame. This time I hope to record some of them on video. Do you know, no one has ever filmed two penguins in the act of sexual intercourse?'

'Do penguins have . . . sexual intercourse, sir?' asked Tanucci.

'Of course they do, Lieutenant,' said Hoffmann, a little impatiently. 'Every living thing on earth has sexual intercourse. Except fish. Fish are different. Even though I am a doctor and not a zoologist by profession, I think I do prefer animals to humans sometimes. I take it you play bridge, Captain?'

'I have done so in the past,' said Roberto.

'The last man didn't, you know. I kept on urging him to take it up. Terrible shame that he didn't. It might have helped him no end. He became rather an introvert, you know, towards the end. And you, Lieutenant?' he asked, turning towards Tanucci, but without much hope.

'I can't play cards at all, sir,' said Tanucci humbly.

'There will be time,' said Hoffman. 'There will be time for everything, you'll see. I could even show you how to use my camera, if you'd like to, that is.'

Hoffmann realised that this was a great favour on his part. Tanucci realised this too, but didn't know quite what to say.

'I know, I know,' said Hoffmann, noticing his uncertainty. 'The Military Code says that cameras are strictly forbidden in military places; but this one has a special imprimatur from Colonel Olivarez himself.'

The sun had set. The little group broke up. Hoffmann went below to check that his photographic equipment had been properly stored. It wouldn't do to have any breakages at this stage; he had been pestering Colonel Olivarez for years to be allowed to use a camera on the island, and didn't want to be disappointed now.

Tanucci went to his cabin to check on his equipment. Not looking after your equipment properly was an offence, after all, and having witnessed Strauss, usually so fearless, being dragged screaming to the gallows that afternoon, he was rather sensitive to the idea of offences in general. He looked over his kit. His lieutenant's uniform he had on; besides that he had the ordinary battledress that the platoon would wear, his blouse marked with the appropriate number of stars to his rank. This included a thick black jumper to be worn beneath the blouse, as well as the woollen underwear that covered the entirety of his arms and legs, and that was only worn in the coldest weather; but December Island would be cold, he was sure. He had left his ceremonial sword behind, for it would not be needed; his only weapon was his Beretta pistol, which, were it not for the fact that he was in a hard walled cabin, he might be temped to clean; but if he were to have an accident with it, and the thing were to go off while he was cleaning it, the bullet would ricochet around the tiny cabin very easily – and that, apart from being negligent use of equipment, as defined by the Military Code, and thus an offence, would also be very dangerous. So instead he picked up his heavy boots, the production of which, thanks to the generosity of the Army, kept a whole factory of blind people in employment, and fell to polishing them.

While Tanucci passed the time thus below, Roberto, who had already seen his own claustrophobic cabin and disliked it, stood on deck, smoking. He wondered how Tanucci, whom he had seen crying tears of hysterical guilt only yesterday, had recovered so quickly. The people in this country, by which he meant the vast majority of them, the ones of which he hardly knew anything, were very odd in that regard. One day they would be complaining about prices, the next they would be cheering tanks in the Square. He thought of this in solitude, and lit another cigarette; but he was not to be left alone for long.

'Hoffmann tells me you play bridge,' said the Chaplain, without preamble, appearing from nowhere.

'Yes.'

'And your lieutenant, could he learn? It would be so nice to have a four. The last tour of duty I did, I spent six months out there without a four. It was hell on earth. I almost wrote to the Chaplain-General about it.'

'I am not sure if Tanucci can,' said Roberto.

'These young fellows are usually happy enough,' said the Chaplain tangentially. 'They almost always are. He's an Engineer, I see, and the Engineers always seem to keep themselves busy, don't they? They watch icebergs and they measure things and they keep temperature charts. We had some spectacular icebergs last spring. Quite spectacular.'

Later, dinner was served. The four officers dined together in uneasy state and then separated for the night. Roberto lay down in his cabin fully dressed. He did not fall asleep for some time. When he woke it was still dark, but the engines were running. The ship was moving: they had started their long journey south into the cold waters of the South Atlantic.

Twenty-four

Fritz was not enjoying certain aspects of life in San Cristobal. The town itself was far to the south of the capital, and rather cold and dreary even in midsummer. It was the sort of place where hardly anything ever happened; there was a small port, and a large central square surrounded by unremarkable buildings, but little else. It was for this reason, doubtless, that it had been chosen as the main training place for the Army's recruits, who were housed in huge uncomfortable barracks. There was little that could have appealed to Fritz less. He had always felt himself to be a city man, and had enjoyed his work in the City in the offices of the Quartermaster-General. But here in San Cristobal he was stuck in barracks and expected to teach raw eighteen- and seventeen-year-olds about how to use guns, as well as the rudiments of strategy. He was amazed at their stupidity. Time and again he had told them about how to clean a Beretta, or an M-12, the two guns most commonly used by the Army, but time and again they got it wrong. He was forever living in fear of hearing an odd shot from somewhere in the building that would announce that yet another cadet had wounded himself or someone else by accident.

On top of that was the tedium of the routine. Everyone was up at six; and at six-thirty every morning, which had never been his best time, Fritz was forced to make the first inspection, checking to see that every one of the cadets was properly dressed; while it was true that the uniform of this particular regiment was rather elaborate, it was still surprising and exasperating to see just how often the cadets contrived to get bits on back to front or inside out or both at once. With these difficulties cleared up, it was then time for The Flag. Fritz had now decided that he rather loathed The Flag, despite what the Army rules and regulations said to the contrary about every man in the Armed Forces' duty to love and venerate it. The tuneless rendition of the National Anthem likewise frayed his nerves. That over, the cadets were sent to take off the uniforms they had so laboriously put on, and were sent for their run; whereupon Fritz would retire to the officers' mess to read the previous day's *Mercurio* (everything arrived late in San Cristobal) and feast off dry bread and rancid coffee, sweetened by a cigar. Outside he would hear the furious shouts of the NCOs, which would only cease when the unfortunate recruits were herded inside to be forced through cold showers, something which they were constantly trying to evade. This was not at all like the breakfasts he had been in the habit of sharing with Roberto, when they had both been in the City.

Fritz was sure that it had been the unkind intervention of Captain Ximenez that had put him in charge of discipline in the barracks. There was no doubt that discipline was poor, and that this was bound to reflect badly on him. Over the weekend of the General's birthday celebrations, discipline had become positively lamentable. Virtually every one of the Army rules and regulations had somehow or another been infringed. Although no one had actually shown open and flagrant disrespect to The Flag – an offence, the form of which he could never quite visualise, but which nevertheless carried the death penalty – they had contrived to do everything else. Apart from the cadets, too numerous to count, who had been in various stages of drunkenness and disorder, there had been other offences that simply could not have been overlooked, much as he had wanted to. The two men put on guard duty had gone to sleep – one standing up, which was not so serious, but the other had actually gone to sleep intentionally, lying down on the ground to do so. Fritz had cashiered him, and the boy had been grateful. What could you do, he thought, when recruits actually wanted to be cashiered? A dishonourable discharge and a month in jail hardly counted as a punishment any more. Another young man, who, Fritz thought, could perhaps be certified as an idiot, had been caught smoking near the ammunition stores. And another pair had been caught in the dormitories during the day: which was against the rules of the barracks, for which he had punished them, in the process overlooking what he suspected they might have been doing there.

Fritz put down his paper and sighed. Within a few moments classes would be beginning; he would have to tell the men once again about how an M-12 worked. If every man had his natural enemy, then the M-12 was Fritz's; that and the Beretta. He dreaded the idea of putting these guns into the hands of boys who were quite clearly incapable of using them. Or rather, he was frightened that they would use them; the only people he would ever trust with guns were those who would never conceivably use them. He himself fell into this category. And the Beretta in his holster was purely there to fulfil the dress code for officers. It was always unloaded. He did not want it going off by accident, and he never had learned to trust the safety catch; how could he, when the safety catch could be so easily neutralised by the flick of a thumb? The M-12 made him even more uneasy. There was something in the phrase 'double action' that almost made him break out in a cold sweat: you pressed a button, and the thing fired repeatedly. All you needed was one drunk young man with an M-12 and you had a massacre. Why they had to go through all this rigmarole with guns was beyond him. As far as he knew, no one among all these recruits would ever fire at an enemy, or be in a war. It was all an endless dress-rehearsal for a play that would never take place.

Fritz put out his cigar and dragged himself off to class, to try yet again to impress on the cadets the necessity of safety with guns. Once again he saw their eyes light up as he told them that last year no less than forty-two men had been killed, not by enemy action, but by themselves or their colleagues, thanks to horseplay with guns.

After that there was another class on the subject of military history and tactics; they were discussing pincer movements, ostensibly – but the real purpose of the class, like so many others, was to drum into their minds the importance of rules and regulations. Each cadet was supposed to know the entire Code off by heart. It was something that the Colonel was particularly keen on.

The Colonel, an ageing sadist who presided over the entire military establishment in the town – and there was little else in San Cristobal apart from a few decaying fishing boats – the Colonel was the bane of Fritz's life. It was the only thing that he had in common with Ximenez, an overwhelming dislike of this elderly martinet. Of course, Fritz hardly ever saw Ximenez, who was working in another barracks doing quite what he hardly hazarded to guess, but it was well known that Ximenez was leading the opposition to the Colonel, such as it was. Because of that, and because Ximenez was the leader of the Young Turk party in the town, Fritz was careful to remain neutral. But he was sure that if the impossible happened and if the Colonel ever went too far, and was lynched by his own troops for doing so, then he for one would not be sorry. The Colonel was a great believer in the birch and solitary confinement, which was the main reason that Fritz was so lax in his own barracks. He had to protect these raw boys, whose main fault was ignorance, from falling into the Colonel's monstrous hands. If anything could be kept from the Colonel, Fritz endeavoured to keep it from him.

He finished his last class at about eleven, and left it with the dispiriting realisation that if the Colonel were to come round and test the youngsters on the Code, all hundred articles of which he expected them to have by heart, he would be sadly disappointed, and greatly enraged. His rages were not pleasant to behold. But Fritz tried to put all this aside, and stepped out of the barracks and within a few moments found himself in the main square of the town.

He had nothing to do until the roll call that had to be taken that night at eleven. Twelve hours of boredom loomed; his life in San Cristobal was made up of stretches of tedium which alternated with stretches of boredom. There was only so much of barracks life he could take. In the City he and Roberto had lived in a barracks that had to all intents and purposes been a hotel; and they had also had the Military Club to amuse them. But the officers' quarters in the barracks he was presently condemned to were about as comfortable as the room he had shared with Roberto in their final year at boarding school. He was expected to share a room with another man, which he didn't like. There was no private bathroom, which he liked even less. The presence of a room-mate made his favourite solitary pursuit – reading Tacitus, Livy and Clausewitz – almost impossible. His room-mate would insist on talking to him in Spanish, a language Fritz never felt quite comfortable in, having been brought up by his Teutonic mother and Iberian father to speak English. It was this sense of imprisonment that made him think he was punished enough for his indiscretion with Mrs Mendoza. She had certainly not been worth all this. In fact, he had quite made up his mind to keep away from women for good – not that there seemed to be many of them in the town: San Cristobal was little better than a penal colony.

The instinct for freedom invariably drove him out of doors whenever he had nothing to do. This happened often. The dreariness of military life had never struck him so forcibly before. In the City, when he had lived in the Cavalry barracks, there had always been something to do. Despite the fact that at twenty-eight he considered himself too old to be a bachelor much longer – his hair was beginning to fall out, and his tunic was getting tight around the waist – despite all that, he had never been bored before now. There had always been Roberto to take up his time. The friendship that had existed between them had been a constant thing in Fritz's life since the day they had first met at school, both aged thirteen. From then on Fritz had more or less been at Roberto's beck and call, forever at his disposal, and quite content to be so. They were rather different in character. Whereas Fritz had always been universally popular, Roberto, even when quite young had had a reputation for arrogance and reserve. Fritz had been the outgoing one, although he had never been one to trust the crowd; he had been the first to meet Elena, although he had immediately relinquished her as soon as he saw that she preferred his friend, and done so without resentment. He wondered sometimes if Roberto had noticed the sacrifice he had made; except it wasn't a sacrifice, because Fritz was quite used to the idea that whatever Roberto wanted he should have. There was nothing deep or Teutonic in their friendship, he sometimes thought – it was simply something that had always been there. It was not that they had stayed up together late into the night discussing philosophy and opening their souls, one to another; or that there was perfect unreserve between them, for there was not. There was just that ease that exists between people who are entirely familiar – for Roberto was familiar with no one else, as Fritz realised, and the same was true of himself to a certain extent. It was that that gave him a sense of responsibility for Roberto and the knowledge that he ought never to offend him. For if Roberto were to be offended by Fritz, and he was the sort of man who might easily be offended, then he would be entirely cut off from all human friendship. This was the reason why Fritz never told Roberto about some matters, the small affair of Mrs Mendoza, for example; he had made up a story about a poisoned *empanada*, he seemed to remember, and pretended to be ill, rather than let Roberto find out what he had really been up to. Neither did he ever ask after Elena; he was careful to make Roberto neither shocked nor jealous, and this carefulness was quite alien to him usually. For like many people who are generally liked, Fritz was constantly offending people. At school he had been constantly in trouble – it was his nature. Then there had been Colonel Mendoza, and that had got him exiled from the

City; and now he was not on good terms with Ximenez, and how that would end he did not know.

Just why he was on bad terms with Ximenez was complicated to explain. They had quarrelled one night in the bar of the Military Club, but that had been five years ago. The subject of the argument had been the old chestnut that seemed to keep cropping up, namely who should have won the Second World War. It was funny, thought Fritz, that people should keep on arguing about it, considering argument would never change the result one whit. Of course, Ximenez had aimed to provoke him, he realised that now. And he had been provoked. Ever since he had been wary of Ximenez. They were diametrically opposed characters, but he was resolved not to think about it, and the fact that he hardly saw Ximenez was a help in this regard.

Fritz now stood in the central square of San Cristobal wondering what to do. It was only eleven o'clock. He went and sat in his usual café, and took out his pocket edition of Tacitus. He was just coming to the part about the collapsible ship, his favourite passage. The waiter came to inform him regretfully that once again there was no coffee, and offered him some home-made spirits instead, concocted out of potatoes, which Fritz wisely refused. He tried instead to settle to his Tacitus, which was an English and Latin parallel text. There was nothing quite like a little Latin for calming the mind – usually. But today his mind refused to be soothed, and he felt restless. He wished that this farce would soon end. They said that there would be trouble once the General was dead: everyone said so – but at San Cristobal there was no news; in the City one could hear a rumour and know that it was fresh and possibly well-founded. In San Cristobal all one had to go on was what people like Ximenez said, which was only what they wanted you to hear. He sighed and shut his book. He looked at his watch again and wondered whether he could go and call on the Harpy.

The Harpy was one of the very few diversions that the town offered. As one might expect of a place like San Cristobal, the Harpy was not particularly diverting. She had long nails and teeth, and was the wrong side of forty. Nevertheless she seemed to have unlimited access to Fundador brandy, and a liking for Fritz. If you were going bald, and getting fat, and he was, then perhaps women like the Harpy were not so bad. Her conversation too was not entirely without interest. For the Harpy, whose real name was Mrs Williams, happened to be Ximenez's aunt. And it was just because he was deeply suspicious of Ximenez that Fritz told himself it was not a bad idea to keep abreast of the aunt. Her husband worked in some sort of agricultural business, selling tractor parts and seeds, and was frequently away from home. But it did seem that the Harpy knew a great deal about her nephew's activities; thus Fritz could justify his visits to the Harpy as undercover work.

He put his book in his pocket and began to saunter across the square in the direction of the Williams's house. Perhaps he would have a Fundador and hear how Ximenez was planning to kill the Colonel. Naturally, he didn't take that very seriously; all this talk of war was fantastical, he thought, simply because he knew that no one in the Army could fight, even if they wanted to; but it was worthwhile listening to the conversation of Mrs Williams, and there was a look in her eye, which he had seen in other eyes, most recently that of Mrs Mendoza. He was waiting for his ideal, his future wife, but wherever she was, she certainly wasn't in San Cristobal; and one had to have something to do in the meantime, even if it was only conversation with Mrs Williams.

Twenty-five

The offices of *The Post* were unnaturally quiet; it was the sort of stillness usually associated with coming storms. Elena sensed it but did not care. A little over a month had passed since Roberto's abrupt departure, but the pain of separation still lingered, always there, sometimes returning with an intensity that she could hardly bear. She wondered if this was what widowhood was like, and if these had been the feelings her mother had undergone when her father had died. But there was no bond of fellow feeling between her mother and herself in this or anything else. It annoyed her to think that her mother was living as if nothing had happened; that her mother continued her harassed existence as editor of *Moda* without thinking of Roberto, but distracted by paper shortages and the collapse of the currency instead. Elena could not forgive her her seeming indifference, her serenity in the face of Roberto's departure. She suspected, and how quick her mind was to form suspicions now, that her mother was actually glad that he was gone. She had never liked him; she had been prejudiced against him from the start; and Elena was in no frame of mind to make allowances for that now.

That anyone should not like Roberto felt to her as if they were slighting her own judgement. She had chosen him for herself, and it was far too late now to think that this choice might have been a mistaken one. She was not, as she had almost hoped she would be, pregnant; but the bond between them was as firm as if she had been. There were people, she knew, who did not like her Roberto. Perhaps they were even glad that he had been given the Army's least enviable posting. But she discounted their opinion, whoever they might be. She knew Roberto as no one else did; she had seen into the depths of his soul.

She had had one letter from him, which he had sent her by the ship's return. It was not, in some respects, very comforting. In it he described December Island. She had not realised how close it was to the Antarctic. He had written of the penguins, the sparse vegetation, the dimensions of the place, a mere two or three square miles. There were no buildings apart from two huts, one for the officers, the other for the men. Of the latter, she gathered that they were not to be trusted, and had been sent there to be kept out of the trouble they would surely get into, and in some cases had already got into, on the mainland. As for the officers, little comfort was to be expected in that quarter either. Even though the letter had been written on the evening of his arrival, she could tell that he was suffering already. If he had written to her hoping to arouse her sympathy, he had succeeded.

There were certain passages that moved her particularly, in which this cold man she loved spoke of his tender feelings for her. This was a comfort, to know that he missed her. Again and again she read the few sentences that told her what she most wanted to hear. He missed her, he longed for her, he wanted to be with her, and when he returned, if he ever did, he would never allow himself to be separated from her again. Absence, it seemed, really did make the heart grow fonder. And in these re-readings a new Roberto developed in her mind and eventually took possession of it. She thought of him now not as reserved, shy and cold, but as ardent and demonstrative; and gradually this phantasm she had created for herself replaced the memories of Roberto as he had been in truth.

Hours were spent in this way. She would sit at her desk, gazing at his photograph, constructing a new future for them both. But always these dreams were menaced by nightmare figures in uniform, the men who had come on two separate occasions and taken him away. She found that she was beginning to hate the Army and the Junta. The Army had absurd ideas about duty and obedience which interfered with her dreams of private happiness. By putting him into uniform it had tried its best to depersonalise and destroy Roberto. Somewhere there sat a man who mulled over files marked with her name and with his, playing with their destiny. That man was Olivarez.

There had been a time when the name of Olivarez had simply been that of an important Government official – it had meant nothing to her. He had been another unreal presence in this Republic of phantoms. But now Olivarez had become real to her: the exterior phantom had joined the other phantoms in her mind, and with the anonymous 'they', had become the villain in the story she had constructed. He was the man who, in sending Roberto to December Island, had ruined her happiness. He was the one who, out of pure malice, had tried to ruin their lives. He was the fairytale ogre. He was so capriciously cruel, and she hated him for it, and she knew that if ever the opportunity came, she would do all she could to destroy the wicked Colonel.

It was in this frame of mind that Father Morisco found her.

There was something rather alarming about this sudden visit. Of course, she knew the priest by sight, everyone did, but there was something unsettling in seeing so familiar a face now so close, towering over her desk. He was as dark and ugly as he always was, but solemn as well, as if he had come specially to break bad news to her, to tell her news of death.

'I have just been to the Palace,' he told her. 'The Presidential one. They told me there that Captain Enriquez had been sent away.' He looked at the photograph on her desk. 'Quite a few of the young officers I spoke to are concerned by the arbitrariness of it all.'

Father Morisco sighed. Elena had a vivid picture of him pausing in the marble corridors, inviting confidences from the tired and weary officers and men, while all the time, in some distant bedroom, the Father of the Country lay suspended between life and death.

'Arbitrary rule,' said the priest thoughtfully. 'Not the rule of law at all.' He thought of Zondadari and the many conversations that they had had together; he thought of the dying General whom he had not been allowed to see. Finally he brought to mind the reason for his present visit. He took a photograph out of his wallet and put it on Elena's desk. It was the picture of a girl, blonde, blue-eyed, smiling. Elena looked up at the priest questioningly, wondering what the significance of this picture could be.

'It is a long story,' he said. 'She's called Nicola Nickleby. She is British, and was here as a tourist, learning Spanish. She was snatched in Palace Square by two soldiers, the Saturday of the General's birthday celebrations.'

'That was weeks ago,' said Elena, who remembered that afternoon.

'Quite. Her parents have been out here since then. They tried all the normal channels, but the girl has disappeared without trace. They went to the Ambassador, and he came to me. They've now gone back to England. The only witness is far too frightened to speak – she's the cook of Isabel de Calatrava. As for Isabel herself, she's been no help at all. She still insists the girl has eloped.'

'And the girl? Where is she now?'

'The girl is dead,' said Father Morisco gravely. 'No one but Isabel could believe she had simply run off. She must be dead. We shall never know the exact truth, I fear, but if she were still alive they would have released her once they had realised she was British. They could not possibly want to upset our allies, could they? They must have killed her before they realised their mistake.'

'Poor girl,' said Elena, looking at the picture again. 'Poor parents.' This was more than a news story. It had the ring of truth. 'Who is responsible?' she asked.

'Olivarez. It was done by Olivarez's men. He is behind it all.'

Morisco was silent. For years the Church had been too kind to the Generals. Now this had happened. This was the beginning of the end. The British Ambassador had said the same thing. Olivarez had let them down. He had deceived them into thinking what they had wanted to think, namely that this had been a respectable regime – but now in the hard light of day they could see the regime for what it was – one that kidnapped and murdered innocent girls.

'Won't the British Government do anything?' asked Elena, who had been thinking of Olivarez.

'They can protest, but there is no body. Our Government can say that the girl ran off to Brazil with some man. They could say that she never entered the country in the first place. They have covered all their tracks so well. And Isabel de Calatrava is such a friend of the Junta, that she wants to keep it quiet for their sakes.'

'What shall I do?' asked Elena.

'Take the photo,' said the priest. 'But be careful, my dear. I know that you don't have any reason to love Olivarez; but remember that Olivarez is a dangerous man, and that picture could land you in jail.'

Father Morisco rose and left the room on silent feet. He knew she was brave, and he trusted his own judgement of character.

Elena looked at the photograph again. The innocent smiling face absorbed her. This girl, like Caballero, was not dead, just missing. There was surely nothing illegal about making an appeal for information about the whereabouts of a missing girl, or in stating the circumstances of her disappearance? Of course, very little was strictly illegal in such a proceeding. But she knew that the laws of the Republic were capricious. There were no laws, only one general principle, namely that nothing should be printed that might embarrass the Junta. And what she had before her was deeply embarrassing to the Junta. It might even harm Olivarez a great deal.

The girl had been snatched on the afternoon of the military parade. Roberto had been with her in the country that weekend, and so he had had nothing to do with it.

She put a sheet of paper into her typewriter. After a little hesitation she began to write as follows.

'The above is a photograph of Miss Nicola Nickleby, an English student and British national, aged eighteen, who has been missing since Saturday 15th November. She was last seen in Palace Square during the military parade to mark the General's birthday. Reports suggest that she was helped away by two officers. Further information about her whereabouts has not been forthcoming; any such information will be gratefully received by the British Embassy.'

Nothing she had written was untrue. Taking the text and the photograph, she decided she would by-pass the usual editorial channels and go straight down to the print room where the latest edition of *The Post* was already set up. It would be a small matter to remove one article and substitute it with the photograph and the few words about it. And as long as there was no one about to interfere, there would be nothing to stop her.

She stayed at *The Post* that evening until all the other journalists had gone home. Then she had the satisfaction of seeing twenty thousand copies of the incendiary photograph printed. The quality of reproduction was poor, but good enough for her purposes. Of course *El Mercurio* had a print run of nearly half a million – but perhaps for once *The Post* was about to make news.

Twenty-six

Carmen, like the rest of the country, was to have an eventful morning the next day. She arrived at her editorial desk at *Moda* very early, leaving Elena still asleep at home, in the hope of getting a great deal of work done. For a start, she had been meaning to deal with the Cookery Editor for some time. This series on nouvelle cuisine would simply have to stop. If it went on much longer it might cost them readers. In a country where everything was served soaked in olive oil, who on earth wanted to eat naked asparagus?

However, the interview with the Cookery Editor took over an hour. Carmen had imagined a few terse minutes on the lines of 'Out with this rubbish' and 'Certainly, Senora Garcia.' But the interview had degenerated into a heated argument about all things culinary. The cookery woman, who had dyed blonde hair and was clearly in need of advice from the Beauty Editor, and whom Carmen now realised she had always disliked, had ground on for what had seemed like hours about cookery, new approaches, editorial policy and 'fashion'. The magazine's title meant fashion, didn't it? Carmen agreed that it did, while wondering why she had ever employed this ghastly woman in the first place.

By the time she had won the argument it was time to get hold of the printers and to complain about the quality of the paper they had been using recently. But even that proved more difficult than she had imagined. The telephones all seemed to be out of order, and when she finally did get hold of the printers, she was rudely told that she had to be the only woman in the country not to realise that paper was imported and that the escudo had collapsed again, and they had to put up with what they could get. Another argument seemed to be in the offing; but Carmen felt defeat looming and declined the contest. The currency had collapsed, which was perfectly true, and there was nothing she could do about that. It was clearly going to be another bad day. Although it was only ten in the morning she was beginning to long for a quiet day spent at home. It was not too late for that. She felt she was wasting her time in the office. She would go home, and perhaps she would come back after lunch.

She left the office and began to walk down the principal street of the City, that bisected the northern and southern sides and ran from east to west, all the way from the Zoo to the Palace Square, but she did so obliviously, wrapped in an insulating cloud of bad temper. It was some time before she realised something rather strange. The entire Army seemed to have taken to the streets. There certainly were a great many soldiers about. Most seemed to be rather foolish-looking teenage conscripts led by equally confused officers. With a start Carmen remembered the terrible days that had followed the coup, when she had first been a widow. But there was nothing to be frightened of now, she told herself. She would take a taxi home, perhaps, and never mind the expense.

Something was happening by the taxi rank. She noticed a clump of soldiers. One, a mere boy, was looking towards her, his face white, as if to say that he at least did not want to be there. His companions were gathered menacingly around a man in civilian clothes, a man who sold newspapers. Perhaps they were going to cut his hair. In the early days the Army had been given a free hand to do that whenever they had wanted to. But few men had long hair nowadays; certainly this man did not. An argument was in progress there on the pavement and Carmen heard angry words. Then for no reason that she could fathom, the soldiers began to turn over the flimsy news stand. That was the last thing she noticed before jumping into a taxi.

While the taxi waited at the next traffic lights – in a country where nothing worked, it was strange how the traffic lights still did – she saw another soldier on the pavement in the act of taking a newspaper out of the hands of an old lady. With a shudder of recognition she saw that it was *The Post*.

It was now clear what had happened. But still she could hardly believe that *The Post* of all newspapers was in the process of being suppressed for sedition.

She got home, paid the outrageous taxi fare, and ran up the stairs. As soon as she got inside the flat she found her daughter.

'Aren't you at work?' she asked.

'Captain Zondadari brought me home,' said Elena.

And there she saw the Captain sitting on the sofa.

'I went out to arrest her,' explained Zondadari. 'As soon as I had done so I brought her back here. It was the least I could do.'

'But what has happened?' asked Carmen.

'Colonel Olivarez has ordered out the troops from the City barracks to confiscate all copies of *The Post*. And he sent some of his special men round to the offices; I'm not one of those, but I did my bit. I rushed round there, and when I met Elena on her way into work I put her in my car and brought her home. After all, I couldn't let them arrest a friend of Captain Enriquez, could I?'

Elena was showing her mother a copy of *The Post*, one of the very last left in free circulation. Her mother read it quickly and understood. Then they burned it; and then they destroyed the original photograph as well; and finally Carmen wondered what would happen if the police or worse were to turn up to arrest Elena. Elena did not think this likely, but Zondadari, who knew that such things could happen and had already done so, suggested that he drive her to the country, as soon as she had packed a few things. He had a military car and was in uniform and no one would stop them.

It really did seem that this would be a good idea: but Elena was inclined to argue that Olivarez, wherever he might be at present, was far too busy with other things to worry about her.

And even if she did leave the City, where would she go? Zondadari could hardly drive her around the country until he ran out of petrol.

Carmen began to remonstrate. If the Army had kidnapped and murdered this English girl, a girl protected by her evident youth and her foreign passport – if they could do that, there was nothing to stop them arresting Elena as well. She would be taken away and never seen again. Now it was Zondadari's turn to join the argument. This case, the case of the English girl, was an aberration, he said. It had been the work of some lunatic. And besides, everyone knew that Elena was the girlfriend of Roberto Enriquez: they were hardly likely to murder the future wife of an important young officer.

Carmen despaired at their obtuseness. She sat down on the sofa, holding her head in her hands, amazed at the blindness of the younger generation. If they had known what she had known, they would not be arguing now.

'You don't surely think that all the Army approve of the action of one or two bad soldiers, do you?' Elena was asking her mother.

Zondadari felt embarrassed. He did not want to have to defend the honour of the Army, or witness a quarrel about it, especially if Elena was in some danger after all.

'Let's switch on the radio and see what the news has to say,' he suggested. 'It will say if there are going to be arrests, or if there have been already.'

And he switched on the radio. There was always news at noon. They would listen to that and then make their decision. There was always something calming about listening to the radio: the radio broadcast reassuring truths. But instead of the expected pips that usually marked the middle of the day, they heard solemn martial music.

'That is the Death March from *Siegfried*,' said Elena suddenly. 'How odd.'

'Someone has died,' said Carmen, her bad temper suddenly dissolving.

The other two heard the music and waited for the words that would surely come, feeling that everything was about to change.

The General had died at the hottest time of the day. The heat had penetrated even the State Bedroom of the marble Palace, and it was already doing its work. The corpse was growing greyer by the minute, and presently would begin to smell. Two other people were in the room when the event had taken place: Messina and Hernandez.

'Well?' said Messina, looking at his rival.

His hand rested on the holster which contained his pistol, the cartridge of which contained fifteen bullets. Hernandez knew that, because he too had his pistol with him, just as all officers did, whether generals or lieutenants.

'Where is Olivarez?' said Hernandez quietly.

'He is chasing newspapers,' said Messina contemptuously.

'I think Olivarez has gone too far,' said Hernandez. 'Don't you think so? And as he is not here . . .'

'He would have been here,' said Messina. 'If he had had any sense. But fortunately for us, General, he isn't.'

Hernandez realised that even though they had said so little on the subject, they had reached agreement.

'This matter of the English girl,' began Hernandez, 'will do us immense harm unless we do something about it. Now that it has been in *The Post*, we have no choice.'

Messina made no objection. The President had been dead only a few minutes, and already Olivarez's fate was being sealed. It was a few minutes to twelve. If the news were to be announced at once that the General was dead, the country would immediately slip into the paralysis of mourning. It would take Olivarez off-guard; he would not be able to put his plans into practice – for neither of the Generals doubted for a moment that Olivarez did have plans and that he, like them, had been waiting for the President's death. But Olivarez, for once, was not there. He had made a fatal mistake: he was not there to give the signal his men would be expecting. They could strike while the iron was hot. They could strike before Olivarez himself did so.

The Indian woman was called in to attend to the needs of her late master, the now disregarded figure on the bed, and the two elderly Generals set to work. Hernandez sent instructions to the radio station, suggesting they play solemn music as a way of preparing the long-suffering public for the tragic news of the passing of their President; and Messina, as quickly as he could, got together a squad of trustworthy men, and set them to arrest the Head of Security. Hernandez felt his old stomach go tight in anticipation: the radio station sent a message, asking him to specify what solemn music he wanted. He immediately thought of *Siegfried*, the only solemn military music he could call to mind. He wondered if the General had liked Wagner; he wondered in fact what he had liked; he noticed that the minutes were ticking away. Soon the country would stop everything, as a mark of respect, and Olivarez would be powerless to act. But these minutes were vital.

Olivarez was at the Army Navigational School, supervising the burning of the confiscated copies of *The Post*, nearly twenty thousand of them, which formed a merry conflagration in the wasteland behind the building. He had felt he could not have rested securely until he was sure that the copies were burned to cinders. There had been enough in that paper to destroy him; Strauss had already paid for that mistake, as had Enriquez and Tanucci, but he had no intention at all of allowing what they had done and failed to do to reflect on him. So he had watched the papers burn, a process that had taken some hours. It was only after noon had come and gone that he saw the job completed and dismissed the chosen men who had supervised the fire.

It was now boiling hot, and when the men, all but one, had left him, Olivarez went into the courtyard of the Army Navigational School and washed his face in the fountain there. There was but one young officer with him, whom he had particularly asked to stay behind, ostensibly to drive him back to the Palace. There was a deathly stillness in the air, and he was tired. It was past noon now, and he thought that the stillness was merely a symptom of the entire City stopping for lunch as it always did. He was not aware of the radio's solemn music, nor of the shops shutting as a sign of respect, nor of the fact that everyone had gone home leaving the City streets deserted, as they felt they were expected to do. Nor was he aware of Messina's men outside the building, waiting for their moment. (Theirs was a dangerous mission, but they had been well paid for it.) Olivarez's mind was on other things; he had just completed a tiresome operation, the failure of which might have destroyed him. He was basking in a sense of his own security.

'Come and wash,' he said to the young man who stood by, knowing and yet not knowing what was expected of him.

The arrest turned out to be simplicity itself. When, after waiting a quarter of an hour, Messina's men forced an entry to the Army Navigational School, they found Olivarez quite taken by surprise and not armed. The Colonel was treated with consideration, allowed to make himself presentable to the outside world, and driven away to the Palace under armed guard. The unfortunate man who had been with him, to prevent his ever speaking of an operation so delicate as the arrest of the Head of Security or identifying the men who had done it, was left dead in the sunlight.

Twenty-seven

Even in San Cristobal, far to the south, it was proving to be a day of exceptional heat. Fritz had spent the morning in the classroom, dinning into unreceptive heads once again the history of the Second World War, an occupation that always distressed him. For though his mother had been a Schultz, and his father had been something of an admirer of Franco, Fritz himself was quite convinced that as in all wars, it really had been the best side that had won. For if a side was any good, it would win. That was logic. Hitler had been doomed simply because he had been a bad soldier and an evil man as well. It was one of the thoughts that he often had which made him think that the world was a good place after all. But such confidence was sorely tried in these barracks where the cadets, almost to a man, seemed to take the opposite view.

Classes had finished as usual at twelve sharp, but because it was so hot, instead of going to the officers' mess to listen to the news on the radio as he often did, Fritz went upstairs, peeled off his clothes and went and stood under a cold shower. All the showers were cold, especially in the middle of the day, but that was something to be grateful for, he supposed. He was also glad that he was on his own too. The cold water poured down on him and he felt the sweat of the classroom being washed away. It was the first time that day that he had had a moment's peace. He even began to sing as the thunderous waters poured down on his head.

It was only when he stepped out of the shower and onto the bare tiles of the wash-room floor that he realised that he was not alone after all. Under the cover of the noise of running water, someone had come into the room and was standing there. It was Ximenez; and suddenly Fritz, wet and naked but for the identification tag around his neck, knew that if Ximenez chose to kill him there and then, and perhaps make it look like an accident, he could very well do so.

He had not seen Ximenez for some time; and perhaps it was this strange, silent and utterly unexpected appearance that had given him the odd idea that the man hated him enough to kill him, and that one day the loathing that Ximenez had for him under the surface would break out into open warfare.

'You're wanted,' said Ximenez, looking at him with sardonic interest, his precise tones echoing around the tiled room.

'Pass me my towel,' said Fritz calmly. 'Who by?'

'My aunt, Mrs Williams,' said Ximenez, throwing Fritz his towel. 'It seems she is having a lunch party and she is a man short. She is desperate for you to come over to her at once. It is twelve-twenty now. She sent me over with the car, to fetch you. I'm sure you don't mind, do you, Captain Rodriguez?'

Ximenez gave Fritz a thin-lipped smile.

'Not at all, Captain,' replied Fritz in the same tone. 'I am merely surprised, that's all; not by the invitation, but by the fact that I should see you here. We don't see you in barracks much.'

'I'm kept busy,' said Ximenez simply. 'We mustn't keep her waiting, must we?'

Fritz, now dry and clad in a towel, led the way down the corridor towards his room. Ximenez followed him in. It was a hot day, but his shower had cooled him. He wondered what Ximenez's game was.

'Tails, I think,' said Fritz, going to a large trunk in which he kept his very rarely worn dress uniform. He had it in mind to spin out his levée.

'How's your uncle?' he asked as he opened up the trunk.

'Fine,' said Ximenez, nonchalantly lighting a cigarette, but to Fritz's eyes looking a little impatient. 'His business has folded, of course. Now that our currency is worthless, you can hardly import agricultural goods any more, can you?'

'I suppose not,' said Fritz, now wearing a stiff white shirt and taking his time over his cuff-links. (He noticed that Ximenez had glanced at his watch.) 'What will he do now?'

'He may come back to the Army,' said Ximenez, affecting ease.

'Really?' asked Fritz, now stepping into the heavy trousers, and experiencing some difficulty in doing them up – for they were old-fashioned trousers, the type that open at both sides, not the front, and the buttons were stiff. (Ximenez, he noticed, was now looking out of the window.) 'It's gone awfully quiet,' observed Fritz. 'Look, Captain, you don't have to wait for me. I really can find my own way to Mrs Williams's; I ought to polish my shoes and possibly have a shave . . . Perhaps I'll turn up there a little late, but she's bound not to mind.'

'Not at all, Captain,' said Ximenez with unruffled calm. 'She said I was to bring you myself; and I always obey her instructions to the letter.'

'Indeed,' said Fritz. 'I had no idea you were such a dutiful nephew.' He was now doing up the buttons at the front of the tight fitting tail-coat. He had put on a few inches since he had last worn the uniform, and he was conscious that he was looking a little ridiculous.

'Let's go,' said Ximenez with great determination.

With this there could be no argument. Fritz had only to put on his shoes and he was ready to go, dressed like a Napoleonic soldier. He had wasted at least twenty minutes of Ximenez's time, and he had discovered that whatever Ximenez wanted to do, he was very impatient about getting Fritz over to Mrs Williams's first.

They went down to the car.

'I wish you'd tell me what is going on,' said Fritz as they got in. 'Is that flag at half-mast?'

'No, I mean, yes,' said Ximenez, driving off at speed.

'This isn't quite the frankness one should use with a brother officer, Captain,' said Fritz.

'Oh do shut up,' said Ximenez.

'Nor the politeness,' added Fritz.

The rest of the short journey passed in silence. All the streets were quite deserted. Mrs Williams was waiting for him, and as soon as he was handed over, Ximenez was off without a further word.

'You look very smart,' observed Mrs Williams, once she had taken him into the house and poured him a drink. 'But a little hot too.'

'Is it a big party?' he asked, noticing that there was little in the room to suggest that it was.

'To a certain extent,' said Mrs Williams.

She took her seat next to him on the sofa, her red nails clutching the narrow glass.

'No, it's not,' said Fritz. 'I wish you wouldn't be so mysterious.'

'I am so glad you at least could make it,' said Mrs Williams. 'All the others have cried off. Even my husband has gone somewhere. You see, something has happened. They've just announced that the General is dead. It was on the radio.'

'Ah,' said Fritz. 'I was in the shower. That's why . . .'

'But you won't go, will you?' said Mrs Williams. 'I mean, you can stay here and have lunch with me? I do so want it.'

There was something so desperate in this appeal that suddenly Fritz realised how serious things were. He went to the balcony. Outside he saw two men, nonchalantly smoking in the midday sun. He realised now that something was happening.

'How long have I got to stay here for?' he asked.

'Until four,' she said. 'It will be over by then, they tell me.'

'What will?'

'The coup,' she said. Then she put a hand on his arm, and said: 'You will be safe here with me, I made them promise.'

'Who promised?'

'Major Williams,' she said, meaning her husband. 'And Ximenez.'

Fritz picked up his glass again, and realised that this rather odd woman with the long teeth and the painted nails had probably saved his life.

'I am your prisoner,' he said. 'Do I still get lunch?'

'What is happening in San Cristobal?' asked Messina.

'I don't know,' said Olivarez. 'What is happening in San Cristobal? You tell me.'

'The penalty for mutiny is execution,' said Hernandez.

'There has been a mutiny?' asked Olivarez sarcastically.

'You know there has been,' said Messina. 'They must have been acting on your orders. They've shot their Colonel. It was that brute Ximenez who did it. He is one of your men. We all know that.'

'It's your fault,' said Olivarez calmly. 'You told the radio station to broadcast the news, and you must have told them about what music to put on, I presume. Ximenez is just one among many, who has his instructions to rise as soon as they hear the sound of the Death March from *Siegfried*. It was kind of you to broadcast the signal for me. You may be in charge in this Palace, but in the Provinces, I am now the President. I am not going to negotiate with you; rather I am going to wait until you negotiate with me.'

Hernandez held his head in his hands and groaned: why hadn't he chosen some other music? The radio man had not suggested *Siegfried*, but he had chosen Wagner, because he hadn't been able to think of anything else on the spur of the moment. And now they had a rebellion on their hands.

'Put him in the cellar,' said Messina.

Olivarez, who had been tied to a chair throughout this interview, was carried triumphantly away. Messina fell to thinking what they could do next.

* * *

When Fritz finally emerged from the shelter of Mrs Williams's house, it was to find that much had changed. The flags were all at half-mast; armed men, mostly cadets, but some adult soldiers as well, stood at every street corner; and black-edged posters had been put up everywhere to inform people that the President was dead, and that Colonel Olivarez had taken his place. Fritz read one of these with interest, then rather than returning to barracks, he decided to walk to Army Headquarters in the town square.

There he found Ximenez in what had been, until that morning, the Colonel's office.

'Where's the Colonel?' he enquired, wondering what had happened to the old sadist.

'Dead,' said Ximenez. 'Shot. Those were our orders. He's been replaced by myself; Major Williams will be Quartermaster.'

'Everything seems to be sorted out,' said Fritz. 'You obviously had everything planned.'

'We expect your co-operation, Captain,' said Ximenez.

'I have no choice, do I?' replied Fritz, lightly, who couldn't feel sorry for the Colonel, but nevertheless thought that this change could hardly be for the better. 'And what has happened in the Capital?'

'Olivarez will be seeing to that,' said Ximenez confidently. 'Everything has been arranged.'

Evening was falling over the City. The Archbishop sat in his Palace, wondering what would happen. Father Morisco was keeping him informed. The various parish priests around the country who had working telephones had in their turn been keeping him informed. The picture was gloomy. The President was dead; in the City the two remaining members of the Junta had Olivarez under arrest. But in the Provinces, Olivarez had been acclaimed the new president. Several senior officers who had protested at the illegality of this action seemed to have been shot. The smooth transition of power that the Generals had hoped for seemed at best precarious.

Before him the Archbishop had the latest news. It was a proclamation that had been posted up around the City, announcing the arrest of Olivarez and a long list of crimes of which he now stood accused. Olivarez, it seemed, had plotted to overthrow the State; he had practised unnatural vice; he had given the orders for the murder of an English student called Nicola Nickleby. The public were assured that justice would soon be done.

'What will happen now, Father?' asked the Archbishop, consulting his oracle.

'The British and Americans will support the Generals, of course,' said Father Morisco. 'But the common troops, the conscripts, the soldiers, even the cadets, and there are so many of them, and especially the younger officers, not to mention the police, they may well join Olivarez, even if for no better reason than they haven't been paid for nearly a month.'

Don Alvaro sighed.

'Will they shoot Olivarez?' he asked.

'Probably, Don Alvaro. He has, as they say, asked for it. But whether that will solve anything, I don't know.'

Similar uncertainty gripped the rest of the City. The news that was filtering in was unsettling. It seemed clear that the garrison in San Cristobal, the largest in the country, was in revolt. Rumour had it that Captain Ximenez had shot the commanding officer, and anyone else who had raised any objection. But to the north, they said, things had not gone so successfully. Some prospective rebels had been shot by their officers themselves; in a few garrisons, the men had run riot. In the City all was yet quiet, but no one could tell which way the City garrisons would move. And what would the police force do? Or the Navy? And on top of all this was the news that Olivarez was under arrest in the Palace.

Few could believe that the high and mighty Olivarez had really fallen so easily. They were inclined to be cautious.

Perhaps Olivarez had merely pretended to fall, and would shortly emerge from the Palace, triumphant, and purge the Army of his declared enemies. Perhaps it would be better to wait and see what would happen.

It was in this spirit that about a hundred or so of the younger officers in the City gathered in the smoking room of the Military Club that evening. Some were friends of Olivarez, inclined to be hot and angry, and ready to throw their lot in with him at once. They had read the proclamation made by the two Generals, and found it disgraceful. If Olivarez was to be arrested and tried and no doubt executed for atrocities, then who was safe? It could not be allowed to happen. The old men, Messina and Hernandez, had held power far too long; it was time they gave way to the new.

The news from San Cristobal, and the execution of the Colonel there by Ximenez, did not dampen their spirits. The alcohol flowed, and anecdotes about that particular Colonel were repeated. He had deserved what he had got. He had been Messina's man, and people like Messina and Hernandez had simply gone too far in their desperate desire to hold on to power.

(Even the Generals had begun to sense this, from the safety of the Palace. The news from the Provinces was very disquieting. The entire garrison at San Cristobal was in open revolt, and there was nothing they could do about that. There was a sense that things were getting out of hand. The Palace was quiet and empty; even the men on guard duty seemed to be unaccountably absent. Others had been called in by Messina, but they were men with strange and unfamiliar faces, men Hernandez felt he could not quite trust. In the communications room, efforts were being made to get into contact with various outlying garrisons, but many were not replying. And worst of all, only a quarter of a mile away, there was this meeting going on in the Military Club. Both Generals had sent stern messages ordering the officers to go home; telling them their meeting was illegal; that there was a curfew; that they should be in barracks, all of which had been studiously ignored by the young men.)

The unofficial and by now illegal meeting in the Military Club had been called to order by Captain Zondadari, who, sensing that there was business to be done, had ordered the staff to shut the bar, which had been done at once. Zondadari carried some natural authority, and when he stood up to speak, all was quiet.

'It really does seem,' he said quietly, 'that the regime is on its last legs. It can't go on much longer and from what we've seen today, it would be best for the entire country – not just for us, but for everyone – if the remaining members of the Junta retired from public life. God only knows, they're well over retirement age anyway.'

There was laughter at this and cheers.

'Then what?' someone shouted out.

'Then,' said Zondadari, 'we shall have to choose a responsible Government, one that people actually want.'

There was complete silence in the room. He had not mentioned the obscene words 'democracy' or 'elections', but the effect was the same. This was not what many of them wanted to hear at all. Perhaps there were ten or twenty who secretly agreed with Zondadari, but for the majority, there could be no turning back now. Olivarez had to be president, for if they were to brand him a criminal it would mean they were all criminals as well.

Into this silence stepped a young police officer, rather out of breath.

'Are you a member?' someone asked him ironically.

The young man, the only person that the Generals had been able to find for the job, looked around uncertainly. He wasn't a member, and had never been in the Club in his life. He saw Zondadari there, standing in the centre of the room, clearly the man in charge.

'Sir,' he said a little apologetically, 'I have been ordered to tell you that this is an illegal meeting and that if you do not disperse very soon, you will all be arrested. There is a detachment of police outside this building.'

Zondadari opened his mouth to reply, but whatever he intended to say went unheard, drowned in the roar of derision that the young policeman had incited. Clearly the Generals had lost the war before it had even begun if this was the best messenger they could find. Something of a riot began to break out. Two rather drunk lieutenants jumped on the unfortunate policeman with the intention of removing his trousers. That accomplished, in the ensuing hilarity, they threw him out of doors, into the empty street where his colleagues were waiting. Then drawing their pistols the young officers began to shoot into the air and around the street, which made a great deal of noise, and made the police who had been sent to arrest them run away.

Those were to be the very first shots fired in the civil war.

Twenty-eight

Despite the despondency that his colleague Hernandez was inclined to feel, Messina did not yet regard the situation as hopeless. It was true that a police officer had been debagged by the young fools in the Military Club, but he now realised that it had been a mistake to try and overawe soldiers, and officers at that, with mere policemen. No one respected the police any more; and if the police had been fired on, that didn't bother him too much. In fact he was rather glad of it. The one hundred and three young men in the Club had effectively put themselves outside the law by their action. As soon as proper troops he could rely on, and not just the police – he had great confidence in the Engineers, none at all in the Cavalry – were ready, he would have the building surrounded until they gave themselves up. If necessary he would have the building stormed. He had tanks after all, which he had bought from the Emperor Bokassa. They had never been used, and if he were to try them out on the Military Club, as he had a mind to do, that would soon bring the fools in the Provinces to their senses. Then a few would have to be shot, and that would be that.

As the next day drew on the officers who were in the Military Club, and who had been there for some time now, watched as the buildings opposite, now prudently deserted by their inhabitants, were taken over by troops. Machine-guns were being set up on the other side of the street. That quarter of the City was now completely empty, thanks to the police cordon that had been thrown round it, and the shots they themselves had fired. Now the prospect of a real fight seemed nearer.

Zondadari, who was nominally in charge of the Club now, wondered how on earth it had come to this.

In the Palace, Olivarez was brought before his captors once more. He had a considerable growth of beard and was not his usual smart self, having spent the night in a comfortless cellar.

Hernandez, ever nervous, had resolved to try conciliation.

'The country is in a terrible state, Colonel,' he observed, drawing on a Silk Cut as he did so. 'Your young friends are defying the law, holed up in the Military Club. The City is paralysed. In certain places there's rioting, or so I hear. It is only a matter of time before someone else is killed. Those young men in the Club, now: they've tried to shoot some policemen. Do you honestly think they'll be allowed out alive? We've got troops we can rely on, you know, surrounding the place – it's more or less a siege already. Their situation is quite hopeless, I am afraid. You see, we are still the Government. All these troublemakers are rebels without a leader. They'll soon think better of it.'

'Will they?' asked Olivarez. 'Can you tell me why there's no electricity in this room?'

Hernandez looked uncomfortable. They had cut off the electricity, and the water supply too, to try and make life uncomfortable for the rebels in the Club, and succeeded in inconveniencing themselves in the process. It was just the thing that Olivarez would notice.

'You are panicking,' said Olivarez. 'How many of the troops are obeying your orders? Tell me that; and tell me who they are. Nothing more than a bunch of subservient NCOs, I am sure.'

'Don't you realise we can have you shot?' said Messina, breaking in.

'You wouldn't dare,' said Olivarez. 'And there isn't a soldier in the country who'd raise a hand against me. You would have to do it yourself, and you don't have the courage for that.'

'We can put you on trial, or we can hand you over to the British,' said Hernandez.

'And I would tell them the entire story,' said Olivarez almost gleefully. 'There are so many things that the Junta has authorised which would make you very uncomfortable if they were known. You are both as guilty as I am. You have no choice but to let me go.'

'Let you go?' said Messina incredulously.

'The longer you keep me, the worse it will be for you in the end,' said Olivarez. 'I am the President now.'

Messina and Hernandez retired to the further side of the huge room. Olivarez wondered if his reasoning had in fact won the day.

'We can defeat the rebels,' Messina was saying. 'We can storm the Military Club if necessary and regain control of the City. That will make the Provinces see sense. We could send the Navy, if they are to be trusted, to shell San Cristobal.'

'But think of the damage to the City,' said Hernandez. 'The Club is only four hundred yards away.'

'I'm damned if I am going to negotiate with Olivarez now,' said Messina. 'Besides we've already gone too far, and so have they.'

The two old Generals approached the chair to which the former Head of Security was now tied. Messina had a look of grim determination on his face.

'If your men return to barracks, then we could think about letting you go. We could have an amnesty, and declare the last two days void. The only exceptions would be those who have actually killed fellow soldiers. They'd have to be shot, of course.'

'But you have already told me that you want to have me judicially murdered,' said Olivarez. 'I will only negotiate with you if you go and give yourselves up to those in charge of the Military Club.'

'You are a fool,' said Messina.

'And you are a brainless thug,' replied Olivarez.

'Oh do stop it,' said Hernandez, who could feel a certain sympathy for Olivarez, even now. The man was from one of the best families in Spain after all. He had never liked Messina, and he had never trusted Italians; for a moment he wondered if he hadn't somehow ended up on the wrong side.

'Surely you don't want a civil war?' asked Hernandez weakly. 'No one would win. We'd just destroy ourselves. The poor General hasn't even been buried yet, and you want to destroy everything we have ever achieved.'

'And what have you ever achieved?' asked Olivarez. 'All you have ever cared about is your own comfort.'

'And you?' said Messina. 'We all know what your habits have been.'

Olivarez preserved a dignified silence.

For a second time the two Generals retired to the other side of the room.

'He'll never listen to reason,' said Messina. 'We've got to cut off the head of this monster called rebellion. Those young fools will all go home once they know he has been dealt with. We can't afford to wait.'

Hernandez was silent.

'Well?' asked Messina.

'As you think best,' said Hernandez quietly, and turned to look out of the window. He felt in his pocket for his pack of cigarettes.

Messina turned to the business in hand. It had better be done at once. There had better be no blood. And Olivarez had been right when he had said that there wasn't a soldier in the Army who would do the job. The fear of reprisal would be too great. But Messina himself was determined not to be a coward.

He took an electric flex from what had been a desk lamp, and tied it into a loop. Then from the desk he picked up a metal ruler. The first he dropped over Olivarez's surprised head; then using the ruler he began to tighten the improvised garotte. Hernandez still stared out of the window; he thought to himself that Olivarez had brought it on himself; that it was too late to feel pity for anyone any more; that there was no going back now. At first he heard Olivarez's protests, then his screams, and finally the gurgle of death. Then there was only silence. His cigarette was finished. The man was dead.

No news had as yet penetrated as far as December Island. The island lay in a sea of tranquillity, under a thin dusting of snow. The sun shone there, it was true, but, as Roberto had been quick to realise, it rapidly lost its power thanks to the sharp wind that blew from the south.

Why anyone should want this island, let alone think it worthy of having a garrison on it, was something of a mystery. It was about three miles square, surrounded by a dark and inhospitable ocean, the home of icebergs and whales. Two military huts lay at the centre of the island, one for the officers and one for the men, but even there one could feel the spray from the sea on a windy day.

Roberto had stopped wearing proper uniform soon after his arrival. It had been no defence against the cold. Instead he wore the clothes that the previous commander, the one who had killed himself, had left behind: thick woolly sweaters, corduroy trousers and a combat jacket. He had stopped shaving too, and had grown a reddish beard, which considerably altered his appearance. He had done this partly out of laziness, partly because the hot water wasn't particularly hot, and partly as an outward sign of penance. He felt, and was beginning to look, like an Old Testament prophet.

There was nothing for him to do; the men were busy enough, running around the island twice before breakfast, under the supervision of the NCOs; or being taught various things by Tanucci; or being given religious instruction by the Chaplain, when they were not playing football. There was very little for Roberto to do there; no one bothered him. His only activity was to observe his companions.

He was interested to note their insensitivity to their environment. The priest was one of those hearty men who always had a bright smile for everyone; the sort of priest who made you depressed simply to meet him. He was a resolutely cheerful man, forever patting people on the back. The sight of the priest had made Roberto take off the medallion of Our Lady of Lourdes that he had worn round his neck ever since his First Holy Communion, and throw it into the sea.

The scientist Hoffmann too seemed remarkably satisfied with his fate, spending hours alone with his penguins.

'There's nothing more enjoyable than watching a female lay her eggs,' he would say. 'It is absolutely fascinating. And that young man is really quite adept with cameras, I find. He is quite useful to me; he has quite a feel for wildlife.'

The useful young man in question was Lieutenant Tanucci, who, true to his nature, was doing his very best to please both Hoffmann and the priest. There was something strange about Tanucci, thought Roberto. He would have thought when he had first met him, that he was simply brutal; but now he realised that this boy who had the gift of not frightening penguins was almost the opposite to what he had thought him. Tanucci was perhaps a paradigm of what malleable people were like. Strauss was gone, dragged to execution; and without Strauss, Tanucci was someone else. Perhaps Strauss's death had produced some sudden change. Or perhaps Tanucci was returning to what he had been before Army life had changed his behaviour.

At night, Roberto would lie on his bed without undressing. Ever since coming to the island he had been unable to sleep. The nights were short now, and he was always up before dawn; but he dreaded the onset of the long Antarctic winter. In the room they shared, Tanucci, he had noticed, seemed to have no difficulty getting to sleep. In fact, the Lieutenant would often drift off to sleep while Roberto tried to keep him awake in conversation.

'Are you enjoying it here?' Roberto would ask.

'Oh yes, sir,' the Lieutenant would reply.

'Why?'

And Tanucci would tell him that he was enjoying the sea air, the isolation. That he was doing something useful for once; how he enjoyed teaching some of the brighter men the rudiments of mathematics and the art of firing guns. There was a certain novelty about observing a colony of penguins close at hand. There were other things that he did not say; he did not tell Roberto that he felt safe on the island, away from Olivarez, away from the work they had been doing and the secret ghosts that haunted him. He did not tell him how he thought of the buried corpses in the Army Navigational School, and how he remembered with such clarity the way he had burned Nicola Nickleby's clothes and passport, or what had happened to Caballero. Those things he remembered still, but they were far away, and he tried to put them from his mind.

When Tanucci fell asleep, Roberto would lie staring upwards into the darkness, trying to think of something normal. Other men could sleep at night, but not he. He would think of his mother sometimes, and the habitual way she had had of looking at him ever since he had grown to maturity. She had disapproved of him, and he in turn, though loving her, had thought nothing of her disapproval. He had always liked to cultivate the belief that women at heart knew nothing about anything important: that important things belonged to men. That was the impression that life in the Republic always gave: but they did have a secret knowledge after all; all along his mother had known about his inner fault; she had known that he was a man who, though wanting to be good, and wanting to do good, had done so not out of love but only out of duty. Even in the days when he had been a good Catholic, even then he had gone to Mass and to confess his sins, because that had been the law; just as he had carried out his military duties with precision, because that had been laid out in the Code. There had been no true merit in anything he had done: he had done it only because he had forced himself to do it; he had never given himself wholeheartedly to anything, except once, that time with Elena, that awful weekend in which the English girl had killed herself, when he ought to have been there. (The only time he had followed his passions, he thought bitterly, they had led him terribly astray.)

His mother had known, but she had never spoken to him about it. She had carried this secret knowledge around with her, in fortitude and silence. Elena had never known it: she had merely assumed that he had been born like that – heartless. Of course, he had made love to her, if you could call it that, because she had expected it, because he felt it was what one expected of a man; but it had been with regret that he had abandoned his hitherto perfect remoteness. He had made an effort to be like other men, he suspected, an effort that had terrified him. For always, he had been walking at the edge of a cliff from which he might fall to his death at any minute. Others did not have this constant nightmare. Fritz didn't. Fritz was able to be happy.

He thought of Fritz; of all the people in the world, Fritz was the only one who had never looked at him with disapproval, as his mother had done, or expected things of him, as Elena did. All the terrible things dated from the day of Fritz's departure to San Cristobal. Terrible things had happened to him, for he would carry round in his mind forever the images of Caballero, the only man he had ever killed, and of Nicola Nickleby, the girl whose life he could so easily have saved. The latter was a sin of omission, the former of commission. And both crimes had been committed for Elena's sake. How he wished now that he had never met her, that he had never grown up; and he was shocked at the disloyalty of his thoughts.

But he did blame her: if she had not told Caballero those things over the telephone; if she hadn't tempted him into going away for the weekend – he overlooked the fact that he had wanted to go, just as he had wanted to kill Caballero – if she had not done that, he would not be here now. And he blamed the Junta and Olivarez. They had used him. They had told him lies. Of course, all Government propaganda was lies deep down; he had always known that. But Olivarez had told him a lie about himself: that he was a good soldier, a man who did his duty, when, all the time, he had been just as bad and as good as Strauss, the man they had hanged. The more he pondered it, the more did he realise that the Army was yet another story that when you grew up you found was not true. It was a lie invented by adults, that left those who had believed it orphans.

The grey dawn would come; Roberto would lie on the bed and watch Tanucci washing at the basin; he himself had long given up washing. Tanucci would stand there shirtless and dutiful – for Army rules and regulations had all sorts of stipulations under the titles of Health and Hygiene. Roberto would notice the two things that the young man had on round his neck. One was a medallion of St Michael, the other was his identification tag, that unpleasant piece of metal which, the moment you were dead, would be broken in half: one part to be left in your mouth, the other to be given to some dry Government official who would enter you into a ledger of the dead, a bureaucratic recording Angel.

'Do you think about Strauss?' he said, thus reminded of death. (Had they put the tag in Strauss's dead mouth, shut the jaws, and broken it in half? Had he counted as fallen in battle?)

'Yes, sir,' said Tanucci slowly. 'But not only about him. About the others too.'

'I suppose this,' said Roberto on reflection, 'is what they used to call being in a state of mortal sin.'

And he thought of Lady Macbeth, and Mephistopheles, both parts that he had played in school plays; and he knew that Tanucci, being Italian, did not suffer what he suffered; for he had been brought up to believe that both the Spaniards and the Scots were introspective and gloomy races.

But Tanucci did suffer; in the afternoon, while the other officers were busy, while the Captain was reading a novel lying on his bed, and Hoffmann was developing photographs, and the Chaplain was reading Aquinas, Tanucci would walk up and down outside the huts watching the men play football, never stopping, because the ground was cold underfoot. Tanucci was not yet twenty, but he was troubled by thoughts of death; not the death of Strauss or the others, those they had killed, but the death that mattered most to him, his own death. He felt that he did not deserve to be alive, for he had now grasped the reality of the life he had been living. He had come face to face with what could only be explained by the category 'mortal sin'. The mortal sins of Army life had undone them both. He and the Captain were both disfigured men.

He wondered sometimes where his own sin had begun. Perhaps it had started when he had first caught Olivarez's eye, and given in to that temptation; from there all other things had led. For once he had told himself that you could not refuse the Colonel his will, everything else followed. He had become Olivarez's man; he had been passed onto Strauss, and he had ended up assisting at the death of Nicola Nickleby. Yet that had been his fault, and how easily that fault had come to him. He ought, he knew, to be dead, just as Strauss was; but he wasn't dead; he was alive, though he did not deserve to be. Somehow or other he had to live the rest of his life in a way that would atone for his sin, in a way that would make him more worthy to be alive. The forgiveness he had received from the Chaplain when he had confessed to being an accomplice to murder, and more particularly the penance he had received, were not enough. You could not wipe out the consciousness of murder by reciting the Rosary; he had tried; you had to do something that involved your entire life. As he walked up and down by the football pitch, he realised that his life was turning in a way that was not of his own volition.

Inside the hut, Roberto was lying on his bed reading *Ivanhoe*, a book he had first read many years ago and which, like Banquo's ghost, now seemed to have come back to haunt him. Literature, even when it wasn't great literature, sometimes had the ability to find one's weak spot. He found himself wondering how he could ever have enjoyed such a disturbing book, when he himself had never done a truly heroic deed in his entire life. He had never sacrificed himself for anyone or for any ideal that was true. He had spent his life following false gods. He was about to put the book down, when the radio sprang to life. He wondered why they weren't being left in peace; but he got up, put on the headphones and began to take down the message.

Later Tanucci came in. He found the Captain smoking, on his bed, nonchalantly staring into space. Another of the false gods was dead. The news of the General's passing had at last reached December Island.

Twenty-nine

News of Olivarez's execution spread over the country, bringing in its wake a trail of despair in all who heard it, which had not been what General Messina had intended at all. The body was exposed in public, in case anyone doubted it was true, but the general rejoicings that had been expected did not take place.

The very best people in the City, the Older Set, whose sons and nephews were still holed up in the Military Club, did not know what to think about it. They did not see the corpse themselves, but received reports from their servants whom they had sent in their stead. In these circumstances, Isabel de Calatrava, who was something of a barometer of public opinion, now that *The Post* was closed, resolved to be philosophical. She knew what it meant, even if the others did not.

'My dears,' she said to the little gathering in her drawing-room. 'I never really liked Mario Olivarez. Of course, he came from an excellent family, but times change and people become degenerate. I hope you don't mind me packing while you are here, do you?'

For she was leaving. The threat of war and the embarrassment of having her house-guest turn into an international incident were driving her away. The British Ambassador had graciously agreed to pay for a truck that she had borrowed from the Military. They were to have half each. And dear kind Maria Enriquez was lending her some storage space for what Isabel had described as 'a few little things' in the huge house she had at Torre del Mar. The dog's disposal had been something of a problem; much as she was accustomed to getting the best out of people, Isabel had not yet found someone to take the unpleasant little animal. Sir Nigel had refused to let her send the poor thing to England via the diplomatic bag. She was glad to go. The fate of Nicola Nickleby was haunting her. Father Morisco had reproached her for this of late.

'Ah,' said Isabel with a little sigh, 'Who knows when I'll see all these things again?'

Five or six really close friends had gathered in her sitting-room. They had heard she was going, and had come to say goodbye.

'They say he was killed while trying to escape,' said one, still on the subject of Olivarez.

'I heard it was suicide,' said another. 'They say he was caught with a young man.'

'I am so glad none of us ever liked him,' said a third. 'And now those young men in the Military Club will have to give up, won't they? My own house is so uncomfortably close to the Club, I don't know what I'll do if . . .'

'Will they give up?' asked Isabel, carefully watching one of her maids wrapping up the china. 'I don't think they will.'

'They say Olivarez was insatiable when it came to young men,' began another lady, who found this part of the case particularly fascinating, never having been aware of the phenomenon until now, despite a long acquaintance with General Hernandez.

'Quiet my dear,' said Isabel. 'There's one of his young men in the kitchen right now, and he's terribly upset about the whole thing. He's having a cup of tea; I'm going to ask him to drive my truck to the country.'

'Oh Isabel, you do manage to get the best out of people,' a friend observed a touch enviously. (No one had offered to drive her things to the country, let alone lend her a truck.) 'I wish I had your luck.'

'People like doing me favours,' said Isabel. 'They do so out of gratitude.'

She turned her attention to the crystal, which had started to rattle on the sideboard. Somewhere not very far away, tanks were beginning to move towards the Military Club.

The Archbishop had come to make one last call at the Palace.

'You have made a terrible mistake,' he told both Generals. 'Those who live by the sword die by the sword.'

'Quite,' said Hernandez. 'That sums up Olivarez.'

'He got his just reward, Your Grace,' said Messina.

'General Messina only did what he thought was right,' said Hernandez loyally.

In the background they could hear the roar of gunfire. The civil war was beginning. Don Alvaro turned and left, filled with grief.

The gunfire had come from the Military Club, where the rebels, growing bored, had decided to open fire on the enemy, as they now called the men who had been comrades in arms only yesterday. The murder of Olivarez had changed everything and the knowledge that he was dead, far from making them think of giving up, had made them reckless. The Generals, they were sure, would do no less to them: thus, they had nothing to lose. So they fired into the surrounding streets, which had no other effect than frightening the civilian population that lived in the immediate area, and bringing Isabel's little gathering to a premature conclusion.

Maria Enriquez also heard the sound. She now rather wished that she had asked for a lift in Isabel's truck, which was going, after all, to what was her house. But she had not thought the situation was that serious. Throughout the day she had been hoping that the shops, which had been shut since the General had died, would reopen, and that things would return to normal. But the sound of the gunfire was enough to convince her that things would not return to normal ever again.

After the initial burst was over she went out on to the balcony to see what was happening. Her car, she noticed once again, was not there. It had been stolen the night before. At the end of her street she could see tanks in motion. It really was time to act. She knew where the Garcias lived. She would go to them. Of course, she did not know them at all, but that was what Roberto would expect her to do. She would have to walk too, and she had better leave as soon as possible, before the streets became impossible. So she went into her bedroom, and gathered the few bits of jewellery she still had, and then put them with the silver into a plastic carrier bag. She looked around the flat and considered if there was anything else that she could easily carry, that might be valuable. There was. She went into the kitchen, and emptied the meagre contents of the fridge and the cupboards into another bag. Then without looking round again, she left the flat, not locking the door.

The Garcia flat was in the southern sector of the City, about a mile away. She knew exactly where it was, having wondered many times when she would get to meet the inhabitants. Before her son had been called away – and thank God he was not here now – she had had high hopes of meeting Elena and her mother. But then Roberto had been sent to December Island, the wedding had been spoken of no more, and that had been that. But now, in this most abnormal of situations, she could very well visit them without being properly introduced. They needed each other now. The Garcias would have a car; and she herself had a huge country house, a place where they would be safe.

The streets were eerily deserted. Everyone who could, and those who lived in the centre of the City generally could, had gone. Isabel, she knew, was going to London. It seemed that Isabel had had the foresight to apply for a British passport some years previously, something she could easily do, having had two grandparents born there. Maria could not approve of that; it seemed so disloyal, to abandon your country just when it was sliding into chaos. It was not the sort of thing that Maria had been brought up to think right. Of course, God only knew what would happen to them, but skeddadling when war broke out was cowardly. She would stay, in Torre del Mar, of course – for the

City seemed to be becoming more like a war zone every moment – but she would stay all the same.

Presently she arrived at the Garcia flat, which, being further from the centre of the City than her own, had retained something of the air of normality. She rang the bell, clutching her two bags, and when the intercom sprang to life she explained who she was, and was bidden to walk up. The lift was out of order. Carrying her load, she did as she was told, reminding herself that of all inconveniences, a broken lift was probably the least she would have to face over the coming days.

Thirty

'Is zeugma a word?' asked Mrs Williams.

'Of course it is,' said Fritz. 'And dictionaries are not allowed.'

'What does it mean then?'

He told her.

Ever since yesterday, when the cadets had been given their freedom to roam the streets at will, armed to the teeth, with special powers to stop and search all civilians, Fritz had found himself at something of a loose end. The General had been dead two days now. Then had come the news of Olivarez's death, according to unsubstantiated rumour, thanks to the personal intervention of Messina himself. After that, there had been a positive snow storm of death warrants; the Generals in the Palace had condemned each one of the rebels in the Club to death; there had also been warrants out for the deaths of several others. The lists had arrived in special editions of *El Mercurio*. It had been a curious experience, reading about people you knew who happened to be under sentence of death from the Junta. One of them had been Ximenez, Fritz had noted. Another had been his old friend Roberto Enriquez. In their turn the rebels were condemning a few unco-operative men themselves. And yet, here he was, playing Scrabble with Major Williams's wife.

'Death,' he said. 'Is that the best you can do?'

'Yes,' she replied, taking up five fresh letters, an operation made difficult by the length of her nails. 'It's a double word score anyway.'

'So it is,' conceded Fritz. 'Where is the Major?'

'I told you. He's with Ximenez. They are trying to work out what they ought to do next. He won't be back for hours.'

'Good luck to them,' said Fritz, failing to pick up the veiled hint contained in her information. 'They have got us into a terrible mess, and they had better get us out of it. Now that Olivarez is dead, I don't quite see what they can do. I mean, you could hardly use the garrison here to march on the capital, could you? It would be a joke.'

'They say,' said Mrs Williams, 'that the Generals are desperate. You see, all the best officers are on our side.'

'Our side,' said Fritz. 'Since when was it our side? I am neutral. You won't catch me joining in.'

'What about your friend Zondadari?' she asked. 'Ximenez was telling me that according to the latest reports, the position of the Club is pretty bad . . .'

'What else has Ximenez been telling you, my dear?' asked Fritz curiously.

'He is my nephew,' she said defensively. 'He can tell me things if he wants to. Go on, it's your turn.'

But Fritz wasn't paying attention to the game.

'What is Ximenez up to?' he asked her. 'Why don't you tell me?'

She looked at him. There was something so appealing about him. No man had ever wasted an afternoon in her company playing Scrabble before. She could not refuse him.

'You mustn't tell them that I told you,' she said. 'But Ximenez has got it all planned. The original plan was that Olivarez was to be President; but now they have killed Olivarez, so that means that when all this confusion is over, Ximenez himself is going to be President of the new Junta. The Major is going to be the Minister of the Interior or something like that; and then he is going to fill the Junta with people he can control. Of course, he doesn't want to have anything to do with Zondadari, because Zondadari is full of stupid ideas, but he may have to have him. And then to counter Zondadari, he has decided to have Enriquez there as well.'

'Roberto Enriquez?'

'Yes. I know you know him, and so does Ximenez. You see, Enriquez is supposed to dislike Zondadari, how they know that, I don't know, but that will put Zondadari in a permanent minority on the new Junta. And of course, the other thing is – they were here discussing it last night – they think that Enriquez himself won't be any problem, and that they will be able to control him very easily. You see, that was why they kept you alive . . .'

Fritz lay back in his chair and thought. He was beginning to see the machinations of Ximenez more clearly.

'Roberto won't stand any nonsense from your nephew and your husband, my dear. He's far too, well, stand-offish.'

'Quite. They said he has a terrible reputation for being arrogant and withdrawn. A man like that is hardly likely to descend to the level of my nephew, is he? Ximenez will have a free hand. And Enriquez is just the man to give the new Junta an air of respectability. And on top of that the Generals seem to have condemned him to death, so he's got to join our side anyway . . .'

'I don't understand how I come in.'

'They know that you are his oldest friend and that you will necessarily be under his protection, should anything happen to you. You'd sort of be his weak point, wouldn't you?'

'But Roberto is on December Island.'

'They'll bring him back,' said Mrs Williams. 'And soon.'

'If I had any sense I would desert at once,' said Fritz. 'I don't like these games.'

'They've thought of that too,' said Mrs Williams archly. 'That's why you're playing Scrabble with me; and that's why there are men outside.'

Fritz sighed a little crossly. He too had noticed that he had been followed on his way there. He looked at his letters. He looked at the board. Then he picked up all his letters and formed a word.

'Disaster,' he read, once he had done so. 'I've used your D. You'll like Roberto when you meet him. He's never arrogant with me, I'm glad to say. I will be glad to see him.'

Tanucci was having a nightmare. He was dreaming that someone was digging up the cellars of the Army Navigational School. A vivid image of naked and rotting bodies came before him. He recognised one of them, and shivered. It was the girl. His body began to shake violently.

'Wake up,' said Roberto, shaking him. 'Wake up. There's been another message. Olivarez has been executed. They are sending a ship out here to get us.'

Captain Enriquez was standing over his bed.

'What ship?' asked Tanucci.

'The Navy have a ship nearby, it seems, and they will be here about noon.'

Tanucci looked at his watch. It was four o'clock in the morning.

'Did you say that Olivarez was dead?' he asked. 'How?'

'The Generals had him executed for treason and other things. It seems that in some parts of the country there's been a coup. And there seems to be a civil war on too. That's why they're coming to get us. They expect us to go and fight.'

Tanucci lay on his back and contemplated the ceiling.

'Fight?' he said. 'Who for? Not Olivarez?'

'Yes, for Olivarez.'

'Do we have a choice?'

'No. The only alternative is to be shot by the rebels. And if the Generals got hold of us they'll probably hang us. So either we fight or we're shot or we're hanged. That is the choice.'

'I think I'd prefer to be shot, sir,' said Tanucci.

'Anyway, get up, and we'll work out what we are going to tell the men.'

Roberto left the room and strode out into the icy Antarctic air. The sun was not yet up, but the grey dawn was not far off. A strange sort of energy had gripped him ever since he had got the message from San Cristobal. He had his instructions now, and the time of uncertainty was over. December Island, they had told him, was to be abandoned. They were ordered home. There was a war on. Olivarez, like Caesar's ghost, was ranging for revenge. The Army had split in two and the first blood had been spilt already.

In a way that he could not fathom this excited him. He had been a soldier for ten years. He had been trained for war. He had learned how to fire guns, how to ride a horse, and he had picked up the rudiments of strategy from outdated textbooks. That had all been theory; but now the time for practice had arrived. He would soon stand in the open and fire at the enemy – the enemy would fire back – and some men would be killed. Perhaps he himself would be among the dead. That did not seem important; even the fear of death that was present in every man seemed then like an anticipation of the great consummation of warfare. He had been imprisoned by the images of his past misdeeds for too long. But now those images could be exorcised by the coming battle.

'You can't mean it, sir, that there's a war on,' said Tanucci, putting his head out of the hut.

'I am serious,' he said almost exultantly, feeling a thrill of pleasure at the Lieutenant's discomfort with the idea. 'They gave me details over the radio. This is a war: in San Cristobal they have executed that awful Colonel Whatshisname. And the same has happened in other places too. And they say the Generals are waiting to hang some of our men, and that they have used tanks against the Military Club. Think of that – a tank battle in the middle of the City.'

'Oh God,' said Tanucci.

Roberto stubbed out the cigarette he had been smoking and said: 'Try and get some hot water going, will you? I'll need to shave.'

'Yes, sir,' said Tanucci and disappeared.

'I think we'll be going to San Cristobal,' said Roberto a few minutes later. 'That means I will see Fritz again.'

'Who is he, sir?' asked Tanucci, who was employed now in cutting off as much of Roberto's beard as he could with a pair of scissors.

'A friend of mine,' said Roberto. 'He's called Captain José Maria Rodriguez.' He was silent a moment. 'Fritz,' he said with deliberation, 'is the last man, now that the General is dead, who actually believes in the Army.'

'What do you mean, sir?' asked Tanucci, in the way barbers always did.

'He is an idealist. He believes in bravery, kindness, all those sorts of things. Protecting the weak, sparing the vanquished, conquering the proud. He reads Latin for pleasure too. He actually believes that there is something called heroism. I suppose that is why I like him.'

'If there is no heroism, sir, what are we doing here?'

'Shut up and concentrate on what you are doing,' said Roberto.

'Yes, sir,' replied Tanucci.

As the Lieutenant snipped away at his beard, Roberto wondered if he had some sort of death wish. Here he was, impatient to join in a war, to fight for ideals he knew were hollow, and in the cause of a man, Olivarez, whom he had never liked when alive and whom he was now glad to hear was dead. But what else was there? What indeed where they doing there? It was no longer possible to believe the old myths about heroism. He had seen where that led. Heroism, attention to duty, had led him to kill Caballero and Nickleby. Those deaths were his fault. That was what true human nature was. All the noble sentiments were camouflage; and he felt that the tenuous feelings he had had for Elena were fast dissolving. He didn't love her; he couldn't. Love no longer made sense.

'Have you ever been in love?' he asked Tanucci, who was now preparing to shave him with a cut-throat razor.

'No, sir,' said Tanucci.

'It's a mirage,' he said.

Tanucci did not reply. He did not want to be told to shut up again. The Captain was a little bit mad this morning. And the Captain was wrong. Love was not a mirage; he knew that, even though he had never been in love, in fact because he had never been in love. What so many called love was not love at all. None of his own experiences had been love. Love was the one thing that separated man from the animals. If I could do one good deed, one thing that was a deed of love, thought Tanucci, perhaps then I could redeem myself. For there was something good in every man; there had to be, for how else could one think, or feel guilty, or feel that you had failed, if it wasn't for the fact that you knew that somewhere there existed something that was pure goodness?

Roberto's thoughts were moving in a different direction. By this time next week, he thought, I could be dead. One bullet, or one bomb, or one grenade, would be enough. He wondered about the pain. They said, he now remembered, that being shot was relatively painless. You never heard the bullet that killed you; it travelled faster than sound; you were simply overtaken by oblivion. If you were hit but not killed, then you would feel it. But they said that the pain was not immediate: there were stories of shot men wandering around for some minutes, wondering what had hit them. How odd, he thought; how like his own military life. Here he was, being shaved, and later he would be packing his kit, cleaning his pistol and performing all the other neglected duties once again. And yet he had been hit by something he could not quite place. How little thought he had given to his life up to now; and now that life might soon be over. Death was a real possibility. Men were already dead, if there had indeed been a tank battle in the centre of the City.

So far the fighting around the Club had been more like a game than anything else. All the windows in the building had been smashed by bullets, but the weather was hot, so that didn't matter. The staff had deserted under the cover of darkness, but the officers had been able to help themselves from the well stocked bar and kitchens. Then the tanks had suddenly arrived, injecting a note of seriousness into the atmosphere. But the rebel officers had soon been restored to good humour by the spectacle of the enemy making fools of themselves.

The tanks had been sent to reduce the Club to a pile of rubble, but they failed in their purpose. One had exploded for no apparent reason. Another had fired its shell at a neighbouring building by mistake, which happened to be a convent of contemplative nuns; and a third had fired a shell which had failed to explode at all.

At this point Father Morisco had appeared on the scene, and persuaded the tanks to withdraw, which they had done, to the sound of cheers and jeers from the Club. And thus the first engagement of the war had been brought to an inglorious conclusion.

Spirits in the Club were high. Zondadari, who, according to some, was only worthy of note because his name appeared bottom of every alphabetical list, found himself the hero of the hour. He had won a battle, and he was the undisputed leader. And even if the food would soon run out, and there was no electricity, and their only water was now mineral water, they did not allow this to dent their spirits. The City outside was now deserted; it belonged to them, if it belonged to anyone at all. They were like schoolboys who had woken up one morning to find that the adults who habitually oppressed them vanished like smoke. The Generals might be in their Palace, but they were out of sight; the only people they could see were a bunch of inexperienced Engineers whom the Generals had sent to occupy the neighbouring buildings. They did not think much of them. Besides, help would soon be on its way. Their friends in the south of the country would soon march to their rescue. It was true that General Messina was marshalling his troops as well, but old men did things slowly; and if the tanks and the

Engineers were anything to go by, there was little to be feared from Hernandez and Messina.

In these circumstances there was little to do except drink too much and shoot at the enemy over the road. There could be little compunction in using the Engineers as target practice; the Engineers were rather a common regiment, and not allowed to join the Military Club. They were also rather stupid. Every now and then one of them would poke his head up over a window sill; and if one were on the watch and could aim straight, it wasn't hard to make sure that that Engineer in particular would never make the same mistake twice.

'Fratricide,' said Father Morisco, when they told him of the deaths.

His was a solitary voice.

Tanucci stood in his underwear in the middle of the hut. It was the type of underwear that covered the entire body, and was perfectly warm, even on December Island. The Captain had gone to wake up the men and explain what was happening to them. Tanucci had been left to sort out their personal equipment. Around him were ranged all the things he ought to pack. This was all he in fact possessed, and it could all be forced into one kitbag if necessary. He didn't count the few things he had in his parents' house as his any more. He wondered about his parents, and his sisters and brothers. He hoped they would be safe. Of course, they didn't live near the centre of the City. The Captain's mother did; the Captain, as everyone knew, came from a grand family. The upper classes were very odd, though. They spoke English to each other and they didn't seem to care about each other in the way normal people did. The Captain did not seem to be at all worried about his mother's safety. And the Captain also had this girlfriend in the City, Tanucci knew that too. (He and Strauss had used to discuss the Captain's private life together – not a very profitable activity, as details were very sparse, and speculation never could get very far with so little to go on. The Captain always remained a mystery.)

Tanucci began to sort out his uniform, and put on the trousers and tunic that he was going to wear for the journey to the mainland. He wondered what they would find at San Cristobal, and he wondered how this particular military adventure would end. Around his neck he still wore the medallion of St Michael the Archangel, along with the military identification tag; and as long as he kept the former on, the latter, he hoped, would never be taken off. Perhaps his life would be spared after all, if the magic of religion could protect him. He had always been superstitious. Of course he believed in God, but the God he believed in was someone he was accustomed to bargain with. It was now time perhaps for a new bargain. If he was spared, and if he was given the grace to be brave – and he felt he needed that – then – what then? What could he do? He considered a moment, and then he made his resolution. He would do whatever God wanted him to do. He would look for a sign; and he had the type of faith, or superstition, or whatever it was, to believe that a sign would be given to him.

From the next hut he could hear cheering. So the men had been told. How odd it was that they could cheer at the news that they were going to fight in a war. But that was what soldiers were for, after all. It was death or glory, or sometimes both together. Of course, Hoffmann would be disappointed to leave the penguins; but there were some things that could not be helped. The Captain came in.

'The men are excited,' he said. 'Fools – but what can one expect?'

War, reflected Tanucci, brought out the worst in people. And it seemed to have brought out the very worst in the Captain. There he stood, shaven and washed for the first time in a month looking impatient, his hand more or less itching to touch his Beretta, dying to use it on someone. Tanucci had never liked him less than he did now.

The ship arrived at noon, and Roberto went on board at once, leaving Tanucci to see to the loading of the men and equipment, along with the NCOs. He was impatient to be gone. It was the same ship that had brought them to December Island in the first place. Aboard was a tall lugubrious officer in a Major's uniform, who introduced himself as Williams. He was about fifty, seemed older, and was clearly a martyr to sea-sickness.

'They sent me to get you,' he said. 'I am instructed to shoot you if you don't co-operate, but I hope that won't be necessary,' he added glumly.

'It won't be,' said Roberto.

'Good, good,' said Williams. 'I knew your father slightly, years ago. Fine man. Can't think why I haven't met you before now. I suppose the fact that I've spent the last twenty years stuck in San Cristobal must be the reason. I suppose you'd like me to explain the situation to you?'

'Yes, I would,' said Roberto.

They went into a cabin, and Williams unrolled a map.

'Now,' he said, pointing with an authoritative finger. 'This is a map of our Republic. There's the City and there is San Cristobal, and that is the distance between them, about a hundred and seventy miles. God alone knows what that is in kilometres. Now the situation is as follows. A certain Captain Zondadari seems to be in charge of the Military Club in the City – there – with about a hundred men under him, all officers, of course. That means, in effect, that the entire City is neutralised until Messina and Hernandez can smoke them out. Quite why they haven't done so as yet is rather beyond me, I am afraid. They are obviously having awful problems getting their act together. So, incidentally, are we. That is where I come in. I, in case you haven't heard, am supposed to be a brilliant organiser. Until last week I used to run a company that supplied agricultural machinery. But that is another story. Anyway, I suppose we will get our act together, and when we do so, we are going to march on the City, save Zondadari and his men, who may well need saving by then, and throw out the Generals. And that, as they say, will be that. You see, here, here and here,' he said, stabbing various points of the map with his finger, 'the garrisons are all ours. We just have to weld them together and we've got an Army.'

Major Williams ended his briefing with a hollow laugh.

Roberto studied the map.

'Any questions?' asked Williams.

'We have four garrisons?'

'Yes, four in all. All, except San Cristobal, in dreadful shape. San Cristobal is in the hands of a good man. At all the others things have got out of hand; there doesn't seem to be anyone in charge at any of them higher in rank than a lieutenant. That is where you come in. You can help lick some of them into shape. Everyone knows that you are a good soldier. Your reputation has gone before you.'

'Am I? A good soldier?'

'Yes. That is why Ximenez sent me to get you. I don't think for a moment he wanted to have you shot. You're too valuable. You see,' said Williams, becoming suddenly confidential, 'we need some English organisation round here' – he stabbed the map again – 'if we are ever going to get here.' And his finger rested on the Capital.

'I don't know Ximenez,' said Roberto. 'But I have heard of him.'

'He's my nephew, actually. He's tough and he knows what he wants and he knows how to get it. That's why we have had very little disorder in San Cristobal, at least so far. What we don't know much about is Zondadari. He is something of an unknown quantity: sprung from nowhere, and between you and me, he may be something of an embarrassment to us later on. In fact we have no intention of getting to the Capital and then having Zondadari taking all the glory, I can tell you.'

'I follow you,' said Roberto.

'I'm sure you do,' said Williams. 'Take a look at this. It is an Army list. You'll see that I have been through it with a pen.

Men underlined in black are ours, those in red are for the Generals, and the ones I've crossed out are dead. It'll give you a good idea of how things stand.'

Roberto flicked through the list. Quite a few familiar names seemed to have been crossed out. The blacks and the reds seemed to be about equal. But many more were unmarked.

'Yes,' said Williams, in answer to his enquiry about them. 'They're the undecided. But as soon as they see that we are on the move and the Generals aren't, they will know what is good for them. Those who refuse to come with us, we shoot. There are far too many officers in this country anyway. What is your Lieutenant like?'

'There's no need to shoot him,' said Roberto.

'Just as well,' said Williams. 'And I suppose your men are the same as most of the men? They'll come with us if we can pay them?'

'That is about it,' agreed Roberto.

'Pay is rather a problem at present,' said Williams candidly. 'We are handing out promissory notes which can be cashed in when we get out hands on the banks in the City. I like to think that it gives the men a stake in victory.'

'Major,' said Roberto. 'This list would suggest that we've only got about five thousand men at most.'

'Oh, much less than that, I should think,' said Williams cheerfully. 'A lot of the men have deserted, you know, not that that does any harm. There's nothing like roving bands of deserters to put fear and panic into middle class hearts, and you don't have to pay them either. Every bit of public disorder reflects badly on the Generals. But we have the pick of the young officers, you know. The Generals are having a hard time getting their act together for that reason. Of course, the Engineers and the police and the Rifle Brigade are solidly behind the Government, but what are they without officers? Messina and Hernandez are already beaten men; they couldn't run the country, and they certainly won't be able to run a war. You'll see. I think I'd better go below now; something tells me that we are about to sail. I will see you tomorrow morning.'

Williams shuffled away. The ship was indeed about to sail, and the motion of the engines was making his stomach exceedingly uncomfortable. Roberto went on deck. There he found Tanucci.

'All present and correct?' he asked.

'Yes, sir,' replied Tanucci gloomily.

'Anyone would think you were sorry to be leaving this Godforsaken island,' said Roberto.

'I can't be sure we are going anywhere better, sir,' said Tanucci.

Roberto laughed.

'You'll cheer up when you reach land,' he said.

Thirty-one

'I thought better of Isabel,' General Hernandez was saying. 'I didn't think she would be so disloyal.'

'Indeed?' enquired Sir Nigel.

'Running away all of a sudden isn't what I expected of her at all,' continued the General dolefully. He was in a self-pitying mood.

'She'd been planning it for some time,' said Sir Nigel cruelly. 'And you did lend her a truck for her furniture and clothes, after all, didn't you, General? And her part in the Nickleby case was far from exemplary. At one point she even denied she knew the girl.'

'You simply can't trust people any more,' said Hernandez, ignoring this pointed remark. 'Besides, I always thought her clothes were frightful. God knows why she had to have them taken to a place of greater safety by truck. Some of our own men could have used that truck. And now there's this!'

'This' was the reason for Sir Nigel being summoned to the Palace. He had been called to explain why the British Government had frozen the Republic's assets in London. He had had a difficult journey to get there, as the entire centre of the City was closed, thanks to the rebels in the Club. But Hernandez had called him all the same, as he had had an inspiration. He was, after all, still Minister for Foreign Affairs. And he was convinced that he would be able to get the British Government to see that right was on the side of the Generals.

'Yes, it is very bad,' said Sir Nigel, resolving to be sympathetic; after all, sympathy was free.

'Bad isn't the word,' said General Hernandez. 'It is much worse than that. The rebels in the Club have now shot over a dozen of our men. Most of them were Engineers; and two at least have been policemen. They've murdered two policemen. Tell that to your Government. You English love policemen, I know. I am sure they will be sympathetic.'

'It certainly is very sad,' said Sir Nigel. 'But why on earth did you send the police and then the Engineers to besiege the Club? They're not meant for that sort of thing, are they?'

'Messina couldn't find anyone else. They were the only troops in the City at the time. One of the boys was only eighteen, for goodness sake.'

'My Government,' said Sir Nigel, delicately feeling his way to saying what was on his mind, 'is still very concerned – and that is putting it mildly – about the disappearance of Miss Nickleby. She was only eighteen.'

Hernandez sighed. He had been afraid they were going to have to go over this again.

'Olivarez is dead,' he said. 'What more could you want? And the man Strauss has been hanged. We have told you all that. What more could you ask for? Very well, we have condemned several more men to death *in absentia*. They will suffer for it, you'll see. Let's see, Captain Enriquez: if you want him shot, then that will be done. It seems he was mixed up in it, you say?'

'We don't as yet have a clear picture,' admitted Sir Nigel. 'The only witness to the kidnapping is rather unreliable.'

'Enriquez has joined the rebels; so whatever happens, we will have him shot as soon as we get hold of him. I hope that will satisfy you. If it wasn't for the fact that she's the widow of a highly respectable officer, I'd have his mother clapped in irons, if that would please you. Believe me, we have done all we can. Tell your Government that.'

'I'm sure you've done your best,' said Sir Nigel soothingly. 'But there are all sorts of details that people are asking about in England. They want to know who authorised the kidnapping of Nicola Nickleby, and why this sort of thing was going on.

They are outraged by your Government's suggestion that Miss Nickleby eloped with an officer or some other man. Apparently the girl was a virgin –'

'We don't have to explain our domestic policy to foreigners,' said Hernandez crossly. 'Besides Olivarez is dead.'

'I know. But they also want to be able to reconstruct the last hours of Miss Nickleby and they want the body. Of course, you've told us that she is dead, but you haven't told us what happened to her. Was she tortured?'

'The men who know that are with the rebels,' said Hernandez. 'And as long as you go on freezing our assets, those men will be free and they will keep on shooting our policemen and Engineers. Which side is your Government on? We need to buy shells and bullets and things like that. We need our foreign reserves; we'd never have put our reserves in your banks if we had thought you would have done this to us. We thought you were our friends. Hardly any of our equipment seems to work, whatever Messina may say to the contrary. But just you wait; when we finally storm the Club or starve them into submission, we'll hang every single one of them as traitors. They're all guilty of murder.'

Sir Nigel sighed at the end of this little tirade. If only London would do the sensible thing and break off diplomatic relations, so that he could go home. But that, alas, was the one thing they showed no sign of doing. They were too interested in the Nickleby girl's case, and what would happen in this civil war. He had the awful feeling that he would never get out of this Republic alive. And he looked at Hernandez, so old, so weary, and wondered if he would either.

'There's no doubt in my mind at all,' said Hernandez, though his looks denied it, 'that we are going to win. What will your Government do then, if it finds that it has backed the wrong side?'

'But if you are going to win, my dear Don Arturo, why haven't you been able to deal with the Military Club yet? They are making you look foolish. No wonder Isabel left. No wonder everyone has gone, except the looters, of course. You should see the Embassy. It is worse than' – he faltered trying to think of a suitably awful simile to convey the desolation of the British Embassy – 'It is worse than Charterhouse ever was,' he concluded.

'The Military Club is making us look foolish,' admitted the General. 'But Messina has said that he will deal with it. You must have seen the Marine Gardens? No? Go and have a look: they are seething with troops from the north, reliable men, and as soon as we can, we'll smash the rebels. But first of all we have to square the Archbishop, and that in effect means having to deal with Morisco. The priest has been trying to negotiate a ceasefire. We can't pretend we don't want peace, and end up excommunicated, can we? But once we've got round that, we'll move. If we have to,' he added quickly. 'They may give up. They can't have much food left.'

'But if you have sentenced the whole lot of them to death, they are hardly likely to come out with their hands in the air, are they?'

'Messina doesn't think of things like that,' said Hernandez wearily. 'He doesn't think much at all, I am afraid.'

The two old men sighed. The whole thing, they realised, had become too complicated for them; but there was no stopping it now.

It was quite true that Messina did not think much. He had not the time, nor the inclination. He was far too busy. He was seeing to the Engineers and the police who were besieging the Club. He was trying to get hold of tanks, helicopters and bazookas. He was listening to men who had bright ideas about poisoning water supplies or pumping in cyanide gas. In short, General Messina was running a war. Above all he was trying his very best to make sure that his first humiliating failure with the tanks did not happen again. All the while, as if to hinder him, Father Morisco buzzed around him, like a fly. The

Archbishop sent messages, and Messina replied, professing filial respect and his abhorrence of bloodshed. But the preparations continued.

As for Zondadari and the besieged rebels, their confidence began to wane when they noticed that the Engineers had gone, and their places had been taken by other troops from the north of the country. Food had almost run out; the supply of drink was low; and as evening fell there was no electric light to cheer them, only darkness.

Don Alvaro, the Archbishop, sat in the same darkness, for his Palace depended on the same supply of electricity. He sat in his private chapel and prayed. He had been doing so almost continuously, and he would do it until the night came when the sky above the City would be illuminated with artificial fires, as it had been on the General's birthday. For the time being, Morisco's ceasefire was holding; but he knew it was only a matter of time, and time was running out.

Thirty-two

Major Williams was talking about strategy; he used the same tone that he had used to lecture his underlings on the uses of manure in his civilian days, when he had traded in all things agricultural.

'The present situation is very favourable to us,' he was saying. 'This will be a ground battle. Of course our enemies have an air force, but they won't dare use it.'

'How do you know that?' asked Captain Ximenez.

'I know that,' said the Major, looking at his nephew with less than avuncular benevolence, 'without having to find out. The Republic has planes, and the planes cost billions of escudos. They're simply too expensive to risk using: we might shoot them down, for a start; and they can't trust the pilots not to desert. So the planes will be grounded. They won't use them until it is far too late for them to make any difference, if at all.'

'Like the Kaiser's fleet,' said Fritz.

'Exactly,' said Williams. 'So there's nothing to stop us putting our men in buses and trucks and driving to the City when we are ready to do so. We could be there in about three hours. It's only a hundred and seventy miles.'

The officers who had gathered for this meeting on strategy buzzed with excitement. Only Ximenez was silent. Ximenez was thinking. And when the others – there were about twenty men present – realised that Ximenez had not joined in their enthusiasm, they fell silent too. There was something about Ximenez that made his opinion important. He frightened people. He was a dark man who never smiled; and he was, though no one had elected him, their leader. He had been the one who had planned the coup in San Cristobal, the one who had shot the Colonel. They now waited to see what he would say.

'We can't do it,' said Ximenez, having savoured the silence, and knowing what it meant. 'At least not yet. We're not organised. We shall have to wait a few days, until all our men are here. To move now would be disastrous.'

'But –' began Fritz.

'Yes?' asked Ximenez coldly, turning a freezing glare onto Fritz. He had always disliked the man, and had recently been doing some research into his background, and found things there that had confirmed his dislike. One day, Ximenez thought, he would settle with Rodriguez once and for all.

'If we wait a few days,' said Fritz, not aware of the murderous hatred he was provoking, 'by the time we arrive in the City, it may well be all over with Zondadari.'

Fritz had said what they all knew to be true. Ximenez stared at him with distaste. Williams shuffled some papers with embarrassment. There was a sudden realisation in the room that Fritz Rodriguez had made a mistake. He was too junior a man to be able to contradict Ximenez or to bear the weight of his enmity. And yet they knew that he was right. Zondadari was waiting for them, and here they were, sitting around in San Cristobal with nothing to do. Yet there was no one who dared point this out, for they all knew, except Fritz it seemed, that it would be dangerous to raise the issue. They were not the ones to stand up to Ximenez. Zondadari might very well die as a result. But no one wanted to offend Ximenez, or support Fritz; they remembered what had happened to their Colonel, and were silent.

If Captain Enriquez had been there, perhaps he would have given them a lead; perhaps then the meeting would have gone another way. But Enriquez wasn't there. He had been expected, but he had not come. The other officers were disappointed, but no one was more disappointed than Fritz. He had been relying on Roberto; for if anyone could stand up to Ximenez, it would certainly be Roberto. And people would listen to him. Roberto knew Zondadari, and he knew most of the men holed up in the Military Club. Unlike Ximenez, he would presumably not be content to stand by while they were murdered by the Generals. Enriquez had the reputation of being a good soldier, and a gentleman. He might also be regarded as slightly arrogant, but all of them there knew that he at least had something to be arrogant about. He was from a good military family, and you could trust a man with such a background. But Ximenez, despite having a name redolent of Castilian splendour, Ximenez was far too like the late Colonel Olivarez ever to be trusted. Yet, here they all were, hardly daring to raise their voices in protest against anything he might suggest. He was their leader, and they would follow him, just as they had always followed their leader in the past. Nothing was changed, and most of them felt a secret shame that it was so.

The meeting broke up, the only decision being taken was that they were to do nothing for at least another week. Fritz left in a thoughtful mood. He wondered where Roberto had got to, and felt that he knew. Surely Ximenez would not have held such an important meeting of the grandiosely titled Army Council without being sure first that his principal possible rival was out of the way. Ximenez was sly, he knew that from past experience; there were no lengths to which he would not go. But the fact was that he had thought better of Roberto. Roberto had always been a man for duty first, pleasure second. God only knew how Ximenez had got around him.

He was now standing in the main square outside the building that Ximenez was using as his headquarters. It was about four o'clock. The meeting had lasted about an hour and a half. It was typical of Ximenez, he reflected, to hold a meeting at the time of day when the smallest number of people could be expected to turn up. Most people in the Republic had lunch at two in the afternoon, after all, following the Spanish habit, and then went to lie down until five, especially in the summer.

Fritz stood there uncertain what he ought to do. Then he caught sight of a slim figure in the uniform of a lieutenant of the Engineers.

'Rodolfo,' he said.

Tanucci smiled. 'Have you seen the Captain?' he asked.

'I was going to ask you the same question,' said Fritz. 'Where is he?'

'Wasn't he at the meeting of the Army Council then? He told me that was where he would be,' said Tanucci.

'Well, he wasn't,' said Fritz. 'What else did he tell you?'

They started to walk across the large empty square that formed the centre of the town.

'He told me he was having lunch with someone called Mrs Williams,' said Tanucci.

'I don't believe it,' said Fritz.

'That's what he told me, sir,' said Tanucci.

'I'm sure he did, Rodolfo,' said Fritz. 'What I can't believe is that he has spent all this time with her. She's rather a harpy and not his cup of tea at all. Of course, I quite like her, but there again, I seem to like everyone, with a few important exceptions. Major Williams spends all his time being Quartermaster-General these days, and running around after his nephew, so he doesn't have time to care what his wife gets up to. But even so: you have only been here a day and this happens. You'll have to look after him better than that, Rodolfo.'

'Are we going to be moving soon?' asked Tanucci.

'No, we are not,' said Fritz. 'Despite the Major's brilliant powers of organisation, we are dragging our feet. If Roberto had been there, perhaps we would have been moving soon. And that is why he wasn't there. Ximenez ordered his aunt to see to that. I dare say she needed no encouragement. She's done that sort of thing before. I wonder if he's enjoyed it.'

'Army life is full of waiting around for things to happen, isn't it?'

'Things are happening. They're just not happening here, that's all.'

'I'm surprised they haven't sent the Captain out to the Provinces somewhere to help organise things. I can't think why they've kept him here.'

'They want to keep an eye on him,' said Fritz. 'This isn't going to be a democracy, you know. It is going to be a dictatorship. Just like the last lot – except there were three of them, and they weren't very efficient. Now we're going to have just one.'

'As soon as it's over I'll get discharged,' said Tanucci.

He had been in San Cristobal less than twenty-four hours, but he had already made up his mind. He had known Fritz for even less than twenty-four hours, and here he was telling him his secret thoughts. But he liked the Captain very much already, and felt the need to confide in him. He was much puzzled by the friendship that existed between Fritz and Captain Enriquez. They were such different characters; Fritz was one of the most friendly men he had ever met, and whatever one could say about Captain Enriquez, you could hardly say that he put his juniors at their ease as Fritz did.

Fritz looked at him thoughtfully: 'Lost your taste for the game, have you?' he asked.

'That's about it, sir,' he said.

'Well, let's go back to your quarters and wait for the Captain, as you call him, to turn up. You can tell me about what you plan to do when you leave the Army.'

They carried on across the square.

As Fritz had guessed, Roberto had fallen into the clutches of Mrs Williams. Roberto had accepted the invitation to lunch for the simple reason that it had been given to him by the Major; and he had been surprised when he had arrived to find the Major not there, and that he was to have a *tête-à-tête* with a woman he did not know. But once he had arrived there was nothing to be done, except get on with the business of eating. That done, he should have gone on to the meeting of the Army Council. That was supposed to be important, as Fritz had told him. But meetings bored him, and he liked to think that he was a man of action and not of words. Besides, he could not think of anything more dull than spending the afternoon listening to the opinions of a group of officers whose judgement he did not consider equal to his own. The time had passed, and Mrs Williams had done her best to entertain him, even to delay him. He began to regret that he had allowed Fritz to force a promise out of him to attend the meeting. He was feeling tired; and he had only just got back from December Island, after all. Men back from lonely tours of duty were allowed a little company of this sort, according to tradition. Her husband was safely out of the way too, which was a further consideration in favour of delay. He did not think her attractive: but she was certainly more interesting than her husband or her nephew, or a meeting of the Army Council.

When he made love to her, as he soon found himself doing, without quite knowing why, her large mouth distended itself in pleasure and assumed the aspect of a case of knives. Such an exhibition of pleasure had been a little off-putting at first, and made him wonder what he was doing there. But there was something compelling about Mrs Williams and the offer she had made to him over coffee. And when that offer had been made, there had been no going back once it had been accepted. He had felt it something of a duty to go to bed with her. For a start he did not like the Major, or her nephew, and rather hoped that if they ever found out about it, they would be suitably annoyed. He did not realise that they had given their tacit consent to the affair.

But even so, he had not spent the best part of an afternoon in bed with Mrs Williams simply because he found the Major tedious or because he was inclined to dislike Ximenez. There was more to it than that. He did not like sex – much. At least that was what he had always assumed. He did not like the complications that it could produce, the way it enslaved you to another person. Taking up Mrs Williams's kind offer was a way of showing that such personal entanglements were not a necessary part of the process. He had wondered about Elena.

He was supposed to marry her eventually. She owned him, or at least she owned part of his future. Yet sometimes he couldn't help wishing that he had never met her. Mrs Williams, did she but know it, was part of his incipient rebellion against that future.

The lady was now putting a lit cigarette into his mouth.

'There you are,' she said after she had done so, and snuggled down against his shoulder.

'Thank you,' he said.

He could hardly call her Mrs Williams, so he called her nothing at all. She smiled up at him, toothily. With the fingers of one hand, adorned with brightly coloured nails, she played with the hair on his chest. He was certainly a very good-looking man, though she much preferred his friend Fritz; but Fritz was only interested in playing Scrabble, as far as she could tell. And even though she had found the Captain rather unresponsive to her passion, and surprisingly inexperienced, she was content with what she had. He for his part wondered what she might be expecting further of him; he felt a little awkward lying there in an unfamiliar bed with a complete stranger, as he was unfamiliar with the etiquette of the situation. He did not want to be rude, but he wondered when he could decently make his excuses and leave.

'When will the Major be back?' he asked.

'Not before six,' she replied.

A clock by the bedside told him that it was only four.

'There's a meeting of the Army Council,' he said.

'Quite,' she said. 'That started at half past two. You could hardly turn up to it now.'

There was no arguing with that, thought Roberto. He sighed. He supposed that this was the type of behaviour that some women expected from men. There was a war on, or rather there soon would be, as soon as they left the stifling boredom of San Cristobal. This sort of activity was supposed to be the affirmation of life in the face of death. Or perhaps it was just Mrs Williams's way of helping the war effort. Only it was meant to be pleasurable, and here he was, wishing he could finish his cigarette in peace and be allowed to go back to his barracks. He wondered if she would let him have a bath, if he asked her. Or would she misinterpret that request? He looked at her red-nailed hand a little uncertainly.

'You're so handsome,' said Mrs Williams, with a fine display of teeth.

He knew he could not get away now. It was in fact not until it was five that he was finally able to make his escape, refusing the offer of tea; he found himself out of the house and in the dull streets of San Cristobal. How anyone could live in such a place was beyond him. He hadn't been there long, but he was already bored to death by the sight of the town. God knew what Fritz had found to do in his spare time over the last few months. As for himself, there was nothing to do except to go back to barracks. He was feeling a little uncomfortable in his uniform and he needed to wash.

It was only when he walked along the road towards the barracks, intent on a shower, that he realised that he had not blushed once during the whole afternoon, nor had he even feared at any point that he might. Whatever he had done with Mrs Williams, he had certainly not made love. He had been quite unmoved throughout. Thus encouraged, he went into his rooms.

'Hello, Fritz,' he said, as soon as he got there, for Fritz was sitting at his desk.

'We found a bottle of whiskey,' said Fritz. 'Is it yours? Do have some too.'

'Certainly,' said Roberto. 'I'll wash first though, if you don't mind.'

And he went through to the bedroom. (His quarters were much better than Fritz's which were on the other side of the town, a reflection perhaps of Roberto's importance and Fritz's relative insignificance. Roberto had two rooms, a study and a bedroom, and a private bathroom. Rodolfo Tanucci was sleeping on a camp bed in the study and acting as a sort of batman.) Presently the sound of water was heard from the bathroom.

'So you see,' said Fritz, turning back to Rodolfo. 'Trasimene showed that numbers aren't necessarily the deciding factor in a battle, and that a very few men strategically placed can defeat a much larger army. And as for Cannae, that is still the best example of a pincer movement in history.'

'Well, of course I can see that, Fritz,' said Rodolfo, forgetting to call him 'sir'. 'But Hannibal still didn't win the war, despite all his brilliance, did he?'

'Overextended supply lines,' said Fritz. 'Fault of men like Major Williams. And he had no Navy. The Romans beat him because they were better organised: a bit like the Hare and the Tortoise, I suppose. Rather sad, though. I always wanted Hannibal to win. But I always pick losers; Prince Rupert of the Rhine is another example – strategy doesn't have a very good track record, but no one has ever won without it, you know.'

Fritz stared into his whiskey. He had drunk just enough to make him aware that he was beginning to talk nonsense. He heard the running water from the bathroom; and it reminded him of the eternal note of sadness. He wondered now what had happened between Roberto and the Harpy. He had seemed quite cheerful when he had come in. Had they played Scrabble all afternoon? But Roberto had never been one for games. If so, was Roberto suffering a certain *tristesse*?

'I wonder how Bobby is feeling?' he said.

'Who?'

'Your Captain. That was his name at school.'

'I've never heard anyone call him that,' said Rodolfo.

'I think I'm the only one left who does,' said Fritz. 'I'll take him a drink.'

Fritz took up a glass, poured in some whiskey, and went into the bathroom. Roberto was still in the shower.

'How was lunch?' he called.

'Awful,' he shouted back over the sound of the water. It had been awful, and he always told Fritz the truth.

'I suppose it would have been,' said Fritz knowledgeably. 'I've eaten there too, you know. You'd think the Major, being our new Quartermaster-General, or whatever he calls himself, would be able to get in a few supplies, wouldn't you?'

Roberto stepped out of the shower, clad in a towel.

'Just turn round a moment, Bobby,' said Fritz. 'You've got a nasty scratch on your back.'

Roberto turned round; and Fritz, dipping his finger in the whiskey, disinfected the wound. It made Roberto wince slightly.

'Nasty,' said Fritz as he performed the operation. 'How did it happen?'

'I can't think,' said Roberto. 'I wouldn't have noticed it unless you'd seen it.'

Yet they were both thinking of Mrs Williams's long red nails. And Fritz knew then that there had always been things that Roberto had liked to keep secret, even from the best of friends. Even so, he hadn't expected this of Roberto. Adultery had never seemed to be his scene before now. In fact Fritz had always assumed, despite his friendship with Elena, that that sort of thing was something of a blank page in Roberto's life. He wondered if Mrs Williams's teeth had done any damage. But Roberto was quickly putting on his dressing gown. Fritz could hardly blame him; if he himself had just made love to Mrs Williams, he too might feel a little shy as a result.

'What have you been talking to Tanucci about?' Roberto was asking.

'Strategy. Hannibal. Napoleon. Religion,' replied Fritz, giving Roberto his glass.

'How mysterious,' said Roberto. 'You always seem to get friendly with people. You seem to have got more out of him than I have in months. You put me to shame.'

'Good,' said Fritz. 'You missed the Army Council meeting, you know. Or had you forgotten?'

'You'll have to tell me all about it,' said Roberto.

They went back into the study. Tanucci was still there. Roberto wondered whether he ought to tell Tanucci to leave them for a while. He supposed he ought to do it politely. He was always having to be polite to people, and he rather resented it.

'I want Tanucci to hear it too,' said Fritz, reading his thoughts. 'I think that sooner or later I am going to need a mathematician, and he's the only one I know for miles around. And he knows things in metres, don't you, Rodolfo? I know things in feet, which is quite a handicap.'

'Is it?' asked Roberto. 'And why are we going to discuss mathematics?'

'We're not exactly going to discuss mathematics, much as I would like to, as such,' said Fritz. 'The real point is Zondadari. I happen to know him fairly well. He is a brave man, a good soldier, quite a lot of people admire him, and he's one of the few completely honest people I know. He is about thirty-five – but you know all that, don't you? The point is, so does Ximenez. Now when all this is over, who is going to come out on top? Is it going tc be Zondadari, or is is going to be Ximenez? Which would be the most popular choice?'

'Zondadari, I suppose,' said Roberto a little uncertainly.

'Of course,' said Fritz. 'He may well be the next President of the Republic.'

'Isn't he too young?' asked Rodolfo.

'Youth is in his favour. There's hardly anyone over forty who would do, when you come to think of it. Virtually anyone over forty has either emigrated, or been put out of the way, or is hopelessly involved with the Generals. It might well have been Olivarez, of course. But Olivarez is dead, and I don't think he had much of a clue about running the country, any more than General Messina has of being Minister of the Interior. Olivarez was an Army man, and you can't treat a country like a recalcitrant platoon, can you? But Zondadari is a man who thinks, who would get advice; a man who would sort things out. And after a few years of military rule, he would probably call elections, and almost certainly win them. That is why Ximenez hates Zondadari and wants him dead. He has no intention of letting the fruits of his labours slip from his grasp, not after he went and organised the coup down here almost singlehandedly. He didn't shoot our Colonel in his office so that Zondadari could become president. That is why Ximenez and Williams are dragging their feet, and we won't leave for the Capital until it is far too late, until in fact the Military Club is a pile of ruins and Zondadari is dead.'

'Is that what happened at the meeting?'

'In substance, yes.'

'And did no one object?'

'I did, but no one supported me. There was no one there who could have got the silent majority to vote Ximenez down or do whatever it takes to stop him. I think I made a fatal mistake as it was, opening my mouth as I did. I am probably a marked man. As for Williams, he is entirely at his nephew's beck and call, and when the war is over, I am sure they plan to run the country between them. Think of that.'

'Is Ximenez so very bad?' asked Roberto suddenly.

'Remember that he shot the colonel of this garrison himself,' said Fritz.

'They say he was Olivarez's special man, sir,' said Tanucci thoughtfully.

'And that makes people afraid,' said Fritz. 'There were all sorts of tales of torture and death floating around here, and they all led back to him. I don't suppose you heard about it in the City, but here people were frightened.'

'These things happen,' said Roberto rather lifelessly, and reaching for his cigarettes. 'The whole country is full of these rumours, I am sure. I can't think that Ximenez is so very evil a character.'

'For God's sake,' said Fritz. 'Just look at him.'

'His appearance is against him,' agreed Roberto. 'But being evil isn't anything to do with appearances, is it, Tanucci? Once you commit a crime, your face doesn't change, does it?'

'No, sir,' said Tanucci, agreeing without enthusiasm.

'What we've got to remember,' said Roberto, speaking with deliberation, 'is that there is a war on. As you know, Fritz, the men we have here are in no shape at all. They need a firm hand, and if they're frightened of Ximenez, that may well be so much the better. I couldn't dislike Ximenez more than you do, and I certainly wouldn't trust him an inch, but a man like that serves his purpose in wartime. War is a nasty business; it's much more than diagrams on a board, you know, Fritz.'

'Of course I know that,' said Fritz, raising his voice a little. 'But now that a war has started, it is our job to get it over with as quickly as possible; and I certainly don't want to see thousands of lives lost or endangered just so Ximenez and Williams can move into the Presidential Palace.'

'I can't see why you dislike him so much, Fritz; especially when you're supposed to like everyone.'

'I like Zondadari and most of the men in the Club,' said Fritz, growing heated. 'And I'm damned if I'm going to sit around and do nothing while they get killed. It's our duty to help them.'

'You see, Tanucci,' said Roberto, turning to the Lieutenant. 'I think I told you, didn't I, that Fritz was the last man left in the Army who actually believed that there is such a thing as – honour, I suppose you'd call it. He's a good soldier; and he's a good man too; the type who would give his life for his friends. He'd be killed for Zondadari. You've heard him.'

'Yes, sir,' said Tanucci. 'I believe what he says.'

'But,' said Roberto, 'he should remember his strategy. Our men couldn't march on the Capital even if we were to order them to do so. Or at least they might get there, but it would be no good at all. Not a single one would get out alive. That wouldn't help Zondadari at all. You can't turn a rabble into an Army in a few days. There is nothing we can do for Zondadari, I am afraid.'

'Our men are as ready as they'll ever be,' said Fritz. 'You know as well as I do that our Army is the most inefficient on the continent. The same goes for our enemies. We must go now while they're still in a state of confusion. We don't need more than a few men anyway. And if Zondadari dies, you will be to blame.'

'Me?'

'If you'd been at the Army Council this afternoon, we might have been getting ready to go to the Capital right now instead of sitting around arguing. God knows what you found more important to do.'

'Oh for God's sake, Fritz, what good could I have done?' asked Roberto, wounded at last. 'Why do you all expect so much of me?'

'Why are you letting Ximenez use you?' asked Fritz in reply. 'I can't understand why you don't see what is happening in front of your eyes. If Ximenez and his uncle take the country over, you will know that you could have prevented it, if you had wanted to.'

'There's nothing I can do,' said Roberto angrily. 'I am no one at all.'

He had expected better of Fritz. Fritz was trying to blackmail him; and right now he felt at his worst. He should have been at the Army Council, and he should have kept away from Mrs Williams, and of course, Ximenez had set him up with his aunt: he was not sure whether that degraded him more than it did Ximenez.

'The men would follow you,' said Tanucci, interrupting the silence. 'You are the one they admire.'

'Rodolfo's right,' said Fritz. 'If you lead, they'll follow.'

'They're better off following Ximenez,' said Roberto. 'I am no hero.'

Fritz made a little sign with his hand and Tanucci took the hint, creeping out of the room. Roberto was silent, abstracted. There was a sudden silence.

'Zondadari and the others need you,' said Fritz. 'You can't think about yourself now, Bobby.'

'I haven't been able to think of anything else for weeks,' he said slowly. 'I've killed a man since I saw you last, Fritz.'

Fritz was silent, taking this in.

'Who?' he asked at last.

'Ernesto Caballero. I suppose you knew him? Yes? I'd forgotten you knew everyone. And that is not all. There was the case of this English girl called Nicola Nickleby. I was mixed up in that. She killed herself when in custody. I should have been there, but I'd gone away for the weekend.'

'I had no idea,' said Fritz. 'I thought, I don't know what I thought.' Then he asked: 'Do you feel guilty?'

'No. That is the worst thing. I just feel slightly ashamed. I feel I want the whole world to leave me alone. I feel that I've let you down.'

'Me?'

Roberto nodded and looked away.

'I didn't know you cared so much about what I thought. Perhaps if I'd been there . . .' Fritz began to say.

'Dammit, Fritz, you know I've never listened to you,' he said sadly, but with anger in his voice.

'You could do so now,' suggested Fritz.

Roberto looked up and saw Fritz staring at him across the desk. He hadn't meant to tell Fritz this terrible secret; he had not planned it, and he had not wanted it. But Fritz had not turned away in disgust; Fritz was doing what he had not imagined anyone ever doing, looking at him with kindness, pity even, but without disapproval. Something stirred in his cold soul. Fritz was true to him. There was some bond between them that not even the knowledge of what he had done could break. They were, after all, what they had always been, brothers in arms against the rest of the world.

'Go on then,' said Roberto. 'Tell me the great plan.'

Thirty-three

Fritz's plan was simplicity itself, and he explained it to Roberto there and then, as they both pored over a map of the City spread out on the desk.

'It'll take about a hundred men, or maybe a hundred and fifty,' he said. 'With more we'd be noticed. And we could go tonight.'

They both looked at the clock. It was a few minutes past five.

'Tonight?' said Roberto.

'Yes,' said Fritz rolling away the map. 'Go and get dressed and then go and tell Ximenez what we're going to do. At least tell him we are going to do it; don't give him details.'

Roberto went to dress with a sense of urgency. From the bedroom he heard Fritz call Tanucci. When he came back a few minutes later, the two of them were discussing guns.

'Get a move on,' Fritz urged Roberto, when he hesitated to listen to what they were saying.

Roberto left.

'Now,' said Fritz. 'I suppose you must know something about rocket-launchers, being an Engineer? I don't, you see.'

'You mean bazookas?'

'Exactly. How do they work? I mean, what can they do?' asked Fritz.

'I never thought I'd have to explain this to a Cavalry officer,' said Tanucci. (For it was well known that the Cavalry despised the Engineers and all things mechanical. In fact it was one of the things that made Rodolfo like Fritz so much, the fact that he wasn't like other Cavalry officers.) 'They're eighty-eight millimetres in calibre, which would be about five inches, I suppose. I don't know, I never learned English measurements. They can fire rockets at a hundred metres a second which can pierce armour that is up to twenty-seven and a half centimetres thick. And they weigh six or seven kilograms. And their maximum range is about eight hundred metres, I think.'

'Then you know all about them,' said Fritz happily. 'I never know what a metre is, but you obviously do. Good. If someone were to fire a bazooka at the Palace from, let's say, the Marine Gardens, would it do a lot of damage? Would it make a terrible noise?'

'Well, yes,' said Tanucci. 'I don't know how thick the Palace walls are – but one could aim at the windows. And the Marine Gardens are certainly close enough. But you need two men to each bazooka, one to carry the thing and another to carry the ammunition and to load it.'

'Eight men would be enough, as long as we can find four bazookas,' said Fritz. He unrolled the map again. 'Now there's the Zoo,' he said. 'If a group of a hundred men turn up outside the Zoo at the dead of night, all in military uniform, what would you think of that? Quite. It's the only place where soldiers do go at night without arousing the slightest suspicion, isn't it? Never mind curfews: we all know how much they are respected. I doubt if the prostitutes who hang around outside the Zoo have gone away because there's a war on – in fact quite the reverse. Now from the Zoo to the Marine Gardens, if you go round the edge of the City centre – all quiet roads – you'll get to the walls of the Marine Gardens, hopefully with no one seeing you. And then you climb over, and within a few minutes' walk you are in range of the north side of the Palace. I wonder if that is the side the Generals have their bedrooms on . . . You could climb the wall, couldn't you?'

'I could,' said Tanucci with confidence. 'And I know how to use a bazooka. It's one of the few things they teach you in the Engineers. And there were a few men I did practice with on December Island.'

'Good,' said Fritz. 'Then that will be your little contribution. I may not know how to fire a gun myself, but I know a man who does, thank God . . .'

Fritz laughed and then wondered if he was not sending this youngster whom he hardly knew to a premature death.

'It might be dangerous, you know,' he felt compelled to say.

'I'd rather do it than attack the Club,' said Rodolfo. 'They say that the Club is surrounded by other Engineers . . .'

Roberto found Ximenez and his uncle together, which was convenient. He was glad he had his pistol with him; but as it turned out, there was no need for it at all. Ximenez and Williams listened to him in silence, but clearly had no intention of trying to stop him.

'You're mad,' was all that Ximenez had to say.

'You've been listening to that young fool Rodriguez,' said Major Williams. 'He knows nothing; type of man who can't even fire a gun. You can't just drive up to the Capital and start a battle without days of planning, you know.'

'If you go to the Capital with anyone foolish enough to join you in your ill-thought-out adventure, you'll all be killed,' said Ximenez.

And Ximenez immediately reflected that this would be a most desirable outcome. He was sick to death of Fritz as it was, and he was beginning to think that Captain Enriquez was more trouble than he was worth. He would certainly not try and stop them.

Within a remarkably few hours the Task Force (as it was later to be called) was assembling in the main square of San Cristobal. It consisted entirely of volunteers, men who for the most part had grown bored with the inactivity of the last few days, as well as a sprinkling of others who thought that Zondadari deserved their help. There were about a hundred and fifty of them in all. Their transport consisted of two buses and thirty requisitioned taxis. As for weapons, each man had his M-12, except for the officers who carried Berettas; and there were also four bazooka rocket launchers, as well as a few machine-guns. It would, reflected Fritz, have to do. Wars were very rarely fought to plan after all.

'The price of petrol has gone up so much in the last few days,' he explained when they were ready, 'that we can be quite sure that the roads will be deserted. We should arrive in plenty of time for dawn, perhaps at around four in the morning. The enemy will be asleep. We will have the element of surprise in our favour. We will all meet up in the Park by the Zoo, which, as you may know from personal experience, is never lit at night. Now, two taxis are going to drive to the Presidential Palace and launch as many rockets against it as they can. They'll make a lot of noise, but probably do little damage; all the same, it will scare the hell out of the Generals, who will immediately call the troops they've stationed round the Club to their aid. The attack on the Palace will be carried out from the Marine Gardens, not from the Square. While the Generals hunt around in the bushes for an attacking army that doesn't exist, we will make for the Club, one group from the back, another from the front. That for those of you who don't know, is called a pincer movement . . .'

'A pincer movement?' said Roberto jokingly, when they were in the bus, heading north at seventy miles an hour.

'Yes,' said Fritz. 'And a diversion, just like in the text books.'

He was studying a map as he said this, and did not look up. Roberto could not see his face.

'The men are very quiet all of a sudden,' said Roberto.

'So they are,' replied Fritz gravely. 'We might all be dead before much longer. Perhaps they've just realised that; or perhaps they've just realised how very lucky we are going to have to be if anything is going to go according to plan. We might run into a tank regiment on the road. It's rather funny isn't it? For the first time in my life I'm actually going to put the theories into practice, against our own men too.'

'Will it work?' asked Roberto.

'About a one in three chance, I'd say,' said Fritz, as if he were discussing roulette. 'It depends who we have to deal with when we get there. We might just find a few frightened policemen. That won't be too hard. Or we might find some troops who are only looking for an excuse to change sides. I doubt that they'll put up much of a fight. But it is all guesswork. For all we know, Messina might have filled the City with his very best men; in which case, we're in for it. I suppose that is what Ximenez is counting on – otherwise he would hardly have let us go.'

'I got that impression too.'

'Are you frightened?' asked Fritz.

'No. I'm too curious about the outcome to feel frightened. Strange, isn't it?'

'Very,' agreed Fritz, and returned to his map. 'Grid patterns can be got round, somehow,' he said to himself.

In the other bus, Tanucci was staring out of the window at the dark countryside flashing by. He had not considered what their chances might be with the same detachment that Fritz had given to the problem. Perhaps they would all die; but there again, perhaps not. He had done exercises like this, but exercises were different. But whatever was going to happen, it was too late to back out now. Worrying would not help. A little sleep would be useful: so he shut his eyes and composed himself to rest.

'It's men like the police and the Engineers I feel sorry for,' said Fritz suddenly.

'What?' asked Roberto.

'I feel sorrier for them than for us. They are conscripts, most of them. We're doing this because we want to. But those poor damn fools are there because the Generals think they're expendable. They are cannon fodder. That is rather awful when you think about it. Most conscripts never seem to be over the age of eighteen, either.'

'You're getting morbid,' said Roberto.

'It's because it is three in the morning,' said Fritz.

But the real reason was because he was afraid that Tanucci was going to die. He was sending the boy to his death, taking advantage of his enthusiasm for using rocket launchers. Perhaps he himself should have said that he would lead the party into the Marine Gardens. But he had never used a bazooka in his life, and what good would that have done? Besides, Tanucci had wanted to go; perhaps he had wanted to go to please him. He didn't doubt his ability, though: Tanucci would get there, that was certain, but would he ever get out again? Perhaps they were all going to their deaths, thought Fritz. And he had planned it all. Perhaps Ximenez and his uncle would be proved right after all.

Within half an hour they arrived at their rendezvous, which was the rather bedraggled park that surrounded the Zoo, at the western edge of the City. It was still dark. For the next half hour the taxis arrived, and finally the hundred and fifty men assembled. Fritz felt his spirits lift.

'I'm told,' said Roberto, 'that the fact that we have got this far without running into anyone is something of a miracle. I don't need to tell you that from here on we have to advance on foot, and without being seen. Fortunately there is no street lighting, as the Generals have been kind enough to cut off the electricity. It is now nearly four and we should aim to attack at four forty-five. The signal will be the attack our men are going to make on the Presidential Palace. When we hear that, we will converge on the Club, and deal with anyone who tries to stop us. In the meantime we must divide up and head for the Club as inconspicuously as possible, in threes and fours. That's the only way we can get through the City without the enemy knowing that we are here.'

The Task Force prepared to scatter as planned. One group,

that of eight men and four bazookas, led by Tanucci, began to prepare for its special mission, loading itself and its equipment into two taxis; the others were to re-form in two groups in three quarters of an hour; one under the command of Roberto behind the Club, and the other under the command of Fritz, in front of it – they were to be the pincer movement. After a few more instructions, which chiefly concerned the exact locations of their next rendezvous, and what to do in the event of taking prisoners or being challenged by the enemy, they parted.

The next three quarters of an hour were the most nerve-racking that Roberto had ever lived through. There was, naturally enough, a curfew in the City. The familiar streets were dark and deserted. The Zoo was about a mile from the Club, but because the City was built on a grid pattern, one could hardly march down the long straight streets without being seen. Thus their route involved taking one block at a time. Fritz had worked it all out during the journey: they were to go left, then right, then left again, and then repeat the operation in reverse order, thus covering the mile in double the distance. At every corner there was the possibility that they might run into the enemy. At each corner Roberto had to take the precaution of looking round the corner with his gun at the ready, prepared to shoot anyone he might see, knowing that there were about seventy men behind him, spread out in twos and threes, who expected no less of him. It was like a game of hide and seek, zig-zagging back and forth. But still they went on, and still they met no one. It was only when they were two blocks from the Club that Roberto encountered the ring of steel that the Generals had thrown around the rebels in the Club.

He was aching in every joint by now, for his progress had seemed eternal, and he had been running bent double, sheltering behind parked cars to avoid notice. And now he saw them: at a crossroads a block away, there were a group of soldiers standing around in the drowsy night air. They did not seem to be particularly alert, he was glad to see. And yet there were bound to be others nearby, and from where he was crouching, next to a Mercedes which had lost its windows, it was impossible to see more. If he and the men behind him were to wait for the signal – and what if it didn't come? Would Tanucci and his companions succeed? – and then attack the enemy they had within their sights at present, there was no way of telling who or what might be around the next block. If he could get from where he was now to the other side of the road, and that would mean crossing the enemy's line of vision, then he might have a better idea. His watch told him that there were still some minutes to go. He wondered if he could dash across the road in the darkness without being seen. But the enemy, there were about twenty of them, had a light, and the road was filled with crunchy particles of glass. He would be both seen and heard. The only thing to do was to think in the way Fritz thought, to approach the situation as if it were a problem that could be solved, and this he accordingly started to do.

The block of flats next to him seemed to be abandoned. Its door was open. He gestured for two or three men, one of whom carried a machine-gun, to go in through the open door, and pointed out a balcony to them. Then he beckoned the only other officer he could see in the gloom, and gave some whispered instructions. Thirty of the men were to go around the other side of the block: thus when the signal came they would attack the enemy from both sides at once, as well as from above, and hopefully without shooting each other in the process.

Thirty-four

Rodolfo Tanucci and the seven men with him had an easier time getting to their destination, the perimeter wall of the Marine Gardens, which lay to the north of the Palace. Their two taxis were able to drive there along a peripheral road undisturbed. That part at least went entirely to plan, and the taxis disgorged eight men and four bazookas along with a quantity of rockets at a little after four at a quiet spot next to the wall. Climbing the wall was relatively easy too, and was something that most of them had done before at one time or another during their short lives. Thus soon all of them were standing in the shrubbery with their equipment. Only then did the real difficulty arise; for, peering out of the shrubbery, Tanucci saw that the wide expanse of the Gardens had been converted into a military camp; and a military camp, which, for that time of the morning, showed every sign of intense activity.

Fortunately they had not been seen. The enemy, Tanucci realised at once, was far too busy getting ready to attack the Military Club to bother to keep a proper look out or to expect to be attacked themselves. For once, inefficiency had saved them. Evidently the enemy had as little idea as they did about what the other side was doing. But even so, it was at once apparent that to attack the facade of the Palace that faced the Gardens was quite impossible.

Rodolfo crouched under the friendly shelter of the rhododendrons and considered what would be the best thing to do. He had expected to find the Gardens deserted; so had Fritz. The others, he knew, would be waiting for the signal. It all depended on him now. Turning back was out of the question; but going forward seemed equally impossible.

As a child, his mother had sometimes taken him to the Marine Gardens on Sunday afternoons. He knew the ground. And using his knowledge, he led the men in single file along the inside of the perimeter wall, still concealed by the shrubbery, until they reached the point where the wall met the sea. Here there was an ice-cream kiosk, and behind it they gathered for a hurried conference.

'Could we fire from here?' one of the men asked.

The answer was an unsurprising negative. Their maximum range was eight hundred and seventy metres, and the Palace was well outside that distance. They were far from the troops in the Gardens where they were at present, but also much too far from their target. The challenge was to get near to the latter without the former noticing – which seemed impossible. Rodolfo looked at his watch and saw that it was nearly four-thirty.

'What about the sea?' suggested another of the men.

There was indeed a sea-wall running the length of the Marine Gardens, and this wall ended in a little jetty, which offered one of the best views of the Bay, the City, and, of course, the Palace. Despite the fact that the jetty was small and exposed, it was well within firing range of the Palace, and its seaward front in particular. No one would expect the Palace to be attacked from the seaward side. And just below the ice-cream kiosk behind which they were crouching, was a slipway and several pedalos. Once again, Rodolfo thought carefully. Then he gave his instructions. Within a very few minutes they had managed to detach two of the pedalos and load one with the bazookas, and the other with the ammunition. The eight men, fully dressed, then began to push the pedalos along as they waded through the water, under the shelter of the sea-wall, so that no one on land could see them.

It did not take long to reach the jetty; and soon they were hauling themselves out of the sea. It was a sultry night, of the type common in late summer, and the sea had been warm, but their soaking clothes clung to them and squelched in the silent darkness. Rodolfo knew they would have to escape by water once the attack was over, and took off his boots and threw them into the water. The others began to do the same. It was now a little past quarter to five, and they were only a few minutes late with beginning the attack.

They started to make their weapons ready to fire as unobtrusively as possible. It was already perceptibly less dark, and they worked hurriedly in assembling the rocket-launchers. Rodolfo looked out over the harbour for a moment. When they had finished what they had come to do, they would have to swim across the Bay for safety. That was why he had thrown away his boots, and his heavy wet tunic and trousers. They could not possibly hope to come back the way they had come. The distance across the Bay, to the Riviera on the other side, was at least three or four kilometres, he reckoned. He had never swum such a distance in his life. He shivered and wondered about currents and sharks, and thanked God under his breath that it was summer.

Roberto looked at his watch and saw that it was nearly five to five, and that the rocket attack on the Palace was late. Perhaps they had run into trouble. Perhaps disaster was staring them all in the face. Fritz, he was sure, would now be at the other side of the Club, a mere three blocks away. He wished he could communicate with Fritz – but they had no field telephone. Fritz would know what to do in the event of the rocket attack not happening. How long would they have to wait until something did happen? It was already growing light. From where he crouched behind the Mercedes he could hear the enemy talking to each other; it was the usual bored conversation that men have on guard duty at night. He had overheard nothing of interest. Clearly these men were not expecting anything to happen now, in the grey light of dawn.

Then he heard the rockets: there was a barrage of sound, then silence, then a renewed barrage, then silence once again. Then came the sound of a siren from the Palace, which was rapidly supplemented by further shots, coming from he did not quite know where; in fact he was hearing the sound of the machine-gun that he had posted on the balcony above his head. Those were his own men firing. He heard the confused babble of the enemy soldiers in the street, who, under the impression that the men on the balcony were friends, could not understand why they were being fired upon. But he had to do something himself, rather than listen to what was going on around him. He crawled forward and aimed at the senior officer of the enemy troops – it was a lieutenant of the Engineers, dressed just like Tanucci. He brought him down with a single shot.

The Engineers, surrounded on three sides, and confused too – for they had confidently been awaiting the arrival of their own men, who were supposed to attack the Club that morning, and their attention had been directed at the Club, not behind their backs – turned and ran the length of the street. It was only at the next crossroads that they regrouped, were reinforced by colleagues, and recovered from their panic. Here a nasty little battle ensued, which lasted some twenty minutes. It was only resolved when Roberto's men established themselves in some of the neighbouring buildings, and were able to fire down from the first floor windows on the Engineers below, using the overhanging balconies to protect themselves from the enemy troops stationed on the roof-tops, who, in firing wildly into the streets, probably did more harm to their own side than to anyone else. When this happened, the senior surviving Engineer blew his whistle, and his men retreated. They had never expected to fight a street battle; they knew that the Army's best regiment was currently stationed in the Marine Gardens, and yet had not come to help them. They were under the impression that the attacking forces had been much larger than they really were; so they considered their duty as done. They withdrew, leaving thirty of their men dead.

Thus did Roberto gain entry to the Military Club, via the back entrance, despite the fact that he was a member of several years' standing. And there in the hallway he met Fritz, sitting in the porter's chair, looking rather pale – for battle and strategy were clearly completely different things – but otherwise quite well.

The rocket attack on the Palace had been a complete success. It had in the first place given General Hernandez, who was a light sleeper, an enormous fright; and though there had been but two bursts of fire which had lasted less than two minutes each, the old General's fright had developed into full blown panic. Messina was somewhere in the Marine Gardens, marshalling the troops that were going to smoke out the nest of vipers established in the Military Club as soon as it was light. General Hernandez, who had never been under fire once in his life before now – and he was seventy-five years old – crawled out of his bed and hid under it, cursing Messina for handling things so badly. For he, like everyone else in the Palace, assumed that the rockets could only have come from their own men, and that either there had been another accident with ammunition, or else their own men were turning against them. He resolved to stay under his bed, and so he did, until his aide-de-camp found him about ten minutes later.

By that time the various noises that had convulsed the environs of the Palace directly after the attack had all but stopped, except for the siren's solitary wail of alarm, which no one quite knew how to switch off. But the damage had been done. One rocket had missed the Palace but landed on the presidential launch that was moored below, holing it above the water line and setting it on fire. Like Cleopatra's barge it burned on the waters. In the building itself, several windows had been smashed, and at least one ceiling had collapsed. No one had been killed: but the Palace siren wailed in the darkness and everyone assumed another more lethal attack would come.

Some troops had rushed, without being told by anyone to do so, to the presidential launch, to see if the fire would spread. Others had fanned out into the further reaches of the Marine Gardens, looking for the enemy. Yet others had taken to a gunboat. No one had any thought of the Military Club and the sounds of war coming from there. The Engineers could deal with that. Far more important was the safety of the Presidential Palace. And in this way, Fritz's diversion proved itself to be a great success.

It was only at about five-fifteen, in the grey light of morning, when, did they but know it, the real battle was all but over, that anyone had the sense to check the jetty. But there was nothing to be found there, for the enemy had been wise enough to throw all their equipment, wrapped in the remaining parts of their sodden uniforms, into the sea, where they had sunk without trace. Yet an air of cordite and recent activity hung around the jetty.

'Could they have swum for it, do you think?' asked one of the officers investigating the scene.

'Are those buoys?' asked his companion.

'Boys?' said the officer, peering across the Bay.

But the level rays of the now rising sun made it hard to distinguish between buoys and human heads. It was further almost impossible to tell whether the round black objects were stationary or moving. The officer was carrying his Beretta, but rather than waste a cartridge on what might not be a real target after all, he called one of his men up and instructed him to use his M-12 on one of the black spheres.

'Any difference?' he asked his colleague.

But it was hard to tell.

'Try some automatic fire,' he said to the men with him, just to make sure, in case there were enemy men in the water. 'That will teach them if there are,' he added grimly.

Meanwhile, General Messina was losing his temper. He was never at his best early in the morning. All his plans seemed to be going wrong. The minutes were ticking away. He wanted to deploy the troops currently in the Marine Gardens, who were real soldiers, and not Engineers, in the centre of the City, but this was proving much harder than he had thought possible. Some of the officers he had counted on had run to the presidential launch and were trying to put out the fire there. Others were in the building itself; others had gone to the sea wall, or were firing across the Bay, or searching the Gardens for intruders. And whenever he gave orders, he was infuriated to find that there was never anyone higher in rank than an NCO to carry them out, and that they were being countermanded by Hernandez as fast as he could give them.

It was not until six that something like order had been restored and his troops were ready for a counter-attack. By that time the Club had been liberated, and the first stage in the fight for the City was over.

Thirty-five

As soon as they had finished firing the bazookas and exhausted their ammunition, Rodolfo and the men with him had jumped into the sea and swum for their lives. The sound of an M-12 being fired, a sound that was familiar to him, had convinced him of the need to swim as much of the way as possible under water, hiding himself in the blackness of the sea, for it was still only early morning. He was not a strong swimmer, but he did his best, and after about an hour he thought he was safe and came to rest sheltering under the lee of a yacht, holding onto its anchor chain. It felt odd to be alone out there almost in the middle of the Bay, and to know that the automatic fire had been intended for him, and that someone had given an order that was meant to kill him. But he was alive, and as soon as he had got his breath back, he pressed on towards the shore and eventually hauled himself onto dry land on the far side of the Bay.

He was now in the southern part of the City, and he seemed to have arrived at one of those private beach clubs that lay below the road known as the Riviera. It was now well after six, for his swim had taken him about two hours, but it was still early, and the place was deserted. He was safe, for the moment at least, because he had put a considerable stretch of water between himself and the Palace jetty. Moreover it was much further round by land, and between him and the men who had tried to kill him lay the Military Club, where, to judge by the stillness of the morning, some decisive action had taken place. If their side had won that action it would mean that he was safely behind his own lines.

For some minutes, he lay there on the beach, beguiled by the peacefulness of the early morning and feeling too tired to move. His mind began to wander, and he thought of the others: he wondered about Fritz and about Captain Enriquez and what had happened to them; and the earnestness of the game in which they were involved seemed remote and unreal, as he lay there in the sunlight, feeling the warmth on his exhausted limbs. There had been seven men with him, men he had known, though not known well. As soon as they had used their last rocket, they had all pulled off their remaining clothes as quickly as possible and had jumped off the jetty, just as he had done. Then there had been the sound of guns, and he seemed now to remember, the vibrations caused by a gunboat. And of his seven companions, there was now no sign. Perhaps they had come ashore on another part of the Riviera; they had all been strong men, stronger, and for the most part, older than himself. He could not imagine that he might have survived the adventure and they had not.

He realised, with a sudden jolt of fear, that he ought not to lie there any longer. He limped up the beach and went into what he supposed was some sort of changing room. What he needed now were clothes, for, apart from his watch, he was only wearing his military undershorts, having thrown the rest of his clothes into the sea, wrapped around one of the bazookas. The first thing he saw in the changing rooms were showers, and by great good luck an abandoned pair of swimming trunks. This would be his first disguise. He stood under a shower to wash off the salt, and then put on the swimming trunks, which made him feel a good deal less like an Engineer. The long military undershorts still needed to be disposed of, and he screwed them up into a ball and stuffed them into a lavatory cistern. Before leaving he stopped to contemplate the military identification tag that, along with his medallion of St Michael the Archangel, hung around his neck. If he were to keep that on, he would in all probability be recognised as a soldier. But if he were to take it off and throw it away and still be caught by the enemy, they would shoot him at once as a spy or a deserter. Besides, he had a residual belief that no good soldier should ever take off his tag – parting with his regulation underwear was bad enough; and if they caught him, they would shoot him, he reflected, whether he was wearing it or not. So he decided to keep it on, and if he was challenged he would pretend he was a young soldier who had gone for an early morning swim, and whose uniform had been stolen by some passer-by. Of course, allowing your uniform to be stolen was an offence, as was leaving a weapon unguarded – but the penalty for that would hardly be death.

He was now very tired, and when a final search of the place revealed that there were no clothes lying around that he could steal, he sat down and thought. He could hardly walk the three miles or so back to the Zoo, their agreed rendezvous, in swimming trunks and without shoes. Theft seemed to be the only available option open to him. And yet in this part of the City, which was remote from the fighting, most of the flats and houses were bound to be still inhabited. There would hardly be any looted or abandoned places for him to take advantage of. A further consideration struck him: if he were to be seen in civilian dress – and a nineteen-year-old out of uniform would be very conspicuous – he would be bound to be asked for papers and his identification cards. What he needed was not clothes, but some sort of disguise.

According to his watch it was a few minutes after seven. If he was going to go anywhere, he had better go now. Soon people would begin to appear on the streets.

He emerged from the beach hut and went up the stairs that led to the Riviera above. There was naturally a gate, but the gate was not hard to climb. Once he was on the promenade, the Riviera, the part of the City where all the hotels were, he tried to get his bearings. This was the most expensive part of the City, and thus rather unfamiliar to him. The Riviera had a superb view of the noble Bay he had just swum across, and the City and the mountains beyond. He noticed the hotels, the expensive blocks of flats and a church. That was the only building he recognised: for many years he had been in the habit of carrying a picture of St Francis in his wallet, for luck, and that picture had been obtained at this particular Church, which was the Church of the Friars. And he remembered that the Friars were Italian Franciscans. He knew that he was in danger of death, for here he was unarmed, in hostile territory, and the enemy would not look kindly on him, when they realised that he had been responsible for the attack on the Palace. And already the suspicion had come into his mind that the men he had not seen since they had all dived off the jetty might well be dead. But now he saw the church in front of him, and recognised it as a familiar place of sanctuary, and he knew in a strange way that he was being provided for.

He crossed the road; the door was open and he went in. All was quiet within, and deserted, apart from one old friar kneeling down at the front of the church, before the main altar, deep in prayer. Rodolfo wondered what he ought to say. Then, with a little cough designed to announce his presence, he went forward on silent and bare feet, to speak to the friar.

'*Padre, mi scusi*,' he began.

The friar, who perhaps had been wrapped in contemplation, had evidently not heard his preparatory cough. He was plainly surprised to find himself looking up at a nearly naked young man, and a reproof was coming to his lips – but the young man had spoken to him in Italian, and there had been the traces of a Neapolitan accent in his voice, which softened the old man's heart. Besides, Rodolfo had a pleasant face, and though not properly dressed, was wearing a pair of religious medals around his neck. But even so, church was church, and the old Franciscan's sense of propriety was strong.

'*Vieni, vieni, ragazzo*,' he said, more or less pulling Rodolfo into the sacristy.

The sacristy, Rodolfo was quick to notice, had several doors, and one of them seemed to lead directly out into the street, and it was only closed by a bolt.

He then told his story, speaking in the language his parents had used at home. He was a soldier, he said, and he had gone for a swim from the beach below the Riviera early that morning, and because there had been no one about he had left his uniform on the beach. But some *ragazzini* had stolen his clothes. He now wished to use the telephone, if that were possible. But none of the telephones had worked for days, said the friar in desperation. Ah, yes, said Rodolfo, I had forgotten; but I come from far away, he added, and how am I going to get back to where I came from without your help? The friar was all sympathy. A young man simply could not walk all the way to his barracks dressed only in a bathing suit, especially if it was a long way. But he was unsure what he could do. They had no secular clothes in the house, except for the overalls used when the cloister was being painted, and he was not sure that they would do.

Rodolfo urged the case of the overalls. The friar remained doubtful, but at last, after much hesitation, said he would go and ask the Father Guardian about it; the Guardian had the key to the cupboard where the painting things were kept. He went to a door that led to the cloister, told Rodolfo to wait, and then disappeared.

Rodolfo did not wait. There were three cupboards in the sacristy, all of which seemed to contain priest's vestments. But there in the last cupboard, looking a little neglected, was what he had been hoping to find.

The Father Guardian, having given Frà Antonio, for such was the old friar's name, a little lecture on Christ's injunction to clothe the naked, came into the sacristy a few minutes later, bearing the painters' overalls. But the nearly-naked recipient of this intended act of charity was now nowhere to be seen.

'He was here,' said Frà Antonio. 'He said he was a soldier, and look, his feet have left a mark on the polished floor.'

The two friars looked down at the footprints, where the remains of salt water had marked the wood.

'Are you quite sure?' asked the Father, a little suspiciously.

'He came to me in church. I think he was wearing just a bathing suit. I was doing my Thanksgiving after Mass, and I looked up and there he was. He had a medallion of St Michael around his neck.'

'Really? Angels wear no clothes,' said the Father Guardian meditatively.

'And he spoke very good Italian, but with a Naples accent. I can't think where he has gone.'

The priest listened to this and suddenly felt that the ground he stood on was holy ground. He had always known that angelic apparitions, if they spoke at all, would speak the Italian of his native city. For years before, as a young man, he too had known the smiling land to the south; he had sat in the majolica cloister of Santa Chiara, in the delicate lemon-scented air, and had been at peace under the shadow of Vesuvius. And he felt now what he had felt then, and he knew that an angelic soldier had been sent to them.

'St Michael,' he said to himself. 'Perhaps it was a vision.'

The vision was now at least a hundred yards away, wearing a Franciscan habit, not running, but walking in what he hoped was a religious way, towards the centre of the City. He had put the brown habit on easily enough, and now was adjusting the cord around his waist, not quite sure which side the knot should be on. Finally he settled for the left hand side, thinking that was the way Saint Francis had worn it in the picture, and he had just done so when a van full of police drove up.

'Where are you going, Father?' asked a voice from the van's window.

'The centre of the City,' he replied.

'There's a battle there,' said the man, who was a police captain. 'But come with us. You'll be safer.'

Rodolfo did as he was told, and soon he was in the back of the van, gathering the skirts of his habit awkwardly around him, squeezed between two heavily armed policemen. The van continued its journey.

'You've no shoes,' said the young man sitting next to him.

'The Italian Franciscans never wear shoes,' he said rather grandly. 'Like St Francis himself.'

He said this in what he knew would pass for heavily accented Spanish. The policeman next to him, who had all the curiosity of extreme youth, and like most conscripts was a boy who loved to ask questions about everything he saw, was making him nervous. And he promised God there and then that if he survived this day he would do his best to become a real Franciscan before he died. It would be too unfair if he were to be hauled out, discovered and shot, after all the effort he had made and all the luck he had had so far. The peace of a cloister, after all the things he had seen and suffered, seemed the most desirable refuge.

'I know that's true,' said another conscript policeboy. 'But you have forgotten your rosary, Father.'

'I was in a hurry to leave the Friary,' said Rodolfo, telling the perfect truth.

'True, true,' said one of the older men. 'God knows how many wounded there may be. Quite a few of our men will have been involved, and it won't have been their fault. We're not trained to fight in wars, even though we do count as soldiers, officially, but we're policemen really. And did you hear the shelling?'

'Yes, I did,' said Rodolfo.

'The daring of it,' continued the man, with a touch of admiration in his voice. 'They picked up three or four of the men who did it about an hour ago. They swam across the Bay, stark naked. Can you believe it, Father?'

Rodolfo could very well believe it. 'And what happened to them?' he asked.

'They walked straight into a welcoming party, who shot them just like that,' said the policeman grimly. 'And they say the rest of them were killed in the water shortly after the attack. They must have known what risks they were running . . .'

The boy next to Rodolfo spoke to him in an undertone, in Italian: 'Your hair is wet, Father.'

'I had a shower,' said Rodolfo, also in Italian.

'Well,' said the Italian boy. 'We have a priest with us, so for the moment we are safe.'

The older policeman who had been speaking before now looked grave.

'They wouldn't kill a priest,' he said. 'That is true. A priest can go right up to the Club and they wouldn't dare touch him; it's as if he was wearing armour. They say that it brings terrible bad luck to harm a priest. They can range freely over the worst battlefields, bringing comfort to the dying, just like angels. If you're lying there bleeding to death and you look up and see a priest, you know your hour has come all right.'

'That is what I have come for,' said Rodolfo, more prosaically. 'To see if I can be of any help.'

Presently the van stopped and they all got out. Rodolfo, affecting clerical politeness, which, had he known more clergymen he would have known to be most unusual, thanked them for the lift and left. Carefully he began to walk in the direction of the Military Club, through streets that were covered with broken glass. He wished that he had shoes.

Evidence that there had been a battle soon became apparent. It was now nearly eight o'clock, yet the streets were absolutely deserted, apart from the dead. Remembering that he was supposed to be a friar, he approached each corpse with reverent care, and in one or two cases bent over them to shut the eyes. All the casualties seemed to be Engineers, members of his own regiment, but he recognised none of them, though he felt that some of them had a ghostly familiarity about them. He had seen corpses before, and had imagined that he was now used to the sight of them. He hoped that these dead soldiers would be pale, white, calm, like sleeping ghosts. They were not. There was little blood on them, showing that their deaths had been quick – for once the heart stops, one can bleed no more; their mouths were open, and their expressions surprised, and their skin an odd blend of yellow and grey, and each dead man seemed small in his uniform.

He had gazed at about ten of these apparitions, thinking that they had been killed by men of his own side, and that they were men who, like himself, had expected not to die. Death seemed so arbitrary. Some were called, others spared. Then he came across a youngster in police uniform, his blue shirt brown with drying blood, and still alive. His eyes seemed sightless, and Rodolfo wondered if he had caught the boy in the very moment of death; but on his approach, the boy focused his gaze on the brown Franciscan habit. Rodolfo took hold of his hand to feel the strength of his pulse; and with his other hand he began to undo the shirt to find the source of the wound. It was not a fresh wound, and he realised that the boy must have been there for some time, slowly bleeding to death on the tarmac. And he realised that he could not leave him – for his wound was not deadly, but it was the loss of blood that was killing him – and that he would have to put himself in danger again, and go back to find the police, or some enemy soldiers who could take the young policeman to hospital.

'I am going to carry you to some of your colleagues,' he said. 'They have a van a few streets away.'

The eyes of the wounded young policeman seemed to register understanding, and Rodolfo began to try to lift him; but the wounded man was larger than he was, and a dead weight. Rodolfo had hardly slept for the last twenty-four hours; he was exhausted by his long swim across the Bay; and no matter how hard he tried, he could not lift him. Perhaps he ought to go back to the police van – but they would hardly come, even if he told them what was the matter. There were bound to be snipers in the surrounding buildings, which was the reason the boy had been left to die; and his priestly disguise was so thin that they would expect it was some kind of a trap. In despair, he tried to lift the young man again, hoping that strength would come to him; but he merely succeeded in propping him half upright. It seemed hopeless: Rodolfo had never been strong, and now even the strength that he used to have had deserted him.

Then he saw a pair of black boots next to him, and raising his eyes he saw the dark figure of Father Morisco.

'Here,' said Father Morisco, lending a hand. Between them they raised the dying man, and carried him the length of a street. The police van was fortunately still there, and the wounded conscript was soon inside it. The doors were shut and the van drove off at speed.

'I don't know you,' said Father Morisco.

'I am Frà Michele,' said Rodolfo, picking the first name that came into his head.

Then as if from all around them, quite suddenly, came the sound of gunfire. Father Morisco turned to see where it was coming from, and when he turned again, it was to find that he was alone.

Thirty-six

The fighting went on for several days after that, and when it at last subsided, it was discovered that most of the centre of the City was severely damaged, and that the ruins were neatly bisected in two parts, along what had been the main road. The Government held the north side, and the rebels the south. In the Government sector lay the Palace, the Marine Gardens, the Cathedral and the Archbishop's Palace, and most of the public buildings. Under the control of the rebels was the Military Club, and the chief residential district, which included the Riviera and its hotels. The front line that lay between the two sectors was a terrible sight: all the plane trees had been cut down to create an anti-tank barrier. And this front line ran all the way from the Bay, right across the City, far out into the countryside, until it reached the border. The City, and the Republic with it, was split in two.

That this had happened was clean contrary to the laws of strategy, according to General Messina. It was frankly incredible: a few hundred men had managed to sow such confusion that they had succeeded in taking half the City, when, by rights, they should have all been massacred within half an hour. What was worse, they had managed to hold it for a long enough time to enable their dilatory friends in San Cristobal to come and reinforce them. And the Government men had not been able to do anything about it. There were many reasons for this, Messina was sure: the Government men had been cowardly, slow to move, badly organised; too many of their middle-ranking officers had been on the other side; the NCOs had simply not known what to do without the officers to tell them; far too many vital platoons had, in the course of the fighting, changed sides; even the police in the south of the City had done so. Thus General Messina had raged and fumed and blamed everyone but himself, while General Hernandez wrung his hands and started at the merest noise that resembled gunfire.

And outside the Palace, where mutual recriminations were the order of the day, the City grew quiet as is often the case after battles; and each side saw to the burial of its dead and the care of its wounded, as is also the custom.

Fritz, who had planned the entire operation, at least until Ximenez had arrived, hot on their heels, having heard the news that they had won, and eager to claim what credit he could for it, Fritz found himself with nothing to do, and rather than waste his time, decided to visit Rodolfo in hospital – for Rodolfo, on the second day of fighting, had been wounded.

'They tell me you are making progress,' he said cheerfully, appearing at his bedside. 'How are you getting on?'

'Slowly,' said Rodolfo, for this was now the second week he had spent in bed.

'If it is any consolation to you,' said Fritz, drawing up a chair, 'they all say that you are a hero, and a living hero too.' (For not one of the others who had attacked the Palace had come back alive.) 'I still don't see how you did it,' continued Fritz. 'I mean, you swam to shore, we know that. Then the next thing was they found you in the Club wearing a bathing suit, with nothing wrong with you except cut feet. How?'

'It was a miracle, Fritz,' said Rodolfo, who had thrown his Franciscan habit down a manhole soon after meeting Father Morisco. The real priest had unsettled him, and he had decided to impersonate the clergy no longer.

'Ah well,' said Fritz, wondering whether this was an attempt at humour. 'Why don't you show me your wounds?'

'Go ahead,' said Rodolfo.

In a spirit of scientific curiosity Fritz pulled back the sheet resting on the cage that covered the wounded body. The wounds had cicatriced satisfactorily, but seemed all the more frightful for it. Rodolfo's abdomen was red and marbled in appearance.

'Nasty stuff, shrapnel,' said Fritz. 'I expect you are glad to be alive.'

'Yes,' said Rodolfo, thinking of the men who had jumped into the water with him; and all those who had been killed later on. 'I have been given a second chance. It's as if God meant it somehow.'

'There's a positive outbreak of religious mania at present,' said Fritz without quite understanding him. 'They say it is common in wartime. During the First World War, the British soldiers claimed they saw angels fighting alongside them in the heavens. That was at Mons. Oh well,' he continued, changing the subject, 'I suppose you will be glad to hear that your Captain is a hero as well. And so is Zondadari, but he was one anyway. It has made Ximenez sit up and take notice, which is a good thing. The three of them are now going to run the Provisional Government. They could hardly do anything less, don't you think?'

But Rodolfo did not seem interested in this or any other news.

'It didn't work last time,' was all he managed to say.

'You're not in pain, are you?' asked Fritz with concern, wondering why all his attempts to be cheerful were proving so very unsuccessful.

'Do you think, Fritz,' said Rodolfo, 'that it is all true?'

'Is what all true?'

'God, and the angels, and the saints, and that God somehow sees everything that is done, and that he remembers it; and that if you make a promise to God, you can never escape it? You know what I mean. Is it all true?'

'I'm the last person to ask,' said Fritz. 'But the vast majority of the people in this country believe it is true. Even Roberto does, from what I can see. There's a certain fatalism in this country.'

'But what about you?'

'I'm not sure what I believe,' said Fritz honestly. 'I never really have given religion a thought. I mean, I am sure there is a God, but I've never seriously thought about religion. Some people do; Roberto used to take religion seriously, but he never used to talk about God, which always struck me as odd.'

'Is there a difference between religion and God?' asked Rodolfo, his lethargy disappearing.

'Often,' said Fritz, glad that at last he had interested the Lieutenant in something. 'You see religion is what people do in church, and God is something beyond that. You can have one but not the other, but ideally, I suppose you should have both. Now someone like Roberto used to go to Mass every week and go to confession and all that, but I was never convinced, between you and me, that he was genuine. He never once reproached me for not going to church, for example. He didn't seem at all worried that I was destined for hell. He fulfilled his duties and that was it.'

'Don't you go to church?' asked Rodolfo, somewhat shocked.

'Never,' said Fritz. 'And you?'

'Well, yes,' said Rodolfo. 'I mean, what else was there for us to do on a Sunday morning? I presume you went off to play polo.'

Fritz laughed: 'Don't be ridiculous,' he said.

'I think,' said Rodolfo reflectively, 'that deep down you have known all along, without having to go to church and do all those things. Whereas so many of us Catholics, we think we know, and yet we don't know a thing. There are so many things that we do, thinking that they are all right, and yet we deceive ourselves. We never stop and think. No one in this country has stopped and thought for a long time. You yourself said that you didn't. If we did, we wouldn't be in this stupid war.'

'You're right, of course,' said Fritz. 'About the war. But what should we know, if we stopped and thought about it?'

'We'd know that it is all true,' said Rodolfo. 'God, and the angels and the saints, and the Ten Commandments, and love your neighbour as yourself.'

'It would be nice if it were,' said Fritz.

'But why don't you go to church?' asked Rodolfo suddenly. 'You can't be an atheist.'

Fritz shrugged: 'Why do you think I'm called Fritz when the name on my papers says José Maria?'

'It's a nickname, of course,' said Rodolfo.

'It was a fiction my parents adopted to make me appear Catholic,' he said. 'José Maria is a good Catholic name. But I have never used it, nor thought of it as mine, and neither has anyone else, because I am not a Catholic.'

'So, you're a Protestant?' asked Rodolfo.

'Neither,' said Fritz. 'I'm nothing at all, but if I am anything I suppose I must be a Jew.'

'No, you can't be,' said Rodolfo.

'It is not generally known,' conceded Fritz.

'Is it on your tag?' asked Rodolfo. 'On my tag, and on every tag I've seen, it says Catholic. I suppose there are a few that must say Protestant as well.'

'My tag says Catholic too,' said Fritz. 'When they see the name José Maria, they assume that. Thank God my parents never went the whole hog and call me Jésus.'

'And does no one know you are a –'

'A Jew? Roberto knows, of course. But whenever I have to fill in a form I just leave the religion space blank, as if I'd forgotten it, and they usually fill it in for me. I suppose if it were well known, I would never have got into the Cavalry, let alone been put up for the Military Club . . .'

'How awful,' said Rodolfo. 'I didn't know that that could happen.'

'My dear boy,' said Fritz, 'think a moment. Could you join the Military Club if someone put you up?'

'I'm an Engineer,' said Rodolfo. 'The Military Club is only for the best regiments.'

'Quite,' said Fritz.

'But,' said Rodolfo. 'I am an Engineer because people know where I come from, and they can tell when I speak that I'm not really officer class. But there's nothing about you that could give you away, is there? I mean the fact that you are a Jew is almost an accident of your ancestry, isn't it? I mean, you don't look like what people imagine a Jew to look like. You don't go to a Jewish synagogue, do you? There's nothing about you that makes you any less an officer than, let's say, Captain Enriquez, is there?'

'No,' said Fritz. 'I have only got one mark and I don't flash that around unless I have to.'

'Where?'

'Read the Bible,' said Fritz with a smile.

'The Bible . . .' said Rodolfo, without picking up the reference. 'I keep on thinking about the sheep and the goats.'

And his animation vanished.

'I'll see you again soon,' said Fritz, sensing that his visit had not been a complete success, and that the next time they might discuss a less exhausting topic.

Somewhere to the north of them, in what was still Government territory, lay Torre del Mar, which was not a village, but a mere name, the only building in the place being a large neglected house built for summer occupation, which, now that autumn was near, was getting rather cold. It was perhaps providential, thought Maria Enriquez, as she put what had been the leg of a Sheraton chair into the wood burning stove, that poor Isabel de Calatrava had left them to look after her heavier pieces of furniture for the duration of the war, along with a rather unpleasant little dog.

Having loaded the fire, she sat down again. The kitchen faced north, and was warm as a result. All the most comfortable furniture that they could find had been moved in there. Maria's visitor was sitting on a Louis Quinze sofa, which he had sat on before, when the sofa had graced one of the reception rooms in the British Embassy. It was now being used as a stand for various kitchen items, and Father Morisco found that he was sharing it with a sack of potatoes and a jar of pickles.

'How are you managing?' he asked.

'Remarkably well,' said Maria. 'We found so many things here when we arrived. I had more or less forgotten having told Isabel that she could put her things here. And it seems she has put Sir Nigel's things here too. Of course, we've used a few of them. I imagine she only sent us the stuff that she didn't want. I mean this dress . . .'

Maria was wearing a frock seemingly designed by Norman Hartnell. (One could never tell whether Isabel's clothes, like her furniture, were real or reproduction.) She had cut off as many of the supernumerary frills as she could, and she used it as her work dress.

'I mean, Isabel is hardly likely to want this again, is she? I consulted Carmen, you know she ran *Moda*, don't you, Father, and she told me that no one wore this sort of thing any more. I suppose Isabel was one of those people who never threw anything away. Which is just as well, because her frocks go down very well with the farmers' wives round here. That sack of potatoes and those pickles were an absolute bargain, if I may say so. And we have got so many of her dresses that we won't go hungry for a very long time.'

'Good,' said Father Morisco, whose sympathy for Isabel was severely limited. 'Of course, the escudo isn't worth the paper it's printed on now. Our accounts have gone haywire, as a result. It is a funny thing, but when there's a war, there are always more Mass intentions. A young man is killed, what do his parents do? They ask the priest to say Mass, or sometimes more than just one. In the old days a Mass offering was ten escudos. Now the priests are snowed under with Mass intentions, because of all the dead, because of all the pious grandmothers who are worried about those who aren't dead yet – and the priests are demanding stipends, as is their right, but in kind. So the clergy won't starve. One Mass will cost you half a chicken sometimes. And ten per cent of that is supposed to go to the Archbishop's curia – that is me.'

'Goodness,' said Maria, imagining Father Morisco dealing with endless poultry carcasses. 'And how is the Archbishop?'

'Still there,' said Father Morisco. 'Dealing with a lot of people who claim to have had visions of late. Did you know, that on the first day of the battle the Archangel Michael appeared not once but twice, early in the morning? Once to a friar at that church on the Riviera, and once to a policeman.'

'Not really?'

'The friar is the imaginative type, and the policeman was a mere boy who was dying of blood loss – he's recovered now – and he may have had a hallucination. You see, he's called Miguel, and he was praying to his patron saint, the Archangel Michael, and suddenly this person appeared to comfort him. In fact I am a little puzzled about it myself, because, you see, I was there. There was this Franciscan friar, and the odd thing is I had never seen him before.'

'But I thought you knew everyone, Father?' said Maria with a touch of irony.

'I know all the clergy of the diocese and all the religious orders. And there are about fifty friars in the archdiocese, and I know them all by sight. And even more odd, I didn't know him, but he knew me . . . Perhaps I am becoming a religious maniac. It may be catching. There's already a cult springing up at the Franciscan church, and this boy, the young police conscript I mean, has been receiving people in his hospital bed. How very strange people are. If I could find a printer that could do it, I'd get lots of holy pictures printed with that prayer on the back – the one to the Archangel, about defending us in the day of battle, being our safeguard against the snares of the enemy.'

'Talking of the day of battle, Father, have you heard anything about my son?'

'He's an important man now,' said Father Morisco. 'He is

one third of the new Government. I haven't heard from him directly, but I do hear about him from other sources, on the other side, you understand . . .'

'Oh,' said Maria. 'Of course we haven't heard anything at all. We know he is alive, because the Government have put a price on his head; that at least is something. But of course, he can't write to us, can he? Unless he writes to someone abroad and then gets them to post it to us there, which might take ages and might never arrive. I expect that is what he has done. If you do hear anything, of course . . .'

'I will let you know on my next visit,' said the priest. 'I will keep my ears open.'

It had in fact been with this idea in mind, of setting himself up as some sort of go-between, that Father Morisco had come to Torre del Mar in the first place. Of course, he had been passing, and might have called anyway, even if this particular idea had not struck him.

'If you write to him now,' said the priest, 'I could take a letter the next time I go over there; and perhaps the next time I come here, I'd bring a reply with me,' said Father Morisco, seeing this as a way in. (There were, he knew, many ways of establishing channels of communication, and this surely was one, by carrying letters.)

'Elena would be very pleased, I'm sure,' said Maria. 'They do allow letters across, I presume?'

'They wouldn't search me,' said the priest. 'I've got to know most of the men on duty. They let me through.'

'There's a man wanting to sell a piglet outside,' said Elena, suddenly bursting into the room. 'Oh Father Morisco,' she said, surprised, wondering what he could be doing there. But the piglet seemed momentarily more important. 'Do come and look,' she said.

Out they went into the yard. A man stood there holding a piglet, a pink screaming mass that wriggled in his arms. Next to him stood a teenage girl, looking a little haughty, as if to say that piglets were not her major interest in life.

'Isn't he sweet?' said Elena.

'Couldn't we just stick with the dog instead?' asked Maria, who thought that the piglet, though novel, might easily outlive its charms.

'Oh Maria,' said Elena. 'I don't want it as a pet, I want it as an investment. It will grow huge, they eat anything and we can keep it in one of the outhouses, and then we will kill it. Just think of that.'

'Yes, dear,' said Maria, looking down at the piglet with new eyes. 'There's something in what you say.' She looked at the farmer, who had been silent during this conversation. 'How much?' she asked him in Spanish.

The farmer said nothing, only shrugged and gestured at his daughter, who immediately burst into rapid speech, at the end of which Maria went into the house and came out with two suitcases. Each was stuffed with clothes. Soon, to the sound of the porcine squeals, there was a rapid survey of the goods on offer. But the girl did not seem satisfied by what she saw.

'Norman Hartnell,' said Maria encouragingly, pointing to labels. 'St Michael.'

But the girl was unimpressed, and Elena, despairing about getting her piglet, rushed inside for more clothes.

'This is more like it,' she said, holding up something which seemed to be made out of black leather, and which she was sure Isabel de Calatrava could never have worn. She looked at the label. 'Zandra Rhodes,' she told the girl triumphantly, wondering who he could be.

The girl was immediately smitten. She would be the first in the entire country to dress in a pair of black leather skintight trousers. The exchange was made, and everyone was satisfied.

'Did Isabel wear that leather thing?' asked Maria, when they were back inside the house.

'I saw it among the Ambassador's things,' said Elena. 'It must have been something used for fancy dress parties or pantomimes. Poor girl, she would have been better off with the Norman Hartnell; or even the Marks and Spencers.'

Then she went to put her new acquisition in one of the outhouses, and to try and think of a name for it. She wondered whether it was male or female, and how long it would take to grow. Months, perhaps; but it might be a long war, and one had to be prepared for that.

'You will stay to lunch, won't you, Father?' asked Maria. 'I'm just about to see what there is to eat.'

Lunch turned out to be one of the very best meals Father Morisco had eaten for some time. There were pickles and ham to start with; and then there were roast potatoes and a chicken, and finally the most extraordinary pudding that he had ever seen that seemed to be made out of old pieces of bread and which tasted delicious.

'I always cook English things,' Maria explained.

'If ever I get my magazine started again,' said Carmen, who by this time had come in from the garden where she had been planting potatoes, 'I will have a special series on English recipes. It's the cuisine of the future. You see this pudding is made up of stuff that other people usually throw away.'

'Maybe I'll call the pig Olivarez,' said Elena meditatively.

'And how are things in the City?' Carmen was asking.

'Stalemate,' said Father Morisco, holding out his plate for more bread and butter pudding.

'And have you heard anything of Captain Enriquez?' asked Elena at last, because up to now she had been frightened to ask. She herself had not heard anything, and it worried her; of course Roberto was still alive, that was certain; but did he still care whether she was alive or not?

'I was coming to that,' said Father Morisco. 'I may have to go to the other side on business for the Archbishop in the next few weeks; it is just possible that I could take a letter through for you, if you wanted to send one, that is. What a delicious pudding. May I have a third helping? I won't be depriving your new piglet of his essential rations, will I?'

'Not at all, not at all,' said Elena happily, content at the thought of her letter, and quite forgetting her new pet, who, by the time she next saw Roberto, might well be but a memory of roast pork.

Thirty-seven

Major Williams had arrived in the Capital only to find that his stock had fallen. Autumn was setting in, and with it the realisation that the war had ground to a halt for the forseeable future. There would be no offensive operations for him to organise for the moment, and he was given the impression that his presence was rather superfluous. However, he was a man much given to activity, and if he could not be useful, he was just as determined to be a nuisance. He took over a large suite of rooms in one of the best hotels on the Riviera and filled it with maps and files, and wrote out numerous memoranda. To reward himself for his business, he gave himself the title Quartermaster-General.

Fritz, who was usually a very tolerant man, found all this rather hard to take. The new Quartermaster-General, like a spider, seemed to get everywhere. Fritz had thought it a good idea to mount some machine-guns on top of the Post Office, but Major Williams had had other ideas. A series of memoranda passed to and fro on the subject, which, as the weeks went by, gradually grew terser and terser. At last Fritz could stand it no longer and went to see Roberto, who was established in another hotel on the Riviera.

'Look here, Bobby,' he said. 'I want two machine-guns. And please don't tell me that I have got to go and see Williams about it, because I have. I want two machine-guns for the roof of the Post Office, which is an important strategic position that commands the front line, but that old fool, who doesn't know the first thing about strategy, won't give them to me.'

'Sit down, Fritz,' said Roberto, who was ensconced behind a huge desk. 'What is his excuse?'

Fritz handed over a sheaf of memoranda. Roberto looked at them, frowning. (He had always frowned, Fritz remembered, even as a boy.)

'Williams,' said Roberto, after a moment's consideration, 'is a pain in the backside. I think you should have had your machine-guns weeks ago. Williams is a pain in the entire Army's backside.'

'Then get rid of him,' urged Fritz.

'It isn't that simple,' said Roberto. 'He is Ximenez's uncle. We can't get rid of him unless Ximenez agrees first. Ximenez is very touchy. Look, there's some Fundador in the filing cabinet and it's probably the last bottle in the country.'

'I am sure Williams hates me,' said Fritz crossly. 'His wife is here with him, you know.'

'Is she?' asked Roberto, pouring out the brandy.

They took their glasses. There was a pause in the conversation.

'This isn't much like a war, is it?' said Roberto.

'No.'

'War is rather a disappointment to me,' he said ruminatively over his brandy. 'A couple of days of frenzied activity, when you don't quite know what is happening, and then you have these long long periods of stultifying inactivity. And everything is so badly organised. No one quite knows what to do with himself.'

'Quite,' said Fritz.

'I'll see Ximenez and see if anything can be done about the Major,' promised Roberto.

'Good,' said Fritz.

'Is anything else worrying you?'

'Yes,' admitted Fritz. 'I am a bit worried about Rodolfo. He has been in hospital for nearly a month now, and he doesn't seem to be making much of a recovery. I mean, his shrapnel wounds have healed, more or less, but he seems rather odd. I suppose it was a bad business what happened to those men who were with him.'

'Do you think he feels it?'

'I don't know.'

'Yes,' said Roberto, to no particular effect.

Both of them considered the seven men who had been with Rodolfo Tanucci. That had been a bad business. Some had been shot in the water; others had been captured more or less alive after their swim across the Bay. They had been killed in a manner that still struck Roberto as gratuitously cruel.

'I would never have chosen Tanucci for that mission,' said Roberto. 'But you did, Fritz, and you were quite right to do so. He saved the day, and did what was needed, and he came back alive, all of which shows that he is much tougher and cleverer than I had imagined possible. But I wish I had told him not to do anything more; he had done enough as it was; I feel bad that he was so unlucky the next day.'

'Shrapnel is very nasty: leg, groin, abdomen and chest. But it isn't that, so much. I think it is more in the mind.' Fritz put down his glass. 'If you aren't doing anything at present,' he said, 'we could go and see him.'

Roberto was indeed doing nothing, so they walked to the hospital together.

'You'll find him much changed,' said Fritz, when they were outside the room.

They went in. Rodolfo was lying on his bed, like a crusader on his tomb, dressed in hospital pyjamas. He was staring at the ceiling, and did not seem to notice their approach. He was paler and thinner than he had been before, and he had that ethereal quality of otherworldliness that often hangs over the dying.

'Hello, Tanucci,' said Roberto awkwardly. 'I wanted to come and see how you were. You're a hero now, you know.'

He leaned over the bed to say this and saw a flicker of amusement pass over Rodolfo's face.

'You don't want to be discharged, do you? Or are you looking forward to going back to the war?'

'I haven't been thinking about the war – much,' said Rodolfo slowly.

'Of course, you have had a grave shock,' said Roberto.

'That is what they keep on telling me.'

'Perhaps you need a period of rest,' said Roberto, without realising what he was saying.

'What do you think he is doing?' asked Fritz in a whisper.

'Look, if there's anything you want me to do . . .'

'There is,' said Rodolfo suddenly.

'Fritz, wait outside,' said Roberto, fearing what was coming. And when Fritz had gone, Roberto sat on the edge of the bed and said: 'Go on.'

'That girl was buried in the Army Navigational School,' said Rodolfo. 'In the cellars. I keep on thinking about that, and that we should dig her up and give her a decent burial. We made a mistake –'

'It couldn't do her any good,' said Roberto coldly. 'And it would do us harm. I'll have the place blown up first.'

'But her parents,' said Rodolfo.

'Just forget it,' said Roberto, unnerved by the way the buried past was coming back. 'Fritz,' he called. 'Come back in.' He was sure Tanucci would not dare mention the subject in front of Fritz – he valued his approval too much – and that if Fritz was there the subject would be closed.

'Finished your secret business?' asked Fritz.

Roberto said nothing, but went to the window, and lit a cigarette.

'I wish you'd be your old self,' said Fritz to Rodolfo.

'I don't want to be,' said Rodolfo. 'I'd like to speak to a priest. But not the hospital chaplain. When I was outside the Club, I met Father Morisco. I want to speak to him.'

'The Archbishop's secretary?'

'No,' said Roberto, turning round. 'That's out of the question. The man is on the other side, anyway, so it is impossible.'

'But he has been over here, you know,' said Fritz. 'He visited some policeman whom he rescued from death in the battle. He gets everywhere. He is the Archbishop's secretary, after all. If he wants Morisco why shouldn't he have him?'

'Absolutely not,' said Roberto. 'I don't trust Morisco an inch. He's too clever by half. There are hundreds of priests on this side of the City. Go and get one of the Italian Franciscans if he wants to go to confession. I presume that's what it is.'

'No, not them,' said Rodolfo. How could he explain himself to one of them? 'I want to see Father Morisco.'

'But you can't,' said Roberto.

'Morisco may come over here again,' said Fritz. 'Would you stop him? And why would you want to anyway?'

Roberto knew he was over-reacting. 'If he comes, I can't stop him,' he said. And he thought of the seal of confession, which would surely mean that whatever Rodolfo told Morisco could never be used to damage someone else. 'I'll wait outside,' he said. 'Goodbye, Tanucci,' he said, trying to sound casual.

Fritz followed within a few minutes.

'Of course, he's got religious mania,' said Fritz. 'Some sort of obsessive guilt because he is still alive and he feels he ought to be dead. I'd relieve him of his commission if I were you.'

'Yes,' said Roberto. 'He seems good for nothing now.'

Thirty-eight

Roberto did his best over the next few days to try and forget about Tanucci, but he was unable to put the thought entirely from his mind. He did not believe Fritz's bland assurances about religious mania; Fritz thought everyone in the country had religious mania, to a greater or lesser degree. Fritz could not understand what the matter was; Fritz could not know what it meant to commit a crime, or more accurately a sin, and to spend the rest of your life wondering when it would catch up with you.

Roberto did not trust Morisco, but he calculated that he could have nothing to fear from the priest, even if he were to find out everything that had gone on in the Army Navigational School. He was too powerful now to be touched by the past. When the war was won, he would be in the new Junta, and he would be above the law. The only enemy he had to fear was the enemy within, the same enemy that had overcome Tanucci, namely the idea that one should regret the past and try and undo it, that one should repent. Roberto had once been religious in a particularly devout way, as Fritz had noticed, but now he did his best not to think about religion, for if he were to do so there would be a chance that he too, like Tanucci, would be overcome with this terrible desire to make amends. Tanucci had proved himself to be brave and resourceful, getting through the City that day unarmed and more or less undressed. But there were other things that were harder to resist, such as the desire to be at peace with God. The bravest men were supposed to shrink at the prospect of putting themselves beyond the divine mercy, and were reputed to give in to the siren voices that counselled repentance. Roberto was determined to resist them. But he knew that of those voices, Morisco's was supposed to be the hardest to withstand.

The Army Navigational School itself was in their part of the City, and to his regret it had not been damaged at all in the fighting. If it had been blown up, it would have been so much the better; no one would be able to dig up bodies there if that happened. He toyed with the idea of arranging some sort of accident for the place, but decided against it. To do so would only draw suspicion on himself, and it would be far better to forget about the whole thing. No one was going to dig up those bodies anyway. Strauss and Olivarez were dead; Tanucci was clearly unbalanced; and the only persons who knew about what he had done were Elena, now on the other side, geographically at least, and Fritz. He regretted ever telling them but they were both people he could trust, he was sure. And more importantly, he knew that though they knew about Caballero, and in Fritz's case, Nickleby, neither understood the meaning of these events. For them, it remained on the level of a mistake; but for Roberto it could only be mortal sin, something once done, that could not be undone, and which shaped and directed the whole of his existence.

As for Tanucci, it was quite like the Italian male, he thought, to want to confess his fault to a priest. He was certain he would never do that; for if he were to confess that one fault, it would be tantamount to confessing that his whole life had been mistaken. He had gone too far for that. Morisco would never succeed with him. And having resolved not to turn back, he had no choice but to carry on going forward.

Strangely enough, a few days later, Morisco tried to see him. The priest, who seemed undaunted by the battle line that divided the City, turned up at Roberto's hotel, desiring an interview with Captain Enriquez. The man on guard duty at the door let the priest in – Father Morisco had always had the knack of getting round men on doors – and it was only by a stern refusal on the Captain's part that the good father, to whom no doors had ever been closed before, was refused admittance into Roberto's suite of rooms. The priest however left a letter; even though Roberto was told that it contained some news from his mother, he ordered it to be thrown away unread. He had made up his mind that Morisco was one of the few men who could pierce his armour, and that even to see him or have any contact with him would be dangerous. And he gave strict instructions that the man was never to be admitted to the building again, under any circumstances. He still felt his resolution against repentance was precarious.

'You know Rodolfo,' began Fritz one day, ill-advisedly, in these circumstances.

'I'd rather you didn't mention him, Fritz,' replied Roberto.

Fritz realised he had touched some sore point about which he knew nothing, and at once let the subject drop. He could see that something in the Tanucci case had deeply upset Roberto. He remembered how Roberto had behaved that day at the hospital. He sensed that all communication on this subject was now shut off. By this time Rodolfo, having been given a suitable medal, had been discharged from the Army; he had also seen Morisco; Roberto was determined that they should mention his name no more.

A further development convinced Fritz that something in Roberto's heart was hardening. He saw it with sadness, realised that he could do nothing about it, and took what comfort he could in his books on strategy. This further developement was Roberto's growing *rapprochement* with Ximenez.

Fritz, who had always liked everyone, continued to make an exception to the rule for Ximenez. It rather wounded him to see now that Roberto was drawing close to his enemy, despite the fact that he knew that Fritz disliked him. This was, he reflected, not entirely unexpected. Ximenez had not succeeded in getting Zondadari out of the picture, and if there was to be a triumvirate, Ximenez had to be on good terms with at least one of his colleagues. Unwittingly it was Fritz who cemented this new friendship; this was how it happened.

'I want to talk to you about Major Williams,' said Roberto to Ximenez one evening, as Fritz had asked him to do.

'Very well,' said Ximenez coolly. 'Talk about him.'

'I don't think he's up to the job of administering our supplies. He's too fussy. He's being a nuisance. He's more a businessman that a soldier. He knows nothing about strategy.'

'That is perfectly true,' said Ximenez reasonably. 'He got the job because he was a businessman and used to run a company.'

'There's a war on now and we've got to win it,' said Roberto. 'We've got to run things efficiently. And we can't have a man who is a civilian at heart doing a soldier's job.'

'I see,' said Ximenez, stroking his dark chin thoughtfully. 'Now let me be equally frank with you, Enriquez. Your complaints against my uncle are completely justified. He is a tedious old fool. I'm sure that I have listened to him in the past far more than I should have done. He was all for caution when we were in San Cristobal, and you weren't, and it turned out that you were right. So, Major Williams must go. But, Enriquez, if he does go, let it be on this understanding – that from now on there should be complete agreement between us on everything. As you say, there's a war on and we have to win it. We can get rid of my uncle. You can send him to December Island for all I care. Let him have his little kingdom. But you and I, Enriquez, we mustn't let these little personal things ruin our work. Do you have anyone you could suggest to take my uncle's place?'

'Fritz Rodriguez,' said Roberto at once. 'Cleverest man in the Army, and hasn't enough to do at present.'

Ximenez was thoughtful. Then he spoke.

'Of course,' he said. 'I know you like Rodriguez, and that's your affair. I have never warmed to him, I must say. I don't like clever men, but if that is who you want . . .'

Roberto considered. Fritz was his best and only friend. It

wasn't Fritz's fault that of late he had found the thought that he knew about the Nickleby girl irksome. He ought never to have told him.

'You won't see much of him,' he told Ximenez. 'He'll be kept very busy by the job.'

'Very well,' said Ximenez, overcoming his reluctance. 'I'll let you convince me on this one. Of course, we'll have to get Zondadari to approve.'

'Will he make any objection?'

'Not if we are agreed on it,' said Ximenez. 'Two to one.'

And so it turned out. Zondadari did approve of Fritz, but it would have made no difference even if he had not. Roberto felt a slight twinge of unease when he thought of the unspoken bargain he had now made with Ximenez. Matters were further cemented between the two of them by the sudden departure of Major Williams to December Island a few days later, and Ximenez's casual suggestion that Roberto might like to drop round on Mrs Williams and lighten her spirits in her husband's absence.

He had in fact already seen Mrs Williams once since her arrival in the Capital. She had smiled at him sweetly, treating him to a fine display of teeth, and congratulated him on the success of the Task Force. She had referred archly to his sudden departure from San Cristobal and chided him for not saying goodbye. He in turn had asked her in the coldest tones that he could manage about how she was enjoying life in the Capital. She had sighed and said that she found the days, particularly the afternoons, very dull, as her husband was never at home.

Now that her husband was permanently out of the picture, he wondered whether he ought to risk calling on her. He too found the afternoons rather dull; but there was an element of risk all the same. Fritz had called her a harpy, and the woman was clearly being put up to it by Ximenez. But when he thought of Mrs Williams, and remembered that he did not like her much, he assumed that he was safe from any entanglement.

Besides, he was growing bored with life. The war, as wars were in the habit of doing, had ground to a halt: the two sides had even stopped firing at each other across the front line. Perhaps Mrs Williams might amuse him. He had not exactly forgotten about Elena; she did cross his mind every now and then, and when she did so, he thought of her as a rather embarrassing dependant. He had no time for sentimental love any more: it would only lead to a fatal softening of the heart. That was what had happened to Tanucci. He would go and see Mrs Williams, she of the nails and teeth, and he would try to exorcise the demons that plagued him by taking an intelligent interest in women.

Mrs Williams, when he found her – and she was living in what had been Isabel de Calatrava's flat, which her husband as Quartermaster had taken over – was all compliance. Her nails and teeth were just the same. She poured him some wine, and was most attentive. He felt himself relax in her presence.

'A friend of my mother's used to live here,' he remarked.

'Goodness, how strange.'

'She fled the country, I believe,' he said laconically. 'My mother has gone to the north. I haven't heard a word from her since. I wonder why not. She is there with the girl she wants me to marry, and her mother.'

'Yes, Fritz told me.'

'Did he?' asked Roberto with a little frown. 'Fritz seems to find out about everyone and everything, even me.'

'Yes, he does,' said Mrs Williams.

'And what else does Fritz say about me?'

'Oh, you know,' said Mrs Williams, forming her large mouth into a girlish smile which hardly suited her. 'Fritz loves talking about everyone. He told me you were at school together. He is very very fond of you, and he says you are going to marry this beautiful girl when the war is over –'

'I really do wish Fritz would shut up sometimes,' said Roberto a little coldly, interrupting her. 'Of course, he's an excellent fellow and really does deserve to be Quartermaster, but all the same I'd rather he didn't discuss my lovable qualities with you or anyone else.'

He had never spoken so harshly about Fritz before.

'Does it upset you so much?' she asked tenderly.

'Yes, it does.'

First Rodolfo, now Fritz, he reflected. All the camaraderie was fast evaporating. He put down his wineglass and looked at his watch.

'You don't have to go?' she asked.

'On the contrary, I have about two hours to kill.'

Why on earth he felt the need for this woman whom he did not like or even find more than moderately attractive was a mystery to him. But he was driven by compulsion. He felt a curious interest in her simply because her teeth were too long, her conversation arch, and her red nails gruesome. Or rather the interest he felt was in his own self. Why was he using her to cut himself off from what should have been the surest path of happiness for a man?

As her red nails coursed through the hair on his chest afterwards, while he lay on his back smoking, he said:

'If ever you tell me that you love me, I'll never come and see you again.'

He watched her hand pause a moment as she took in the meaning of his words; pause, and then continue its wanderings.

Mrs Williams soon became something of a habit. His mornings were always filled with tedious business at the hotel he had made his headquarters, where he was either holed up with Ximenez, or deciding some trivial matter, or engaged with Ximenez in persuading Zondadari to do something he did not quite agree with. Thus the mornings would pass; winter advanced on them, and the war stood still, awaiting the coming of spring. The afternoons he would pass at Mrs Williams's or with Fritz. And because Fritz was in the habit of organising things carefully, as befitted a Quartermaster-General, he fell into the custom of seeing Mrs Williams on Tuesdays, Thursdays and Sundays, and Fritz on Mondays, Wednesdays and Fridays. This should have been an ideal arrangement, but like all human things it turned out to be less than perfect; for as Mrs Williams's usefulness increased, he found that his tolerance of Fritz was beginning to wane.

Naturally Roberto still knew that Fritz was the best man in the Army, and that there was no one better outside it either. And he also knew that Fritz loved and trusted him as no one else did. But this too had become a weight, for despite all Fritz's friendship, he did not tell him of the afternoons he spent with Mrs Williams. It was his secret; he was also very careful not to let her scratch him with her nails, as she had done that first time at San Cristobal. It would not do to have Fritz know how he spent his afternoons, for he was ashamed of it. Fritz knew too much about him already; Fritz knew about the Nickleby girl, and though there had never been the shadow of a reproach over that, Roberto dreaded that one day Fritz might come to disapprove of him.

A second area of silence was the question of Tanucci. That too was another reserved area between them. Roberto was sure that Fritz knew where Rodolfo had gone, but, though he was sure that Fritz wanted to tell him about it, he was equally sure that this was a subject he would never discuss. Tanucci's desertion meant that he was now the only one involved in the Nickleby case left. Tanucci had betrayed him, in an odd sort of way, by his talk of confessing to Morisco, or whatever it was he had wanted to do. But this was something that Fritz could not understand, and he was merely puzzled by Roberto's strange attitude to one who had been a comrade, and briefly a friend.

Despite this, there were many many other topics that Fritz could and would talk about. Some of these topics Roberto came to dread. Some afternoons they would walk by the sea, along the Riviera, and Fritz would talk of his romantic longings.

'As soon as the war is over, I would like to get married,' Fritz would say. 'I'll soon be thirty, after all. I'd like a girl of about twenty-five. The trouble is there don't seem to be any about. All the respectable women have left the City. I don't blame them, really, as there are enemy troops not two miles away from this spot. The trouble is, even when I did meet girls of the right age, none of them seemed to like me. Why not? It's not because I am revoltingly unattractive, is it?'

'No, Fritz it's not that,' Roberto would reply wearily.

'I suppose it isn't. Men who have been a lot less prepossessing than me have married beautiful women before now. My father was one for a start. So were my uncles. Perhaps if I stopped worrying about it, I'd find someone, but the trouble is –'

'Fritz, for God's sake talk about something else, will you?' Roberto would say, exasperated. This train of talk would remind him how it had been Fritz who had first met Elena, and how it had been Fritz who had been supposed to have taken her out, yet been ill at the last moment. If only that illness had never taken place, Fritz might have married Elena, and that would have taken care of them both.

'Yes, I knew it. I'm boring. That's it. That is the secret of my failure.'

'Fritz, you're not boring. No one seriously thinks you are boring. Just help me to get this cigarette alight. The wind's rather too strong today.'

Fritz obediently opened his tunic to provide the necessary shelter for Roberto's lighter. But as soon as that was done, he would fix upon some other topic.

'We could end the war, if we wanted to, quite soon.'

'How?'

'By negotiation. I reckon Hernandez and Messina must be sick of it and each other by now. Hernandez is very old and from what I gather his nerves have gone to pieces ever since the rocket attack on the Palace. All he'd ask for is a hefty pension and a free passage out of the country.'

'How could we pay him even that? The escudo has ceased to exist. He'd want it in US dollars.'

'The Republic has got assets in London.'

'And the British have frozen them.'

'They'd unfreeze them; they only did so to stop the Generals spending the money on arms.'

'And who would do the negotiating?'

'The British Ambassador.'

'He's a fool, Fritz, I've met him. And I wouldn't trust him an inch,' said Roberto, remembering the Nickleby case. He could never negotiate with anyone British now.

'The Archbishop, then,' said Fritz.

'They say he's a saint. That rules him out.'

'Father Morisco would be the man, then,' said Fritz at last.

'I'm damned if I am going to negotiate with anyone,' said Roberto at the mention of Morisco's name. 'Morisco is a snake. And I am determined to see Messina and Hernandez hang, and I don't care how old they are. They deserve nothing less and when the spring comes we will blast their Army to kingdom come. We don't have to negotiate, because we're going to win. And now I want to go back to my hotel. It's cold out here.'

Nothing daunted, for Fritz had known him since he was thirteen, and was used to these tantrums, Fritz would return to the attack once they were inside the hotel lobby.

'So, we've got to win the war,' he would say.

'Of course,' Roberto would agree, regretting the way he had lost his temper.

'Well, why don't we do just that? Why don't we go ahead? Why don't we go on an offensive?'

'It's the season,' Roberto would reply mechanically. 'We have to wait for the spring, and it won't be long.'

'We could easily hit the Presidential Palace from a number of points. Just a few bombs – enough to blow the roof off. That would put the wind up Hernandez: he would be on the next plane out, and Messina wouldn't be able to last long without him.'

'Fritz – we're not going to blow up the Palace. It would cost the earth to rebuild. It's our city too. And they would only retaliate in kind. They'd level this hotel. Do be reasonable.'

'I am being reasonable. I suppose Ximenez has talked you into this.'

'He has not. I have got sense, and I can see things that you can't. You don't know a thing about war. This isn't a game. This isn't Hannibal and his elephants, you know.'

'I do know. You don't need to tell me that, Roberto.'

And Roberto would realise how unjust he had been, and feel himself forced to apologise, something that he hated doing.

During the few moments that he got to himself, Roberto would sometimes reflect on the evident dislike that existed between Fritz and Ximenez. It troubled him a little. In a time of war, when such little things could be magnified, personal animosity could be dangerous. Of course, Fritz was the sort of character who had *ideés fixes* about things like strategy and Hannibal, and other harmless topics, and it stood to reason that he could do the same with people. And the same could be said for Ximenez; there was something a little maniacal about Ximenez, and Roberto never forgot that Ximenez was the man who had shot his own Colonel in cold blood. Ximenez was equally a man for *idées fixes*. And the two of them had clashed at the famous meeting of the Army Council in San Cristobal. And even before that there had been a history of dislike, but quite why, Roberto could not imagine. Why should Ximenez dislike Fritz so much? Fritz was so easy-going, he was quite sure that Ximenez had started the feud. That was a question that disturbed him, but his interest in it was not as great as the interest he felt in the wider question raised: he wished Ximenez could be more tolerant, more self-controlled; and sometimes he wished that Ximenez was not a man he was forced to work with.

As the winter advanced, the weather got steadily worse, but still Roberto and Fritz would walk on the Riviera. Roberto would look out to sea and see the Presidential Palace, inviolate on the other side of the Bay, and his heart would grow heavy. At such times, Fritz's proximity and cheerfulness would make his heart even heavier.

On one such walk they were caught in a squall, and took shelter in a church porch.

'This is the church where the Archangel Michael was supposed to have appeared,' remarked Fritz. 'They have got his footprints in the sacristy.'

'Surely you can't believe that sort of rubbish?' asked Roberto.

'A lot of people do,' said Fritz. 'It is quite a common belief, not just in Christianity, that men dying on the field of battle are comforted by heavenly visitors.'

'I won't be,' said Roberto.

'I've never thought about death,' said Fritz. 'Not even during those days when we were fighting. I felt too busy. I was worried about other people. When we were in our pincer movement, I kept on thinking you would be killed.'

'Well, I wasn't,' said Roberto. Then, relenting, he added: 'It was kind of you to think of me then, Fritz. I'm not worth the trouble. I remember once thinking that one of these days you would sacrifice your life for someone. I think you would. But don't do it for me, Fritz, do it for someone else. Do it for Zondadari or for someone you admire. But not for me.'

And saying that, Roberto decided to walk back to his hotel alone. Fritz watched him go, not understanding what was the matter with him. Perhaps, he thought, he was missing Elena, or even his mother. That sort of sacrifice must be hard. It was remarkably dedicated of Roberto, he thought, to forgo the company of his nearest and dearest when he might have brought them over to this side of the Republic without insurmountable difficulty. Fritz looked at his watch. It was still early in the afternoon. Perhaps he would go and see his old friend Mrs Williams for a cup of tea and some Scrabble.

Thirty-nine

As the days passed and the letter she had sent to Roberto through Father Morisco produced no tangible result, Elena grew more and more disappointed. She wondered if perhaps the letter had never been delivered; perhaps the priest had lost it, or even purloined it, for reasons of his own. Father Morisco had the look of a man who might well have plenty of reasons of his own. But she had no way of finding out what the priest had done with her letter, as there was no working telephone at Torre del Mar, and as they had no petrol, which ruled out driving to the City to investigate. Besides, even if she were to get to the City, that would be no guarantee of finding Father Morisco; he might be anywhere, and from what she had gathered from his last visit, frequently was. All she could do was wait patiently until the priest visited them again. He had promised that he would come back, after all. And she used reason to try and calm her fears. If anyone could get a letter through to Roberto, that man was Father Morisco. Maria had told her as much. It seemed that Father Morisco had friends on both sides of the divide, and could come and go as he pleased.

In the meantime, she waited. They had been at Torre del Mar long enough now to make the experience of living in the country lose its novelty. So she settled down to wait, and as she carried on her daily tasks, she did them in the consciousness that this was merely an interval, and that she was waiting for her real life to start again. Waiting had become something of an art with her. In the old days – before the war – she had waited for Roberto to ask her to marry him. She had waited for smaller things too: she had spent hours waiting for him to phone her. She had then waited for him to come back from December Island. Now she waited simply for him to acknowledge that she still existed. While she wondered about what he might be doing, about whether he was thinking of her just then or whether he was thinking of her at all, she carried on with the dreary task of living. She fed her pig and watched it grow day after day – but still no Father Morisco came. She cooked meals in the kitchen, all the time alert for the welcome sound of a car. She read books, of which there were plenty in the house; she read Dickens and Scott and tried to think of people who might be worse off than herself. But on that score her imagination failed her. Men, it was true, had been killed, mothers had lost sons and wives husbands – but at least they had known they had been loved. She had no such assurance, and continued to live in a state of uncertainty.

Her only comfort was Maria. Maria would look at her with serious eyes as they sat quietly at night, and she could tell that Maria knew what she was feeling.

'If he has any sense, my dear,' Maria said more than once, 'he will love you the way you deserve to be loved.'

This was all the comfort she had. Her own mother tried to be more practical. Apart from filling her day with plans for a new magazine that she would start when the war was over, which would deal with organic gardening and English cookery, with overtones of self-sufficiency (for Carmen could sense that something as lacking in weight as *Moda* simply had no future), Carmen had other plans. Father Morisco had told her when he had been there that the City was for the moment quite safe, and that there was no fighting; in particular, the district where the Garcia flat lay was far away from the front line. It was therefore possible, though it would be difficult, to go home, if that was what they wanted to do. It would mean selling their jewellery for US dollars and buying a flight out of the Republic, and then re-entering the Republic by land on the other side of the front line. It would be complicated and expensive, but it could be done. The simpler method, driving to the border, crossing it, and then recrossing it south of the lines, was impossible, as all the neighbouring countries had closed their frontiers to prevent refugees seeking expensive and troublesome sanctuary. But there were still a few flights from the airport to be had at highly inflated prices.

Elena refused even to consider this course of action. Roberto had not asked her to come to him, and she would not go until he did so. For at the back of her mind was the realisation that he might not want her, and that her arrival on his side of the lines might be an unwelcome surprise. Carmen knew this too; that was why she had suggested it, hoping that it would bring her daughter's uncertainty to an end. But Elena preferred to remain uncertain; she preferred that to an end she dared not think of.

At last, one day, early in the morning, while she was feeding her pig, Father Morisco arrived, almost a month to the day since his previous visit. When he saw her his expression was grave. He refused to answer her questions until they were both in the house and sitting down.

'You delivered my letter to Roberto?' she asked at once.

'Yes, my dear, and no,' said Father Morisco gently. 'I left your letter for him and they did say that they would give it to him; but you know how things are in this country; you can never be sure that people mean what they say. I wasn't allowed to see him myself. I was only able to get into the ground floor of his hotel – he's set up his HQ in a hotel along the Riviera, you know – they wouldn't let me see him. He has become a very important young man these days.'

'And so, you have brought no reply,' she said flatly.

'None at all, I am afraid, my dear.'

'If he'd known it was you, I'm sure he would have seen you, Father,' said Elena.

Father Morisco would have liked to have agreed with this sentiment. He had wanted to see the Captain for reasons of his own. But he was sure that Enriquez had known he had called, and he was unable to give Elena the reassurance she wanted.

'What about the prospects for peace?' said Elena.

'They say that peace is in the air,' said Father Morisco. 'There is a lot of talk of it in the Capital, you know. They say it is because it is winter. Some people expect the fighting to start again in the spring, but, and this is something you mustn't tell a soul, there are men on both sides that want to patch up the quarrel before the spring so that that fighting never happens. You see, General Hernandez – do you know General Hernandez, my dear?'

'Not at all,' she said.

'General Hernandez,' said Morisco, 'is seventy-five years old. Even if he won the war, it stands to reason that he wouldn't enjoy the fruits of victory for very long. And the idea of fighting in the City is not his cup of tea. Just imagine the damage that a few serious bombs could do. They have done enough damage as it is, and smashed enough windows. And of course, but for different reasons, Captain Zondadari thinks the same way. He is a good man, Zondadari; he's a member of lots of Catholic organisations, and I know him quite well. He would have no objection to letting the Generals leave the country, if that is what they wanted to do, and giving all their men an amnesty. And then his idea would be to call elections. But you see, the problem is that General Messina is all for renewing the war if these negotiations don't produce any result; and Captain Ximenez won't hear of peace at all.'

'And what does Roberto think?'

'Captain Enriquez, from what I've been told, seems to be on Ximenez's side rather than Zondadari's. That's why we have deadlock: Zondadari can't do anything as it is two to one against. That is why your Captain holds the key to the situation, and why I would so like to speak to him. And we have so many opportunities at present. The British Amabassador is disposed to help. You see, Hernandez would like to go and live in England, and we seem to have solved the Nickleby case, and that means the British would have no objection to his presence.'

'You have solved the Nickleby case? How?'

'One of the guilty parties came and told me all about it,' said the priest. 'And naturally, and this is quite in accord with Canon Law, he was given absolution on the condition that he made restitution as far as possible. That meant giving the injured parties, chiefly the girl's parents, the information they wanted. The girl was killed, as I supposed, a few hours after being taken. But she wasn't murdered, she killed herself. She was raped, and then she killed herself in despair. They buried her body in secret, and at present we are unable to recover it.'

'But why did they arrest her?'

'They thought she was someone else,' said the priest. 'It was as senseless as that.'

'And the guilty men?'

'The guilty man was hanged very soon afterwards. The man ultimately responsible, Colonel Olivarez, well, we know what happened to him. And then a third man, the one who took part in the arrest, he is now doing penance for his sins. The British, it seems, don't want him; he was merely an accomplice. The British were far more interested in the men at the top.'

Father Morisco was silent. He thought of Tanucci, and the bravery of his choice. And he thought of Enriquez, and wondered what sort of man he could be, and how much Elena really knew about him. Enriquez, he knew, was now more or less immune to prosecution, thanks, ironically, to Father Morisco's own efforts. He had persuaded the Ambassador not to follow up the British claims against Enriquez in the interests of closing the Nickleby case and getting on with the job of negotiating a peace. But now the Nickleby case was closed; the British Government were satisfied, and they would give Hernandez asylum, they would unfreeze the assets they had frozen, and provided Enriquez could be made to see sense, the whole thing could be brought to a conclusion. A conclusion was much to be desired, though whether it would end anything, the priest was not sure. He was worried about Enriquez. What sort of man was he? Could the government of the Republic be safely left in the hands of men like Enriquez and Ximenez? Of course, Enriquez was not guilty of murder as such, he told himself, but even that was not much consolation.

'Father,' said Elena suddenly, 'do you mean that you think that Roberto actually wants this war to go on?'

'I am afraid I do.'

'But why?'

He could not answer. The Nickleby case was undoubtedly at the root of it all.

'I wish to God,' said the girl, 'that I had never, that I had never . . . I can't say that I wish I had never met him. I mean that I had never become so deeply involved with him. But I wanted to. He didn't. It was me all along; and now I feel that I never really knew him at all.'

'What do you mean?' asked the priest gently, looking at her with that expression that had brought secrets out of the most hardened consciences.

'Of course, we have made love,' she said. 'I mean, we've known each other for five years, and it is considered normal in those circumstances, isn't it? At least it is nowadays. We did make love, but only once. At other times, there were other things, but not very often; he would always dash off to the confessional afterwards, you know, because he felt guilty – at least I think he did. He never told me what he felt, and oddly, I never wanted to ask him. Never once, until right at the end, did he say that he wanted to marry me. It was never clear that what we were doing was a sign that we were eternally joined together . . .'

'The only sign of that is marriage,' said the priest. 'That is the unbreakable bond between a man and a woman, and sex is just part of that bond.'

It rather amazed her to hear the priest use the word 'sex' with so little visible effort. It was as if he was used to dealing with the concept every day.

'But sex,' she said, trying to articulate a concept that she had imbibed from the pages of her mother's magazine, which, despite the Generals' strictures, had occasionally sailed a little close to the wind, 'sex is important, isn't it?'

'It is,' said Father Morisco. 'All physical things are important. I don't mean food and drink, but physical things – we are in the body, you know. We are not just souls that happen to be attached to bodies. Your body is yourself. To give your body is to give yourself. But things beyond the physical are more important. Sex is a sign of love, but it can't create love unless love is there already.'

'I always hoped,' she said forlornly, 'that if he made love to me then he would eventually come to love me as well.'

'And did he?'

'I don't know; I loved him. I thought I'd met the man I was going to marry. But he was so . . . withdrawn. I know why, I think, now. And it is a very silly reason. When he was quite small he very occasionally had tantrums; but as he grew older, he learned to control himself; but he knew that if ever he grew angry or sad, or whatever, or passionate in any way, the most awful, or so it seemed to him, thing would happen to his face. He would go bright scarlet, and he couldn't bear to be seen like that. I've seen him in that state, only once. His face was almost purple, and the blush went right down over his chest and his back. Isn't it odd to think that a man like Roberto, who has every natural gift, should be so concerned about what other people might think of him? And he was. He always used to wash his face in cold water on the oddest occasions; I thought it was strange, but I didn't know. No one knew. And yet he always pretended that he didn't care a damn about what people thought. But he cared so much; he even cared what I might think. He didn't want me to see him blush; and what he didn't realise was that I was in love with him, and that anything he might do would make no difference. And for five years he succeeded.'

'But didn't he blush during those other things you spoke about? The things that made him rush off to confession?' asked Father Morisco curiously.

'He was as pale as marble,' she said. 'Except that once, at the end. He would always be so unmoved. I used to wonder whether he didn't prefer . . . men. Fritz Rodriguez was his particular friend for years, but Fritz isn't like that at all, so I never thought that was possible.'

'What is Fritz like?' asked Morisco. 'I know him, but I never see him in church, and he's not a member of any Catholic societies, as far as I can work out, and I have been through all the records.'

'Fritz,' she said, 'is one of the best men alive; and he'd be the only person that Roberto would listen to.'

'I see,' said Father Morisco, storing this information for future use.

Father Morisco stayed to lunch yet again, and when he left he took with him another letter for Roberto from Elena and one from his mother as well. This time he was determined to make sure that they were delivered and did not meet the fate of the last letter. He also determined to cross the lines the very next day. Winter was the shortest of seasons, and though the weather was now dull and rainy, in a few weeks it might well be brightening up, and even a few clement days might have the unhappy effect of turning men's minds to war. The need for peace seemed more urgent than ever, and now he felt it might just be possible.

Crossing the lines, in other words, crossing what had been the City's main thoroughfare, presented little difficulty for him. He said Mass at dawn the next day, and after breakfast with Don Alvaro, he set off. The soldiers on the Government side of the road let him through, because they knew him; and because he was a priest and known to the rebels, no one shot at him as he walked across the sea of broken glass that divided the two sides. Others were less lucky than Father Morisco: on each side of the wide road small groups of women were gathered, doing their best to shout messages from one side to the other, their words often lost in the breeze. No one allowed them across; but Father Morisco was different. Unknown to them, General Hernandez himself had given orders that the priest was to be allowed to cross at will; and Captain Zondadari had said the same thing to the rebel troops, so the priest had the special status of confidential go-between.

By eight that morning Father Morisco found himself in the presence of Captain Rodriguez. Despite the fact that he hardly knew the Captain, he found that he was being greeted like a long lost friend, his hand warmly shaken, and being conducted to the most comfortable chair.

'I know why you have come,' said Fritz as soon as they were seated.

Father Morisco arched an eyebrow. If that were true, then Captain Rodriguez was a very perceptive young man. Father Morisco always liked to think that his plans were far beyond the comprehension of ordinary mortals. It was the one little vanity that he allowed himself. But all the same, he was much disposed to like Captain Rodriguez. Only yesterday he had heard the confession of Elena Garcia, and the secrets of her heart had taken a long time in the unfolding; he did not quite understand it all, but he felt that this young man might well have a significant part to play in the future. And he really seemed very pleasant. He had a nice face; and though he was balding, and seemed to fit a little too snugly into his uniform, and he was not a handsome man in the way Enriquez was, he certainly was engaging.

'You know why I have come?' he asked.

'Yes, to tell me how Rodolfo Tanucci is,' said Fritz.

'He is well,' said Father Morisco. 'He is enjoying the life, and they are very pleased with him. He is quite transformed. I think he will make a very good friar. But you look puzzled, Captain.'

'It seems odd to me, that's all,' said Fritz. 'I mean, he was the very last person I'd have expected to want to be a Franciscan. He's tough, you know.'

'And so is spiritual warfare, Captain. Perhaps one day you will hear the entire story from Rodolfo himself. There is a story there, you know. It is always the same story, though, in all these cases. At certain times in our lives we feel that our lives don't belong to ourselves any more, but they belong to someone else. It is like falling in love. And with Rodolfo, that day, when he so narrowly escaped death on several occasions, he felt that he had been redeemed from the grave and that somehow he belonged to God.'

'Italians are good at those sort of revelations,' said Fritz.

'But,' said the priest suddenly, 'I have in fact come about something else. I want to ask your help. You can do me a favour, and more importantly, a favour for us all. In fact, I think you can save us all from absolute disaster.'

'If I can, I will,' said Fritz.

'Of course, I know you will,' said Father Morisco with a chuckle. 'You're not a freemason. I checked. We have a list of all the known freemasons in the Republic in the archives. I'm not sure if it is up to date, though. Neither you nor Captain Enriquez are freemasons. But to business,' he said, and suddenly grew serious. 'I have spoken to the British Ambassador, and to General Hernandez, and to General Messina as well. General Hernandez is quite happy to retire into private life in the country of his choice, under certain conditions, of course.'

'That's good news,' said Fritz. 'I had heard as much.'

'From Zondadari, no doubt. The delicate part concerns your side. Of course, Zondadari wants peace; that goes without saying. He does not want to become a professional warlord, any more than you do. Yes, I did a little research on your character before taking you into my confidence, you can be sure of that. I've also spoken, only once, to Captain Ximenez. I've also tried to see Captain Enriquez, but he refused to see me.'

Fritz was thoughtful.

'Zondadari is a nice chap,' he said at last. 'But I am afraid he doesn't carry as much weight as he ought to. I like him and admire him. He's a brave man, but his parents came here from

Spain after the Civil War. They were on the wrong side. A lot of people hold that against him. They think he's not quite one of us, and that makes him socially awkward. There's a lot of that sort of feeling in the Army I am afraid to say . . .'

'So Zondadari is not like Captain Enriquez?'

'He is quite the opposite. Roberto went to the best school in the country, and his father was an excellent man. Everyone knows who his mother is. That counts for an awful lot. No matter how much good sense a man like Zondadari talks, people are unwilling to listen. Of course, he is in this triumvirate that they've set up, but he's like Lepidus. The other two are the ones that really count: they are the Mark Anthony and the Octavian; Zondadari is their messenger boy.'

'Quite, and that's why I have come to you,' said the priest. 'Ximenez won't hear of stopping the war. I can't think why, but he's bent on carrying things on until the bitter end. He wouldn't even admit that if he wins, all he'll win will be a heap of smoking ruins.'

'Ximenez wants to rule the country,' said Fritz. 'It is as simple as that.'

'But if Enriquez can be persuaded to see the benefits of peace, then Ximenez would have to give way. It would then be two to one – but in the opposite direction, so to speak. The trouble is that Zondadari himself can't seem to get through to Enriquez at all. He has tried, but . . .'

'And you think I can?'

'At the very least you could persuade him to see me,' said the priest.

'I am not sure I can persuade him to do anything he doesn't want to do himself, these days,' said Fritz. 'But I suppose I can try.'

'I would be very grateful.'

'I usually see him this afternoon,' said Fritz. 'I could leave a message for you here, if I'm not here myself, this evening, to let you know what he says.'

'Good,' said Father Morisco, standing up to go. 'And before

I forget – the diocesan records have a record of everything, but I couldn't find any record of your baptism, Captain.'

'Were you looking for it?'

'Yes, I was. Just out of curiosity, you know. But I couldn't find it at all. And when you get married you have to produce a baptism certificate, you know. I remember one odd case where a man who couldn't had to be done again. It can always be done, but it is a little troublesome, you know. But perhaps you were baptised in another diocese?'

'I don't think so,' said Fritz. 'Perhaps there are simply no records of it. Perhaps I will have, as you say, to be done again, if I get married.'

As he was seeing the priest to the door, he asked: 'Can anyone look around the diocesan records?'

'Good Lord, of course not. Some things there could do enormous damage. Things like the evidence used in annulling marriages. Can you imagine it, if it became public knowledge that someone's marriage was dissolved on grounds of non-consummation? Some things are meant to be secret, Captain.'

'I couldn't agree more, Father,' said Fritz.

'And finally, these are for Captain Enriquez,' said the priest. 'Give them to him this afternoon, please. Goodbye.'

Fritz was left alone with his thoughts and two envelopes. The handwriting on one of the envelopes was Elena's. He had only seen her handwriting once or twice before, but he recognised it immediately. How odd to think that he hardly knew the girl, and yet he could remember such a small thing about her. The other letter was clearly from Roberto's mother. Yet, even though these two letters ought to give Roberto endless pleasure, Fritz had a sense of foreboding. He feared that Roberto would be annoyed by Father Morisco's mission. He had been annoyed by the priest before and he had refused to see him, presumably because he had not wanted to do so. It was hard to make Roberto do anything he did not want to do, Fritz knew. But this was an important matter; the fate of the country rested on it, and it was surely worth running the risk of making Roberto angry in a case such as this. But even though he knew he had to speak, Fritz felt a secret fear. He had never felt fearful up to now, even when he had run the risk of being killed. But this was a different sort of fear. Roberto had changed of late, he had grown cold, reserved and withdrawn. He had been those things with others for most of his life, but never with Fritz. Fritz realised he had annoyed him, but he had not meant to or wanted to, nor had he quite realised exactly what he had done to do so. If he were to annoy him again – and Roberto had already told him that he did not want to hear Morisco's name even mentioned – what might happen then?

The more Fritz thought of how the good understanding that had always existed between them had been eroded, the more he considered that it was the work of the baleful influence of Ximenez.

'Ximenez hates me,' he had said to Roberto one day.

'Then he must be very vengeful and very petty to expend so much energy on you,' said Roberto unfeelingly.

'It was because I opposed him at that meeting of the Army Council at San Cristobal,' said Fritz. 'You weren't there,' he had added.

'So you keep on reminding me. But I doubt if Ximenez has given a thought to the matter since,' he had replied, knowing, however, that this was unlikely.

This had not been the friendly reassurance that Fritz had been looking for. He persisted in his view that Ximenez loathed him. He had seen it in his eyes at that meeting. But before that even, the day of the coup, when Ximenez had made such elaborate arrangements to get him out of the way, he had sensed it then too. Fritz pondered the events of that day, and in particular pondered the way Ximenez had surprised him when he had been having a shower. That made him feel particularly vulnerable. If Ximenez were to realise that Fritz was Jewish, it would be quite possible for him to use that against him. There were no anti-Jewish laws in the Republic as such, but there were some laws, and even some Army rules and regulations, left over from the 1940s that could be given that interpretation. Fritz had never given such vague ordinances about how all officers were expected to live in accord with Christian principles much thought before. But Ximenez was vengeful, and just the sort of man who liked to settle old scores. And Ximenez would be just the man to poison Roberto's mind against him.

Father Morisco would be back that evening, expecting progress. Perhaps the best thing to do would be to deliver the two letters at once, in the hope that that would put Roberto into a good mood. Accordingly he walked the few blocks to Roberto's hotel, was admitted by the guards, for everyone knew him, and made his way to Roberto's office. It was deserted, as was his bedroom, so he left the letters on the desk, where he would find them as a pleasant surprise. Then he went away.

Forty

Roberto found the letters about an hour later, when he returned from one of his morning conferences with Ximenez. Elena had never written to him before, and he opened the first envelope in a spirit of idle curiosity, not realising that it was from her. By the time he had read the first few lines, the chance of throwing it away unread was already gone. He read it in appalled fascination, this long letter from a girl he now felt he hardly knew, but with whom he had once briefly imagined himself in love. She was, as he had always assumed, in Torre del Mar with his mother. The letter told him what he most dreaded to hear, namely, that somewhere beyond the sphere of his control was someone who pinned all the hopes of her existence on him. But she was a stranger to him; and more importantly, the man to whom she wrote was a stranger too. He felt that this letter could be addressed to anyone, except him. The Roberto she imagined had ceased to exist.

He put the letter aside, and picked up the other. This was from his mother. It made unpleasant reading. 'You are under a serious moral obligation,' she wrote, 'to make clear to Elena what your intentions are. The last we heard was that you were engaged to her; but your present behaviour, Roberto, is not at all like that of an engaged man. I know that you know that we are capable of looking after ourselves here at Torre del Mar and that we are in no way dependent on your help. However, that is not the point. You still should feel enough concern about your future wife to write to her at least to ask whether she is still alive. Or at the very least you should write to her to break off the engagement if you feel it has become a burden to you. But to leave the poor girl in this state of complete uncertainty, without any news of you for months, is quite quite wrong. I know there is a war on, but all the same, you mustn't forget your personal duty. It is most unlike you . . .'

Maria's letter continued in a similar strain for some pages. He skimmed its contents, felt himself grow a little uncomfortable, and went at once to wash his face in cold water. His mother was one of the few people who could still make him blush; his conscience was not completely dead after all. Perhaps, he thought, he ought to write back. But what was there to say? How on earth could he renew his promise to marry Elena when he was in fact Mrs Williams's man? How could he break the engagement off, without making himself appear utterly unfeeling? What would his mother think? Did she know that they had gone to bed together, he and Elena, that weekend of the General's birthday? If she knew that – and could Elena have told her? The letter did seem to hint at it – then she would certainly regard that as a seal to the promise that he had made to her to marry her. He wished to God now that he had never met the girl, or at least never entangled himself so deeply. The idea of the girl and his mother ranged against him was quite unsettling. He was glad that there was a front line between the two of them. And then he wondered how the letters had got there.

He sat at his desk and tried to concentrate on other things. In a few weeks perhaps, if the weather improved, and as the days got longer, they would attack the enemy. He considered the plans that Ximenez had put before him. Details about men and machine-guns, platoons and mortars, swam before his eyes, as he tried to concentrate on the papers on his desk. But after a time, he was drawn back to Elena's letter. A second reading produced a softer impression. He was not vain, but if he had been, he would have been flattered. There was much in what she wrote that spoke of pure and innocent feelings. For months he had lived among people he had disliked or been brought up to despise. He had deliberately started an affair with a woman he disliked in order to kill such feelings, to cauterise his heart. Fritz was one of the only people he respected, but even Fritz was beginning to drive him mad. But as he re-read Elena's letter, he began to realise that she deserved better. He wondered if in fact he would reply. The old fantasy crept into his mind. One day all of this would be over, and perhaps then he could, despite all and after all, settle down to what was called a normal life. He could leave behind war and plans for war, and be happy and at peace. The world he had deliberately turned his back on tempted him once more.

This mellow mood settled on him, and he was almost glad when he saw Fritz that afternoon. For the first time in many weeks, he felt he was enjoying Fritz's company. He had forgotten how Fritz could make him laugh, or at least smile. Fritz told him a story about Major Williams, as they had lunch together.

'So, he's decided to number all the penguins. Naturally, Hoffmann was delighted.'

'Is Hoffmann there too?'

'Oh yes. As soon as Hoffmann heard that December Island was being re-garrisoned, he asked to go back. He simply couldn't keep away. Anyway, the Major sent all the men off to catch the penguins and number them. You see, penguins can't fly and can't leave the island either.'

'Are they easy to catch?'

'That's just it. They have been trying to catch and number them for weeks and so far they have only done seventeen. Whenever they pounce on a herd or whatever you call it of penguins, they get one, but it seems they always get the same ones. And there are thousands of them. Hoffmann is quite in despair and the Major gets crosser and crosser.'

'How funny,' said Roberto, not that it was, but he felt in the mood to be amused.

Fritz was pleased with the success of this anecdote, which

Mrs Williams had told him over a long game of Scrabble. They had finished a bottle of wine over lunch, and something of the happier times they had experienced in the past seemed to have returned.

It was raining heavily outside, and instead of their usual afternoon walk, up and down the Riviera, they went back into the hotel; it was a cold day, and there was nothing to do. Roberto suggested they try the hotel's Turkish bath as a way of passing the time. Neither of them had ever had a Turkish bath before, but provided they could do so on their own, they were both willing to try.

The experiment was a success. They had the place to themselves, as Roberto had told the hotel staff not to admit anyone else, and as he lay on the marble slab in the steam room, Roberto felt the refreshing heat all over his body, which was a pleasant contrast to the cold and darkness of December Island that Major Williams was even then suffering. He was quite unaware of the effect that the heat was having on his skin, making it go a pale shade of scarlet. While he lay there, Fritz rubbed his shoulders.

'Roberto,' said Fritz at last.

'Yes, Fritz?'

'I want to tell you something. But I think it might make you a little bit angry. Can you guess what it's about? Or rather who it is about?'

'Not Rodolfo Tanucci?'

'He might be part of it, I suppose.'

'What has happened to him? I haven't heard a word about him, except that he was discharged, and given a medal.'

'He went off to become a friar. You know, a Franciscan.'

'Good grief,' said Roberto. 'Throwing his life away.'

'From what I gather, that day he swam the Bay, he realised that God had saved him from death, unlike the other poor blighters. So he decided to become a friar. I suppose the fact that there's a Franciscan church on the Riviera might have had something to do with it. But people do funny things in wartime.'

'They do,' agreed Roberto. 'Why haven't you become a priest, Fritz?'

'I'm an unbeliever, that's why not.'

'But you could convert. That's not hard,' said Roberto half-seriously. 'You wouldn't change much: you go round being kind to undeserving cases all the time. I've noticed. I don't just mean myself. You're too damn good, that's your trouble. You might as well become a priest. You're almost one already. You'd make a better one than any of the ones I've ever met.'

'But think of the things I would have to give up.'

'Like what? Money? You haven't got any money, and for the last few months the army has paid you in IOU slips. And the other thing I've noticed is that you don't mind taking orders from people. You are the ideal candidate.'

'There's women,' said Fritz. 'What about them?'

'What about them?'

'I like them,' said Fritz.

'How extraordinary. I suppose Tanucci had never given that a try, so that didn't dissuade him. You much prefer Tacitus and Livy and Clausewitz, I'm sure.'

Roberto was more than half serious as he said this; for he had never thought of Fritz and women before now. He wondered if Fritz had some secret life of which he knew nothing. He realised now that he had always implicitly assumed that Fritz was as inexperienced as he was.

'It is quite true that I like Tacitus and Clausewitz and Livy,' agreed Fritz. 'But I also like sex, or at least the idea of it, as well. I can't think of anything nicer than a bit of military history followed by –'

'I see,' said Roberto. 'I've known you all these years, and now I see you as you really are. All this talk of pincer movements and encircling and battering things down – it seemed you were talking about tactics, but I was missing the point. Thank God you didn't become a priest. You'd have brought ruin on the Church. And now, you can stop rubbing my back. I'm not sure where your hands have been. I'll rub yours.'

'I always thought,' said Fritz, as he got used to the sensation of Roberto's knuckles rubbing into his shoulders, 'I always thought, when you were younger, when you were at school, that you might have become a priest.'

'Why?'

'You were always quite serious, you know. And you were very virtuous. You always did as you were told. You never got the cane, not even once. I was always getting it.'

'You were always getting caught,' said Roberto.

'But you didn't want to break the rules, did you? You kept them because they were there. I always wanted to know why we had to do stupid things that had no logical explanation, like eating cod liver oil capsules. You just did.'

'I suppose it was because of the way my mother used to tell me about my father,' said Roberto. 'All that disciplined example. And to think that he died because he caught a cold and didn't mention it until it was too late.'

'That is rather sad,' said Fritz thoughtfully. 'But you Catholics have the same sort of idea. Single-minded devotion. You are very single-minded, Bobby. You always were.'

'And you?'

'Not really. I always like to do lots of things at once.'

'And I suppose I must be the opposite,' said Roberto. 'I am only ever interested in one thing. Not so very different from Rodolfo Tanucci. He discovered God, and everything else faded out of the picture. I noticed that happening when we were on December Island.'

'What do Catholics really think of their religion, I wonder?' said Fritz. 'Do they love it or do they hate it?'

'If you were a Catholic you would know,' answered Roberto. 'We do both; we love it and we hate it all at once; at least I think I do.'

'And the priests?'

'Same answer. Priests are men who have power, after all, although they hardly ever use it nowadays. They can excommunicate you – or maybe you have to be a bishop for that. But they can touch something that no one else can.'

'I see,' said Fritz. 'Everyone I know is a Catholic, but I'll never understand it.'

'I don't understand why you aren't a Catholic,' said Roberto suddenly. 'I mean you are one to all intents and purposes, aren't you? You get called José Maria by lots of people, and they simply assume you are. You don't go to church, but that is quite average for a lot of our men. It wouldn't cost you anything to become a Catholic. And I can bet you, if ever you get married, you'll be baptised first, so you can have a proper wedding. I mean, it's not as though you believe in any other religion, is it?'

'No,' said Fritz. 'But all the same. My mother refused to speak German, you know, even though it had been her language. I'd feel I had let them all down. I am supposed to be Jewish in an odd sort of way.'

'Oh what nonsense,' said Roberto. 'You are about as Jewish as I am. In other words, you're not Jewish at all. I've never thought of you as a Jew, and you haven't thought of yourself as a Jew. You're just an agnostic, and one day some clever priest will get hold of you and you'll see what will happen then. You'll be a Catholic. There's something a little bit inescapable about Catholicism. You can't get away from it. I suppose that is because, deep down, no matter how much you try and convince yourself that the priests are liars, deep down you know it is true.'

'What is true, though?' asked Fritz.

'God, and the angels and the saints, and loving your neighbour,' said Roberto.

'That's exactly what Tanucci once said to me,' said Fritz. 'I suppose it must be a phrase from the catechism. But what about all the things we were taught about at school – I mean things like Papal Infallibility? I can see how that may be logical, Roberto, but I don't see why it has to be true. I mean, all sorts of sane people get on perfectly well without believing that, don't they?'

'God comes first, Fritz, before all the doctrines. You can't get away from God. But I wish to God it wasn't true, though,' said Roberto. 'I wish to God that this was it.'

'Don't you want to have an immortal soul, then?' asked Fritz.

'No, I don't. I've lost mine.'

'I don't believe you,' said Fritz. 'What could you have done to have lost your soul?'

Roberto did not answer, but kept on rubbing Fritz's back, and Fritz could not turn round to see the expression on his face. He was not sure how serious their conversation had been. Silence followed.

'I wanted to talk to you about a priest, actually,' said Fritz eventually.

'Not Morisco?'

'Yes,' he said, feeling Roberto's hands slacken.

'Go on, then,' said Roberto.

Fritz sat up on the marble slab. Roberto was silent, staring ahead, not looking at him. Fritz noticed that Roberto was completely red. He had never seen him like that before, and put it down to the overpowering heat in the Turkish bath.

'He came to see me,' said Fritz quickly. 'He wants me to persuade you to see him. He wants to interest you in some sort of peace proposals. Apparently he has spoken to Hernandez, and he has also spoken, more than once, I think, to Zondadari.'

'And do you think I should see him?'

'Yes, I think so. If we are going to negotiate, then we really have no choice, except to do it through him. He's our only link with the other side. Hernandez wouldn't trust anyone else.'

'Precisely,' said Roberto. 'Now let me tell you what I think. Hernandez and Messina let Morisco through to our side. Morisco gets a hearing from Zondadari. That is just what our enemy wants – disunity in our ranks. They are using Morisco. Messina is clever – Hernandez isn't – but Messina is, and Morisco isn't allowed through without Messina's approval, I am sure of that. Messina killed Olivarez with his own hands. That was unforgivable. He has no intention of making peace, because that would be the end of him. Quite a few people want him dead. But he is sending Morisco, who may be genuine in his desire for peace, for all I know, over here, because he has spotted the weak link in our chain.'

'What do you mean?'

'Zondadari, of course. Morisco will flatter Zondadari into thinking that he is a man of peace, the man to restore democracy and justice and all that nonsense, and that will be the ruin of our side. There are enough idealistic fools among us to follow Zondadari's lead. And then we'd be ruined.'

'Do you really think so?'

'Ximenez thinks the same.'

'But what do you really think?'

'I certainly don't think much of democracy,' said Roberto. 'It is mob rule, or at least it would be here. This isn't a country like England. Half the population can't even read or write. And I think Zondadari is a fool to listen to Morisco.'

'So you won't see Morisco?'

'No. I won't.'

'And the war will go on?'

'Yes – and we will win it.'

Fritz sighed. There was silence between them.

'That seems to be that,' said Fritz conclusively, sensing failure.

Forty-one

The next afternoon was one that Roberto, by force of custom, devoted to Mrs Williams.

'My husband is having trouble with penguins,' she told him.

'So I have heard,' he replied.

'Oh, have you. I thought it would amuse you. The Major wants me to go back to San Cristobal. He says there's no reason for me to be here if he's not.'

'And will you go back?' he asked.

'Not if you need me, Captain.'

'You'd better stay,' he said, though he didn't really want her to. 'At least for the next few weeks. After that I might be a little busy. It will be springtime then.'

'That's what I have heard too; you will be busy in the spring.'

'Who told you?'

'Ximenez, of course.'

She passed him his cigarettes; she had got to know his ways, and knew his habits by now. She knew when he wanted to smoke, and could anticipate his need.

'The Major never smoked in the bedroom,' she remarked, as she watched him light one.

'I'm lower ranks and I do,' said Roberto. 'And from what I can gather, there were plenty of other things the Major didn't do in the bedroom as well.'

'Oh, I'm not complaining,' said the Major's lady. 'Quite the reverse.'

'Good,' said Roberto. 'And now, if you'll let me go, I think I'll have a shower.'

And he put out his cigarette before he had smoked half of it.

When he was dressed, he went into the sitting-room, and there he found Ximenez.

'I have a key,' said his colleague, seeing the look of surprise on Roberto's face. 'I thought you would be here, and I've been waiting for you patiently. I wanted to talk to you urgently, and this place is as secure as any other.'

'What is the matter?' asked Roberto, sitting down, lighting another cigarette.

'Zondadari is the matter,' said Ximenez, getting straight to the point. 'He is a traitor. He spent hours yesterday afternoon speaking to someone who is in direct contact with our enemies.'

'I suppose you mean Father Morisco?'

'Yes.'

Roberto was silent.

'You don't seem as shocked as I had hoped you would be,' said Ximenez.

'What do you want to do?' asked Roberto coldly. 'Get to the point.'

'It is what we have got to do, Enriquez. Zondadari wants to negotiate with the Generals. That is just a ploy to force us to postpone our next campaign. We can't afford to waste time like this. We must have Zondadari arrested and put out of the way. We don't have a choice. We certainly won't be able to fight a war in the spring with him on our side, will we?'

'Zondadari is not important. No one pays any attention to him,' said Roberto. 'You know that, Ximenez.'

'As far as I can see, you only need one man to start talking about democracy and freedom, and a hundred fools will listen to him. Zondadari is a fool, and he is a dangerous fool. He already has his sympathisers. We've got to deal with him, and now. If we leave it to after the war, it may be too late. Can you imagine what will happen if we were to have elections? Can you imagine what will happen to you? They might well re-open all sorts of past things, mightn't they? Olivarez might be dead, but there are plenty of his colleagues still alive. We can't allow Zondadari to open up a hornets' nest.'

'What do you mean by putting him out of the way?' asked Roberto.

'You know what I mean,' said Ximenez.

'Just Zondadari?'

Ximenez was silent for a moment; then he began to speak carefully.

'There are others who have had proven contact with Morisco. Yesterday your friend the Quartermaster spent about half an hour in secret conversation with Morisco. Did he tell you that?'

'Are you trying to tell me that Fritz Rodriguez is a traitor?' asked Roberto in disbelief. 'Are you going to have him shot too? You must be mad.'

Mrs Williams came in.

'Get out,' said Ximenez.

Mrs Williams went out again.

'Rodriguez is very friendly with Zondadari. Did you know that? They are in this together.'

'Both you and I are very friendly with Zondadari too, on the surface at least.'

'But he has also had at least one meeting with Morisco. That makes him a traitor. Anything you may happen to let slip in front of Rodriguez about our plans might well be going back to the Generals via Morisco.'

'If you touch Fritz,' said Roberto, feeling he was becoming angry, and putting his hand on the butt of his gun, 'I will kill you myself, do you understand?'

Ximenez laughed.

'Very well,' he said. 'Have your beloved Fritz. I won't lay a finger on him. I hadn't realised how attached you were to him. But what are we going to do about Zondadari? And just remember, I sent my uncle to December Island so you could have his wife.'

'That is not true. We got rid of your uncle because he was an embarrassment. And Mrs Williams's morals are her affair.'

'And so are yours,' retorted Ximenez. 'I don't care how you spend your afternoons, whether with her, or alone in a Turkish bath with a jewboy. But I do give a damn when the whole Army has to put up the same jewboy as Quartermaster just because of your favouritism. We are as badly organised as ever we were. Your Fritz spends his time at his desk reading a book, or else he's with you, or else he's up to no good when your back is turned. You're the laughing stock of the Army, Enriquez, and for your own good, as well as for ours, you'll get rid of Rodriguez.'

Roberto was too angry to speak. He could feel that his cheeks were burning, and knew that this would be taken as an admission of guilt. It was so unjust. He had promoted Fritz because Fritz was a good soldier. And Ximenez's implication about how they had spent the afternoon in the Turkish bath disgusted him beyond words. How awful to think that his friendship with Fritz should be so misrepresented. But he could not speak; nor could he look at Ximenez, but he gazed out of the window until the terrible burning in his face should subside.

Mrs Williams, who had been listening at the door, came in.

'You're vile,' she said to her nephew. 'I don't know how you could say such things about Fritz. Not a word of it is true.'

Roberto knew that: but true or not, was this what people were saying?

'Tell Captain Enriquez about your afternoons playing Scrabble with Rodriguez,' said Ximenez.

Roberto spoke from the window.

'You'd better leave Zondadari alone,' he said.

'I've warned you about him, though. It isn't my fault if things turn out the way I have predicted,' said Ximenez.

Ximenez left the room. They heard the door slam. Roberto left the room for a moment to wash his face in cold water, and then came back.

'My nephew is extraordinarily unpleasant,' said Mrs Williams. 'I do apologise.'

'What is this about Scrabble?' asked Roberto.

'Fritz and I play some afternoons,' she said.

'Is he your lover?' he asked.

'No.'

'Was he your lover in San Cristobal?'

'No.'

'Does he come here often?'

'Fairly often.'

'And does he know that I come here too?'

Mrs Williams could think of no reply to make. Roberto felt that he could not believe her denials. There was something horrible about the thought of Fritz making love to this woman.

'Why does Ximenez think Fritz is Jewish?' he asked her coldly. 'What have you been telling him?'

'Nothing at all,' she said.

He could not believe her. If the vision he had of Fritz making love to her was horrible, there was something horrible too about the way he himself had done so, for three afternoons a week, over the last two months. He did not want to see her again. What a fool he had been. Neither did he want to see Fritz again. Had he stumbled on a part of Fritz's secret life? They had made a fool of him. Ximenez plainly thought that his aunt had been playing a double game. And how on earth could Ximenez know that Fritz was Jewish, unless Mrs Williams had told him so? It was such a well-guarded secret, after all. But if Fritz was her lover as well, she would have discovered his secret. The thought of how they had both been used by this woman made him feel almost ill.

'Penguins,' said Roberto bitterly.

'What?' she asked, puzzled.

'You told Fritz about the penguins and the Major, didn't you?'

'Yes, I did but –'

'Goodbye,' he said, and left her.

He still felt overwhelmed by the effect of Ximenez's intervention, and though he knew that that was what Ximenez had wanted, he was quite unable to reason himself into a calmer frame of mind. His face was burning no longer, but its usual calm and fair colour. But his mind was in turmoil. The more he thought of Fritz and Mrs Williams, the more probable did it seem. He had known her in San Cristobal, after all; and he had continued his acquaintance with her in the capital. In fact Fritz had known her before he himself had met her. He had been making love to Fritz's mistress. And Fritz had known. It was shaming. He had been ashamed of his penchant for Mrs Williams from the start, but now, to think that Fritz had known about it all along, was humiliating in the extreme. Fritz would have to go. It would be better that way. Besides, as Ximenez knew that Fritz was Jewish, it would make it quite easy for Ximenez to get rid of Fritz if he chose to do so. And that would be most unpleasant.

He returned to his hotel. He had sweated so much that he rather wished to have another shower. But as soon as he got to his suite, he found the person he least wanted to see just then, waiting for him.

'Roberto,' said Fritz. 'Something terrible has happened.'

'I know. Ximenez has told me.'

'I have just got a letter from Ximenez,' said Fritz. 'It asks for my resignation as Quartermaster. It says that I'm incompetent, and that sort of thing. It says that if I don't resign quietly, then he will have me removed from the Army, dishonourably discharged, on the grounds that I've infringed Article Forty-five.'

'The man's devilishly clever,' said Roberto in the rather distant tone of voice he used when he was trying to keep calm. 'Remind me about Article Forty-five.'

'It's the one that says that every officer that behaves in a conspicuously unchristian manner is to be discharged. It's the catch-all rule against adulterers, homosexuals and Jews.'

'And what can you do against that, Fritz?' asked Roberto

bitterly. 'He'll have Mrs Williams testify against you on two of those counts. I presume she told him you were a Jew.'

'Mrs Williams?' asked Fritz. 'What has she got to do with it?'

'You have been her lover, haven't you?'

'Of course not,' said Fritz. 'Are you crazy? The woman's a harpy. I mean, she's perfectly pleasant to play Scrabble with, but it would take a braver man than me for that.'

Considering that Fritz, who had once tended the scratches Mrs Williams had made on Roberto's back, knew about Roberto's affair with the lady, this was not exactly a tactful thing to say. Roberto's face remained like granite. But Fritz was far too concerned by the monstrous attack made on him by Ximenez to notice. It was what he had always feared.

'You don't think that just because of what I said yesterday, I would go to bed with Mrs Williams, do you?' said Fritz. 'Believe me, I haven't had anything like that with anyone since before San Cristobal. And Mrs Williams –'

His voice trailed away. He remembered what he was saying. He could tell he had offended Roberto.

'But they can't prove that I am a Jew,' he started to say, returning to the far more important matter. 'I could deny it; being circumcised isn't proof that you're Jewish. And the fact that I've never been baptised isn't proof either. But they can always do research in Germany I suppose, into my mother's family. And as for me being an adulterer, of course there was that affair with Mrs Mendoza, which got me sent to San Cristobal, but they're hardly likely to dredge that up, it would punish Mendoza more than it would me, and generally people like adulterers. And as for me being a homosexual, that is so ridiculous that I don't even need to bother with that one.'

Roberto thought about the Turkish bath, where they had been completely alone, and where he had instructed the staff not to let anyone else in while they were there. That could be used by Ximenez against them.

'Roberto, you will do something, won't you?' said Fritz, in

appeal. 'You will speak to Ximenez and get him to leave me alone?'

'Do you promise me you only played Scrabble with Mrs Williams?' asked Roberto.

'For God's sake,' said Fritz. 'Is that all you can care about? Can't you see what Ximenez is doing? He's trying to destroy me.'

'I'll phone him,' said Roberto.

He picked up the telephone; and waited to be put through. Fritz sat down miserably to wait what his fate would be. Roberto lit another cigarette.

'Ximenez,' said Roberto at last.

'I was expecting you to call.'

'Why are you doing this to Rodriguez?'

'Perhaps I don't like Jews,' said Ximenez.

'What on earth makes you think Rodriguez, José Maria Rodriguez, is a Jew?'

'I can smell them a mile off,' said Ximenez.

'Look, you may be the world's worst anti-Semite, for all I care, but I want you to stop this ridiculous nonsense right now,' said Roberto. 'It is disgraceful. He is a fellow officer, for God's sake.'

'But he is a Jew,' said Ximenez. 'I know. When I found out he was circumcised, I investigated.'

'Lots of men are,' said Roberto.

'Not in the Republic, they're not. It's quite unusual. Besides, his mother was a Schultz who came here from Germany; and she never spoke German. Classic Jewish persecution complex. German Jews always try and deny they are German. And often they deny they are Jews too.'

'I'm not going into that now,' said Roberto. 'There's no law against being Jewish and a Cavalry officer.'

'So, how many Jewish Cavalry officers are there? Or Engineers for that matter?' asked Ximenez. 'You don't have to answer that. We simply can't have these people in trustworthy jobs. He has to go. He's an alien.'

'You're persecuting Rodriguez for no reason at all,' said Roberto. 'I want you to leave him alone.'

'Of course, if you want to keep him on, I'll be quite happy to do so, and to drop the whole thing. We all have our personal preferences, however strange they may be. But that depends on you.'

'What have I got to do?'

'Agree with me on Zondadari,' said Ximenez. 'Think about it and ring me back, if you can.'

The phone went dead. Roberto was thoughtful. If he were to agree to Zondadari being sacrificed on Fritz's behalf, that would not be the last sacrifice; others would surely follow. He could not protect Fritz indefinitely.

'Fritz,' he said. 'I can't protect you.'

'Why not?'

'The price is too high,' said Roberto. 'He wants me to help him get rid of Zondadari in return. Shoot him. And I can't do that.'

'Yes,' said Fritz. 'You can't do that.'

'You'll have to resign as Quartermaster and take whatever job you're offered. I am sorry, but that is it. You'll just have to keep out of Ximenez's way. The man's unbalanced. You shouldn't have trusted Mrs Williams,' he concluded.

'I didn't trust her,' said Fritz. 'Do you honestly think that I would go to bed with Mrs Williams, when all along I knew that you were doing so three afternoons a week? What sort of man do you take me for? And as for Ximenez knowing that I am circumcised, he knows that because he once walked in on me while I was having a shower in San Cristobal. Mrs Williams and I have played Scrabble and nothing more, do you understand?'

Roberto felt he was going red again. He realised that for once in his life, he had offended Fritz, not the other way around.

'I see that Ximenez has won. I knew he would. He's always hated me, and now he's succeeded in getting rid of me at last. But if you, Roberto, had any guts, you would stand up to him, you and Zondadari, and you wouldn't let this happen. It's disgraceful. I wish to God I'd never pretended that I wasn't a Jew.'

'Then you'd never have got into the Cavalry.'

'Damn the Cavalry,' said Fritz. 'I'm damned if I am going to resign. Let Ximenez try his worst. Let him have me charged under Article Forty-five and let him find me guilty of whatever he wants. You don't have to help me, Roberto.'

'Fritz, for God's sake, calm down. You can't do that. You must resign. You don't want the whole country to know you are Jewish, do you?'

'Why not? I am, after all.'

'And what happens if they bring up all your peccadilloes? I mean that Mrs Mendoza you mentioned. You don't want to be branded an adulterer, and dishonourably discharged, do you? And what if they try and say that you are a homosexual?'

'They can say I am homosexual,' said Fritz. 'But no one would believe them. They can say what they like on that score.'

'Never mind you, what about me?' said Roberto. 'Think of all the people who could suffer with you. I mean yesterday, we were alone together in that place, and the man on the door had his orders that we weren't to be disturbed. Just think if that becomes public, and people begin to talk.'

'So, I should accept an unjust demotion to God knows what because if I don't it might embarrass you, is that it? People might say that the high and mighty Captain Enriquez was for years and years the friend of a Jew, and that's not all we hear, they were more than just friends . . . Oh what would they say? If I'd known you were so ashamed of me, Roberto, I would never have forced my company on you.'

'For God's sake, Fritz, be reasonable. What good would a dishonourable discharge do you?'

'You seem sure that Ximenez can carry out his threat, then?'

'Of course I am,' said Roberto. 'He'll ruin you and he'll ruin us all.'

'You're frightened he'll ruin you, aren't you, Roberto?' said Fritz. 'Why are you so frightened of what people will say? What have you got to hide? Why have you suddenly gone scarlet in the face at the thought somebody might think you are queer? For all I know you might be; it has crossed my mind, but I honestly never gave a damn about it. The fact that you couldn't bring yourself to make love to Elena for years and years, oh yes, I noticed, and now you can only seem to be able to do it with a woman old enough to be your mother, is pretty damn suspicious. But I never cared. You were my best friend, but now, I am not going to give a damn about you ever again. You obviously care more about your own reputation than you do about me. Well then, enjoy your reputation on your own. Goodbye. I'd better go and clear my desk at the office. You won't see me again.'

Roberto had never seen Fritz so angry or so offended before. He sat at his desk, stunned. With automatic hand, he opened his packet of cigarettes, only to find that he had smoked the last one. He had just lost his best friend, he realised. Outside, on the Riviera, Fritz stared out to sea, already regretting what he had said, and tears coursed down his cheeks.

Forty-two

Having lost his temper, Fritz spent the rest of the day trying to recover it. He arrived at his place of work only the next morning to find that his books had been thrown into cardboard boxes, and someone else, a friend of Ximenez, by the look of him, was moving into his office and into his job.

'I looked for you, yesterday,' said the NCO who had acted as his secretary. 'But no one knew where you'd gone. Apparently you have been transferred to some other work.'

'What other work?' asked Fritz.

'The Catering Corps, I am afraid,' said the NCO. Then he added apologetically: 'There have been signed orders to that effect. They've come from –'

'Ximenez?' asked Fritz.

'No. From Enriquez.'

Roberto had not quite realised when he had taken the step of having Fritz transferred to a posting that would be out of harm's way, that Fritz's departure would be so sudden. It gave him a shock the next day to see unfamiliar faces in the Quartermaster's offices. It was as if there had been a sudden death. He sat in his hotel as a result and wondered what he could do. He had handled things so badly. Even Mrs Williams seemed to think that, for she was packing and going back to San Cristobal. His afternoons from now on would be empty, at least until the fighting started again, and when that might be, he did not know.

He felt relieved in some ways that Mrs Williams was going; she had not been worth quarrelling over. But it was not simply that he had unjustly accused Fritz of being involved with Mrs Williams. There was more to it than a simple misunderstanding. So many things had been said in that quarrel which would be hard to forget. Had Fritz really thought he was a homosexual? And how on earth had Fritz known about the timidity of his relations with Elena? He supposed that Fritz could have guessed that quite easily, without her having to tell him. He and Elena, until that fateful weekend of the General's birthday, had never spent the night together under the same roof. He had spent most of his time with Fritz. He had never done anything with her that fell into the category Mortal Sin, until that weekend. But why? Was he a latent homosexual? His oldest friend had thought that of him. And his oldest friend had known all along about his affair with Mrs Williams. What had she told Fritz about him over their games of Scrabble? How could he ever see Fritz again, when Fritz might know of his most private habits? He did care excessively about what people thought of him after all. Fritz knew him well, and had been right when he had said that. And the fact that Fritz was right about so many things made him want to see him again less and less.

This desire to get Fritz out of the way until the whole thing should be forgotten, and their quarrel treated as if it had never happened, had compelled him to treat him even more unjustly still, by transferring him to the Catering Corps. The very fact that they were in the City now, and not still sitting in San Cristobal, was due to Fritz. He owed Fritz so much, yet this was the way he had repaid him. He was acting ungratefully, and Fritz was justified if he was offended – but what else could he have done? If he hadn't had the good idea of having Fritz transferred before Ximenez could court-martial him under Article Forty-five, or whatever he wanted to do, his association with Fritz would have destroyed him, not to mention what would happen to Fritz himself. That of course was all part of

Ximenez's plan. Ximenez knew that he could use Fritz as his rival's Achilles heel. It was only too clear what sort of man Ximenez was. And the worst thing of all was that Roberto, though he knew what Ximenez was like, and though he disliked his methods, saw no alternative but to stick with him. He had had a choice between his best friend and his natural enemy – and he had chosen his enemy, because his enemy was his natural ally in the course he had chosen.

As for the question of Ximenez's anti-Semitism, much as it disturbed him to find himself so closely associated with a man with such marked Nazi tendencies, Roberto felt it was wise to ignore that. Of course, Fritz was, technically speaking, Jewish, having had a Jewish maternal grandmother, but he did not look Jewish (though what Jews were supposed to look like, Roberto wasn't quite sure); nor was there anything Jewish about him, in the religious sense of the word. It was impossible to think of Fritz as a Jew when he had known him so long. Fritz himself didn't consider himself to be a Jew – and so he could hardly be outraged if he was persecuted for being one, considering he had denied it implicitly for so long. He was not Jewish; to be accused of being Jewish could not hurt him. Thus reasoned Roberto, while he hoped Fritz would call him, so that something like normality could be restored between them.

Fritz had decided to do no such thing. The dreary office he was exiled to, once the domain of a second-rate hotel manager, was a daily reminder of the injustice of his treatment. A week passed, and instead of growing calmer, Fritz found himself growing uncharacteristically angry. That Ximenez had proposed to have him shot, and that Roberto had prevented it, Fritz did not know. That he had been moved out of Ximenez's way, to the Catering Corps, where no one would notice him, in order to preserve his life (so Roberto had thought) he did not know either. Nor had he any idea why Roberto was so traumatised by the realisation that Fritz had known he had been Mrs Williams's lover. He could not see what that particular fuss was about. Sex was simply sex, as far as Fritz was concerned. Mrs Williams was not his cup of tea, but if she was Roberto's, that was nothing remarkable. It was all a matter of taste.

Thus while Roberto expected Fritz to be grateful to him, Fritz himself thought that he owed all his misfortunes to the stupidity of Roberto. On top of this was the further wound that came with the realisation that, though he was his oldest friend, Roberto simply had not understood the anguish Fritz suffered from knowing that Ximenez wanted to attack him on the grounds of being Jewish. Roberto had seemed to imagine that he could have shrugged this off. But you simply could not shrug it off: it was the most deeply personal attack that anyone could make. Fritz had indeed never imagined himself as Jewish except in the most peripheral sense of the word: he had grown up knowing that he was not a Catholic, nor a Protestant, but instead someone who didn't quite fit into the expected religious categories. Maternal piety had had him circumcised, something he had always hidden; but he had thought that it made no difference; that he was fundamentally like the others, not some terrible alien who would be ineligible for membership of the Military Club. The fact that everyone had always liked him cancelled out the consciousness that his mother's mother had been a German Jewess and that somehow made him different. And yet now Ximenez knew about his grandmother and was trying to show that he wasn't one of them after all – and Roberto had not given Fritz the wholehearted assurance he had expected. Roberto had failed him. He felt betrayed. After all the friendship he had shown Roberto, Roberto had done nothing to protect him from a Nazi like Ximenez. The parallel with what had happened to his grandmother's family did not help. In these circumstances a deepening of the breach was inevitable.

It came about a week later on a windy afternoon, when Fritz, too angry to do any work or even to read a book, went for a walk on the Riviera. The sea was grey and choppy, and the weather, which until a few days ago had shown promises of spring, had relapsed into wintry coldness. It was a depressing day, and Fritz walked up and down the Riviera near the Franciscan church, cursing life, hunching his shoulders against the wind, his eyes cast to the ground. In these conditions, they might have been able to pass each other without speaking, or even noticing each other, but Roberto, also taking a walk in what had once been a favourite shared spot, felt a slight softening when he saw Fritz, and felt guilty at the prospect of passing him by without a word.

'Hello, Fritz,' he said.

Fritz looked up.

'So it's you, Roberto,' he said, seeing the traitor before him.

'What have you been doing with yourself?' asked Roberto, feeling a little at a loss, for it was not every day that one met an estranged best friend.

'You know what I have been doing,' said Fritz bitterly. 'You gave me the job. The bloody Catering Corps.'

'Ah yes,' said Roberto, and then to justify himself, he added: 'I had to think of Ximenez.'

'That makes it worse,' said Fritz. 'You know that Ximenez hates me, and yet you let him do his worst to me.'

'That's not true,' said Roberto. 'If it hadn't been for me –'

'You liar,' said Fritz, overwhelmed by bitterness.

They stared at each other, and Fritz saw a look of hatred in Roberto's face.

'You don't know what you are saying,' he said. 'You are a bloody fool, and I won't do anything to protect you again.'

'I don't want your protection,' shouted Fritz. 'I wish to God I had never met you. You are just as bad as Ximenez, and when it comes to taking sides, you'll be on his, not mine; and more fool you. Between you, you'll destroy the entire country. All of this will be a heap of ruins.' A gesture of the hand took in the Riviera, the Bay, the Presidential Palace across the water. 'And if ever you get to the Palace, God help the rest of us. I'd much rather the Generals won than you. I don't like men who betray their oldest friends. And you know what I am saying is true. I can see it in your face.'

'You've gone mad, Fritz,' said Roberto, quite unable to control the colour of his face any more.

'No, you have.'

'I could shoot you,' he said in his anguish.

'Because you know I am right, that's why.'

Roberto's hand went to his gun. Fritz saw what he was doing, and immediately feared something awful was going to happen. He himself was carrying his Beretta, but it was unloaded, as it always was, to prevent accidents. Roberto seemed quite strange now, his face almost purple, as it had been during their last quarrel, only more so. Fritz heard the click of the safety catch being released, and he realised that Roberto was going to carry out his threat. At once he pushed him against the railing of the promenade, to make him lose his balance. Roberto's hand tightened as he fell. The gun went off, and at the sharp sound of the report, Fritz jumped over the railing, and fell onto the sand below.

'For Christ's sake, Fritz, come back,' shouted Roberto, as soon as he got up, quite unhurt. 'Don't be a fool.'

But Fritz had broken into a run, and was soon out of sight behind some beach huts. Roberto, realising that the case was hopeless, put away his gun, and walked away.

Fritz leaned against a beach hut, trembling. Once again he felt close to tears. The friend he had loved and trusted most in the world had now tried to shoot him. First of all Roberto had refused to protect him against the loathsome Ximenez, now he tried to do this to him. And Roberto knew that he never carried a cartridge in his Beretta. He knew he was defenceless. But Roberto clearly didn't care about that any more. He had become an embarrassment to him. Roberto had chosen Ximenez. There would be more fighting, and if they won, what would happen then? There was no reason to go on living; for if they won, Ximenez was bound not to rest until he had done his worst. Ximenez was a Jew-hater, Fritz realised, and he, although it was not a way he had ever thought of himself before now, was a Jew. It could not be disguised: he was not one of them, or someone who simply had an unusual maternal grandmother, but he was a Jew, and even though all that seemed ancient history now, there was no escaping from it after all. He was on the outside, and nothing could overcome that. Why should things be any different now? Would the Gentile ever stand up for the Jew? Would Roberto?

He wished he was dead. If his gun was not a mere useless toy, he might have used it on himself there and then.

The beach was deserted and cold. Out in the Bay he could see a gunboat, and beyond it, the Palace. This was the water that Rodolfo had swum across. How wise he had been to take refuge in a friary. There seemed to Fritz then to be no goodness left in the world. The other side was as bad as this one, but at least there, on that side of the Bay, there was no Ximenez.

Although he could not shoot himself, there were other things he could do. There was no one about, so there was no one to see him take off his clothes and start to wade into the freezing water. He would swim until he drowned or until he reached the other side. Rodolfo had swum the Bay, but that had been in summer. Wading in further, Fritz commended himself to the waves, now surging around his waist. He would die, or he would desert to the other side. He did not care what the outcome would be. In he plunged.

Forty-three

'Our plans,' said Ximenez, 'are simple. I have worked it all out. It is essential that we move now, before they do. This' – a hairy thumb jabbed the map – 'is the present front line. With some bigger guns brought up from the Provinces we can cause enough trouble there to make sure that Messina and Hernandez concentrate their forces there. Then we can make an assualt, here, to the west of the City, and here, wheeling round to the north, and here as well.'

'The Marine Gardens?' asked Zondadari. 'How do you propose to attack the Marine Gardens?'

'Boats,' said Ximenez calmly.

'But the enemy have lined the sea wall with machine-guns,' said Zondadari.

'Our casualties will be heavy,' said Ximenez smoothly, not intending to back down to Zondadari in front of Enriquez. 'But you can't make an omelette without breaking eggs.'

Roberto had not spoken.

'Enriquez, what do you think?' asked Zondadari.

'What do you expect me to think?' asked Roberto, lighting another cigarette.

Zondadari wished that Enriquez were not quite so arrogant. It was a great pity. He hoped that his own children would not grow up to be like him. But the upper classes were full of men like Enriquez, he reflected, men who wore a continual scowl, smoked too much, and were rude to the people they considered to be their social inferiors. What a pity Enriquez had become one of them. Before this war had started Enriquez had enjoyed a far better reputation as an abstemious young man, shy rather than arrogant, a good Catholic, a good athlete, handsome, a mother-in-law's dream. To think that he, Zondadari, had done his best to help Elena Garcia the day the General died. Would he do the same again? Enriquez was looking terrible, in Zondadari's opinion. Even his strikingly handsome features seemed coarsened. He seemed to have heard too that he was having some sort of an affair with Ximenez's aunt, of all people. Zondadari shivered. How awful; and how strange to think that he had once thought that Enriquez was the type of man who wanted to do the country some good.

'This plan will entail an enormous amount of people getting killed,' Zondadari said at last. 'I mean civilians as well. When you talk of wheeling round to the north for example, that will damage vast amounts of the City and the suburbs, all of which are heavily populated.'

'There are always casualties in war,' said Ximenez.

'But when the war is over –' insisted Zondadari.

'Quite,' said Ximenez. 'When the war is over, they will realise that we are men who are not to be messed with. How many men and officers have the Generals got? I don't know – but when they see us coming, they'll realise what we are like. And when we win we can hang every one of the enemy officers who stay around to see what happens next. Every single one of them. That way we will stamp our authority on the country.'

'I didn't realise you were so adamant,' said Zondadari. 'We can get want we want now by negotiation.'

'What you want isn't necessarily what we want,' said Ximenez.

Roberto was still silent. It was now several hours since he had parted from Fritz. Fritz would now never speak to him again. His anger had deserted him, and now only sadness remained. He had hardly been following what Ximenez was saying. He looked up at Ximenez with dull resentment. It had been Ximenez who had destroyed his friendship with Fritz.

That had been the price he had had to pay. He had sold his soul and lost all the good things he had ever possessed, and for what? So he could sit around in a smoke filled room and plan the death of thousands?

'Hernandez and Messina will be hanged for murdering Olivarez,' Ximenez was now saying. 'And so will everyone who has made common purpose with them.'

'Isn't it time we forgot Olivarez?' asked Zondadari. 'At the time we didn't know what we know now.'

'What is that supposed to mean?' asked Ximenez sharply.

'He means,' said Roberto slowly, 'that if most of our men had known what Olivarez was really like and what he stood for, they would never have got involved in this war.'

'Olivarez was a good soldier,' said Ximenez. 'I won't have his memory attacked. And you agree with me, Enriquez. Everything Olivarez did can be justified, and was justified.'

Roberto thought of Caballero for a moment; then he saw the body of Nicola Nickleby; and lastly he thought of Fritz. All these pictures seemed to say one thing: they represented the claims of humanity in the face of the ruthless quest for power.

'I think we should negotiate,' said Roberto, putting out his cigarette. 'Zondadari may be right. And I think your plan is badly thought out, to say the least.'

'I suppose you're going to say that Rodriguez could have worked out a better one?'

'He most certainly could have,' said Roberto.

'I knew it!' said Ximenez. 'Your friend Rodriguez has been working on you. But he is a traitor. Did you know that he was caught trying to desert to the enemy earlier this afternoon? And you know what the rules are about that, don't you?'

Fritz's swim had been a complete disaster. He had swum out from the shore for about a hundred yards, his eyes blinded by the salt water, his body growing steadily more numb with the cold. It was almost impossible to see where he was going, as the swell was sufficiently large to stop him seeing ahead for any distance, except intermittently. But on he swam, confident that if he only kept on, he was bound to reach the other side eventually, or die in the attempt. He wondered what such a death would entail, and whether he would be killed slowly by cold and fatigue, or die of a heart attack. He wondered what would be waiting for him on the other side of death. He felt he ought to pray, but he knew no prayers apart from the Hail Mary and the Our Father, and he was damned if he was going to die with Christian words on his lips.

Then two things happened. He noticed, as he was lifted by the swell, that the gunboat was much closer than he had imagined possible. He must have swum very close to it without realising. He knew he would have to swim around it, and do so without its crew noticing him. But as he was changing course, he encountered what felt like a severe electric shock. It was a jelly fish, perhaps even a Portuguese man-of-war; despite the numbing cold, he screamed aloud in agony. Writhing in pain, he did his best to swim on, and shortly he found himself colliding with the boat's anchor chain. He clung to it helplessly, and within a few moments he found that strong arms that he could not resist were dragging him on board. Wet, naked, shivering and in pain, he was dumped on deck like some exotic fish, surrounded by unsmiling faces and drawn guns.

'Of course, he will have to be shot,' Ximenez was now saying. 'If he hasn't been already.'

'Where is he?' asked Roberto.

'Army Navigational School, I suppose,' said Ximenez. 'That's where delicate cases always go, don't they?'

'I'm going there,' said Roberto. 'Zondadari, why don't you come with me?'

Zondadari got up to go with him. Enriquez seemed to have been changed by this news. Within a few minutes they were together in a car. It was a short drive, and when they arrived at the once familiar building, Roberto left Zondadari to deal with the officer in command, and himself secured entry to the cells in the basement. There he found Fritz, in a cell that had been used for similar purposes before. He was sitting on the floor, leaning against the wall, wrapped in a thin blanket. He did not look up when Roberto came in.

'He hasn't spoken since they brought him here, sir,' said the soldier who was acting as gaoler.

'Why isn't he properly dressed?'

'They picked him up out of the sea, sir.'

'Get him some clothes then.'

'We can't, sir. He might try and hang himself. We've been told to watch him at all times.'

'Very well. I'll watch him for the moment. You go.'

'Very good, sir,' said the man a little uncertainly, and withdrew.

'Fritz,' said Roberto, sitting down next to him.

'Why don't you leave me alone?' said Fritz. 'Or have they sent you to shoot me? I'd be glad to get it over with.'

'Fritz –'

'They are bound to shoot me tomorrow morning,' said Fritz. 'At dawn, I suppose. Just like the poor Emperor Maximilian.'

'I've brought Zondadari here, and he and I will get them to release you.'

'I don't want to be released. I want to die.'

'But why?'

'Because nothing I have believed in up to now is true after all,' said Fritz.

'Look, Fritz, I know we have quarrelled, but quarrels can always be repaired. These things aren't important.'

'This is the place where that English girl was killed,' said Fritz. 'And Ernesto Caballero. I knew him.'

'I wasn't responsible,' said Roberto quickly. 'I – I mean, I was there, and I could have prevented it, I suppose, but the English girl killed herself, you know, and Caballero could have been released if he had wanted to be. But does that matter so much now? So many other people have been killed since then.'

'It isn't all Hannibal and his elephants, after all,' said Fritz sadly. 'You told me that, but I couldn't believe you. I thought you were different.'

'Fritz, for God's sake, you don't have to let them shoot you, do you?'

'We used to be such friends,' said Fritz. 'But now we are on different sides. And my side has lost.'

Roberto felt despair gnawing at his entrails. He had come to save Fritz from death, and here he was, refusing to be saved.

'I won't allow you to be shot,' he said.

He went to the door of the cell, and told one of the men on duty to call Captain Zondadari at once. Within a few minutes, Zondadari was there, tall and pale. He looked at Fritz.

'This man is suffering from shock,' he said. He gave various instructions to the men on duty, about fetching towels and hot water, and sugar. Then he bent over Fritz and touched his shoulder. It was stone cold. So were his feet. Further examination revealed huge welts on the stomach.

'Get a doctor,' said Zondadari, when the man came back. 'And tell him this man has been stung by what seems to be the tentacle of a Portuguese man-of-war. There's some sort of antidote that he'll have to have.'

Then Zondadari set to work, forcing Fritz to drink the sugar dissolved in hot water, and trying to restore the circulation to his limbs, by rubbing them with a dry towel. Roberto stood by, helplessly.

'He'd have died if he'd been left here all night,' remarked Zondadari.

The doctor arrived and administered an injection. But Fritz seemed to be losing consciousness. Finally, Zondadari, with a natural authority that no one dared challenge, wrapped Fritz in blankets and carried him up to the car. They drove off, heading towards Roberto's hotel.

'No one will disturb him in your bedroom,' said Zondadari briskly.

Fritz was put to bed.

'He is still stone cold,' said Zondadari.

'Is he going to die?' asked Roberto.

'You know nothing about first aid, do you?' said Zondadari. 'He could very well have died. He could have died of cold. That place was freezing, and he'd been in the sea. Try and see if you can get any warmth into him.'

'How?'

'There's only one way,' said Zondadari. 'Rub his feet and hands.'

Roberto did as he was told.

'I think Ximenez has gone mad,' he said later. 'His plan will be disastrous if he loses, and even worse if he wins; and I think he wants to go ahead with it soon.'

'What can be done about that?' asked Zondadari.

'Could we have him arrested?'

'No one who had any sense would dare do it,' said Zondadari. 'It would take a brave man, even a foolish one.'

Roberto could now feel that Fritz was returning to life.

'It has to be done, though,' he said.

'I had hoped you would say that, Enriquez,' said Zondadari. 'Fritz has persuaded you at last.'

Ximenez had heard what had happened at the Army Navigational School. It was as he had expected. He had no objection to Enriquez saving his friend's life, as long as he got what he wanted in return, namely support for his plan. Enriquez could keep Fritz; the important thing was that Enriquez supported him against Zondadari, and the war went on. Power was within his grasp; and he began to look at his plans and dispositions again, and think of moving the day for the attack yet closer.

Forty-four

'My dear,' said Father Morisco the very next morning. 'You really shouldn't be here, you know. Things are going to get very dangerous and quite soon too. I've tried to persuade the Archbishop to leave, but he won't hear of it. But you, my dear, must go back to Torre del Mar at once.'

He was speaking to Elena who had that moment come into his office in the Archbishop's Palace.

'But I've only just arrived,' she said.

The priest looked stern.

'And I used up all the petrol we had getting here. I can't possibly go back at once. And surely things aren't going to get dangerous between now and lunchtime, are they?'

'Of course, I don't want to alarm you, my dear, and I know you'd be worried about that young man of yours, but things might very well get dangerous between now and lunchtime,' said Father Morisco gravely. He paused and thought a moment, and then continued: 'Captain Enriquez is such a nice young man,' he said, in a rather odd tone of voice that Elena had never heard him use before. 'He is a very handsome young officer, isn't he? I imagine you would think him much handsomer than Captain Rodriguez, now, wouldn't you? What a terrible pity it is to think what war can do to young lives. Between now and this evening, something could happen to your young Captain. Oh, I've seen bodies lying in the streets, and they are unrecognisable. Death is a great disguiser, as Shakespeare said –'

'Father Morisco, what are you talking about?' she said, interrupting him.

But the priest continued relentlessly: 'To think that he could stop it if he wanted to. That's the pity of it. Roberto Enriquez could save his own life and the lives of countless men; think of all those widows and orphans that there are going to be, and how it could all so easily be avoided.'

'Father Morisco, do tell me what you mean, please,' said Elena.

'Did you know that it is illegal to ring church bells in wartime?' he asked her suddenly.

'Is it?'

'At least it always should be. In European wars it always was. They only rang the bells when they were about to be attacked by the enemy – sign of invasion, things like that. Now you, and most people in the Republic, don't know that. The commanders on the other side don't know that, it seems. Only a few hours ago, bells were rung on the other side, and I heard them. I wasn't the only one who heard, but I was the only one who understood.'

'It was a signal?'

'Precisely. The Angelus bell is always rung at seven in the morning. One of our priests on the other side rang it at the right time, but with one chime too many. That was the signal he was to give me when he noticed that the other side were getting ready to attack us. Everyone else must have thought that some foolish priest had miscounted the rings; but I know that it was a warning.'

'But when?'

'I don't know,' said Father Morisco with a sigh. 'I don't know what is going on there at all, or what the priest saw. There's no way of me finding out. Perhaps if your Roberto could see you now, it would make him think twice about this attack. Perhaps it would remind him of all the other people who suffer when soldiers go to war.'

'Couldn't you get across to him somehow?'

'He won't see me. And I tried to cross this morning early and they wouldn't let me across. They had their orders.'

'Could I cross?'

'But how? No one is allowed to cross. If you tried to swim, you'd die of cold. And they have started patrolling the Bay. No one can cross by the road. If they won't let me across, they won't let you. Short of catapulting yourself over, or crawling through the sewers, there's nothing we can do.'

'Nothing?'

'We're doomed,' said the priest.

During the ensuing silence, he looked at her out of the corner of his eye.

'Of course, there might be a way,' he said. 'For someone who was brave . . .'

Father Morisco had divined the bells correctly. An attack was coming. The rebel troops were moving into their positions – hurriedly and in disastrous order, but moving all the same. They had received their orders late the previous night, orders that had not been expected for days, if not weeks, and which, arriving so early, had hardly been believed. But Ximenez, fearing that time was running out, had decided to pre-empt any opposition from his own side, and attack as soon as possible, before it became too late. He feared Morisco's overtures for peace; he feared Zondadari, and he feared Enriquez might fail to co-operate. It was time to get started; and once started, as everyone knew, a military campaign could hardly ever be stopped by anything short of a miracle.

Fritz had spent a reasonably quiet night and revived with the coming of morning. By ten, he was sitting up in bed eating a hearty breakfast. Roberto was lounging in an armchair, watching him. The room was remarkably hot, thanks to two electric fires, and Roberto had taken off his tunic and his holster, both of which lay on a table, disregarded, his gun hidden by his tunic.

'You saved my life,' said Fritz, biting into his steak.

'I am glad I did,' said Roberto.

Their quarrel, and all the bitter words they had spoken, were forgotten.

'What will happen now?' asked Fritz.

'You'd have done the same for me,' said Roberto. 'I remember it coming up in conversation once, in San Cristobal. We agreed that you would sacrifice your life for me.'

'Amazing how you remember things, Roberto.'

'And as for what is going to happen now, Zondadari and I will have to deal with Ximenez.'

'Are you sure you want to do that?' asked Fritz.

'I am absolutely sure,' he said.

'It could be dangerous,' said Fritz.

'It's not like you to worry about things like that, Fritz,' said Roberto. 'But I am sure.'

And he was. As he had sat there last night, making sure that Fritz did not die in the night, not that there was any danger of that, but because he had felt the desire to make amends, a new clarity had come to his mind. There was something he had to do; it was not duty, it was something higher than that. He had always been a man for keeping rules, but now he knew that there were certain things that rules could not cover, and the case of Ximenez was one of these. Ximenez had to be stopped; he had co-operated with him for far too long already, and if ever he were to deserve what his friends had tried so much in the past to give him, then he had to stop Ximenez.

There came a knock on the door, and as if on cue, Ximenez entered.

'That man,' he said, looking at Fritz, 'should be in prison. He is a deserter.'

'He went for an innocent swim,' said Roberto, not getting out of his chair. 'You had no business having him arrested.'

'He'd better get up and get dressed at once,' said Ximenez.

'Fritz, stay where you are,' said Roberto.

'We can discuss all this later,' said Ximenez. 'He'll have a fair trial, and if it was an innocent swim, he'll be acquitted with honour. Right now, Enriquez, our troops are taking up offensive positions; in fact they have done so already.'

'What?'

'Within a few hours you'll be hearing the guns. As soon as it is dusk. And please don't say that you weren't informed properly. You left the meeting before it ended.'

Wearing the Archbishop's wellington boots, and clutching a plastic bag full of oranges, Elena was following Father Morisco down a wet smelly tunnel. It was the City's main drain. They had entered it by climbing down a shaft in the cellar of the Archbishop's Palace. The smell was overpowering, but, the priest had assured her, not deadly. The drain debouched into the Bay on the other side of the front line, and its end was shut by a grille, at which at least two policemen were permanently on guard. The oranges were for them, and had cost the extraordinary price of two US dollars each.

'I think we're in luck,' said Morisco at last, putting out his torch, now that they could see light at the end of the tunnel. 'That boy –' and looking ahead, Elena could see the figure of a young policeman, actually leaning against the grille '– that policeman is a friend of mine. I visited him in hospital. He almost died in the earlier fighting. He was all alone, bleeding to death on a pavement, when he prayed to St Michael, and the angel sent someone to rescue him. They pumped him full of new blood in the hospital, and he's been a great friend of mine ever since. He's grown fond of oranges.'

'I've heard the story,' said Elena in a whisper.

They went on, and when they were behind the grille, Father Morisco coughed, and the youngster turned round.

'Miguel, I've got some lovely oranges,' said the priest, 'if you'll let us through.'

The grille was opened at once.

'Thank you very much, Father,' he said, taking the oranges, preparing to share them with his colleague.

'You see,' said Father Morisco happily, once they were in the open road, and the drain was behind them, 'there are no doors closed to me.'

'You are gambling with men's lives,' Roberto was now saying. 'This attack of yours is senseless. It is hurried, and it isn't mature. All you want to do is to prolong the war for your own ends.'

'So, Enriquez, you understand what I am up to. My ends are your ends too. If there is peace, you will lose as much as I do. If we hand the country over to Zondadari and Morisco, think what will happen.'

'I'd much rather have them than you,' said Roberto firmly.

'You have no choice,' answered Ximenez. 'You were there, working for Olivarez, here in the City, just as I was in San Cristobal. The first thing Zondadari would do – or any democratic government would do – is to string us both up.'

'There's nothing worth fighting for,' said Roberto. 'But there may still be something worth dying for. And I'd rather die than see you win this war.'

'I see that you won't be persuaded,' said Ximenez coldly. 'You can both consider yourselves under arrest.'

Ximenez drew his gun.

'You can't arrest me,' said Roberto, knowing that these words were empty, because his own gun was on the table, and Ximenez stood between him and the table. But it was worth attempting to bluff his way out of it.

'I can,' said Ximenez.

'You are not my senior officer.'

'You are a traitor and a pacifist, and you automatically lose your rank as far as I am concerned. As for him,' he said, gesturing towards the bed, where Fritz lay, a helpless spectator, dressed in Roberto's pyjamas, 'he is already under arrest. You, Enriquez, happen to be sheltering a deserter.'

Ximenez kept his gun trained on Roberto; then he backed towards the door, and opened it; this was to be the signal for the men he had outside to come in with the handcuffs. But the people outside were not there. Instead Father Morisco came in.

'I told your men to go away, as they would not be needed,' he said. 'Wonderfully obedient they were. I've brought a young lady to see Captain Enriquez.'

Elena came in.

'Hello, Roberto,' she said.

His face lit up on seeing her.

'Put away your gun, do, Ximenez,' he urged.

Ximenez looked at the girl, then at the priest, wondering what he ought to do. In that one moment of uncertainty, Fritz, who had been watching the table, on which Roberto's gun lay, covered by his tunic, leaped out of bed to grab it. At this sudden movement, Ximenez wheeled round, and pulled the trigger. He missed his target. Roberto, seeing the opportunity, flung himself at Ximenez and threw him to the ground. There was another shot. Father Morisco, who was a strong man, threw himself at Ximenez as well. Soon he was disarmed, and Fritz had him covered with Roberto's gun.

'Roberto,' cried Elena.

Roberto had gone very pale. The second shot had found its target. She tried to support him in her arms, and he looked up at her and smiled calmly.

'Fritz,' he said slowly. 'He's ill. Look after him.'

'Oh Roberto,' said Fritz, coming to help her. 'Bobby,' he said, reverting to the old schoolboy name.

But Roberto would hear them no more.

Forty-five

The funeral was over; the Archbishop and Father Morisco had retired to the sacristy to disrobe; the crowd of mourners, led by the dead hero's mother and fiancée, had dispersed; only Fritz sat on in the dimness of the cathedral, far from the altar, as befitted one who could watch but not take part in a religious function.

A week had passed. Outside the cathedral they had already started to roll away the barbed wire that had divided the City for so long and clear up the broken glass. That was being done by the conscripts, who, now the country was at peace, would soon be sent home, their war games over. For Zondadari was now President, and things had changed.

Someone had joined him on his bench. It was a young man wearing the habit of a Franciscan friar; his appearance was typical – he could have been any young cleric; the well-washed face, the badly cut hair, and the teeth that betrayed his birth amongst the lower orders. Not officer material, as one of the older Generals would have remarked, Fritz thought. Indeed not officer material at all.

'I wondered if I would see you here,' said Fritz. 'I hardly recognise you; of course they did tell me that you had joined. How does religion compare to the Army?'

'I prefer it,' said Rodolfo.

'I suppose you do,' said Fritz. 'You weren't a bad soldier, you know. Roberto once said to me that good soldiers would make good members of religious orders. The way you swam across that Bay – that was brave.'

'I only did it to save my life,' said Rodolfo shortly. 'There's nothing particularly heroic about self-preservation. It's throwing your life away, or at least risking it, that is really brave. I didn't have a choice. It was Captain Enriquez who was the hero.'

Fritz considered this in silence.

'What are you going to do now?' Rodolfo asked him.

'Zondadari has offered me a civilian job,' said Fritz. 'Something in the Education Department; I have told him that I'll consider it – leaving the Army is quite a step. Elena Garcia has gone back to work for *The Post*; but I've got to find something new to do. The Army is finished for me, I think.'

'How is Elena? And how is his mother?'

'I feel I hardly know them,' he answered. 'They are strangers to me. Now that Bobby is dead, they will live separate lives from mine.'

He had thought of trying to revive his old friendship with Elena, but he had realised that any such attempt would be fruitless. Roberto had died and taken the past with him. What once might have been, when he had first met her years ago, was now an impossibility.

'There are so many illiterates in this country,' said Rodolfo, 'that I imagine you would have plenty to do in the Education Department.'

'That was what Zondadari said to me,' said Fritz.

It was odd to think of Zondadari as President; or of General Messina, now in exile, like Napoleon, on December Island. Hernandez was in England, keeping Isabel de Calatrava company. Ximenez, in less comfort, was in jail, awaiting trial. Yes, in the Education Department there would be a great deal to do.

'Come on,' said Fritz, standing up. 'I'll buy you a drink.'

Soldier and friar made their way down the length of the cathedral, and out into the Square.

'Do you know any Latin?' asked Fritz, as they stood in the sunlight.

'A little.'

'Tacitus, now,' said Fritz, taking out a pocket edition, the one he always carried with him. 'I was just reading the bit about the collapsible ship. I've marked it.' He opened it at the right place; it was marked with a letter that he had received from an old friend, one Mrs Mendoza, only that morning. 'Now that is a good story,' he continued. 'If I was in the Education Department I could do my bit for Tacitus.'

They walked on across the Square, discussing Roman heroes and ancient heroic deeds.